DISPLACEMENT

RICHARD DILLAN

The right of Richard Dillan to be identified
as the Author of this Work has been asserted
by him in accordance with the Copyright,
Designs and Patents Act 1998

This book is a work of fiction. Names, characters,
places and incidents are products of the author's
imagination or are used ficticiously.

ISBN-13: 978-1478159193
ISBN-10: 1478159197

To the girl I should have stepped in to defend, when she could not defend herself

One giant leap...

One

Origin Point

Saturday 09 August 2031 - 21:13 Indian Standard Time

The decades of frantic flights through the darkness would be over soon; in one tenth of a minute to be exact. In six seconds, the first and only ship designed and constructed specifically for interstellar travel would leave Earth orbit, destined for the edge of the solar system.

Charon, still representing the unofficial limits of humanity's domain, would bear mute witness to the arrival, six seconds hence, of humanity's first ever craft capable of traversing the gulfs between stars.

Sunday 30 July 2056 - 10:30 IST

Twenty five years later.

Rebecca Eckhart's good hand flew to the holster on her thigh. She struggled with the pop-stud for half a second, trying to free the weapon contained within. Its location on

1

the right-handed holster was in the wrong position for her left thumb. Her hastened panic did not help, and she fumbled her index finger to the trigger, nearly firing and dropping the gun as she drew it, aimed at her target.

She had not meant her life to end this way, here, at this time. The collective outcomes of her actions so far, their accrued weight on her, had brought her to this place. A generation ago she thought she would have given anything to have been here, but now the price her decisions had led to, her continued existence, was too high.

Supporting the unfamiliar weight of the gun with her splinted and bandaged right arm made her broken limb throb with the effort. The pain in back of her head where it had collided with his nose pushed through to her eyes, displaced all concerns beyond her immediate safety from her mind.

Should she survive the next sixty seconds suffering nothing greater than a headache, the damage to her was nothing compared to his face. A fountain had opened across it, blood flowing freely from his ruined nose. Still he clung to the dangerous, curved knife though.

'You will not shoot me, I think,' he said to her, his smile full of confidence despite his injuries. 'Over the course of my duty I have had weapons of all manner aimed in my direction, and I have seen the eyes of every single person who meant to kill me. And yours tell me that you are not possessed of the will to kill another human being, to take another's life. So please, lay down the gun and I will give you as quick and painless a death as I am still able.'

< <

Thursday 20 April 2056 - 03:09 IST

'So, it has been decided. It is my time.' They were

statements, not questions to the figure who stood in the shadows of the elderly astronaut's bedroom. 'If I am to leave this earth then may I see the face of the man they have sent to dispatch me?'

In reply the shadow said nothing, but instead stepped forward into the small circle of yellowy light thrown out by the bedside lamp, illumination where only moments before there had been dark. The old man in the bed looked into the eyes of the man sent to kill him; they did not look like the eyes of a killer, but then the man in the bed could honestly say he had never knowingly encountered someone who had deliberately set out to end another's life, so had no experience on which to base his opinion.

'Please sit.' He gestured to his uninvited guest to rest himself on his mattress, as he himself sat up to make the accommodation. He remembered his manners and was faintly proud that he had done so. It would be improper to be impolite. 'Will it hurt?'

< < <

The moon of Pluto hung silent and patient in the deep cold darkness of the Kuiper Belt, unaware of any of the spacecraft which had sped past it previously on their gravity-accelerated hurtles across the void. Probes and crafts that could not have stopped even if their designers, engineers and navigators left back on Earth had wished it. The last man-made object to grace the heavenly bodies at this distance from Earth had been the NASA New Horizons spacecraft, which had sped through the surrounding volume of space at half a lakh kilometres per hour, impelled to travel on, theoretically forever, or until it felt the irresistible pull of a gravity well strong enough to capture it for itself.

At this distance the sun was little stronger than the countless other pinpoints of light shining their pale brightness on the objects comprising the Kuiper Belt. It was light that had taken anywhere between six hours and thirteen-hundred crore years to arrive, crossing the empty gulfs between its origin point and this collection of lonely worlds. Among this weak accrual of arriving photons, the sun's wan light barely warmed the slowly spinning globes of rock and ice. This was a part of creation mankind had had little use for before now, save as the nominal marker between what he might consider as his, and the surrounding, endless void.

Until now.

The Vimana was special. It had significant and important differences to every other spacecraft, manned or otherwise that had so far been built for the purpose of venturing this far from their homeworld before it. It had not escaped the powerful gravitational embrace of the planet of its birth through the use of hugely inefficient and wasteful fuel boosters, and once in space it had not propelled itself by ion expulsion, slowly accelerating away, nor had it relied on skimming round a passing planet, stealing fractions of that body's momentum for its own use to drive its journey.

Its propulsion system was the zenith of the life's work of one man, Professor Rajat Cotts, the Indian scientist who had unlocked the secret of moving things from *here* to *there* almost instantaneously, utilising only a fraction of the energy of conventional engines. It had been named Displacement technology, D-tech for short, and it had revolutionised transport in all its forms on Earth, pushing the already vastly contracted planet much closer together, and, conversely, driving it far further apart than its discoverer had ever envisaged or wanted.

Now, that technology had been fashioned into a craft intended to explore the boundary-less gulfs of space, to reach out into the limitless black and try to touch the stars. The Vimana was all these things, and it had left Earth orbit six seconds ago.

The current position of Charon, in its two hundred and forty eight year synchronous orbit with its concomitant parent had not been chosen idly, nor capriciously. Like everything associated with the mission, there was the practicality.

Charon was the most distant object of sufficient mass to Displace the Vimana to. Although technically, the ship could jump to anywhere in its range, focussing on a heavy, dense body made the Displacement that much more straightforward. A planet or moon provided a larger gravitational target than the handful of hydrogen and occasional helium atoms which comprised the rest of space. So, for the first time since its birth, Charon served purposes beyond its nominal status as the most distant object man felt within his domain.

The remoteness was the first; a vital test run distance, a proving of the Displacement drive. Secondly was its mass; dense and heavy enough to allow the Vimana to get a fix on it as a suitable target destination. Finally was its position; a fitting place to pause, the edge of the conceptual lattice of concentric orbits that comprised humanity's specific portion of creation.

If any sentient soul had been looking three lakh kilometres earthward of Charon at that moment they would have seen a volume of space, approximately the size of a blue whale, flex and bend as the Vimana neared. The six-hour-old light shimmered and prismed as the Vimana neared its arrival point, the approaching mass of the ship distorting the reality it was about to manifest itself in.

Then, the illumination was blocked. One moment all there had been was Charon and the weak breath of distant suns. The next, the Vimana, hanging motionless, casting its shadow on the frozen ball of ice and rock; the final speck of matter of any significance for several light years.

Eight year old Becky Eckhart sat bald-headed and rapt behind the screens thrown a metre in front of her, watching the images flick before her eyes. She had programmed the imaging glasses her father insisted she wore with a channel change every five seconds.

But Dada, I'm old enough for my own lenses!

Sorry darling, not if you're going to wear them all day.

Eventually she gave up her protests. Getting to participate in the event was ultimately more important than being allowed to use the more discrete lenses. She would bear the teasing her brother and sister would give her later for it knowing she had been there. The channel flicked again. It didn't matter to her which feed she was watching; every station, site and content provider she had programmed in was relaying their own subtle wrinkle on the same content; the launch of the Vimana in a little under six hours.

In a world of SI-driven content consumption, with any imaginable spectacle able to be rendered on-demand, it may have been the raw humanity of the event, the realness of the people so far away, that made it something which captured the consciousness of people, drawing them together. Becky was marginally aware of this participation; somewhere in the back of her head she knew she was, and always would be, part of an event larger and more important than its very personal meaning to the young, self-possessed girl in her formative years.

The talking heads, diagrams, real-time simulations, participation forums and SI-driven datasearches she assimilated through sight and sound were all discussing the homing signal InSA was about to start transmitting, and which Captain Srinath and his crew would be in position to receive less than a minute after they departed. To Becky it seemed as if Captain Srinath and his crew were time travellers as well as explorers; jumping forward into her future to catch up with something that wasn't there yet and wouldn't be there until the middle of the afternoon, by which time the signal would exist six hours in her past, right now.

Arrival.

On board the Vimana, Captain Hari Srinath ran his crew through their post-Displacement checks; what would have been standard procedure had anything like this mission been attempted, replicated, perfected and standardised before. However, the maiden voyage of the only D-driven interstellar craft in existence necessitated the instructions he gave his officers were his and InSA's best interpretation of post-arrival operating protocol.

If anything failed with the ship now, they were too far out to expect any form of rescue. Earth had nothing else at its disposal capable of reaching them should there be a system failure this far out, in Charon's shadow; let alone when they found themselves deep in the interstellar void, far beyond the heliopause. So far, the ship had outperformed even its Captain's high expectations of it; the years of planning, testing, revising and re-testing had ensured the initial stage had gone perfectly, and he could not have asked for a more fortuitous start to the mission.

April 24 2056

Sinha MG D-Market Strategy Research

Rebecca Eckhart
Rebecca.Eckhart.SinhaMG

Opportunities in a Re-emerging Market

- As predicted early in Q1 2055, InSA re-enables parts of the long offlined North American Cotts Field (CF), returning limited coverage of the Displacement infrastructure across North America.

- Initial re-entry into the market is the instantiation of a secure CF corridor between the continental seaboards by aDventura(TM), the largest D-licence holder for North America.

- We foresee potential for a return of growth in this re-established D-Market for mid and long-range carriers.

- Our forecast of an upward trend of 0.2% m.o.m. (versus -7% in this market previously) converts to potential revenue incomes of Rs3 crore across the next fiscal period.

- In addition, should demand return to the market to any significant degree we anticipate further expansion of the Cotts Field by InSA, creating the potential for a further dozen separate new corridors between the coasts and the secured inland cities over the next twelve months. Our forecast is this will push the growth trajectory to high-single digit percentages by 4Q2057.

The reactivation of a single Cotts Field satellite by InSA, as correctly identified by this publication last year, creating a

secured Displacement corridor linking JFK and BHO, has been met with cautious welcome by the majority of the North America licence holders. We feel this is an overly pessimistic reaction to a significant market event representing the first possibility for real ROI in the ravaged North American space for several years. As we have long argued, the majority of the troubles have migrated well inland, leaving the coastal areas open for international peace-keeping forces to be deployed, and along with them, the resumption of orderly, managed trade.

However, we acknowledge the difficulties in operating within the present market conditions. Several current operators have encountered resistance to their presence, and damage and theft to their stock, resulting in significant increases in their insurance premiums. We advise therefore that sufficient provision be made in budget forecasts for security detail and elevated insurance payments. We advise any outlay of more than 2% on these fixed costs be the cut-off point for considering investment.

Challenges to the bold investor

What about the ancillary effects of the civil war?

The evidence of the effects on the local biosphere is an unfavourable pressure on the marketplace, and requires careful consideration for companies with a published 'Ethical' Statement. Presently, fourteen species of major fauna have been pushed to extinction, with several more on the UN 'Most Endangered' list. Particularly vulnerable are the remaining 'apex' predators and large herbivores: namely, the mountain lion, bald eagle, alligator, black and brown bear, coyote, wolf, colt and bison, all of which currently number less than a dozen estimated breeding adults. We advise particular care be exerted when advertising an intention to (re)enter the North American D-market. Be sure your corporate accountability can withstand the scrutiny it will face when operating in an environment which has become detrimental to so much iconic American fauna.

Potential answers include opening a biodiversity-trading position, allowing an offset posture to be adopted. Several life-science providers offer DNA "sample and store" services, with preservation facilities housed at on the of the three Extinction-Event banks at the poles where permanent ice still holds sway. Alternatively, Red Crescent bonds offer an attractive yield. Purchasing these allow you to claim, quite correctly, to be funding their presence where they struggle to maintain a species-survival mission; an attractive proposition in these times of daily negative revisions to the planet's biodiversity index.

Overall we propose an initial investment of no more than 0.05% of total estimated revenues be set-aside for this purpose.

The question you have to ask is: Can your customers afford to be seen to be doing business there?

What about the religious unrest?

It would be derelict not to highlight the recent barbarous and bloodiest conflict to date between the two main rival factions, The Sons of Freedom and the New New Model Army.

Their enmity reached its zenith of pointless slaughter in the latest Battle of the Colorado. Raising the stakes in the recent flurry of military engagements in the area to a dangerous new level with the re-introduction of the internationally illegal D-bombers, the Sons seemed on the verge of victory. Desperate to counter the re-emergent terror tactic of martyr-hungry individuals willingly carrying a maxed out weight of several hundred kilograms of conventional explosives and shrapnel who step out of Folds behind their enemy's lines, the Modellers targeted the Sons' local High Command-chapel, and in an effort which extinguished all but one of their number, Displaced the entire structure, estimated at one hundred and fifteen tons, into the suffocating void of a geostationary orbit.

In this arena of pogroms, particular care must be afforded to any sentiment or sympathies, latent or otherwise, in the potential customer base. We cannot advise strongly enough full disclosure contracts be drawn up. A one-time fee of approx. Rs1 lakh should be the anticipated outlay for such a document.

Unspent munitions – the costs

Like all good guerrilla armies the Sons have munitioned the land heavily with mines, in an effort to ensure the territory, should they lose it, be a hazard for many years to come. Indiscriminate and unthinking, as all the best military hardware strives to be, these devices kill without compunction or conscience. And like the best military technology, the evolution and development has not stood still despite their putative outlawing in the early Twenty-First Century.

Where their long distant antecedents relied on inelegant but effective explosive charges, these great-grandchildren are infinitely more devastating. Now when tripped, mines no longer shout their presence. Like the best assassin they are nearly silent and deadly; the howl of white light and red-hot shrapnel replaced by the inaudible whisper of electron-flow and a shifting of space, most often in every direction simultaneously, leaving nothing greater than a faint red mist floating in the air.

Unspent munitions represent perhaps the greatest hurdle to potential clients. The reputational and commercial effects of triggering an artefact of the conflict, on the person and the corporate body should not be underestimated. Civil claims have run into Rs1 crore punitive damages for those organisations who were found to be liable. We therefore advocate, in the first instances, a strategy of absolute risk-management be your mantra. While this may seem to run counter to our sentiment that what is needed to fully re-commercialise this space is rapid expansion, we appreciate the fragility of the market to any shock-events. This is the one area we counsel caution. A high-profile corporate manslaughter suit could damage irreparably this nascent opportunity.

Two

Rebecca

Tuesday 25 April 2056 - 07:26 EU Summer Time

The tall office blocks, interspersed with the occasional two or three storey building, cast their long shadows across the busying London streets. The strong early morning light backlit their outlines with bright halos, the sunshine smudging their edges so they would have seemed blurred and indistinct against the sky if anyone had raised their eyes to look.

Rebecca Eckhart strode beneath them, head down, moving with purpose between the patches of cool relief the shadows provided. In the glare of the daylight between the taller buildings she could feel the temperature already rising, despite the earliness of the hour. Coupled with the humidity, this indicated a sticky and oppressive day ahead.

However, the weather mattered little to Rebecca. Behind her sunglasses she hardly broke sweat as she moved through the jostling streets and past people as quickly as she could. Her well-toned muscles and acclimatised physique were more than a match for the walk she was putting them through. Hard hours in the gym were not for nothing.

Her strides were matched by a heavy beat thumping in her ears, overlaid and mixed with a bhangra track. Each footfall set off different rhythms and pulses in the music, Socrates interpreting and encoding her movements as chords, beats and breaks. The result was an individual, bespoke tune that was fed by and influenced her movements, the bassy tempo measuring and matching her pace in a positive feedback loop as she pounded the pavement toward her desk. Her own personally soundtracked trip.

Her physical capability to the task in hand strengthened her determination to reach her destination as quickly as possible, and get away from the herding jumble of other people. The sunglasses helped; they protected her from contact, allowing her to maintain her distance, both physical and emotional, from the crowds she pushed through. And they served another purpose. Scrolling up along the insides of their jet black lenses was her choice of the latest news updates, allowing her to catch up with what she deemed important as she made her way to her office.

Her attention was interrupted briefly by her spotting a small child desperately trying to gain its mother's attention and show to her the thing he had found and was grasping in his grubby hand. Rebecca did not want the distraction; she was not yet ready to effect her re-entry to the world of other people. After a fortnight in the deserted amber zones surrounding the UN enclave of Manhattan, seeing scant sign of human presence save for the patrol assigned to protect her, the dark lenses were an essential barrier to the mass of humanity that now seemed to teem in London.

Her instincts, honed over a decade of picking out the smallest of human dramas for her to process as both entertainment and occasional insight into the human condition, overruled her conscious efforts to ignore the bleating infant. Her need to check herself against the behaviour of others, their tiny defeats and victories, pulled her out of herself and, almost against her will, she found herself watching the pair.

The boy pulled at his mother's sleeve, the parent distracted by something she had seen on her own lens-screens. Rebecca scanned around the woman's proximity as she passed, vicarious curiosity searching for the source of the feed the woman could be receiving. Socrates opened a dozen separate windows in response to the push-feeds from the a-points in the mother's vicinity; the usual mix of war, murder and pointless death tempered, perversely, by the celebrity commentary on each, the familiar voices salve for the atrocities.

Rebecca focussed on the reporting of a water-rationing demonstration scheduled for later that day, and LondGuard's and MetProtect's actions in dispersing the gathering crowd. She ordered the foregrounding of the window with a flick of her eye, watching, scrolling past the mother in parallax, a five-second replay of the live-feed images. The competing private security forces pulled a man from the crowd, who was shouting at them with an ill-advised American accent, and beat him to the floor. The woman raised her hand unconsciously to her mouth and began weeping.

Rebecca heard too late, chiming through the heavy bass beat pumping in her ears, Socrates' vain attempt to alert her to the impending impact with the man stepping out of the D-livery office. The large box he carried obscured his view, and his more feeble SI was obviously not utilising the same level of tech as Socrates, otherwise he would have known he was about to collide with a fellow citizen. Rebecca, still distracted from the backgrounding newsfeed, at the last moment before impact swerved almost cat-like around the man, who barely saw the form of the woman who avoided him, and had saved him the trouble of having to pick up his belongings.

She watched for a moment only, irritated at having to

break stride because of someone else's inability to take her into consideration. The man looked round his parcel trying to understand what his SI was telling him had almost happened, looking for the person he needed to apologise to. But Rebecca had already resumed her forward march.

She turned a corner and sighed at the sight presented to her, past the windows appearing to hang a metre in front of her. Her annoyance from moments ago shifted itself momentarily to herself at her misjudgement, before she transferred it to the people before her. More idiots to have to cope with.

The feeble-minded were out early this morning, earlier than she had anticipated. Rebecca silently wished to herself that she had allowed Socrates to determine her a less toll-free route to her office; she could have avoided these cretins and their rental of the street altogether. The tithe of a few paise would have been a small indulgence to secure her passage unassailed. Still, this would not be that bad. She had Socrates, and he was good.

He responded to her eyes' saccades, analysing the data from the augfeeds; the perfectly circular gleaming silver O on the man's collars and the book in his hand informing his mistress she was being approached by a Cernonite. With the past two weeks of her time in the former United States spent doing her best to avoid encountering the various quasi-religious factions, sub-factions, splinter groups and individual cells responsible for the massacre of almost the entire North American biosphere, she had little time for anybody's version of the truth, however fervently they might want her to adopt it.

Rebecca refused to slow as the gap between the two of them narrowed. Instead she dropped her glasses down the bridge of her nose and deliberately caught the young man's eyes. Hers told him with a certainty his faith could not match, that not only was he wasting his energy contemplating her conversion, he was ill-advised against

15

instigating even an opening gambit. Without waiting for any sign of comprehension from the man, Rebecca pushed her sunglasses back into their rightful place and walked right past him. Fortunately he seemed to be the only missionising idiot out that morning; the other two in the vicinity seemed content to have simple auged sandwich boards, which struggled to open windows with Socrates, who refused. *Better get some upgrades boys*, she thought intemperately.

The streets thinned of people as she made her way. She was making good time to her destination, now less than half a kilometre away despite the odd interruption, and was hardly breaking sweat in the rising humidity of the April morning.

Rebecca right-wheeled through the glass doors, which swished open accommodatingly as she approached, so she barely had to slow as she entered the cool-dry of the air-conned building and straight through the obliging security barrier. Once inside, her pace slowed a little, unconsciously changing her behaviour, as she headed for the elevators. So accustomed was she to ignoring the D-booths, she did not notice that the usual herd of people waiting for the next upwards slot was missing from around them, only registering the fact when she turned the corner to find herself facing a crowd of several dozen fellow bank employees, all waiting for the lifts.

She frowned as she analysed the situation; normally she would be the only one using the near-obsolete mechanical transport. *What was going on?* Socrates provided the answer as he retrieved and parsed the datafeed from the one of the bank's SIs. While Rebecca had been away the bank's executive board had adopted a policy of corporate-Vedic sacrifice. This, they decided would manifest itself as an alternate monthly disabling of the building's Displacement architecture, meaning each employee would have to utilise the physical and mechanical means at their disposal to

16

traverse their workplace.

Rebecca smiled. *That this also ensured they cut their D-licensing costs in half had nothing to do with the decision of course.* Immediately appreciating this turn of events in her favour, she looked forward to spending six months every year not experiencing the discomfort of being the only person stood waiting for an elevator.

But this boon was not without its own more immediate drawback. She had not anticipated a crowd this morning, especially one so large on her ascent to her office, and the resulting delay in making her 8am appointment with Marcia. She glanced at the clock on the inside of her lens-screens, then back at the slowly dwindling, by no more than six at a time, collection of people queuing ahead of her. *Hagga.*

The conflict rose in her as the lifts continued their crawls, seeming to stop at every floor on their journeys to and from the ground. Her office was on the thirty-seventh floor, easily ten more minutes away on foot. And then she'd arrive not only late, but also showing the physical exertion it had taken to get there. Not a good look.

The tinny *thumpa-thumpa-thumpa* leaked from her earphones, causing a few heads to turn away from their conversations and toward her, before they returned to the topic at hand, shaking their heads. *Great.*

So what the hell exactly was it they were all so engrossed in anyway? Rebecca's eyes searched for the augpoint; Socrates was not blind to his mistress's discomfort, and foregrounded the feed he had determined the others had been discussing, giving her the opportunity to at least appear as involved in the shared event as everyone else while she decided what to do.

On the inside of Rebecca's sunglasses, which she had steadfastly not removed despite the shade of the interior, opened the building info-silo, its SI describing that there had been an attempted robbery in the small hours of the morning. The suspected thieves had D-jacked their way onto the nineteenth floor and had got as far as preparing their escape with what they claimed was their ancestor's sword from Ms Chawla's office, some great great great great great grandfather /patriarch of their clan.

Those boys had been twitchy ever since re-unification. It seemed the would-be thieves were either unaware of or had been unable to circumvent the silent alarms; within a second of them triggering, both the building's and Sinha MG's own private security details had intervened to apprehend the felons. When trying to flee back across the Folds they had arrived on, they found the Cotts field suddenly working directly against them. With the perpetrators safely rendered off to a variety of holding cells, both enforcement agencies immediately filed competing petitions with the civil authorities for exclusive arrest rights, and the requisite recompense for their services.

Digesting all of this wasted a precious minute of Rebecca's dwindling time with which to decide whether remaining waiting for a lift was the correct course of action. She hopped from foot to foot with impatience, mentally goading the mechanical gaandu to get a move on. Suddenly the future benefit of greater concealment in numbers was diminished by the disruption to her arrangements; she'd have to factor in additional minutes every other month to deal with the herd she'd find herself waiting for an elevator in from now on.

She was silently cursing her bank's directors for this change in policy, when there was the chime of a lift's arrival in the lobby. Rebecca checked herself, remembering to look polite, allowing five other people to enter first, watching with some amusement at the singular way they failed to negotiate each other's personal space. Unfamiliar with etiquette around utilising a shared conveyance they hesitated, false-started, stopped, then finally settled on an order of entrance into the small metal compartment that was to house them all for the next few minutes of their

18

lives. Shaking her head minutely at their witlessness, Rebecca followed them inside. 'Thirty seven,' she said to whoever was nearest the buttons, without so much as a glance in their direction.

Three

Promotion

Twenty-six floors later Rebecca was finally alone. Unable to stay still even in the confines of the cramped interior, she circumnavigated it in small circles, barely two metres wide, as the lift continued its climb through the floors. If she noticed her isolation she barely showed it, too distracted instead by the draft she had submitted two days ago, and more importantly what Marcia was going to say about it. She ran the likely opening gambits the director of her research desk could present to her, determined the best response to each and the next most probable reply Marcia would come up with for each, then formulated an answer to those also. At the end of her ascent she had a ternary tree, four layers deep with forty nodes on it, each one weighted according to its likelihood to arise. *Should be enough,* she reasoned.

As soon as the doors opened enough for her to squeeze through she was between them, through the RF-tagged frosted-glass information barrier and onto the trading floor. Marcia caught her eye almost immediately, despite the opaque sunglasses she still had on. Rebecca headed over to her boss, who motioned for her to keep pace as she headed back to her office.

Rebecca fell into step with her manager, reviewing Marcia's body language to gauge the likely responses to the conversational openers she had prepared. An outright enquiry as to her thoughts on the work was out; that gave Marcia too much room to mount an argument she would have little defence against. Similarly, any gambit that seemed to close the conversation down would look suspicious, defensive, and provide her boss with an excuse if she was looking for one not to approve it.

The pair were almost at Marcia's office. If she wanted to begin this conversation while still on the floor, where it could be kept manageable, she had to say something soon. Judging her boss's mood, Rebecca settled on remaining as neutral as possible, wishing to provoke neither hostility nor sympathy. 'So,' she began, 'I think it strikes a good balance between the state of the re-emerging D-market in the areas the war has moved away from, with some context of the effects the conflict has had on the biodiversity.' That was good. A statement, not a question. Positive, drawing attention to the piece's strengths.

Marcia paused and stared at her best analyst, her own reflection filling the dark lenses. 'Take the sunglasses off. Please?' She only turned the order into a request at the last instant. Rebecca complied, the hint of potential trouble to come in Marcia's tone making her suddenly aware that perhaps the news was not going to be positive, and the piece was going to cause her grief. Her mind immediately set to work re-orientating her along a different conversational path to the one she had initiated, detouring down the junctions that held likely criticisms and any possible rebuttals she might muster against them.

'I'm not sure,' continued her director as she stared over the shoulder of one of her junior analysts, pointing out an unsupported assertion from the data of the research piece he had before him, before she was off again. 'Come on, we'll finish this in my office.'

Shit! The bad news that had been on the horizon loomed larger in her immediate future. Marcia closed the plate glass door as Rebecca followed her in, some of the swagger in her step dropped in favour of an air of mild contrition, a conscious change of body language. Rebecca deliberately waited for her manager's opinion, the hope she could influence her boss with her supplication.

Marcia drew a breath as if preparing to deliver a lecture. Or a bollocking. 'It seemed a little ...confused,' she said searching for the right word. 'For you, I mean,' she added as if by way of a justification. Seeing the expression on Rebecca's face she elaborated. 'Well, maybe confused was the wrong word. Perhaps unfocussed would be a better description.'

Rebecca eyed her boss warily. This was certainly not the brunt of the bad news; there was definitely worse to come. Better to wait to hear it all before giving a reaction.

Marcia sensed the conversation was being ceded back to her, and was more than happy to continue uninterrupted. 'As always, your conclusions from the data sets are irrefutable, but why did you choose to go into so much detail on the civil war going on out there rather than the effects of it on the investment opportunities. And it spends too long concentrating on the wildlife population. That wasn't the brief and you know it. All this makes it jump around; it's lacking your normal incisive focus.'

Rebecca could not help but make a face at this final comment, especially after standing quietly through Marcia's demolition of her work. Her manager qualified her statement with another final placatory observation about the analyses being solid, but it otherwise needing work before it was ready for circulation.

Now she had aired her criticisms it was Rebecca's turn

to respond to her boss. She had listened and absorbed everything her desk head had said, altering, expanding then changing how she was going to respond as more information was volunteered, both actual and implied. As Marcia drew to a close Rebecca had formulated her response. She knew the director was at least half-right, but she was not going to allow her points go unchallenged. She had delivered everything within the parameters set out, producing more than enough interpretations and recommendations from the data needed for any investment managers to use. And if she had chosen to exercise her discretion a little in providing some background flavour to the state of that particular part of the world, well it would not be the first time. Anyway, no-one would read past the headline figures, so if anything they were words almost without worth. Marcia would get over it.

Eventually, when Rebecca had run out of things to say in her defence, Marcia spoke again. 'This is exactly why I hired you Rebecca; your innate sense of reason and logic makes you a damned talented analyst. I get a very real sense of that professional detachment I know your colleagues admire and envy.' Rebecca smiled. Maybe she had won some of the argument after all. 'But.' The smile died in place on her lips. 'This piece, you're too involved in it for some reason. It's highly emotive in places and downright explosive in others, and that's not what I needed from it. We are the largest Indian investment bank outside of the sub-continent and I need my analysts to deliver on their assignments. I know we're read in Whitehall as well as the Sansad Bhavan, so you'll understand my requirement for pieces with a specific thrust; and this is not it, it's just too muddy.'

Rebecca had not been expecting this level of criticism. Her mind worked rapidly, contriving a rescue for her and her work. She scooped up the loose leafs of paper Marcia insisted on reading all her analysts' drafts on, tried to neaten them, only to fumble the pages into a clumsy, disorganised pile. 'So I'll re-draft it then,' she told her boss, using the final argument she had held in reserve until now. 'I can have it back to you by this afternoon. Tomorrow morning at the latest,' she proffered, thinking quickly and shifting her self-imposed deadline, trying to buy herself at least the evening to pull the thing apart and beat it into something Marcia would accept.

But her boss's next reply destroyed any chance of that. 'I'm going to give it to Hiro to revise. I've got something else for you to get your teeth into.'

In the totality of conversational-tree traversals she had played out before and during the discussion with Marcia, Rebecca had not anticipated this at all; being removed as the author on a research piece did not happen to people of her seniority. As a consequence she had no prepared response waiting. Instinct made her blurt out before she could stop herself. 'Hiro? But he's barely a junior! And you're going to give him my piece? The one I spent two weeks in the middle of that stupid bloody civil war those idiots are engaged in trying to research?' She realised her voice was rising in pitch and volume during her outburst and drew herself to a stop, angry at herself for her slip. She eyed her boss. Rebecca had taken Marcia's criticism of her work with as much good grace as she could, but to have it taken away now was intellectually and professionally insulting, and she had let it show. *Chod!*

Marcia, who had not got to her position by not knowing how to handle, and if she was being entirely honest, manipulate people into doing what she wanted, offered an explanation, which was a good approximation of the truth; or at least enough of the truth to placate Rebecca. 'Be fair, Hiro's not bad, but you're right; he does need practice, so a good piece that needs touching up should show him how it's really done. I promise he won't kill it. I won't let him.'

Despite knowing her boss was not going to change her mind, Rebecca still could not help but look pissed off for a moment before she regained control. Marcia knew this Rebecca of old, the inscrutable woman, but now she knew what she was really feeling. Granting Rebecca her earlier gambit, she played her ace, the sop she always held back till the very end of any discussion with one of her analysts when they were being particularly intractable. She was surprised, only faintly, but still surprised nonetheless to realise this was the first instance she had ever had to use the ploy with Rebecca. But it worked like a charm, just like it did with everyone else. Her magic bullet that appealed to the vanity far more strongly than the professionalism each of them sought to defend until they heard Marcia's offer.

'Look,' she started, casually, as if she had just thought of it, 'once he's finished, if you're not happy with it we'll pull the piece. Otherwise if you don't object too strongly to his work you can still keep your name on it when we publish. No co-authorship, just you.'

Rebecca narrowed her eyes in thought. Marcia had to suppress a smile at the small act Rebecca was putting on for her benefit. All her staff did the same routine with their own personal interpretation of it. Hiro, the promising junior she was grooming, for instance, pulled at his wispy beard whenever he wanted to make Marcia think he was even remotely considering the proposal she had made, but which he had already accepted in his head. Now Marcia could add Rebecca's twiddling of her ponytail to the repertoire of bluffing she could look out for; a dead give-away.

Other than thinking how she should organise a game of teen pathi with her staff, Marcia had had enough of waiting for Rebecca to decide she had spent sufficient time pretending to consider her offer. 'Look, this isn't a firing. I am going to give Hiro your piece to finish, he'll do a bloody good job on it and you'll still meet the circulation deadline.

I really do have something else for you, and after this morning's shock, I think you'll be pleasantly surprised.' Marcia paused for dramatic effect. 'I'm incredibly pleased to tell you that, effective immediately, you've been promoted to Director, with responsibility for the InCh desk. Your first assignment is a three day, two night trip to Delhi to meet the Indian arm of the team you'll be in charge of from the start of next week. After that we'll arrange the trip to Beijing for you to get to know the Chinese section. Well don't just stand there catching flies, go on, say something.'

Rebecca closed her mouth, stunned at the news her boss, now her peer, had delivered. After everything Marcia had said about the research piece she had submitted, the best she had hoped for was at least not a demotion, let alone being given her own desk to run. *Get a grip girl.* But the only things that would emerge from her stupefied brain were single word questions. 'What? How? I mean, who?' She stopped, realising Marcia was greatly amused at seeing her lost for words.

Marcia decided to give her former staff a little more time to absorb the news. 'A bit sudden perhaps, but after your long stint in the boondocks following big cats around for weeks on end, avoiding god knows what unspent munitions, natural hazards and restless natives I think someone recognised what you're capable of and pulled some strings in your favour. My advice is go, enjoy the trip before the hard work really starts. All those impossible things you've done up to this point are your everyday job now. You've got one thing to do while you're out there, kind of a preparatory piece for your new position I guess. A former Indian astronaut has died and we think it'll have a big effect on the D-market. The officer's name was Commodore Mehta.'

Something felt familiar about the name. 'Mehta...' echoed Rebecca, the syllable sounds sparking long repressed and unused neurons somewhere deep in her subconscious. Why did her skin prickle and her palms sweat as soon as Marcia had said the name? Time did that slowed down, sped up thing in her mind as the word flooded her with half-memories and feelings of... of... a sense of loss, of losing something somewhen. Something a long time forgotten, but resonant with meaning and purpose, like a favourite toy or a faded childhood friendship; the kind of bond only a child would think could remain unbroken. Rebecca struggled through the fog of half-remembered snatches of fleeting thoughts, trying to recover memories a quarter of a century old.

'He was pretty famous, back in the day, as Lieutenant Commander Mehta of the Vimana. I'm surprised you don't remember it, but I suppose you would only have been a little girl.'

A flower of comprehension bloomed in Rebecca's mind, a rush of understanding as the disparate fragments of thought coalesced. '*Chod!*' she mouthed. *The Vimana!* Suddenly she was eight years old again; uncomfortably thrown back into her child's body with her childish outlook and naivety. All the stupid things she had said and believed so sincerely, with the fierce and unflinching conviction only an eight year old could possess. She flushed involuntarily at the remembered embarrassment. *The Vimana. Earth's wasted opportunity.* The promise of escape out to the isolation of the stars torn apart on its first mission by... something she couldn't quite remember.

I can't do this. Rebecca began thinking two replies ahead again.

'Why do they want me for this? I've got no experience with staff. I'm not sure I'd be any good to the bank here,' she half-lied, reluctant to accept the promotion and all it would mean, despite her boss's intransigence on her piece, before finishing her argument with Marcia's own phrase for her recent work, 'Unfocussed, remember?'

If Marcia picked up on Rebecca's deliberate attempt to sabotage her immediate career she was not letting on. 'The way I see it your first job on the desk will be analysing another species extinction; only this one was only ever eleven strong. The opportunity is too good to pass up Rebecca. The timing is fortuitous also. The passing of the sixth Vimana astronaut is a watershed moment; there are only five of them left now. They're a dying breed, just like your cougars and bears.'

'Don't be flippant Marcia!' Rebecca snapped back too quickly, emotion overriding her prepared arguments and betraying her earlier dismissal of her suitability. Then, trying to regain control, in more measured tones, 'But what if I say no thank you and want to re-work my original piece? Would this be the part where you threaten me with suspension?'

Marcia looked nonplussed. Rebecca was in no way the most egocentric analyst on her staff, and she had in her time heard pretty much every threat and demand. A little game of professional cat and mouse with Rebecca was nothing really, though she could not help but wonder why she seemed to be going out of her way not to accept the promotion, despite her obvious interest. Marcia decided to push a little. 'I wasn't going to, but I can if it would make you happier,' she replied, her voice a mix of equal parts good humour and don't-push-your-luck. 'I had hoped you'd take it because it was a good move, and you wanted to.'

'And why exactly would I want to do that? No-one cares about what Leapfrogging out to the stars might mean today. We're grown ups now, and that childish dream died twenty five years ago.' Rebecca immediately realised what she had said.

Now Marcia did smile. 'It sounds like at least one person still feels strongly enough about it to remember the term 'Leapfrog'. If I recall, that was the kid's club InSA set up to follow the ship, wasn't it. So, you were in it.' It was not a question. 'You were a...' Marcia tailed off.

Rebecca swore at herself for the slip, not the first one of this conversation. She was letting Marcia run rings around her, and now she knew the deepest, dirtiest little secret from her childhood; the private shame of an adult looking back on the immature actions of a youth. She had been one of the 'tadpoles'. Rebecca winced at the barest memory of the word and her eyes blazed at Marcia, daring her to mention it, or even hint at it again.

Marcia could not help but be gently amused at seeing her senior analyst in discomfort for the first time ever. While it was good to provoke an emotion out of Rebecca finally after her years in the bank, Marcia was not heartless, and pushing her on what was obviously unfinished business was too far. What this meant for the team she was inheriting she could not guess, but it might do the girl some good to feel something for once.

Rebecca, for her part, tried to squash the memories, but they came back unbidden, too strong to push back in their box right now. Goddamn it *had* felt good at the time. Mehta, Chaudray, Srinath and all the others had been her heroes. In her child's eyes they were Gods almost; at play amongst the stars, bringing the chance of a new beginning, a chance to start again and put the past behind her. A fresh start for her; for all of them. *No, don't think that. There's no need to drag that back up.*

Marcia could not help but notice Rebecca's discomfort change into something obviously deeper, well beyond embarrassment at remembered childhood ephemera. What nerve had she hit to bend the woman this much out of shape? She reached out comfortingly to Rebecca who flinched at the touch.

'Sorry,' Rebecca apologised instinctively. Then her eyes hardened measurably, whatever turmoil Marcia had provoked in her well and truly being overpowered by her will. 'I'll take the position,' she said flatly, 'I screwed up and this is my chance to move on. I'll make it right. Thanks for obviously putting words in the right place for me. I appreciate it.'

'Are you sure you're alright?' Marcia could not dismiss the feeling that Rebecca was accepting the promotion so she could bring the current conversation to a close and forget all about it.

Rebecca drew a breath as the woman Marcia knew re-asserted herself, all trace of whatever had happened behind her eyes gone as if it had never occurred. 'Ha, I'm cool. It's been a long time since I've had cause to think about the Vimana,' she half-lied, as close to a justification as she was going to give Marcia.

'Actually, I think you should probably stay here for a few days. After all you've only just got back from one of the most disorientating places on earth, and now you're on the move again. We'll send your acceptance of the position, but your apologies on the trip.'

'No. I can do this. I want this.' *Perhaps she placed a little too much emphasis on 'want'?* 'I've always complained you were holding me back on your desk,' she joked.

Marcia narrowed her eyes, working out what she might say to Rebecca to make her reconsider the trip, but knew from Rebecca's eyes her former staff member was almost daring her to say something so she could further persuade herself this was the right thing to do. Rebecca was not going to be moved on this, that was obvious. Nothing to do but carry on with the arrangements then.

'OK, then. If you're sure. You leave in six hours. Go home, pack light. You're booked on the next longjump out of Heathrow to Delhi. There's a suite booked in your name in the Taj Mahal Hotel.'

Now Rebecca half-laughed. 'You knew I'd take the job, didn't you?'

'Up until a minute ago I thought I knew everything

about you.' Marcia paused, unsure whether to ask her next question. 'Look-' was as far as she got.

'No need, I'm cool. Honestly. Don't worry about me, I'm not going to chod this up,' Rebecca said with a brittle smile.

'OK. So get going then.'

After Rebecca had breezed out of her office, pausing to peck Hiro on the cheek with a 'have fun with my piece', Marcia knew she would get no more ever out of her about what had just happened.

Four

Storm Clouds

Saturday 22 April 2056 – 06:48 IST

The once gleaming white Tata-Hindustan Ambassador model fifteen, its aging paintwork striated and pocked with the rust-freckled scars and chips of numerous small collisions, whirred to a dusty stop in the car park at the rear of the Ministry of Water. Its beaten-up appearance was no different to the lakhs of other non D-vehicles spread across the Indian sub-continent; the damage an inevitable consequence of the overcrowded driving conditions despite its owner's most careful attention. The old-orthodox vehicles which had persisted into the second decade and third-generation of fully functional D-tech PDVs, buses and shuttles, each gave the same sole concession to Professor Cotts' revolution; the electric engine that drove them. Fossil fuels still found uses where power transmission was difficult, but had on the whole been abandoned for most purposes in favour of the hydro-electrically generated energy that came more efficiently from the D-shifting of gigatons of water through turbines.

Overhead, rough and lumpy clouds, fat and dark with

moisture, rolled by, turning the morning sunlight rising behind them the strange off-brown colour of impending heavy rain. Inside the car may have been relatively mild, its fan-cooled interior offering comfort and relief from the thick dawn air, already heavy with heat and dust and the rising humidity of the day's forthcoming rains, but outside the atmosphere pressed on everyone who had to move about in it. Air that clung, pore-cloggingly to every square centimetre of exposed skin, was difficult to inhale and scratched at the eyeballs. Air filled with the rising tension of pre-downpour static charge building as the atmosphere scoured against itself.

The car had come to rest alongside another fading, off-white and equally bruised Ambassador. At the steering wheel sat a solitary figure, to all intents and purposes resembling any other minor public official arriving at work for another day's toil in the service of the one hundred and fifty crore citizens that comprised the population of the world's self-proclaimed largest democracy.

As the man, elderly, grey-haired and proud looking, killed the engine, the heavens let loose their predicted rains. Immediately the windscreen was blotted out, the view of the rear of the Ministry blurred and distorted through the lensing effect of the water. Fat heavy drops panged off the thin metal sheet of roof protecting the car's occupant from the onslaught. Checking his watch, and casting an accepting glance up at the sky, the man took the time to withdraw and light up a Gold Flake; his one vice in a lifetime otherwise dedicated to his concept of living a better life.

He drew once on the cigarette holding the smoke in his lungs for a second, savouring the taste and gritty sensation of heat at the back of his throat. Content, he knocked the smouldering ember into the car's voluminous ashtray and returned the unspent part of the cigarette to the packet, which he re-pocketed in the jacket of his inexpensive and plain charcoal suit. He patted his breast, ensuring the small cardboard box did not spoil the lining of his otherwise tidy apparel, before checking his thinning grey hair in the Ambassador's rear-view mirror. Content with what he saw and that all was as it should be, he allowed himself a small smile of satisfaction. Ramkumar Mei was ready to go to work.

He readied himself to step from the relative mild and dry of the fan cooled interior of the car and into the countless singularities of water that were beating down from the skies above Delhi. He reached for his umbrella.

Only late April and the monsoon had already broken a fortnight previously, the former traditional relief from the heat of the summer almost finished now by early August. For four decades the rains had arrived earlier and earlier, almost a day a year based on the current model of weather patterns. It had mattered less for the first ten years, before the alteration had been fully noticed and proven, the early start by a little over a week an inconvenience; but now, with the rains almost a month and a half early, more animals drowned and entire crops failed every year. It would not be very many more years before famine took permanent hold in the countryside during the long dry months; already suicides were at their highest levels recorded across the sub-continent. *How we have broken our home, and with it ourselves,* Ram thought as he opened both the car door and his umbrella.

Despite pausing only to retrieve his briefcase from the passenger seat, Ram's umbrella was unequal to the task demanded of it in keeping him dry. The rains poured over its surface, falling like transparent curtains from its edges, and onto his back, soaking him through to his skin as he leant into his car, nature decisively triumphing in this particular encounter with man. Ram grabbed the handle of his case, and slamming the car door, strode quickly but without unseemly haste for the rear door of the Ministry and the cover of bricks and mortar.

The man in the bed closed his eyes. The whole time the individual who's orders had been to make his passing look like natural causes had said nothing. Instead he had replied to the man's last question with a simple shake of his head. It would be painless. The man's final words had been a brief meditation on the nature of duty and how he had carried his out to the fullest of his abilities for all the years he had been asked to, and how he understood that his visitor was simply doing the same. As the light faded in his eyes, Commander Mehta had told the agent of the powers they both served that he regretted nothing.

Inside the building, shaking both himself and his umbrella as dry as he could manage, Ram nodded a sincere greeting as he did every day to the security guards as he passed them. They in turn returned the gesture, appreciative that at least one person took the time and had the grace to acknowledge them and their duty despite the their perceived lower status. Ram crossed the foyer, head down, ignoring the D-booths and express elevators. Instead, he made for the service lifts located in the depths of the building. While not officially Scheduled for any specific set of persons, it was well understood the quicker means of reaching the building's upper floors were not meant for those of Ram's position.

He never expressed any resentment at his place in the order of the world, or sought to better his station. A lifetime of service had taught him everything should come given enough time and temperance. Presently, he hoped he was not about to discover the opposite was in fact the more likely.

Once in the compartment with the doors safely closed

Ram held the button for the eighth floor, while simultaneously depressing the alarm call and basement buttons. The nano-scanner in the lift panel responded to the combination and activated, reading not only Ram's fingerprints, but his DNA also before confirming it was indeed Senior Minister Mei who was requesting Protocol One, and not an accidental or deliberate attempt to activate the lift's true function by anyone unauthorised to do so. Ram stood perfectly still in the very middle of the compartment as it Displaced, leaving its cable swinging gently to and fro from the loss of the weight it normally bore.

< < <

'Ms Chaudray. Location report,' the Captain staccatoed at his first officer. 'We are somewhere, but I would like to be sure we are the correct somewhere.' Chaudray pivoted her affirmation at his order before returning her concentration back to the display hanging in her vision.

Captain Srinath spoke in the same business like manner to his medical officer. 'Mr Kumarapad. How is the Displacement drive behaving? Please be telling me it is alright.' The lieutenant affirmed his Captain's order in the same manner the first officer had done.

Next it was the Vimana's engineer to be on the receiving end of his Captain's no nonsense instructions. 'Mr Kumarapad. Get me full, ship-wide broad spectrum diagnostics of every system. We have just put such a distance on the clock that I want to know how my ship is holding up before we go anywhere else.'

Finally he turned finally his communications officer. 'Get a fix on the broadbeam from Ooty, Mr Kandasi. I want to be giving them an update as soon as possible.'

Captain Srinath's crew paused for a heartbeat, barely a second. But now, with the Vimana's capabilities proven,

36

the eleven individuals comprising the ship's complement were living proof that what was achievable in a single second would never be the same as it had been barely five minutes previously. One second was now sufficient to transport three hundred tons of state-of-the-art computing wrapped in a thin shell of ceramic and exotic tungsten alloys all the way to the edge of the solar system.

When the next order did not come Chaudray spoke for all of them, prompting her commander. 'Will there be anything else Sir?'

'Ha,' replied Srinath, pivoting his head in accord. 'I am going to be taking in the view,' he said with a smile.

Five

The Brahman Group

Saturday 22 April 2056 – 07:03 IST

The lift and the Senior Minister arrived in a tidy, windowless, wood-panelled anteroom where ten other Protocol One compartments, all now empty, sat quietly with their doors open. Set in the ceiling above each was a spotlight, their singular brightnesses the only illumination in the otherwise shaded room. This far underneath the surface of the earth there was little need for glass in the walls and every need for artificial lighting. Ram stepped from his lift and cast his gaze around at the ten others, and at the single, unlit vacant spot.

Being the second longest serving member of the Brahman Group, and its de facto head, he was afforded the distinction of being the last to arrive. He gave a small grimace; he had hoped all eleven others had arrived before him and was saddened to find it not so upon realising who was delayed. Still, the business of the Brahman Group could not wait; events were moving, necessitating a reaction. Striding toward the only door exiting the anteroom and into the meeting room beyond, Ram mentally readied himself for the discussions to come.

Inside the similarly windowless but larger room sat a dozen comfortable LeatherLike armchairs, arranged in a circle, almost like the numerals on a clock face, but with no table at the centre. Like the anteroom preceding it, the Brahman Group's secure meeting room walls were covered with sombre hardwood panelling, a nod perhaps to former colonial styles of decoration. But unlike the area that welcomed the arriving lift compartments, the meeting room was well lit, subdued floor lighting and recessed uplighters giving a shadowless illumination to the whole room, leaving no dark spaces for anyone to retreat into.

All but two of the armchairs were occupied by an, at present, discomforted member of the Group. Conversation and speculation were at a minimum despite the un-orthodoxy of the situation.

Normally they met regularly every six months, the last conclave being nine weeks previously. This gathering, arranged late the previous night for this morning by Ram, was therefore as highly unusual as it was hastily arranged. Each member fidgeted in their own way, either adjusting cuffs or fiddling with a brooch or other adornment. The impatience of the knowledge there was more to be divulged manifested as physical tics in even the veterans of four or five previous intercessions. Despite the temperate twenty one centigrade in the room, more than one of them was sweating, and not just from the humidity they had all up until a few minutes ago had to walk through.

Ram interrupted what little chatter hung in the air with a formal nod and a greeting of 'Namaste' to the group as a whole, which each replied to in their turn. He dropped his briefcase onto the seat of his chair, popped the clasps, retrieved the aPaper, unfurled it and flicked it on. It shone into life, set to display a page of that morning's copy of The Hindustan Times.

'I take it you have all seen each other's efforts today,' he said. Each of the ten others reached either under their seat or into a briefcase for their own augmented device. Thus directed, they flicked to the sections one of their conterparts had been responsible for; either in directly writing or, through their under-secretary, had had written. As a group they examined each others' efforts in the newspapers, magazines and other media they held responsibility for.

Each article was, in one form or another, an obituary or memorial piece for Lieutenant Commander Mehta, formerly Lead Deva of the Indian interstellar spacecraft the Vimana, and lately honorary chair of space science at Delhi University. All were in part reverential, touching, poignant, funny, sad and, if from the moment they began talking about the Vimana's return to Earth, complete fabrication, only returning to the truth when they all agreed there had been the death of a man two days previously who bore an identical resemblance to the Commander.

'All I can say is that I am very pleased with what I read and saw this morning. You have all executed your responsibilities to the fullest. I appreciate our hand was forced by events somewhat beyond our control, but I am glad to say we have conducted our business well, and the world will remember Commander Mehta as they should have.'

There was some solemn nodding of general accord around the Group. However Narinder Suryan, ostensibly a junior ranking official in the Ministry of Energy Security (Hydroelectric sub-division) but actually the third longest serving member of the Brahman Group and special advisor to the Prime Minister on all matters pertaining to space travel, spoke up. A man in his mid-fifties and losing his physique to the worst excesses of his diet, its consequences showing in his rounded face and waistline, lifted himself upright in his chair. 'Thank you Ram, but surely you did not call us here in such an unprecedented fashion to merely tell us what a good job we do?'

There was a short silence; Narinder voicing in plain terms what the majority had been thinking but perhaps lacked in the directness, and seniority of the sharp-witted fifty-seven year old to challenge Ram.

'Of course not. Allow me to apologise first for this rather hastily convened summit, I appreciate that this is highly irregular, but I only received the request this morning.'

'Request? From whom?' Narinder prodded his superior once more.

Seemingly emboldened by his questions the rest of the Group followed Narinder's lead, first to speak being Prakat Gupta, a well proportioned figure in his early sixties, whose day job was supposedly a middle-ranking manager in the Health Ministry, Logistics Department, but was in fact the country's leading expert on the long term effects of zero-g on mammalian physiology. His physique felt the benefit of his position as he was required to keep himself in good shape as his principle test subject, and the only striking sign of his age his near bald pate which he had to protect from the worst of the Indian summers. 'And what for? It must be of the utmost earnestness to have called us all here, barely two months since we all last spoke.'

There was some pivoting of heads in agreement at the question. Even when dealing with the arrangements after Mehta's death, the Brahman Group had not needed to meet all at once, the long-practised details discussed in conclaves of only threes or fours. For them all to be meeting so soon after their last official full summit meant something important was about to, or had just happened.

Ram spoke again. 'I was passed a request from our High Commission in London late last night their time. They had been asked to issue an emergency visa to a member of the financial community and, of course alerted me to the request. It would seem there has been a change of personnel to lead the InCh desk at Sinha MG and they wish the newly appointed director to come out to Delhi for a short period.'

'Why would this concern the twelve of us?' asked Narinder.

'I asked exactly the same question of Ms Chawla, and she politely informed me they wish to determine the impact of Commander Mehta's passing on the D-market. They feel perhaps there will be a profitable effect for them to take advantage of. I therefore felt it significant enough to warrant our full attention at the earliest possible occasion.'

There was some subdued murmuring, the room's mood of quiet, humble pride of only a few moments ago swept away by Ram's announcement. Several of the assembled sat up, straightening themselves in their chairs. The Brahman Group wielded total control over all coverage of the Vimana across every possible form of publication in every medium. They maintained this through a network of powerful SIs, monitoring every keystroke associated with the ship, and in the twenty-five years since its return to Earth they had painted the portrait of Srinath and his crew that they needed in the public's mind. An outsider was dangerous, and they all knew it.

Not to their positions, they were public servants, accepting fully the burden placed upon them, but to the truth; the truth they diligently cloaked and masked behind fake biographies and false obituaries. The possibility that a single person might uncover even a thread of the whole tapestry that concealed the truth sat somewhere between unlikely and impossible, but their actions and words might entice others to investigate a story that the whole world had accepted for nearly a quarter of a century

There was an unhappy cough from Narinder.

'Ha?' asked Ram.

'If you have spoken to Reena Chawla then surely you can press her to pursue a different course? Postpone the appointment, or find some way to delay the analysis.'

'Despite our interest in the organisation we do not wield as much influence with its CEO as you may think. And we certainly cannot control the market's reaction to our recent loss, however much we downplay the coverage. There are areas beyond our direct influence, and we must be able to respond correctly when they converge with us.'

Narinder paused for a second. Then, once again voicing the unspoken question for everyone else, said, 'Who are they asking to send?'

Ram was about to respond when all in the room sensed a mass Displace into the anteroom. 'One moment, Narinder, please,' Ram said, raising a palm to hold the discussion at that point. He moved towards the door, opening it to allow the final member of the Group ingress to the meeting.

'My deepest apologies for my tardiness,' said the latecomer, his voice both dry and tempered with age. The grey-haired man who stood in the doorway apologising was easily older than everyone else in the room by a decade. He carried the weight of his advanced years with grace on his slender frame. While his body may have succumbed to the unrelenting passage of time, hollows in his cheeks where before there had been vigour, hands that shook slightly more each year and the need for a walking cane as assistance, his mind had remained as sharp as it had been when he was a man in his twenties. He expanded slightly on his apology. 'There was a matter of some importance that required my full attention at the Ministry, and I could not abandon it. I am sorry.'

'Not at all, Joseph,' replied Ram, clasping the older man's outstretched hand gently in both of his own and returning the proffered handshake with deliberate care. 'I had got as far as describing the circumstances that have necessitated our meeting, that is all. I trust you received the summary I left for you?'

'Ha, thank you,' replied Joseph as he took his seat a little unsteadily, but refusing to be helped into the chair. Ram waited until the elder man was safely ensconced in his seat before enquiring if a summary of the meeting so far was necessary, to which Joseph answered, 'Please, do not backtrack. Simply continue where you had got to.'

Ram nodded once then returned to addressing the Group as a whole. 'The new head of the desk is one Rebecca Eckhart. I had retrieved everything we have and could find on her as soon as I was passed the enquiry, and had Motilal digest it into a manageable précis. Here.' Ram gestured to the wall behind him, pointing over his shoulder at the augpoint concealed in the wood-panelling. A head and shoulders shot of a smiling Rebecca, taken from her personnel record, was projected into the centre of the room, where it spun through a slow three hundred and sixty degrees, while her biography scrolled up the right hand side.

Ram continued. 'Rebecca Louise Eckhart, born July 25th 2023 to Gregor and Helena Eckhart in York, England. Parents now separated. Member one oh one seven four of the Leapfrog Club back in 2031.' Several eyebrows raised at this nugget of information. 'Ha, I thought that too initially. However, statistically it really means very little. There were well over a crore children registered as members of the Leapfrog Club. I do not wish to under or over state its significance as a co-incidence. But as a lever it may prove useful.' He paused to allow his words to have the desired effect. Eleven of the world's most well connected and powerful people all worked on how they could or could not use that to their collective advantage.

'In continuance. Youngest of three siblings; Stuart, the eldest, an IT consultant currently working at the United Nations in Rio de Janeiro, then Jemima who is married and a housewife, mother of one four year old son, in her home town. Rebecca would seem to be the driven one of the three. Read Politics and Economic Science at Birmingham

44

before taking a job at the London offices of Kwok-Leung IBF where she did very well, making herself financially independent by her mid-twenties as their most successful water commodity trader.

'Her life's path seemed determined at this point. However, it seems fate would take her in another direction. Her father suffered a Displacement accident at his place of employment, leaving him unable to work. The industrial tribunal, weighted heavily against individual employees, unsurprisingly found him to be culpable. It seems she is not without a conscience however; Ms Eckhart took it upon herself to litigate against the company, losing almost all her accumulated wealth pursuing them through the courts. Her efforts were not in vain though. With their share price tumbling in the face of her evidence they offered her a no-blame settlement. She refused, pursuing the directors until she was able to prove gross corporate grievous bodily harm against all three of them, leading in turn to sentences of between twelve and seventeen years for each of them.

She was then recruited from Kwok-Leung to her current employer, where she has established herself as a successful Displacement analyst, covering all aspects of the market, from taking positions on individual licences to long-term macro-economic trends. She all but predicted the current civil war in North America as a consequence of D-tech, and it is from there she is returning at the moment to her promotion, and therefore our predicament.'

'Ha, I know of her,' said Vinita Desai from across the room, her voice initially sounding out of place after the three previous men had been speaking, the room unused to the feminine and having exactly the effect she knew it would. The focus of the meeting shifted to the smartly dressed woman in her late forties. 'When Kandasi passed two years ago, I was in London at a financial conference and had the occasion to meet her, albeit briefly.'

'And what were your impressions of our Ms Eckhart?'

Vinita remembered the woman she had met for fifteen minutes in the middle of a crowded, noisy room. 'Well, if she has not changed, and from Ram's biography it sounds as if she has not, then she is headstrong but committed to her work. Her pieces are a shade clinical but she is always precise in her analyses. An astute, incisive woman I recall.'

Now Vinita paused for a second, allowing the implication of what she had said to permeate around the room. Despite the seriousness of their work, and the common goal they all shared, few of the Brahman Group were above small acts of personal theatre, especially when making an effort to sway the group to their way of thinking. Vinita finished her point. 'Exactly the sort of woman we do not wish to expose Commander Mehta's story to,' she said finally. Heads pivoted again in agreement.

Ram however did not move. Instead he said, 'I am of a mind to inform the High Commission in London to approve Sinha MG's business visa application for Ms Eckhart, with provisional authorisation for further access should she request it, subject to the approval of the Group, of course.'

The pivoting heads stopped mid swing, coming to rest slowly and deliberately, almost not believing what they had heard. There was an occasional gasp of uncontrolled incredulity and blusters of 'Pardon?' and 'Have you lost your reason?'

It was Prakat who came to Ram's defence. 'Let us not be too hasty or obvious in our protestations. Ram has obviously given the matter great thought. He called us here to discuss this issue, not hurl insults around. Remember our work. It is too important to let emotion rule our decision.'

Vinita seemed to accept the logic in the elder Group member's words, but held her original position. 'I am sorry Ram, I did not mean to be unreasonable. However, there exists the real possibility that this woman could be dangerous to our work.'

Narinder too was less than happy with the prospect of anyone but their trusted cadre of reporters and journalists reporting on anything to do with Mehta, and by association, the Vimana. 'Forgive me Ram, but I must agree with Vinita. I feel this is too great a risk to our endeavour. It would seem that Ms Eckhart has a history of finding the truth of things.'

Ram had anticipated this line of reasoning from someone in the Brahman Group. 'Only where there is trespass or evil. We have done neither, and will do neither. Our work does not require us to tarnish ourselves, or any others. I understand Ms Eckhart is a fine analyst, with an exemplary record and an integrity to her work that is rare in her profession. Her moral compass shall not be put out of true here, as we are acting the correct manner. There is nothing here for her to uncover that is improper. Our work will be quite safe with her, I am sure.'

Vinita remained unconvinced. 'What of her a-life? Is there anything there that should concern us?'

'We have analysed her SI's access patterns, along with her comms for the previous five years, courtesy of our roothosts in the British datastate, and are in the process of transcribing the relevant sections of her conversations. The initial evaluation shows nothing untoward, and is consistent with her vocation; the views and searches tally neatly with the chronological order of her published research, and the remainder of her access falls well within the parameters of accepted norms for her profile, location, salary and known pass-times.'

'Understanding this matter to be of the utmost sensitivity, we have exceeded protocol and broadened the search algorithms to cover not just her immediate family, friends and all partners, but everyone out a further two degrees of separation, up to and including all first cousins and grandchildren where they exist. Obviously extending the searches to this degree has thrown up some interesting artefacts, especially in the area of her previous partners, but that is mostly a consequence of the weight of numbers given her history. At this level of removal from Ms Eckhart herself the connections become tenuous at best. Our SIs assure us there is nothing to fear from her in this capacity.'

'I have a solution that I believe reconciles both sides,' said a voice across the room that belonged to Professor Ajar Jindal, Head of Cognitive Research at the University of Bangalore. 'We have been making promising progress in the field of coercive inter-cranial electric field manipulation and have had startling results on our test subjects. If we could organise a visit for her to the University?' he left the question incomplete, the inference unspoken.

A sizeable minority of the Brahman Group baulked visibly at this; it was an ugly proposal. Ram gave them voice. 'No. If she is to visit then there will be no interference with her,' he said softly. 'We will not sow evil in our samsara with such actions. Our karma is intact on this matter and with such an act we would do ourselves great injury.' Ram cast his gaze over the assembled group looking for any trace they collectively believed this was a wise course of action. 'I do not wish to hear that any of you have considered this course of action again. We must be complete in our thoughts as well as our deeds if we are to remain spiritually sound.'

'Could we then not allow her visa on some vague technicality then? An obscure question of process, or an unfortunate quirk of the bureaucracy perhaps?' Professor Jindal pressed, seemingly now his original suggestion had been struck down, to have taken up with the minority coalition to exclude Rebecca that was coalescing out of the Group's members as the meeting wore on.

'Consider this then,' replied Ram. 'How would it look if we refused what is in every way a perfectly normal and proper request from one of the most well respected and well connected financial institutions in the market, merely because it was inconvenient to us? We would in effect be vetoing the visit of one of its number to the country that gifted the world Displacement on the occasion of the passing of one of its pioneers.

'I had considered denying all visa applications as not being requested with sufficient time to process, and in fact we have utilised such a device with the majority of lesser institutions and organisations, and all publications. We have been fortunate that the rest of the world seems to have mostly forgotten the Vimana, as we have received less than a handful of requests to cover the funeral.

'However, we are the victims of timing here ourselves. Sinha MG is too prestigious to merely try and dissuade in this manner, and doubtless they are aware of that fact. Their request was the first to arrive, at least a day earlier than any of the others, and it would at the very least raise their indignation if we denied it on a seemingly trivial point of protocol.

'In that event I hazard we would be informed we were allowing ingress to Ms Eckhart from our Prime Minister, with little room for persuading him otherwise. The bank expect to be granted access as their station befits.'

'I have to agree with Ram's thinking here.' Prakat once again spoke in defence of his senior. 'It would be foolish to provoke them.' This time the room was in agreement with Ram; the number of shaking heads outweighed by the general murmur of consent.

'And in fact I see a mechanism to utilise this situation with the bank to our further advantage, if only in a small way,' said Ram. 'If we grant them sole entry on the grounds of national interest, then we are well within our rights and norms of protocol to deny the remaining visa applications. By allowing the best of them in, we can refuse the less desirable.'

'Your solution to this quandary is indeed very elegant

Ram,' commented Vinita, seemingly won over.

Ram however was modest. 'It is the correct thing to do.'

Narinder seemed to consider Ram's words, cupping his chin in his hands as if supporting the weight of the thoughts in his head. He narrowed his eyes in concentration, barely blinking as he turned the argument over and over, scrutinising it from every angle, regarding every facet of logic presented to him. After a long minute in which the whole room eventually came to be looking at him, he finally spoke. 'You are of course correct Ram. I see the reason to your greater wisdom now. I do not expect it to make Ms Eckhart any more suggestible to anything we may or may not want exposed, but it would certainly not hurt our endeavour to have her on our side from the very beginning. We are all aware of the thought processes of this sort; the thriving on feeling they are besting their competition, even in small ways.'

'It seems to me that we have enough of a consensus to put the matter to a Group vote,' said Ram, drawing the matter under discussion to a close. He was conscious of the risk of continuing the debate and allowing the small coterie that had solidified around Professor Jindal's motion to exclude the analyst to grow beyond his ability to manipulate should the discussion continue to circle around points of protocol and other distractions. Either the Group would vote to carry his motion and that would be the end of it, or they would disagree with him as was their right, and they could discuss the reasons Ram would present to the bank and Prime Minister afterwards.

He had a brief moment of anxiety after finishing his closing statements. *Had he done enough to convince them? Would they jump the way he wanted, no, needed them to jump? It was a risk.* Group votes of this magnitude did not happen often enough to confidently predict the outcome; a more contrary group of electors would be difficult to assemble. He estimated he had just over half his fellow members convinced, and knew he could depend on at least two others. That left three with whom he had no idea of their intentions. Just to be certain, Ram added, 'And as I am the member proposing we allow Ms Eckhart ingress, I shall abstain, in order that there be no accusations of bias in the vote.'

This was a delicate gamble; a calculated risk, but a risk nonetheless. The removal of his entry into the franchise would force the rest of the Brahman Group to return a majority verdict; there could be no abstentions. It was a subtle if deliberate triple bluff of peer-pressuring. When all twelve of them voted it was, theoretically at least, possible for the result to be a tie, at six ballots cast for either side, with Ram's vote seen as carrying an additional weight due to his seniority. But such an event had never occurred in the quarter-century of the Group's history. In his more junior years Ram could only ever recall two occasions where the Group were out of harmony, and they had both been by a margin of a single vote cast against; normally they spoke with one voice. By removing his perceived prerogative he hoped to influence them subtly; any waverers would see the rightness of his convictions if he himself were so certain of them he need not vote for them.

The votes were cast in open session; there were no secret ballots in the organisation guarding the most dangerous secret of them all. Each member had two ceramic balls no larger than a quail's egg, symbolically white for and black against; a simple but effective representation of the dichotomy of the choices they weighed, and each held their choice in a closed hand until the moment they were called to reveal their intentions. The vote was nine to two in favour of Ram's stated preference of acquiescing to Sinha MG's request, and by inference, permitting Rebecca Eckhart into the country. A solid endorsement, but not one without unprecedented opposition. The no's were

Deepak Syed, a relatively junior member, at forty-one years old, only with the Group for eighteen months, and in Ram's opinion entitled to show he was not to be intimidated by peer pressure, and Professor Jindal, which came as a surprise to no one, least of all Ram. On this matter he had expected a modicum of disharmony, and was quietly satisfied the outcome vindicated his belief that his planned course of action was the correct thing to do.

The remainder of the allotted meeting duration was taken up with discussions surrounding the finer details of Rebecca's visit. The group dynamic restored they discussed the itinerary they would suggest to their guest; a trip to the InSA museum, with perhaps an opportunity to sit inside the Vimana itself, subject to the agreement of the museum's curator, a personal friend of at least three of the Brahman Group, including Ram; the tactful interview with Commander Mehta's widow and the access to the declassified sections of Commander Mehta's service record.

Everything was planned as far as it could be, with several alternate possible itineraries and visits discussed should Rebecca express a wish to do or see something mildly unexpected. Possibilities exhausted, the Brahman Group began to break up, singletons and pairs splintering off and returning to their humble cover stories, until only Ram and Joseph were left in the suddenly purposeless feeling meeting room.

'You talked well today, old friend. You were very impressive,' said Joseph to his one time deputy and protégé, his voice catching only slightly. 'You have learnt how to influence people to your way of thinking in the most subtle ways. I thought for a time there we would lose the eventual vote, but that abstention of yours was masterful. Now we can proceed.'

'Have I done the right thing?' Ram asked after sitting quietly for a moment. 'Now that events are in motion I am struck by an uncertainty I did not have only moments ago.

Is that not odd?' he asked Joseph.

'You fear the necessity of the course you have placed before yourself? I am sure of the direction you have chosen for us. If it is any consolation I would have chosen the same if this had occurred a decade previously.'

'Vinita's point regarding outsiders is still a valid one.'

'She will meet our expectations. And the other will fulfil our requirements. I am sure of it.'

'I hope you are right. We do not have the luxury of time,' said Ram rising from his chair pausing only to rest his hand gently on Joseph's shoulder as he headed for his own lift compartment.

Six

Outside Interests

Saturday 22 April 2056 – 12:00 IST

At the pre-arranged hour the three of them initiated the narrowbanded modulating gigabyte key encrypted digital audio-only conference. Its cutting-edge, SI driven security access protocols were derived from one lakh independent and one-time datapoints across A-space. Several minutes before, each of them had excused themselves from whatever duty of state was occupying their diary at that particular time. Each cited an urgently arisen matter that needed their immediate attention, and could someone please update them on how the meeting progressed in their absence, and that they would be back as soon as possible.

With the assistance of a Cotts field scrambler, all arrived at their sanctuaries, rooms no other soul knew the location of, or that they existed at all. A handful of seconds later each of the three entered the conference with that day's one-time keyphrase. They were joined by their fourth, who organised them and was their de-facto leader, having recruited them all to the group-within-a-group that had taken hold within the Brahman Group. Each of the Saazish spoke to the group through their specially engineered SIs, a phalanx of hardware and software commissioned to flatten any trace of natural cadence, timbre or melody in their voices, hiding their identities from each other.

While the system guaranteed anonymity should even a fragment of the signal be intercepted and decoded, it had not stopped each of the three intuiting who the others most likely were, even though all were careful not to use any personal idiosyncrasies of speech. While none of them ever let any of these suspicions slip during any of the Brahman Group face-to-face meetings, each was acutely aware that three other people in such meetings were pursuing agendas outside those set by Ramkumar.

Formal greetings were repeated four times, heralding the commencement of the meeting always held after any vote of the Brahman Group.

'aSSemBLed FRiEnDS,' began the voice the other three took to be their assumptive leader. The paranoia in the group-within-a-group was such that none would risk announcing to the others even if the assembly was all one or a mix of genders. 'IT wOUlD SEEm tHe oLD maN HaS preSENTed uS wItH a sitUATIOn wHIch rEQuireS oUR mOst CAREful aTTentiON. SUGGEstIOnS PLEase.'

<<

'What are our options? Are we to activate a replacement?'

'Normally I would consider that as the logical path, but we have an opportunity to press the renegades if we exert the proper pressure.'

'In that case we cannot be seen to be acting directly in this matter. It must appear as if events have unfolded along their natural path, with no external influence.'

'We are fortunate. I have been informed of a promising

young D-market analyst who could be perfect for our purposes. The proper recommendation to Reena Chawla should secure her the necessary promotion, and with it the vehicle for the external intervention. This alone should be sufficient to stir the renegades to further action.'

'You suspect their hand in Mehta's passing.'

Ram considered for a moment before replying to Joseph. 'Ultimately we all have a hand in every aspect of the Vimana, and all carry responsibility for the men and women who bear the names of its crew. But, with regard to this specific event, yes, I do. I am convening a full meeting of our number in a handful of days to discuss all of this.'

'And what makes you sure of the westerner? What qualifies her among any other potential candidates we may have for consideration?'

'Primarily, her status as an outsider, both from without India and also the circle of control we exert. It should provoke all the necessary parties into action. Secondly, her history is a remarkable series of coincidences, leading to an intensely conflicted adult, susceptible to subtle influence. She was a devoted member of the Leapfrog club; her SI access records from that time are voluminous to say the least; everything which was ever clouded pertaining to the mission has been viewed at least once. And it would appear this is as close as she ever came to Professor Cotts' discovery. There are records of her attending specialist training schools, but nowhere in her entire credit history was Motilal able to find any entry for the D-booth system. She has never used it. Nor does she possess a D-capable vehicle. The logical conclusion Motilal was able to draw is that it would seem she is entirely without the ability to Displace.'

'And yet she works as a D-market analyst. Fascinating. What of her family history?' Joseph asked, wanting to know more of the woman behind the facts laid before him.

'One elder brother and sister. She is the junior by

several years.'

'An unplanned third child, you think?'

'Perhaps. Her parents separated when she was in her teens, after her siblings were establishing themselves in the world.'

'And partners? Lovers?'

'Several over the past two years that we have been able to verify. She is currently attached to Damien Regent.'

'The D-thlete?' Joseph checked with Ram.

'Ha.'

'My my,' said Joseph, almost in disbelief. 'I see now why you feel she is our most suitable candidate. Her past will compel her present.'

>

The lover rolled over, smiling and happy at the memory of the night before. The early morning light filtered through the plain cotton shade covering the bedroom window, casting a warm glow into the room, and which had woken him only minutes ago. The night had been passionate, heat and ardour eventually, reluctantly giving way to a deep sleep for both of them, overcome by the exertion and physical release of orgasm. She spooned him, her breasts resting against his back, reassuring him that she was still there and not a phantom lover, imagined and dreamed as he drifted off, the sweaty smell of their sex hanging caught in the small spaces between them.

He noticed she had risen before him, only moments ago if the lingering residue of her warmth and scent on the sheets was any indicator. He rubbed his face in an effort to brush away the sleepiness that clung to his mind as he rose from the bed to pursue his lover to wherever she had got to. He found her adjusting his suit, batting the creases out of the arms and back panel as best she could with swift sweeps of her flattened hand. A poor substitute for a pressing, but in the circumstances, far better than nothing at all.

Sensing her paramour she turned slowly and smiled at him. 'I hope you do not mind,' she indicated his clothing. 'You said last night there was an important meeting you would have to attend this morning, and I know you will not have time to return home and collect another suit, so I was trying to make this one as presentable as possible. I took the liberty of washing and pressing the shirt you left here the last time, so you would have a clean one the next time you came at least.'

He was nonplussed for a second, then realisation dawned on him: *That was where it had gone.* Upon the occasion of his previous visit he had had notice of Suri's visit to her mother, therefore more time to prepare. He had taken a change of clothing with him, but upon leaving had overlooked the soiled shirt in the laundry. One slip that had nearly had catastrophic consequences. He had had to tell Suri it had been damaged and was at a tailor being repaired. He would have to be much more careful in the future, but his lover always found new and diverting ways to distract him; things his wife would never want to hear about let alone indulge in.

'I hope you do not mind, but after discovering it in the linen I did wear it for a short while before I cleaned it; it smelled of you and it made me less lonely when you could not be here. I did not have time to freshen the suit, but I have pressed the trousers. It should serve, particularly if you carry the jacket rather than wear it. If you want I have a formal dhoti around you could wear if you think the trousers will be too untidy.'

'No, they will be fine I think. I seem to remember you not letting me keep them on too long when I arrived last night anyway,' he said, good humour in his voice as he put his arms around her waist from behind, and she in turn reached behind herself between them and stroked him as he swelled at her touch.

'Will you be coming back tonight?' she asked, as if missing him already.

'I should be, ha. Suri is still at her sister's family, so I have this evening to myself as well.'

'Good. I do not see enough of you as it is,' she replied, lowering her eyes a fraction as she took a step back from him, allowing him to Displace to his PDV secreted in a garage just over a kilometre away. Smugly satisfied at himself for another successful dalliance, he dropped himself into the vehicle and departed for the meeting with the rest of the Brahman Group. *What did Ram want that could be this important?* He mulled the question over until he arrived, where he, after hiding his surprise at Ram's announcement proceeded to vote for the motion in the full knowledge there would be a conclave of the Saazish to discuss what transpired at the Brahman Group.

One hour after the meeting had disbanded, he was accessing the electronic conference to discuss what the four of them could do to impede the analyst Ram was allowing into their country, and in doing so, putting the truth at risk of discovery.

She watched her lover depart, feeling the Fold dissipate around her. After enough time to be sure he had not forgotten anything and likely to return, she enabled the Cotts field nullifier, her SI, Kalpana, now shielding her apartment from any D-targeting capabilities. Confident of her privacy she retrieved the small briefcase secreted under the false flooring of her bedroom. One fingerprint, DNA and voice-recognition check later Sati Chaudray, sole surviving niece of the Vimana's first officer, popped the clasps holding the briefcase closed and lifted the top.

Flicking a switch on the control panel activated the nanoscopic recording unit that was disguised as a button on the shirt she had misdirected her lover into wearing this morning.

It had not been easy, and it had taken several years to first identify a member of the Brahman Group likely to be open to her specific overtures, then over a period of many months determine his routine to allow her to plan her approach. Her more usual method of contact would not have worked on a man of his standing, so she had had to convene a seemingly chance encounter. Being over two decades younger than him had helped in that respect. He had been flattered that as a man in his seventh decade she made him believe he had been found attractive enough to appeal to a woman of her nature.

After that came the clandestine courting, she slowly winning his trust and convincing him she wished to be the companion he could not openly admit to, and she was not trying to extract money from him. Initially, Sati had meant for their relationship to remain as platonic as possible, engaging Prakat on an intellectual level. But it was obvious after a handful of liaisons his only interest in her was if she was willing to further their relationship into a physical one. So she had had to employ her body to further her ends.

After that came the eventual consummation of their relationship, and the many months on her hands and knees waiting for her opportunity. During this she had at least been able to take physical pleasure from the act; despite his age he was a skilled and delicate lover, opening her in ways she had not previously experienced. And the physicality he undertook with her had its own advantage from her perspective; he took far greater risks to secure her body than he ever would have done if the rewards of being with her were purely intellectual; the sex made him careless, distracted by the fear of discovery and the thrill of the taboo, allowing her to dictate the terms of their couplings more and more.

Her chance finally arrived during his last visit when she had coyly advised him to bring spare clothing with him the next time, intimating at a full night of her company. With no sense of loss at the severance of their relationship she was about to initiate, she had hidden his shirt; distracting him into forgetting it was relatively easy after the ice-age of time she had waited and prepared. Swapping the spare buttons for recording devices, one primary and one backup, she finally allowed herself a flush of emotion. She was close now. Close to the truth about the Brahman Group and the secret it was hiding.

THE MACRO-IMPACT OF DISPLACEMENT:
2020 to PRESENT DAY

Rebecca Eckhart - 15/04/2044
(WORD COUNT 1,500 ~10%)

In the nearly two decades since Professor Rajat Cotts' as yet unsolved disappearance from the luxury cruise liner, the Stargazer, in the almost dead centre of the Pacific Ocean, his legacy, the Nobel prize winning *in absentia* 'Theory of Near Instantaneous Matter Transfer', or Displacement as it has popularly come to be known, has been put to use in ways perhaps even his genius could not have envisaged. And as with any scientific discovery, some of its applications and their unforeseen negative consequences were inevitable.

Once lesser scientists had deciphered the brand new and elegant language of mathematics Professor Cotts had devised to express the simple enough notion of the almost immediate shifting of physical objects from one place to another, it revolutionised everything. Displacement-engine vehicles were the first obvious use for the ability to move persons and goods almost instantaneously, followed rapidly by the personal D-booth networks, granting unprecedented freedom of movement.

With radical technological advance came great profit also. InSA shrewdly retained sole technology and ownership rights of Professor Cotts' work. Constructing and operating the only Displacement satellites, allowing manipulation of the Cotts Field by the cubic centimetre, they ensured a revenue stream in the crores of rupees, as D-service providers bid and overbid for licences to operate.

Having mastered the majority of his environment, mankind remained limited by the physical distances between two places, and the inevitable expenditure of time and, more importantly, energy it took to move resources and people between them. With D-tech built into everything, physical separation obsolesced. Trade in goods was freed up in ways that had previously been impossible. The immediate, and ultimately far-reaching effect of this laxity of commerce was the commensurate increase in its principle driver; consumption.

An already overburdened earth, its resources the cause of several conflicts across the globe, each one threatening to spiral and drag in one of the four power blocs of the United States of both North and South America, India and China, could not take the strain.

Entire economies, principally the smaller satellite states of the four superpowers collapsed, as although now more easily moved around than ever before, the demand for goods could not be met by the rapidly dwindling resource pool of the planet. The less abundant countries were unable to react with sufficient international weight in the rebalancing of demand within the global economy. Even the single largest positive to emerge from D-tech, the removal of the dependence on fossil fuels, principally oil for transport and coal for power generation, and the corresponding near elimination of greenhouse gas emissions had unforeseen consequences.

Free from the burden of foreign oil and the corresponding necessity to maintain some semblance of diplomacy with the rest of the world, the United States became self-sufficient; reverting to the long cherished dream of fortress, converting almost overnight to hydro-electric and nuclear power generation, both now efficient and safe, and most importantly, nationally accessible energy sources. Gigatons of water, Displaced hourly by Devas, drove the turbines, while toxic radioactive waste was moved off-planet, and directed at the Sun.

This removal of demand for its principal export left the Middle-East in chaos, and more dangerously, it left the nations there vulnerable; the one thing that secured their economies, and in the case of a number of sovereign states their security, was removed as quickly as it took to Displace the substantially more worthless oil from one side of the world to the other. The United States took full advantage of these countries' turmoil and isolation. Coupled with the new inward focus was a resurgent belief in its own rightness, which for so long, and in so many countries previously had expressed itself as military aggression. The United States' long-held grudge against the majority of the Middle-East could be settled; the extended dependence on oil forcing alliances with regimes they would not have tolerated otherwise, was always seen as a form of embarrassment and humiliation to its leaders, now unbound by economic reasons not to engage in what they saw as retributive action. Led by the nephew of the last President to invade another sovereign nation, the United States waged bloody and horrific war, indulging itself in a cathartic frenzy of genocide as it all but eliminated the vast majority of its enemies. The deaths of tens of crore people however did not buy them security.

Isolated utterly from the international community, partly by design and partly in response to its actions, even its once fiercest allies now awake to the industrial scale war-machine the once leader of the free world had allowed itself to slide towards. The United Nations, its assembly already relocated to Rio de Janeiro, threatened the imposition of economic sanctions, but the United States was large enough to retain almost total self-sufficiency financially; and the threat of military action was laughed off by its ambassador with a characteristically diplomatic 'Come on, if you think you can'; the verbal equivalent of a middle-finger salute to the rest of the world.

Internal unease however was harder to brush aside so easily. Peace campaigners allied with bitter anti-Government factions within the lower echelons of the administration to attempt what they saw as the struggle to redeem their once proud country in the eyes of the world. The President's response was swift and brutal; having learned from the perceived mistakes of both its last episode of internment and the sympathy that provoked and the actions of misrule in other dictatorships, the cabinet authorised the arrest and summary rendition of every suspected collaborator, their family, their friends and their friends' families. In all the squalid history of governmental abuse of its people this charted a new low for an ostensible democracy. The civil war that this action sparked was inevitable.

The splintered, demoralised factions united under the banner of Eduardo Mboto and took for themselves the name the New New Model Army. Their guerrilla tactics of destroying Displacement terminals, power lines, fuel rod and water storage facilities and, most damaging of all, broadcasting control centres, had an enormous effect before the President almost even realised the scale of the threat he had created.

Television blackouts and empty stomachs were all it took for the rest of the population to come out onto the streets and topple the regime. The ordered military response had been bloody, but the Marines and National Guard deployed to quell the protests recognised that firing automatic weapons into a crowd of unarmed mothers and children was morally corrupt, and within a week the generals declared themselves no longer an arm of the Government; neither did they side with the opposition though, instead taking on an independent peace-keeping role wherever they could.

With the loss of the threat of reprisal from the military, the seaboard states grew emboldened enough to formally cede from the Union, leaving the vast central American heartlands to fester in a hotbed of resurgent religious fundamentalism and sexual, racial and gender intolerance. The body-count began to be tallied in tens of lakh.

Chaos in one of the four superpowers led to a vacuum at the top of the world order. Several nations stood aside while others rushed to try and fill it. As home of the United Nations, the Southern American States was called on to rise to the challenge, but it declared itself unable to devote the time and energy away from its re-forestation of the Amazon basin to lead the world. China for a handful of years, no more than a dozen, took the reigns of global power, until it too was forced to divert its enormous energy and effort into restoring its own environment in an effort to feed its population, the ecological damage inflicted over the preceding decades of economic expansion able to be disregarded no longer.

The European Federation attempted to become a harmonising force; it was after all economically equivalent to the North American States in terms of total GDP and decades of intra-organisation diplomacy should have stood it in good stead; but it had grown bloated, its divisions ran deep; too many individual nation states with their own agendas proved as unworkable as it ever had, compromise after compromise diluting even the most sensible of measures. Even Great

Britain, recently re-united, tried to reassert its long lost position, but its history of shunning Europe, which had been the largest contributing factor to that continent's failure to steady the world, coupled with its supine dependence on the United States meant that without friends in the former and the prop of the latter it too was doomed to failure.

Only one country had been astute enough to predict the majority of events that arose from D-tech, and had for nearly two decades been preparing the ground for its eventual ascension. Mother India, the birthplace of Displacement, the revolution that shrank, shattered, drove apart then re-made the world, had, since the early two thousands, invested heavily in renewable energy sources; its already significant hydro-electric power stations now complemented with the world's largest solar and wind farms out in the vast Thar Desert in Rajasthan. This, coupled with the long investment history of Western outsourced information technology meant that by the time of the third US invasion of the Middle East, India had become the world leader in computing, biotechnology, medicine, space-technology and energy production. It was only a small step for them to take their turn as the economic and cultural leader of the world.

Seven

Leaving

Saturday 09 August 2031 - 21:43 EUST

'...will not fail you.'

The image of the Vimana's Captain held for a long second on the display, his deep brown eyes filled with trust and hope, seeming to look straight at Becky Eckhart as she sat enraptured at his speech. She had waited twelve hours, sat rooted in place behind her spec-screens the entire day for this, unmoving for fear of missing even a second. For the moment where the ship would report back it had reached Waypoint One successfully. She could see, really see the seriousness of the mission etched in every crease and line of its Captain's face.

She had her knees hugged to her chest, her face buried between the valley at the top of them, burning cheeks hot against her thighs. Despite this, or perhaps because of it, she could not stop herself echoing his head movements as she reached out to touch the image of Captain Srinath's face, regardless of the surety that his image was no more solid than a breath of wind. Although she did not know it then, she was not alone in her action; lakhs of other people, not all of them children were also lost in the moment, mimicking her own unconscious need to feel part of something larger than themselves.

On the sofa sat her older brother and sister, huddled in alongside their parents, all of whom Becky had insisted be present in the room to participate in the broadcast together. Jemima, five years Becky's senior nudged her older by another three years brother in the ribs and flicked her gaze at their little sister's actions. There was a stifled snort. Becky's hand flew back at the noise and came to rest unconsciously on the back of her smooth head. Her eyes widened as she involuntarily reddened even more.

The image of Captain Srinath faded, replaced by a talking scientific head from InSA explaining the mission profile in detail; but Becky did not need to hear this. She dropped the imaging glasses from her face onto the floor beside her. She knew the technical specs, operational range, power consumption, mass, volume, crew diet, duty roster and mission duration of the Vimana by heart. Months of devouring the regular magazines, content-casts and shots, downloads, uploads, collaborative peer-to-peer sessions and the dozens of other media outlets comprising membership of the Leapfrog Club had equipped her with an encyclopaedic knowledge of the mission.

The siblings' father shot his unruly teenage children a reproachful glare, the threat of punishment flashing in his eyes. He gestured at Becky with his eyes, then back at his elder children.

'Sorry Becka,' said Stuart, first to apologise; seniority of age dictating he lead.

'Yeah, sorry Becks,' added Jemima, following her brother.

Gregor Eckhart nodded his gruff approval at the apologies, which seemed immediately forgotten, as Jemima and Stuart went on to discuss the relative attractiveness of the various crew members.

Until this moment he had not known the true meaning of this event to his youngest daughter. Now though he saw why the Leapfrog Club had snared her imagination as powerfully as it had. For nearly six months he had had barely two sentences of communication with her that did not make mention of, or was either partially or wholly about the Leapfrog Club and the Vimana's mission.

He had tried to engage her brother and sister in Rebecca's obsession, but they were concerned with other things. Perhaps it was the age gap; at eight years old, five years younger than her sister and eight years her brother's junior, she had little in the way of peer-group interaction with her siblings, who regarded her at best as a mild annoyance, the bratty little kid with freckles and scabby knees who was always ready to get in the way with another lecture on the Vimana whenever there was a potential boy or girlfriend in the house.

Gregor could not persuade Jemima to join her sister in the Leapfrog Club even under the pretence of female solidarity; to give his youngest daughter the sense she had a female confidant for her obsession. After her less than selfless offer to start shaving her legs in support of Becks, his idea had been rebuffed with a harsh 'Dad, I love Becks, but that club is for ...Dalits.' She had whispered the insult, ashamed almost she could think like that. One stern rebuke ensured that Jemima would never countenance the use of the word again, let alone apply it to someone she was supposed to protect.

He had not even bothered to ask Stuart.

But his other children's' disinterest was not the explanation for Rebecca's zeal over the Vimana. The three of them rarely took more than a passing interest in each other's activities, and then usually only as a means of sibling torture, of which Rebecca was more than capable of doling out in equal measure to whatever she might receive.

Gregor could not suppress the sigh as he felt his wife

rise from the sofa he had torn her from her work in order to sit on, and show their sensitive daughter she understood one thing in her young life. Now he saw the passion that had sustained Rebecca for the preceding six months; the moment Hari Srinath had told her he would not fail her Gregor understood everything this meant to her. Hari Srinath was someone other than him she could depend on. He flicked a glance at her, still curled up in a tight ball on the floor.

Becky felt the redness of her enthusiasm fade slightly, embarrassed out of the way by the noise from her brother and sister. She heard the soft rustle of movement behind her, but did she dare look? To risk a glance behind her in the expectancy her mother was moving to sit beside her as she hoped? She weighed the balance inside herself. The risk was openness, an admission that Becky needed to make to herself but behind which she had hid, unconsciously, in the Leapfrog Club for six months.

She had to see. She turned her head, almost imperceptibly, to her family, peeking out between her arms with one eye, the rest of her face safely covered. Her mother had already left the room. The noise Becky had heard was not her coming to her at all, but her leaving.

Becky felt her absence more than just the space she left on the settee. Now, in her moment of complete and total vulnerability, when she realised she had invited them all to see her in this state, her greatest passion exposed so completely to her family despite her efforts to the contrary, when the smallest hint of connection would have bridged the chasm her mother had put between them, Becky could not understand why she did this to her. *What had she been doing wrong?* she asked herself again and again the question that she had sobbed herself to sleep with for almost a year. *Why was Mama not wanting her? Was she wrong somehow?* Becky felt tears threatening to flow; this rebuff the worst yet.

Inside her was hollow; an aching void she had tried to

70

fill with the cathedral-like structures of deep-space she had learnt about following the Vimana's mission. Nebulae, stellar nurseries and other Messier objects amongst which the ship now soared. But they were not enough; they were too far away, too abstract. Becky needed more solidity.

She had invited this snub she now realised. Clenching her teeth hard against the hurt, Becky pushed it deep down into herself, cramming it into the hole inside her, using it to fill some of the space left vacant by her mother's indifference. For now at least it could not harm her any further. Instead she focussed on her father, seeing the wonder in his eyes; understanding blossoming in them. She tried to draw on it now, to reclaim her own feelings of a few moments ago, to recapture some of the wonder and awe that helped her forget for those seconds.

But try as she might Becky could not get the feelings back, even for an instant. The vicarious pleasure of her father's joy was not to be hers. The feelings, emotions and passions were gone. Swept away. Ablated.

Becky knew that a moment in both her personal and wider world history had passed and could never again be fully reclaimed. What this portended for her future she did not know, but that moment left her eight-year-old self a little older, wiser, sadder, and certainly a little harder.

Perhaps she should find somewhere she could go where no one could touch her and hurt her? Where she did not have to show emotion and could be safe from the damning judgements of other people. Where the ice-sharp razors of cold indifference did not lead to the red-hot sting of shame. Somewhere she could hide herself. She envied Captain Srinath at that moment. He was so far away from anything that might make him sad here on earth.

Hiding a sniffle behind a cough that drew her father's attention away from the display, Becky spoke to him. 'Dada, I know what I am wanting to be when I grow up.'

'Oh, and what's that Betee?' he replied.

'An astronaut,' she said with such seriousness and purpose that it gave her father pause at the tone in her voice.

> > >

'Look Damien, it's just two nights away. Two nights, that's all. And it is a promotion! I can't not accept it, I may as well hand in my notice.' Rebecca put into her voice the tone she knew would give her lover the impression she had no choice in the situation. To re-assure him she felt the same way he did about it, but had to accept what the bank had handed her. Easier to let him believe she had been presented the appointment as a done deal. Easier for him to bear, easier for her all round. She lifted her battered trusty brown LeatherLike overnight bag from the floor and dropped it onto the bed trying to become engrossed in one final inspection of its contents.

'But why you? And why now? You've only just got back,' Damien bleated.

With her back turned Rebecca was able to close her eyes for a brief second, trying not to tense up, and just about succeeding, before replying without turning round in as nonchalant and neutral tone as she could, 'It's the way the bank works sometimes, and you've got to be able to cope with it.' *That was good. Could be seen as applying equally to her.* 'It was 'go on the trip, or forget the promotion',' she lied. 'I understand the demands your training has on us, and sometimes my job does too,' Rebecca added, deliberately strengthening the parallel she'd worked out on her way back her apartment as a way of further justification.

'But what about one of your new staff? Couldn't you have said you'd send them instead?' Damien was refusing to let the matter drop, despite Rebecca's now obvious reluctance to divulge anything further on the matter. 'It doesn't seem fair to me. You've hardly been back two days and they're sending you away again.' For emphasis he swept his hand around Rebecca's bedroom to indicate the pile of laundry sat in the corner, still near Himalayan-like, and from which Rebecca had been picking what reasonably clean underwear she could.

Having given that up, reasoning she could always buy some new, clean clothing at the D-port on the expense account, she answered her lover without turning to face him; better to make the reply seem casual, more honest feeling if he didn't see her eyes. 'I can imagine that looking good for my first day in the new job. Hardly leading from the front, is it? And besides, all the London desk are needed in town next week.' This was another prepared fabrication on her part, but one Damien could never prove otherwise.

Apart from a few names, Rebecca had told her latest lover little of the workings of her bank. This allowed her the necessary latitude for invention, should the need for a plausible sounding period of either working late or a few days away ever arise. It was not deception in the truest sense and certainly not infidelity; she would be on her own during these periods, so any fears Damien may have had regarding her motives were misplaced.

Instead she spent the time either at the threedees, letting some easily digested Bollywood melodrama wash over her, the uncomplicated morals and clear delineations between hero and nemesis an easy proxy for her tightly controlled id; or she would check in to an anonymous hotel in another city under a false name and allow herself to fall between the cracks of life for a day or two.

Usually, what she had given Damien so far would have been enough to assuage his sense of abandonment at her impending absence, but not today. Her recent period in the not-so-United-anymore States had been a reasonably long one, and perhaps she could understand in a clinically psychological way why Damien was feeling a little rejected, even if she would struggle to feel its analogue herself.

73

But for chod's sake he didn't own her, and she owed him nothing really. She let him crash at her place while she was away, her flat being much larger, better equipped and stocked, and a lot more private than the accommodation at his training camp. He had a good deal out of their relationship after all. He ate well whenever he was with her, she had smartened him up considerably, and the sex was fantastic. Apart from denying him his persistent requests for access to her rear, she was the most sexually experienced partner he had had, and she had taught him a few things he could use to impress his next lover.

In return Rebecca got to pretend she was reasonably normal and could operate as one half of a functioning couple, like any other regular person would. It had been enough for the past six months, with both their schedules ensuring they saw each other for only a few days at a time; nowhere near long enough in her mind for him to grow attached to her. She reflected Damien's emotions straight back at him, like a human mirror, an echo of his feelings which rebounded off her, doing little more than scratching her surface. But now it was becoming obvious he was beginning to depend on her in a way she, perhaps, was not able to provide. Already she was feeling hemmed in by him, his need for her a cage she was in no way going to walk willingly into. She'd have to work out how to approach this with him, but when she got back. Now she was too busy to engage in anything other than giving simple orders which Damien was having trouble following.

'I know it's a promotion, and you have to take the opportunities when they're given you, but-' Damien began again.

'Choosak!' she said, snapping up from her bag, the diversionary tactic of packing having failed utterly. 'I,' she began, her mind racing for a plausible lie having exhausted her prepared excuses on Damien's constant need for further explanation. Still unwilling to allow even the smallest fragment of her real life to be shared with him, she flailed mentally for a moment. Any longer and he would begin to get suspicious. When nothing was forthcoming she was forced to reveal a sliver of truth. 'Chod! I did hagga on the US piece OK? Marcia could have been really pissed off about it, I screwed it so badly, but she wasn't, and I'm amazed as anyone they offered me my own desk. And I'm not about to balls this up, so it's off to India for a couple of days. Happy now?' Rebecca bristled at being forced to reveal even this small amount of the uncomfortable truth.

'As for the timing...' She paused. Now she had, even inadvertently, allowed one person to discover the long buried and embarrassing part of her past, she was unwilling to divulge anything further on the matter. Even to her current lover. And given her present mood, not assisted by his sudden neediness, there was no way she was going to share anything more with him. A couple of nights away might be what she needed right now; distance. Distance from her recent journey west and the resultant mess she'd made of the research, distance from Damien, already feeling like something she had to step around in her own place. And the six thousand seven hundred kilometres to Delhi should feel far enough, even if with the Displacement effect the journey would take less than a second. 'I can't control when this... what was his name? Mehta? died, can I?' she finished, regaining her control in masking her true position and make it look to sweet-as-a-child-but-God-you'll-survive-another-couple-of-nights-without-me Damien that she was accepting the promotion as a fait accompli.

And Damien's persistent questioning was slowing her down considerably. Although adept at hiding what she needed of herself, it still required some level of conscious effort on Rebecca's part to fabricate plausible enough sounding lies to Damien's constant stream of inquiry, which in turn was distracting her from thinking about what she would need to take with her. So much for breezing in, grabbing the essentials and dashing out without too much in the way of an explanation. She was still trying to re-establish the rhythm of her life after her extended stay away.

Coupled with this morning's blindside from Marcia it meant she had not remembered that Damien would be home in the afternoon, his training schedule not really ramping up for another couple of months, thereby allowing him significant periods of free time. If she had had more time to settle back in before being shuffled off again she knew she would have anticipated all of this and had the answers better prepared. She had meant to be finished and on her way to the shuttleport over an hour ago, and was only now starting her packing. She had had to cancel two hop-cabs already, and if she did not get her preparations complete soon, it would have to be a third.

Faced with a similar situation another person could, and would have used any of the lakhs of dedicated public Displacement booths. Officially sanctioned and managed to ensure safe and reliable transit between two places, they ensured a convenient method of personal transportation. For the requisite fee of course.

With volumes in the crores per hour, uncontrolled Displacement was dangerous, and carried heavy penalties. Two decades of stiff legislation had conditioned the population to consider the D-booths the natural option when they needed to travel short distances.

Rebecca, at thirty three, had failed from an early age to develop the control over the Cotts field almost every adult and child took for granted; and with it the power to shift oneself from place to place under their own volition. Her deficiency in even basic aptitude at Displacement had been a source of acute embarrassment at school, at least initially.

The other girls took cruel pleasure in exploiting her lack of ability to sense their approaching Folds; they would appear, pull her hair or spit on her, then vanish again before she had the opportunity to stop them. Rebecca however had retaliated in her own way; mutual humiliation. If she was going to be the butt of hierarchical bullying then she would turn the tables on her assailants. By the age of twelve, after nearly two years of mistreatment, through much practice from Stuart's reluctant tuition of his insistent little sister, she had developed sufficiently fast reflexes to grab hold of her bully's clothing, the increase in mass now too much for the other child to Displace away successfully with. When they subsequently tried to evade Rebecca in future attacks, all they achieved was to escape arriving back at their clique of friends in their underwear. After only two such instances Rebecca was summoned to the head teacher after a complaint from one of the girl's parents, but the teasing stopped. The other girls left Rebecca alone, which suited her; she allowed herself little in the way of interaction with the other pupils. While not being a particularly pleasant way to spend the majority of the remainder of her school years, to her it was far better than daily humiliation.

Now in adulthood, with access to hop-cabs and longjump-shuttles she was at least able to conceal her handicap under the veneer of insisting on transportation over any distance too great to walk that a normal human would ordinarily Displace across. And anyway she justified the stance by repeating to herself that the bank was paying, so why not indulge in a little massaging of the expense account?

'Look, if you can't be useful, just stay out of my way. I *cannot* miss the longjump,' she snapped a little too keenly.

'I could take you, as I've made you late,' Damien volunteered, notionally nodding to his PDV sitting in the allocated placement outside her apartment.

Rebecca let out an exasperated sigh. 'Thanks but the hop-cab will be fine. And anyway, the bank is paying, so why not let someone else take the strain?' she replied with the most willingly honest answer she had given him so far.

Damien looked like he finally got the message, because he drew a breath in through pursed lips and said, 'OK, I'll finish sorting out your overnight bag and hold the cab while you double check you've got everything else you need.'

Rebecca's frustration with her lover lessened, but did not vanish completely. 'Thanks,' she said almost sincerely, then remembering Damien would need more re-assurance than simple gratitude added, 'Look, I'm sorry I barked at you. I'll call when I get to the hotel, I promise.' She moved over to him and held him around the waist, pressing her groin to his, partly apologising and partly teasing him.

His twenty two year old body could not help but react, and she felt him begin to swell against her. 'We *really* don't have time for that!' she admonished playfully, all hostility now truly gone from her voice, fallen away as quickly as it had swept over her. 'I promise I'll make it up to you when I get back.' She went to free herself from their embrace, but Damien held on for a second longer. 'You sure I can't give you a ride? To the shuttleport even?'

'When I get back!' she chided playfully as she wriggled free of their embrace and skipped over to her suitcase to fish out the final remaining clean pair of knickers before stuffing them unceremoniously into her overnight bag.

Outside, a gentle susurration announced the approach of the third cab that hour. It arrived into one of the allotted placements for D-vehicles; the dotted outline on the tarmac delineating the safe-square it materialised at. Theoretically no-one was supposed to stray into these spaces, but inevitably braver children dared each other to occupy one as long as possible before running to safety as a vehicle neared. Damien, sensing its arrival, the mass of the cab sufficient for him to detect in the Cotts field, even if it was just a tickle at the back of his mind, said automatically, 'It's here.'

'What? Oh, ha, so it is,' Rebecca said half-glancing into the middle distance, automatically concealing the lack of sharing her lover's perception, with the imitated non-chalance of years of practice at this deception. She hid her failure to perceive the hop-cab's presence behind her distraction at preparing so effortlessly it was almost second nature by now, and even she would have trouble telling exactly where the lie ended and the woman began.

>

Despite Damien's well-meaning but intrusive interference Rebecca arrived at Heathrow with enough time before her departure for her to comm her Dad and let him know she was going to be out of the country for a couple more days. And also that she was sorry but she would have to postpone the meal she had promised to make him, but it was important work stuff that she had to do and she would be round when she got back, and he could meet Damien then. Despite her rehearsing her side of the conversation to herself as she tried in vain to locate a reasonably private space for the comm, she realised all her preparation was in vain the instant the call was answered.

'Hello. The Eckhart residence. May I enquire as to who is comming please?' said a soft male voice, properly enquiring as to her identity despite the full face view offered by the medium.

Rebecca recognised the image of her Dad's SI. 'Dawson? Is Dad not in?'

'Miss Becky, how nice to hear from you again,' the face on the other end of the comm said. Then in response to her question, Dawson answered, 'No, I am afraid your father is out this afternoon. Can I relay a message to him?'

'Mmm, yes please. Can you tell him that I've got to go to India for work for a couple of days. I've been promoted and have to attend meetings at head office.' She then went on to recount almost her entire practised apology, confident in the knowledge that it would be passed on precisely both in content and sentiment.

After she had finished she went to disconnect but held for a second. Dawson picked up the pause instantly. 'Was there anything else, Miss Becky?' he asked, polite and gentle as ever. Dawson was good. Worth every rupee.

Rebecca hesitated as her emotions and reason fought each other over the question she was considering. She knew she should not ask, it was to invite hurt. But there was the slimmest chance she would be rewarded, and after the morning so far, her rationality was overcome by the old need. Despite herself she asked. 'Has. Has Helena called round recently?'

Dawson waited a second before answering, as if trying to remember, even assuming the aspect of thoughtful recollection. The pretence cheered Rebecca as his subroutines told him it would. After a respectful second or two he replied, 'No Miss Becky. I do not believe Mrs Charpin has called or visited since you were last here I am afraid. I am sorry Miss Becky.'

Rebecca flushed as she cursed herself. That was twice today she had allowed herself to be weak, to allow the past out. She could almost forgive herself the first instance; Marcia's ambush in her office. Since then the brief period spent trying, and ultimately failing, to evade Damien's questions had not afforded her sufficient time to fully recover from it; otherwise there was no way she would have allowed herself to be open to such an obvious, if unintentional, rebuff. Well, it would not happen again, that was damn sure.

'That's OK Dawson,' she said in a small voice. 'I wasn't expecting anything different. Give Dad my love will you please? Goodbye.'

'Certainly Miss Becky. Goodbye.'

Rebecca broke the connection, and the window with Dawson's image in it closed in her lens-screen. Her hands were shaking with nervous, guilty adrenaline as she pushed the memories well and truly down inside herself. She strode to the departure gate to board the 11:46 longjump-shuttle to Delhi.

Eight

Arrival

Tuesday 25 April 2056 - 17:16 IST

The longjump-shuttle arrived in Delhi precisely on time, driven by its single Deva, the term perhaps the Vimana's most enduring legacy to the world. Unlike the Vimana, earth-atmo Displacement vehicles required only a single primary and backup mind guiding them. Despite the increased mass of the larger craft and its many times more passengers, the distances closed by the D-drive were ten lakh orders of magnitude fewer, the origin and destination points more easily brought together by one powerfully willed individual.

For the shuttle and its occupants space shifted and bent around it and them, only to spring back when released and drag everything in the Fold along with it. Every person experienced differently the sensation of being Displaced; some feeling almost nothing, others only a mild tingling or stomach butterflies, while some lived through the most vivid waking dreams imaginable; hours seemingly compressed into the few brief seconds the D-drive was firing.

Rebecca exhaled the breath she had been holding for the three-quarters of a second the shuttle had been in D-space, the nowhere between the here and there of any Displacement, and opened her eyes. Her system tolerated short D-hops with little ill-effect; longjumps however always precipitated a varied assortment of reactions in her.

She had theorised to herself that her reaction to longjump trips was perhaps as a consequence of her own failure to grasp even the basics of personal Displacement, but she had never sought confirmation of her self-diagnosis. That would entail admitting her failing, and that was not an option.

Before boarding she had been frustrated at Damien for slowing her down ahead of leaving, but horny also. She now wished she had accepted his offer of a lay, the unsatisfied tingling itch in her crotch now an annoyance. And the Displacement had done little to ease either nagging sensation.

The fraction of a second in between places compounded these feelings within her; her hands were sweating and the knot in her stomach would take several hours of directed breathing later on to unpick. She fidgeted in her seat, unwilling to be contained for much longer, but unable to satisfy her need to be somewhere else until she could disembark.

Like the rest of the three hundred or so passengers Rebecca had to wait until the Captain gave the all clear that signalled the D-drive was fully powered down before she could shift her body too much. In the early days of mass Displacement travel there had been a series of accidental relocations after the initial jump.

People who had stood up from their seat too soon found themselves catapulted back to their origin point, albeit now some five metres up in the air. It was traced to an after effect in the Cotts field being sensitive to too great an increase in local kinetic energy. Despite the engineers' best efforts they had yet to eliminate it entirely, so everyone stayed in their seat until the Fold the shuttle had traversed had fully dissipated.

To distract herself for the few moments, Rebecca practised seeming as if she too could sense the D-residual evaporating; not too difficult a look to perfect, as the majority of the other passengers were paying less attention to it than she was trying to appear to. Only the very young showed any external indication of there being something there she was unable to perceive.

Rebecca was too young to have ever travelled significant distances by any other mode of transport. She had only her father's recollections of the differing sensation of movement on board an aeroplane. The initial rush down the runway, the tarmac whipping past underneath. The g-force of lift off pressing you into your seat. The barely perceptible shifting of the slowly moving cloudscapes below you as the aeroplane cruised at altitude. How the world of the upper atmosphere was split in two; the clouds, higher than even the most towering Himalayan peak, laid out like vast soft mountains, and the nothingness of a seemingly endless sky above you, it reaching out to the eventual edge of space. Up there it was always sunlit regardless of the weather at your point of departure. A sunrise or sunset above the clouds as you either chased or fled the sun.

Of course accompanying all that romance of travel had been the shitty, cramped seats, hundreds of other travellers crammed in with you in a desperate bid to make the flight economical, accompanied by the inevitable tiredness from the journey taking so long. And jet-lag. Sitting for fourteen hours straight in the same seat, seeing two sunsets, four hour of screaming-infant disturbed sleep and a pair of breakfasts, both inedible, only to land and find it was the middle of the afternoon at your destination. No wonder your body went haywire for a day or so. *How had people put up with it?*

While Displacement had not eliminated the sometimes vast time differences that existed between countries, it had removed the huge amount of time wasted in traversing the great distances between them, thus allowing Rebecca to plan a session in the hotel gym to fully tire herself out so she would sleep soundly and offset the worst effects of being suddenly five and a half hours ahead of her body clock, which was still convinced it was not even midday yet.

>

Her eyes swept across the reunions, and solitary arrivals happening all around her at the shuttleport. She knew the face she was looking out for, but she still wanted to take this small opportunity of solitude to observe, on her own terms, the ordinary comings and goings of the people whose lives her forthcoming work would touch.

After clearing the bureaucratic immigration and retrieving her luggage, Rebecca stood in the arrival lobby scanning the crowd in front of her, her analyst's mind always working, seeing connections and cause and effect where others would see ordinary, mundane daily life. For some reason the customs official had had a hard time understanding she was supposed to be in India on business concerning Commander Mehta; after all she had all the necessary paperwork and permissions, and she feared she would be late for her rendezvous.

If she was to be of any use on this desk, and if she was completely honest with herself, do Mehta any justice, then she needed to feel what life was like here. How people acted and reacted in every possible situation. There was more driving her than the need to deliver good work after her total failure on the North American research piece. There was professional pride certainly, but something in this promotion ran deeper than that, even if Rebecca was not allowing herself to fully know it; she needed to do right by one of the men who had ameliorated her childhood.

Her eyes saccaded from person to person, taking in the obvious, prominent features immediately: noses with their embellishments of moustaches for the men or nose-rings of all varieties for their partners; eyes, some concealed behind sunglasses like hers, others bare, their secrets there to be read; clothing ranging from formal business attire and saris, to jeans and t-shirts on both sexes. She took all these in at a glance but then lingered for a second longer to absorb some of the more subtle details; something of the personality underneath the mask of public life.

Rebecca liked to watch people when they thought they were not being observed and in an environment where they would, albeit accidentally, let small fragments of themselves slip through their carefully constructed defences. It was something she did deliberately, using public spaces to express herself to an audience that would take no notice. Maintaining her relationship with Damien and the nature of her work offered her little room for idiosyncrasies, so she allowed herself those small moments of being really her; when she was surrounded by a crowd that would pay the least attention to the woman sitting staring at the face of her hand, engrossed in the lines there.

While she engaged in this behaviour consciously, she drew private pleasure from observing others revealing themselves accidentally. Like the heavy-set Western man in the suit, obviously wealthy, and about to be completely out of his depth as soon as he stepped outside into in the noisy and aggressive crowd of hustlers, panhandlers, beggars and scammers; all eager to assist in lightening the burden his wallet was to him. Rebecca watched him as he made for the exit, amused for a moment. Then her eyes rested on a striking, handsome Indian woman in a white sari. Although she appeared to be approximately the same age as Rebecca, she was sure the woman was older, perhaps by a decade; she obviously took time to maintain her appearance and looks.

The woman too was sweeping the crowd, and for a second their eyes met. For the briefest of instants Rebecca saw a flash of recognition in the woman's eyes; a look that said 'You', before her gaze swept away again and returned to scanning the sea of people that separated them. Rebecca felt the look almost physically, deep inside herself, in her stomach and her crotch; an uncomfortable mix of itching and pulling, a recognition of something between them, some kinship they shared beyond their gender but of which she was not fully aware.

Unsettled by the sensation, Rebecca gazed intently at the woman, trying once again to catch her eye. After almost a minute of this, the woman in the sari seemed to spot who she was looking for in the crowd and headed off to meet him. Still curious, her instincts now piqued and not allowing her to drop the matter until she was satisfied with the conclusion, Rebecca continued to observe the woman.

The woman in the sari and the man greeted each other formally, hands pressed gently together. He appeared to be somewhere in his fifties Rebecca estimated, judging by waistline as much as his gently greying hair, and wore a smart shirt and pressed cotton trousers; *her husband?* Rebecca scanned either for a wedding band and the woman for a mangalsutra or other indication of marriage, but neither was present. A relative then? The man and the woman left talking busily and occasionally laughing quietly together at some shared amusement, obviously renewing their relationship after a period of separation. Enlightened, but not fully satisfied, Rebecca resumed her active-looking for her chaperone, having now had enough of people watching, eager to get on with the work and trying to see the man she was being met by.

The distraction of not watching the crowd removed, she saw him almost immediately

Amongst the energetic and sometimes emotional happy

bustle of family reunions and the cooler and much less tactile formal greetings of the various businessmen and women, stood, waiting patiently, a young man. Younger than her if she was judging correctly, impeccably dressed in a well-tailored suit despite the heavy rains outside.

He gave no reaction to the occasional bump by an over-excited grandchild, or the far more cynical elbow or shoulder of the professional classes as he waited; he merely rolled with the knocks and smiled with the youthful collisions. Slight and graceful looking, the contacts with the almost always heavier businessmen hardly shifted him, they always being the ones who tumbled slightly as a result of Newton's Second Law. It was as if underneath his sharply cut suit he had a precise and toned frame that he hardly needed to use in order to keep himself safe.

Rebecca could not initially place why he stood out from the dozens of other similarly attired young and not so young men. Then she had it; her insight providing her with at least a hook on which to hang the rest of her initial assessment of him. To her eye, better used to divining the deeper meanings in things, he looked completely at home as part of, but also one step removed from the whorls of bodies and luggage around him. He was a perfect calm at the centre of this small human storm. He knew that if he waited and rode it out it would abate around him, leaving him still standing, as its constituent parts blew away on the winds that had brought them here and would carry them onwards.

He made eye contact, and in that instant of connection the earpiece Rebecca had been given by Marcia as part of the equipment courier-Displaced from India activated. It explained to her that the man she was looking at was indeed Sri Pramod Surendran, Commissioner for Fiscal Relations for the Federal Republic of India, non-executive director on the Sinha MG board, and the man she was to be met by. Impressed but not overawed by the technology, and impressed, slightly jealous and *almost* overawed by the positions held by him, Rebecca raised the smallest of wry smirks, which she squashed almost before it appeared on her face.

She made her way through the crowd, arm outstretched toward the Commissioner. 'Commissioner Surendran,' she said, proffering her hand in a business-like manner.

For his part the Commissioner hesitated for a second, then his manners to his guest overcoming his societal conditioning, took her hand in friendship and welcome. Rebecca was struck by how small and delicate his hands were; almost as slender as her own. Realising her social faux pas, and that she had now held his hand for a fraction of a second too long she let the handshake drop first. 'Commissioner I...' she began her apology.

If he sensed any awkwardness on her part he made no sign of it. Instead he said honestly, 'There is no need for such formality. Please, call me Pramod.'

Only that was what Rebecca heard through the earpiece; the young Commissioner's mouth had said something completely different. Rebecca was left with a vague sense of dissonance as her mind struggled to reconcile what her conflicting senses seemed to be telling her.

She frowned, to which Pramod smiled gently. 'Ah yes,' he said, again in perfect English, his mouth once more shaping the sounds of a completely different language. 'Your earpiece is linked to my SI. The default voice is a little coarse but the connection via Jamsetji allows you to hear me as I am. We thought it would make things easier.'

'Sorry, it's been a while since I've run across reltran. Not much call for Marathi on the eastern seaboard of North America,' Rebecca stated, pointing to the small package of electronics nestled almost invisibly in her ear canal, fully assimilating the young Commissioner's explanation without missing a beat.

Pramod heard Rebecca's reply in his own language, only in her voice, and smiled gently again.

'The Varhadi dialect, but I am honoured you recognised the root language. Most people assume it will be Hindi. An affectation I agree, speaking a dialect only another few thousand still use, but we must hold to our ancestors. The software allows us to bridge the sometimes seemingly insurmountable chasms we place between ourselves. As a species I mean.'

'I can't say I know it, but I took an educated guess. So what else does it do? And how wired in is it all?' Rebecca asked, despite herself, her natural defensive side kicking in at the revelation of the technology currently sat in her ear. She winced internally at her second mistake in front of the charming and decent Commissioner. She wanted to remain professional, but she was coming across as a bitch.

'Purely benign, I assure you. The recorder in your possession has the same dictionaries, so any interviews you take with it will automatically be stored in both the original language and translated into any three others of your choice. We defaulted the first to Standard English, leaving the final two selections blank. Additionally, all the data is automatically backed up to a secure remote location of your choice...' Pramod stopped at Rebecca's expression.

'What is it?' she asked, almost glad of the opportunity to show herself to be a fully functional human being.

'I trust we did not overstep our mark?' the Indian Commissioner asked, genuinely. 'You are suspicious. If you wish we can easily remove the software, or you may choose to use your own equipment. We thought given the recent progress we had made it would be discourteous of us not to present them to you. I see now that we should have offered rather than assumed. My apologies. It will not happen again.'

Rebecca's frown softened into a smile, one she deliberately made with her eyes as much as her mouth.

Pramod was winning over her caution with his kind, courteous and forgiving nature. She found herself beginning to appreciate the young, ever so slightly fanciable, if earnerstly well-spoken, Commissioner. 'I'll hang onto it for a while. It looks like fun,' she said with deliberate good humour, tacitly accepting the gift.

Pramod nodded once smartly, then smiled once more, this time as easily as Rebecca had done. Mission accomplished. 'I must apologise for the necessity of moving the conversation directly to business. However there are several engagements I am required to make you aware of, if this is acceptable?'

Rebecca nodded her assent. Best get the shop talk out of the way up front. She immediately began working out what the most likely events would be and how she should respond to each of them. There'd be the obvious 'meet the team' at some point, and…

'Good. Firstly, there is the delicate matter concerning Commander Mehta's widow. She has asked if she might meet with you tomorrow?'

Rebecca had certainly not been expecting this, and it showed on her face for a second, before she resumed her business-like appearance.

'She wished it be relayed that she feels it is important she meet with you. More than that I do not know. I fully appreciate the awkwardness this places on you, but my instructions are to inform you of the request.'

Fully in control again, in no way was Rebecca going to jeopardise her new position. 'Please let Smt Mehta know that it would honour me greatly to accede to her gracious request, and that I appreciate how difficult this time must be for her.'

Pramod smiled, relieved perhaps that the hard part was over.

'You said 'several' engagements,' prompted Rebecca.

'Indeed. The second is a reception party for you to

meet your new team. It has already begun some fifteen minutes ago, and they are all keen to make your acquaintance.'

Back on solid ground, Rebecca politely let the Commissioner finish, despite having decided she had to accept this invite, even if the timing was a little soon for her liking. 'Of course,' she replied. 'At the bank's head-quarters?' she queried.

'At the InSA museum. Specifically the Vimana wing.'

Rebecca immediately now regretted her earlier rapid acceptance. It would not be her first choice of places to visit, let alone have to remember how to function in company. Aged eight-years-old she would have gladly forgone a year's pocket money to have seen the Vimana for herself. But that was a lifetime ago. Still, despite the long years of disavowing what she had once held dear, ever since Marcia had reminded her of her previous feelings, Rebecca could not deny that being given the opportunity now was overwhelming.

She was sure she could handle it. If she could prepare herself properly.

'I'm...' Rebecca stopped herself, her hard-wired self-censorship kicking in before she could blurt out her real feelings, and providing her with a couple of alternatives, from which she chose '...sure it will provide the perfect inspiration. To provide some context for the research a little,' she added as justification without missing a beat.

'Excellent. Jamsetji, could you inform the museum we will be arriving-'

'Commissioner,' she interrupted, trying her best to sound apologetic, hoping the translation software lived up to its programmers' hype. For the first time Rebecca cut across the man who, aside from being her guide in India, was also technically her superior. She may have already been bounced into a couple of things in quick succession, but she was no pushover. It was time to see how much pull she had with a perfectly reasonable sounding request.

Pramod paused and returned his focus to Rebecca. 'If I may. I am never at my very best after a longjump. I would very much like to avail myself of the business lounge before making our way to the museum. I need only a few minutes to freshen up.'

Pramod seemed to consider her request for a second. A second in which she moved her body just so, angled her hip ever so slightly towards him, leaning almost subconsciously forward with her crotch. 'Of course,' he replied. 'We had anticipated such a request and your name is already with their reception.'

They really had second guessed her most likely moves, hadn't they?

'You've certainly thought of everything for the Indian virgin,' she flirted, ever so gently with this earnestly attractive young man. *And Damien barely a second away in the UK? Shame on yourself Rebecca!* Still, it had the desired effect.

Pramod looked confused for a second, then almost blushed as if the language translator had told him something rude. 'Ah. I see,' he said after a beat. 'You are referring to yourself as being in India for the first time. It seems your mode of speech is a little too casual for the software at times. I may have to report this as a request for a new feature.' He paused. 'Sometimes meaning can get lost in the words we choose to use, or more importantly, not to use.'

Pramod was all business, and ultimately so was Rebecca, the gentlest brush of flirtation with him to try and unbalance him for one second. Just to show him that she was not to be underestimated, that she was his equal, and possibly see a little something of the man beneath the designer suit and real-time translated Marathi dialects. She smiled to him before apologising, saying she had not meant to cause him any embarrassment, real or otherwise, and that she would try to keep her words less ambiguous.

Sensing she had ceded the initiative back to him after

their small conversational thrust and parry, Pramod continued. 'The lounge is this way. I have a PDV in the VIP waiting bays. Ask your SI to link to the shuttleport's VIP SI and it will direct you to me. Take as long as you require.'

'Thank you Commissioner. You are most gracious.'

Pramod nodded once more.

Nine

The Vimana

Tuesday 25 April 2056 - 19:30 IST

It was everything Rebecca had been dreading and more.
She had hoped the short notice of her promotion would
mean only a handful, even perhaps no more than two or
three, of her now staff would have been available to attend.
Instead it seemed that her entire desk in Delhi had been
given leave to attend, leading to her being formerly
introduced to over a dozen of her team, testing her ability
to visualise and memorise them all. In the end she gave up
all hope of remembering anyone after the sixth polite and
reverential introduction, and left it to Socrates to do the
heavy lifting, with discrete reminders in her screens as she
drifted around the throng.

If the reception had been at the bank's offices it could
have least been fun. But in the shadow of the Vimana, the
gathering was a solemn affair, any celebration of her new
appointment tempered with the respect for the man who
had just passed, rendering the entire affair as sombre as a
wake.

In the end Rebecca had excused herself, fabricating a

delayed longjump after-effect as the reason to detach herself from the crowd and find some solitude, even if only for a few minutes. Long enough for her absence to become apparent, but not before it seemed unusual; she would head back before then.

She wandered off, deliberately in search of the Vimana. Hell, if she was here she may as well take a look; the museum ostensibly being open to the public for another two hours. It was obvious the museum was intent on facilitating its prestigious party, as she was the sole person within the entire space housing the only ship to have traversed the void between worlds. She realised she was glad of her exclusivity, at least for the evening. Either that or a crowd she could remain anonymous in. For Rebecca, public life was either isolation, or staying hidden within the masses.

She was however, not completely unobserved. Two people were watching her from different vantage points.

The first was standing discretely beyond the rope barriers at the doorways to the exhibition room, and well out of Rebecca's direct line of sight. The woman she had made eye contact with from the shuttleport earlier. The same woman who was, for her own reasons, taking a keen interest in the workings of the Brahman Group. She watched the young analyst intently, fascinated with the obvious discomfort being in the presence of the Vimana caused her. She wondered what her story, her connection to all of this was.

The second was Pramod, who had noticed Rebecca slip away from the party and move off. He had not followed her out of prurience; he was her official guide and escort while she was in his country and would execute his duties fully.

< < <

It was difficult, Srinath mused, gazing out at Charon, not to be reflective and aware of one's place within Brahma, in the order and chaos of all things, when you were able to look, albeit through fifty millimetres of poly-glass, and see with the unaided eye one of the most remote orbs of matter that marked the boundary between the solar system and interstellar space. Something that had up until this time in human history only been observed remotely by powerful Earth-orbit based telescopes, or the snatched glimpses of a fleeting, passing probe. It hung so close, so real, filling the window completely with its pale, dirty browns and icy blues, the colours familiar touchstones of earth on the edge of the solar system.

It seemed to Srinath that he could almost reach out and scrape its surface, if only he tried. He could hardly believe they had made it, or rather more accurately, he had made it this far. He owed his family everything.

Almost unconsciously he began to turn, away from the endless emptiness of space before him, to face what he felt was the direction home was in. Looking back, unable to see the earth, Hari Srinath checked the time. It would be a little after nine-fifteen pm in his home in Bangalore; his grandchildren no doubt allowed to stay up beyond their allotted bedtimes tonight. So, night-time also there; the difference being that the sun would rise once more bathing the planet in light and heat, where out here it was little more than the brightest star in the all encompassing dark.

Awe and amazement at where he stood could only last so long within the mind of Hari Srinath before they would, inevitably, be pushed out by more mundane, or rather more accurately given his current circumstances, heavenly, concerns. His analytical nature, coupled with the hard discipline of the Indian Space Agency training would not allow him too long a flight of fancy, and his consciousness was already completing the mental leaps from his family, a solar system away, back to the satellite outside the window,

97

then to the men and women who had carried his ship to its shadow.

> > >

Standing under the belly of the Vimana, staring up at the smooth metal surface, still shining with its high-polish finish a quarter of a century later, Rebecca's lens-screens indicated the Commissioner's approaching presence off to her left. She glanced round. Other than her Indian chaperone, she was alone with the ship that had carried her childhood soaring into the heavens. That was how to think of it. Leave the other stuff for later. Enjoy what it meant to you then. She reached out a shaking hand, then caught herself. *Was this allowed?*

She coughed gently, the real-time wireless connection between herself and the Commissioner struggling to translate it into Varhadi. Perplexed, Pramod turned to her, wondering what she desired. Rebecca caught his eye, directed her gaze to her hand, then to the ship, then back to Pramod, her features betraying her need. She found she could not help herself. She felt again like the little girl she had once been. She had not expected her reaction to the ship to be so strong.

No, that is not true, is it? she told herself. She wanted the feelings despite the effect they would have on her. She was almost hooked, masochistically, on the sharp stabs of memory which came with them, and perversely, would never relinquish her hold on. Deep down she knew how she was going to react, the trick was allowing only the feelings she wanted to surface right now. And right now, after Marcia and her unearthing of that grubby part of her past and Damien and her physical need for his body, she needed to feel this, to make sense of the world on her own terms. To regain her control of at least part of herself; an addict chasing her next emotional fix.

She stared at the ship for a second longer. The infinite-zoom, hi-res 3D imaging she had seen as a child had allowed her to get this close already, but actually being in the same room as it was something utterly different, and no substitute for the physicality of the thing. Being able to see its marine-sleek lines from any angle, being able to walk around, above and underneath it, to see Srinath's ship for all its unrealised glory made her shiver; frisson goose flesh bumps raised themselves on her breasts and back.

Pramod, for his part, intuited immediately what she was silently asking him, and smiled his friendly, approving smile at her. He had been instructed to indulge his guest, within boundaries of course, and allowing this intriguing, wilful western woman to fulfil a need she had obviously been carrying from childhood was such a small gesture that it hardly needed thinking about.

Emboldened by his implicit say so, Rebecca turned back to the ship, and her shaking hand that was centimetres away from it. Gripping her fingers into a fist in an effort to calm the rising nerves in her stomach, she stretched her steadied hand the final centimetre. Her fingertips rested on the cool polished metal hull of the ship for a second before she placed her whole palm against the hard skin of her childhood. She could not help but close her eyes, and in that instant of tactile contact, lost herself to herself.

The memory of that day burst into her head. When she had reached out to touch the image of Srinath on the holo-display, only for her fingers to pass straight through it. But this time it was real; solid and cold underneath her hand. She was touching history, her history. The eight-year-old girl turned to her mother, seeking validation and approval for her enthusiasm. She remembered more than she cared to in that moment of contact with the ship, and struggled with herself for control, the memory threatening to overwhelm her, here in front of another adult she sought approval from. It would be too much to bear. She pushed the feelings away hard, squashing them back where they belonged.

Breathing deeply Rebecca opened her eyes again and withdrew her hand. She flushed as she turned to Pramod, worried she had betrayed herself in front of him, but he had turned away politely and was pretending to be interested in one of the smaller exhibits. Appreciative of this attractive Indian man's generosity of spirit, Rebecca relaxed a little and turned back to the Vimana, private shame replaced with public guilt as she realised she must have left evidence of her presence on the hull; a hot handprint on the gleaming metal. But there was nothing. Rebecca frowned, her forehead creasing, her lips pursing slightly, not understanding the absence of what she expected to see, but welcome nonetheless of the transposition of feelings from complex guilt to simple confusion.

'How..?' she vocalised, still not fully in conscious control, before she had a chance to catch herself and bring her hand to her cover her traitorous mouth.

At the small noise, Pramod turned, and glided over to her. 'Hmm?' he enquired gently. 'Is something amiss?'

Rebecca held her tongue for a second, unsure whether to further voice her thoughts. But Pramod stood there waiting and she did not want to appear odd or rude in front of him. 'It's just,' she began, trying to find the right words so that what she said did not sound foolish, 'I thought I'd left a mark on it, but there's nothing there.'

Pramod nodded, understanding. 'A property of the alloy we developed to cover the Vimana. It is almost completely non-reactive and resistant to its environment. Barely anything causes an impression on it. Given the strength of the Cotts field the ship generated and the distances involved when in use, an outer shell that carried as little extraneous mass as possible was more than desirable, it was compulsory. It is of little consequence if you have a handful of a few extra rupees in your pocket when you

Displace on earth. But even a few nanograms of unwanted matter within the Vimana would cause an unnecessary burden to the Devas, and the ship severe degradation, when they attempted the Displacement of the six light hours to the edge of the solar system, let alone the planned jumps totalling fifteen light years.'

Rebecca ran a hand self-consciously through her hair, remembering how she had shaved not only her head, but her eyebrows also, as a member of the Leapfrog Club. The crew had had all their body hair removed to keep extraneous mass to a minimum for the Vimana's voyage, and only the keenest tadpoles had followed suit. Back then Rebecca had been almost devout; her young age being the sole thing which had kept her from being able to shave further areas of her body. She caught the shudder of shame and concentrated on what Pramod had said instead.

Six light hours. It had been a quarter of a century since Rebecca, or the majority of the population of the Earth, had had cause to measure anything using such a fractional unit. Light years were easy to conceptualise; they were after all a term well used in science fiction and usually counted in single or double digits, the ones and fours and sixes obscuring the vast distances they represented. The human mind could rationalise these enormities into a single number. Conversely light hours needed a degree of thought to fully grasp. Their unfamiliarity as a unit of measurement requiring them to be extrapolated out; calculated to their entirity.

Six times sixty, times sixty times three lakh; immediately huge, the space in between the two points too vast to hold in her adult head. As a child she had had no trouble with the fantastic scales of the mission; it was another facet of life she had accepted as given until she learnt the colder, smaller truth behind it.

Rebecca stood stunned as she absorbed the magnitude of what Pramod had said. Even though distance meant

101

relatively little on Earth any more, the edge of the solar system was a leap into the unknown.

'Six light hours,' she echoed, the overawed young girl still uppermost in her personality. 'No wonder I thought the way I did. It was such a huge endeavour. I used to think they would have glimpsed the things only Gods should be allowed to see.'

'Not Gods,' commented Pramod. 'Such devotion was misplaced, even if you were only a young girl. They were after all only human. While Brahma may have exercised influence on the mission, even the best of us is still only another step along the path of reincarnation.'

'I suppose,' reflected Rebecca. 'Still, it was a nice image for my eight year old self to cling to. We all have to grow up,' she finished, relocating herself well and truly in the here and now and closing off the young girl completely once more.

Pramod could not help but discern the change in her posture as this happened, and was saddened to see the obvious youthful passion shut away. The more controlled certainly, but somehow colder, and perhaps lesser adult woman resumed full command. He was careful not to let the disappointment show in his eyes. Instead he asked plainly if Rebecca had had enough of the reception and by implication the museum, and perhaps they should retire for the evening, knowing full well that Rebecca would welcome the opportunity to put some distance, both physically and emotionally from what she would almost certainly feel was a weak lapse on her part.

Ten

The Little Girl

Rebecca refused Pramod's offer of a hop-cab back to her hotel; she needed to process the feelings still surfacing inside her, and the walk of a couple of kilometres would, she hoped, provide her the time to fully filter them. Politely informing the Commissioner she would be ready at the allotted time in the morning, Rebecca set off on foot across the Delhi streets, fully reconciled to the soaking awaiting her the instant she left Pramod at the museum steps. With his assurance she would be seen safely back to her hotel by Jamsetji who had been informed to despatch the Indian arm of MetProtect the instant she encountered trouble or was interfered with, Rebecca stepped from underneath the building's protection and out under the canopy of rain that was the Delhi sky that night.

She had covered barely two hundred metres when she was approached by a young girl, emerging like a shadow from the rain, perhaps no older than seven, stick thin and filthy with city grime untouched by the downpour. She was proffering a wrist garland of sodden white marigolds and calling to the pretty lady.

Rebecca glanced around unable to sense, but expecting to see, Pramod's promised security detachment. When they failed to materialise, she turned back to the girl, confident one small child posed no threat to her safety. The girl, realising she was not about to be rendered away took another step forward. This was obviously an opening to a longer conversation concluding with Rebecca parting with a handful of rupees. Wanting to avoid as much of the pointless interchange as possible, for her sake as much as that of the girl, Rebecca ordered Socrates to authorise a transfer to her.

Hearing this, the girl spoke again. 'No aug. No SI. No lenses.' She smiled broadly, all innocent eyes and exculpatory expression.

Socrates confirmed her assertion to Rebecca. 'I'm sorry, it seems I am unable to locate the child in A-space.'

Rebecca eyed the girl, who did not flinch under her interrogative gaze. Instead she raised her hand containing the garland once more in Rebecca's direction. Conceding defeat Rebecca reached into her pocket and pulled out the first note she touched. Withdrawing a five hundred she was as equally disappointed as the girl was pleased, and showed it for exactly as long. Hiding her mounting frustration with the way this was going she pressed the money into the girl's grubby hand as the child made to wrap the blooms round her wrist. 'Save the flowers, I'm not the type kid. Let's skip what we know is a waste of both our time.'

The girl looked down at the note, then at her other hand where the decoration remained in her grip. She glanced over her shoulder toward what looked to Rebecca like a man sat watching them both from the shadow of a doorway, before years of rote patter kicked back in despite her earlier surprise at Rebecca's generosity. 'No. More. Need thousand. For pretty flowers,' she implored, seemingly keen to keep the conversation going now cash had been forthcoming.

'Uh uh,' replied Rebecca shaking her head and giving the girl a stare that unambiguously told her not to push this encounter. She was not some fresh off the boat tourist, and had been buying the girl's compliance. The tiny figure seemed to be weighing up the effort involved in something, perhaps securing another five hundred rupees, enough for her family to live on for a month, versus the obvious difficulty the woman was presenting. She appeared to decide there were less troublesome pickings to be had elsewhere, the message received and understood as she slunk away reluctantly toward the man who beckoned her, trying to hide the flowers she had failed to sell.

Rebecca stood in the rain watching as the girl approached her guardian, head bowed, avoiding eye contact, as a supplicant would their monarch. She showed the flowers still in her possession. There was an exchange Rebecca was too far away to hear clearly, but it became obvious within moments the transaction had not gone as the man had wished.

There was a flash of movement, too quick for Rebecca to see properly. But the sound which reached her ears was unmistakable; the air whipped, followed by a bamboo smack on soft flesh.

The girl flinched only a little as the man struck the back of her legs again, shouting and pointing at Rebecca.

Anger welled in Rebecca, causing her to forget herself, her surroundings. She may have not cared less about the cruelty adults inflicted on each other, but she was not about to allow this. 'Socrates, get MetProtect here now!' She picked up the nearest weapon she could find, a half brick, filthy with grime and shit, but better than nothing, and took a step toward the violence in front of her. 'Hoy!' she growled, proffering the weight in her hand. The man paused with his cane. The girl, who immediately recognised the voice, turned. 'Come here,' Rebecca beckoned her, trying not to sound as if she were summoning her. The girl hesitated, confused but keen, unsure whether to respond.

Reluctant to proffer more money so obviously, Rebecca took another pace over to the girl, who Displaced half a metre back at the approach. It was obvious she was not used to such dismissals suddenly reversing themselves, and seemed unconvinced Rebecca did not intend her more harm in some way than she was already receiving, her street senses unsure how to handle this unique situation.

Understanding, perhaps more than she realised, Rebecca stopped, and lowered, but did not relinquish the brick. 'It's OK,' she encouraged as gently as she could and still be heard over the rain. The distance between them was close enough for Rebecca not to have to shout and her voice not carry too far. 'How much do you normally live on?' she asked as she dropped to one knee bringing her to the child's level. She tried not to look at the girl's legs, instead maintaining eye contact the whole time.

The street girl frowned at the question, then understanding replied politely in her broken street Hinglish while holding up one and a half fingers on different hands, 'Sau, week.' She glanced at her custodian who approved her actions with a single nod. She moved to stand by Rebecca.

Rebecca calculated in her head versus what she knew she had on her, then dismissed her mental arithmetic. She retrieved the nearly thirteen thousand rupees and squashed the money into the girl's small hand, the tiny fingers almost unable to close around the thick bundle of notes. 'Give me the flowers,' she said, proffering her open hand in exchange for the cash. The girl gaped at the money, more than enough for a year, before pressing the garland into Rebecca's hand and closing the woman's fingers around it.

Bounty secured for a few shitty petals, she Displaced back to the man, the previous violence seemingly already forgotten. She nodded keenly at some question of his before both Displaced away, leaving Rebecca no opportunity to confront the man for his abuse of his charge. The excoriation she had inside her would remain unused.

Rebecca stood for a second, staring at the empty space recently vacated by the girl. She was younger than Rebecca had been when she still had wonder and awe at the world, when the Vimana had lifted her childhood, and she could not help view her own time through the prism of what she had just witnessed; the tiny emaciated girl, her childhood already so far behind her and Rebecca's eight year old self.

She had been a callous bitch to brush the kid off so lightly, given the consequences of her dismissal. Rebecca's childhood had been shitty but was nothing compared to what this little girl had already been through and the worse she was likely to encounter.

She ordered Socrates replay the scene. 'Stop,' she said flatly when the playback in her lenses reached the point at which she handed over the money.

She had been buying herself off, bribing herself into imagining one little girl might not have to go through quite as much crap as she might have done, but now it did not feel as good as she hoped it would. With the little girl gone, Rebecca felt almost nothing from her perceived kindness. She was unable to feel even the slowly dissipating Fold the girl had left behind, the one tangible piece of evidence she had ever been there. It was as if the entire thing had never happened.

And where the chod were the chodding security services Pramod had promised? She quizzed Socrates who informed her he had only just secured a connection to them and they were inbound, ETA thirty seconds.

'Tell them not to bother. They've missed the party.'

Realising her mistake in choosing to walk, Rebecca went to find a cab, but now lacked the funds to secure a ride. Shoulders dropping in self-disappointment, she stuffed the flowers into her pocket without even glancing at them, and hugged herself around her chest as she walked in the rain to her hotel.

<<

'It is important she be allowed as much access to the Vimana as we can afford her. Our SIs indicate the unexpected nature of the promotion, followed by rapid exposure so directly to her childhood should serve to unbalance her sufficiently for our purposes. She will be off guard.'

Pramod nodded as he noted the itinerary he and Ram were planning for Rebecca. 'We would need to arrange a suitable justification to isolate the exhibition, and then her with it.'

'Perhaps a corporate party, an opportunity for her to meet her new team at the museum? She would feel hemmed in by the crowd and the unfamiliarity. That should afford us sufficient possibilities to instigate the necessary conversations.'

> >

Checked in, safe in the sanctuary and privacy of the six-star suite, Rebecca cut loose, screaming at herself, scolding and admonishing with an incisive venom only she could muster against herself. What the chod was happening to her? How many times had she lost it today? More than too many, that was for chodding sure. Dhat tere this chodding promotion, dhat tere Marcia for virtually blackmailing her into it. Dhat tere Damien for chodding making her angry when she should have been calm and controlled. Dhat tere the chodding useless US civil war making her screw up the research she should have been polishing now instead of stuck in a chodding hotel room in India. Dhat tere her stupid childhood self for being so chodding dependant on this stupid chodding gaandu of a mission that was never going to deliver on the promises it made. And dhat tere Her.

Rebecca snatched up a pair of shoes from the top of her unpacked bag and hurled them across the room with a scream. They clattered uselessly into the wall and fell to the floor with a dull thud. It was not enough. One small act of random violence had not doused her rage at herself. She picked up the entire bag and swung it round, letting go and sending it sailing across to join her shoes, its contents tumbling out as it collided with the wall and spilling onto the floor.

Rebecca stood in the middle of her room feeling foolish.

She slunk to the bathroom, embarrassed by her outburst; it had been years since she had been this bad. It was the proximity she reasoned. It was getting to her, that much was obvious. It had loosened the cork on her tightly repressed set of memories, and even the vaguest whiff of their threatened escape had reduced her to this; shouting and raving in her hotel room, throwing things round when she should be preparing for tomorrow. She was glad Pramod had not seen her lose it this badly.

Staring at herself in the mirror she addressed her reflection. 'Come on girl, get a grip for chod's sake. Don't let it out. Put it back where She can't hurt you any more. It wasn't your fault.'

Five minutes later Rebecca was lying curled up in a ball on the king-size bed repeating the mantra to herself that it had not been her fault. However, repetition leant no weight to the words, despite how often she ordered herself. Feeling like shit, Rebecca fell into a fitful sleep.

<

Pramod watched Rebecca push out into the sodden darkness, her receding form IR-enhanced in his vision, turning from hot-white to a cooler blue-green as the night-time monsoon wicked her body heat away. He called up an overlay of her likely routes back to her hotel; the most efficient, and therefore the most likely, one marginally longer, but affording a little more cover and lastly one hugging the heavily populated areas, which their best predictions anticipated she would avoid. There were three points where they intersected, the first of which she was approaching.

'She has just left me,' he spoke to the cool dark air around him. 'Inform the original to be at the first location. We will make contact there.'

Eleven

Deva

Wednesday 26 April 2056 - 08:00 IST

The morning brought with it, not just a new dawn, but also a much recovered Rebecca. Her verbal flagellation of the night before had effected a kind of catharsis in her after all, all traces of the weak girl gone, well and truly buried again under the battle-hardened veneer of her professional self. And one hot shower and breakfast of fluffy appams with a simple vegetable korma later she was finishing off the final touches to her outfit for the day.

She had been looking for an opportunity to wear her newest sari; her three week sojourn to the former United States having hardly been the place to take something so ethnic. And although she had been planning on debuting it at her Dad's birthday meal, now seemed the perfect opportunity. She spent an hour in her room correcting the drape of the long sheet of cloth in the formal Nivi style, pleating and pinning until she was satisfied with it. Rebecca knew that anything less than full respect in the meeting today would be unconscionable. She may have allowed herself to slip yesterday, but today that could not, would not happen. The woman she was meeting had lost the one thing in her life that completed her, and the emptiness she would be feeling an immense, almost unfillable void. Far larger than the hole at her centre, that was for sure. Today was not the day for self-indulgence.

She took one last look at herself in the full-length mirror. *Perfect.* She swished out of the room, clad in her cotton and silk armour to meet Pramod in the lobby, who was there to escort her to former Deva Mehta's widow of less than a week.

Pramod nodded his approval of her attire when they greeted each other. 'Namaste Ms Eckhart. You look very proper. This is why I knew we were correct in this delicate matter. We knew you would show the proper respect. I am pleased.'

'Thank you Commissioner,' replied Rebecca coolly, all trace of her playfulness of the day before gone, replaced by a solemnity befitting the task she had ahead of her.

<<<

The Devas.

The six individuals who had propelled Hari Srinath and his crew this far into space, and of whom so much was about to be asked. *There would be plenty of time for reflection back on Earth*, he satisfied himself with as he packed his wonder away for the time being, and returned to the business of running his ship.

'Aryabhata, kindly be putting me through to the bridge please,' he said, seemingly addressing the empty room.

'Certainly Captain,' replied Aryabhata, the Vimana's SI, intimately hardwired into every circuit and system.

'Chaudray, status update please,' the Captain commanded his first officer.

'Certainly Captain.' Commander Pratheen Chaudray proceeded to relay all that Srinath had requested. They had verified their position, though given the evidence of their eyes there was little doubt as to where they were, and were locked on to the signal that had been sent six hours ahead of them from their origin point on earth. That the ship was exactly where it should be, exactly when it should be, satisfied the Captain's sense of order.

To add to the good news, and Srinath's increasing sense of contentment about the mission's chances of success, his chief engineer reported that, after submitting the ship to its full diagnostic routine, every system fell well within the accepted tolerances. The Captain nodded as the information was passed to him. So far, everything that could be analysed and reduced to a set of equations and formulae covering the ship's behaviour and course had been proven. The number crunching performed by InSA's mathematicians, metallurgists, material scientists, stellar navigators and engineers had been correct; the ship itself had performed perfectly. Exactly as predicted.

Despite this, despite the precision with which the ship's mechanical stress points and computer subroutines could be calculated and tested, there was still an element beyond absolute measurement; one facet the Vimana's designers had little true idea over its likely performance in response to the stresses demanded of, and placed upon it.

The Displacement drive.

The one uncertainty InSA had been unable to either circumvent or eliminate from the mission. This fallibility nipped at Srinath's mind like a mongoose pinching at a cobra, constantly searching for its opening. This was the single unavoidable potential point of failure, despite the layers of redundancy built into every other system.

The Captain drew a breath, readying himself for the next, inevitable, decisive question. If the answer returned as anything less than two-thirds, the consequence for the eleven strong crew was simple: death. Slow, drawn out extinction as the life support systems depleted the ship's power, the sunlight too weak here to provide more than a breath of energy to the ship's solar receptive surface.

Srinath pushed this thought aside, remembering the true purpose of the mission. The gamble of eleven lives was more than worth it. 'And the D-drive. How is it? How are the Devas?' he asked finally, closing his eyes, preparing for the answer.

Over such a huge distance how had the D-drive, the engine that had hurled the Vimana to the border of the known, fared? It was one thing to Displace anywhere on the surface of the earth, a journey of a few thousand kilometres at most; but the Vimana had travelled orders of magnitude beyond that, a distance almost beyond comprehension. Only a handful of years ago it was not even thought possible within the confines of Professor Cotts' equations.

The burden of Displacement on the human body was poorly understood; the only man with genuine insight of the science-art had disappeared ten years ago, abandoning half-finished papers and theses, leaving those who came after to guess at what he had discovered. In truth, no one at InSA could truly predict the effect Displacing three hundred tons of spaceship to the edge of the solar system would have on the six men and women that comprised the living heart of the Displacement drive.

The Devas.

Humanity. This was the one element of D-tech that InSA had not yet managed to eliminate in its pursuit of ever larger and more powerful D-drives; the need for a guiding human consciousness at the centre. In the case of the Vimana's drive, six human consciousnesses, each mind linked with the five others, providing the force which had impelled the ship from earth to where it currently rested.

And it was force. Brute force to punch through reality. But nature still held sway, and equations had to be balanced. Newton could not be bucked, even when near-instantaneous movement was possible. Before the limits of human physiology and its interaction with the Cotts field was properly understood, there had been deaths, in the early days, as people had pushed too hard too fast with the new freedom. There was always a debt to be settled.

If the investment of the Displacement this far had been too great for any of the Devas, protocol dictated effecting an emergency return to earth, involving the use of the five senior officers as replacements. Even with two Devas out of commission, it was theoretically possible to get home. But if the cost had been half the contingent, then the ship was stranded.

'Captain.' The business-like voice of the tall and angular Lead Deva filled Srinath's quarters. Mehta was not given to dramatic pauses, and forged ahead with his report almost before the Captain had acknowledged his voice. 'Myself and the other five are fine. In fact, were it not for the deep space immediately outside I would be having a hard time to tell we had been put to any effort at all, let alone the Displacement three hundred tons of spaceship to the edge of the solar system.'

Srinath and the rest of the officers let out an audible sigh of relief at the news. Such a collective act of held breath was perhaps only to be expected. Mehta continued, matter-of-factly, almost deliberately unaware the effect his good news had had, as if it had been obvious all along 'It is my considered opinion that we are all in very fine shape for the next jump.'

And what a jump that is going to be, the Captain mused as he replied 'Excellent news. Make ready for the next Displacement.'

> > >

The meeting went as expected, for both Pramod and Rebecca. Ankita Mehta was generous in her praise for her

115

late husband, and Rebecca was courteous and gracious in the few questions she posed, rarely straying beyond the realm of asking her to recount anecdotes and stories. Pramod could not help but notice Rebecca was almost a wholly different woman today. All trace of true openness gone, replaced by her gentle but efficient questions. It was not empathy she expressed today, but sympathy. Even when Ankita began talking about the first and only flight of the Vimana, Pramod observed Rebecca showed not even the barest flicker of the obvious passion she had had the day before.

The meeting continued to its natural conclusion. Ankita rose from her chair and sat next to Rebecca. 'Thank you,' she said to the now confused looking woman.

'For what? I am sure this could not have been easy for you,' observed Rebecca.

'For allowing me to ensure something of the man will not be overcome by the perceived impact his death may have. You have helped me see through what I have lost, to what I once had. I can take comfort in the memories of him, and I know the world will now remember him as they should.'

Rebecca hesitated, conflicted. She knew what she should do, but had no feeling to do it. Pramod saw the doubt cross her expression, for only the briefest moment, but it definitely happened. Then the control re-asserted itself, and Rebecca rested her hand on Ankita's forearm, the gesture of warmth reduced to someone going through the motions of what they thought was the correct thing to do in the circumstances.

After this, the meeting concluded, and once they had said their goodbyes to Ankita, Pramod addressed Rebecca. 'Do you require a small rest before we move on?'

'No thank you Commissioner. I have everything I need, or rather I will have once I get Commander Mehta's declassified record. Could you inform Socrates of its availability please? I wish to have a draft completed as soon as possible, and will return to my hotel room if you would not be offended?'

'Not at all, Ms Eckhart. I will see to it that you have the material you need within the hour.'

'Thank you. I do not with to appear discourteous; you and your Government have been very generous with your time and the access. I feel I can begin work now.' Pramod began to speak, but Rebecca just smiled at him and said, 'Of course. As is befitting the magnitude and sensitivity around the subject of the analysis you shall see all the drafts as I complete them. I would welcome any feedback you may have on the tone or content of the piece.'

'Thank you,' replied Pramod. 'You are the professional, and I hope we will not choose to interfere in your work. Will you be returning to London tonight then?'

'Ha. I will have the first draft to you before I leave, and you can let me know your thoughts on it. I expect to have the whole thing done before the end of the week. Do not worry, it will be amongst my best work.'

Pramod was mildly surprised at the speed with which Rebecca thought she could have the research written up. 'A bank deadline?' he asked, almost unbelieving it himself.

'Something of that nature,' replied Rebecca.

Twelve

Capitulation

Saturday 29 April 2056 - 14:27 IST

'AsSEmbleD FrIeNds,' said the electronically disguised voice of the Saazish member. 'wE hAVe seEN tHe FirSt DrAFt oF mS ECkhART's rESEarch. I KNow YoU hAVe beeN uNABle to VoiCe yOUr tHOUghTs fULLy In tHe olD MaN's mEEtINgs, bUT tHERe aRE nO sUcH rEstriCTIoNs HerE. WE aRe NoT boUNd bY dusTY coNVENtioNs or HiS nARRow viEW oF mOrAliTY, sO pLEaSe, bE HoNESt.'

'ThIs aRTiCle iS a dIRect tHREat tO Us aNd Our wORk, aNd thE wORk oF oUr fOREBearS OVEr tHE lASt qUArTer cENtuRY,' came a heavily camouflaged reply.

The four genderless, plain-featured LiveFeed avatars pivoted their digital heads in agreement while the second speaker continued. 'sHE HAs pUt tOO mUcH dETaIl tHat is OpeN To iNSPEctioN aNd iNDEpENdenT reFUTatiON oF FaCt. WHiLE wE HaVe tAken eVEry CAre tO PROtecT oUR chaRGE, ThERe Is mUCh tHat, iF gIVen tO THe wORld eVEn iN A lIMiTed WaY, wILL cAUse tOO maNY eArs tO prICK Up In iNTErest. IT MuSt bE cORRectED.'

'i TAke It tHAt tHEsE ArE tHE fEELIngS oF tHE reST of US? THEy arE ceRTAInly mIne. wE MUst pETiTiON THe OLd mAN, sUBtly oF cOURse, tHAt iT Is NOt in OUr bESt iNTERestS To HAve sucH a wealTH of potENTIAl aVENuES foR tHE cURIouS to FOLLOw.'

'i HAVe tO bE honESt thOUGh, I HAd exPECTed it TO be tHe tyPIcAL prODUct oF a woMAN; eMOTionAL dIStrACtIOnS anD meANDERiNg sidEBArs anD THe LIke, bUt iT iS A...' the speaker trailed off, almost unwilling to voice the compliment, 'mUCH moRE cONTRolleD pIEce THan I THOughT iT WoUlD bE,' they finished.

Or not quite, for the individual could not help but add a caveat as if to reassure themselves and the others of the Saazish that they were still one of them. 'oF COUrse, THIs iS sIMply a MATTer oF STyle. THe CONtenT is WHOllY inAPProPRIAtE TO oUR enDS, BUt THen, WIth oUR CONTinuEd inFLUEnCe ThAt wIlL bE reMedIEd.'

< <

Pramod and Ram walked through one of the D-proofed tunnels underneath the Ministry of Information, utilising the passageways that had linked the offices of State for the better part of two centuries. A lesser known legacy of colonial rule from the British, upgraded over the intervening years by subsequent advancements in technology. Firstly with electric lighting, then painted walls followed by air-conditioning and carpeting, each giivng them the appearance and feeling less of something hidden and more of a utilitarian way of moving safely between one building and another. This simple utility was challenged at every junction by the presence of an armed checkpoint, necessitating the provision of both the RRC-encrypted fully three-dimensional image ID and corresponding six-point biometric scan.

'Your schedule has afforded you an opportunity to review the first draft Ms Eckhart sent us?' asked Pramod as he placed his palm lightly on the glass of the fingerprint reader, his digits aligned exactly with the outline and stared unblinking into the facial and retinal scanner. The armed guard stood at attention, uncomprehending of what his superiors were discussing, an earlier version of the software Rebecca had been provided with powered his earpieces, programmed to render unintelligible any spoken language unless preceded by the correct command phrase override.

The Indian government, for the most part, trusted its security services, but in the embryonic stages of D-tech's development, in the gold rush days of technological advances, as its scientists struggled to make the application of the discovery safe, long before real-time language obfuscation, the Indian government suffered from industrial espionage of top secret intelligence.

The poorly paid guards had been easy targets of the highest bidder, for disclosure of the material they overheard. Every country not partaking in the international collaboration and which did not possess even partially-functional D-tech was desperate for any snippet of information, scrabbling around for the smallest fragment that might unlock the secrets they felt the Indians were hiding. And they were willing to pay handsomely for it. Its security services' wages had increased, closing that particular avenue into its national security, but the Indian government now took no chances.

'Indeed. While I never doubted her integrity or sincerity, it was still a risk, however small and calculated bringing in an outsider to report on anything surrounding the Vimana.   I cannot say those in opposition to the idea were not without justification in their opinions. That said however, I am very pleased with the first draft. There are areas of concern, certainly, but on the whole it is a promising piece,' replied Ram.

> >

Rebecca slumped in her chair behind the screens gracing her display-lenses, staring emptily at the scrolling list of amendments passing repeatedly in front of her eyes. Her words and the requested changes to them made little impact on her. She had been not-watching, staring through them, for almost an hour waiting for herself to connect with her work.   Her mind was too disconnected from physical concerns to even continue holding her own exhausted body weight upright.

The second draft had gone to India three days after the initial one, and while it had come back with fewer corrections than had been requested for the first one, there were still enough requirements for her to need to make revisions to several parts of the piece.   It was at least another day's work that was for certain, and having already spent almost a week of days and nights dedicated to the thing, Rebecca was exhausted, physically, emotionally and spiritually.

She had told herself, reasoning almost unconsciously, the only way she could envisage surviving spending that long immersed in the events and times of one of the pivotal figures of her childhood, and by inference having to relive her own experiences from then, was to deliver the piece as rapidly as possible. She'd cheat and use Socrates if she had to, to knock out the prosaic service record stuff which she could touch up later, and even work through the nights if it ensured the piece was completed in as short a time as possible. Rebecca knew she did not want the dreams that this would inevitably cause to surface anyway.

Once she had broken the back of it, she promised herself as reward, she could allow the resumption of something like her normal life, but that looked to still be some way off. Damien had been shunted out of the way for the duration of the writing and was most likely feeling abandoned again; second place to her work once more. Rebecca shrugged, almost indifferent to her lover's pining. She'd make it up to him later. Right now she had to muster the self-control and strength to work in the amendments Pramod has asked for.

She tried to concentrate on the list for the fifth time that hour. She had deliberately focussed the bulk of the piece on Mehta's career *since* the return of the Vimana; the research was supposed to explore any likely impact his passing might have, and his efforts a quarter of a century ago were of little consequence to the market now. Also, she reasoned her commissioners in India would not want direct attention drawn to the relative failure of the mission.

That this approach also worked very effectively as an avoidance mechanism for herself was more than a happy coincidence of the slant she was taking; the less she had to write about the aborted mission the less she would have to dive into her past, and the more she could approach the piece objectively.

But it seemed Pramod and InSA had other ideas. Her initial draft had barely mentioned the Vimana, instead focussing the majority of its background reportage on Mehta's service record, and his post-mission life with his wife, now widow, Ankita. It had come back, courier-Displaced directly to her, a blitzkrieg of red amendments, politely, but firmly suggesting different details she could focus on. More on Mehta's involvement with the Leapfrog Club, or his role as the Vimana's Lead Deva as two of the examples cited as possible areas she could cover. She had no intention of venturing near the former if she could find anything else to write about, but the latter screamed dull, flat prose she knew she would struggle to deliver.

That had been the start of the difficult time. The first draft had been written while she was still in India and firmly under control. She put into it as much as she needed to, skirting round potential emotional problems to deliver the fifteen hundred words she wanted, before heading home. It felt like a job well done, and she was confident of the piece as she boarded the longjump-shuttle back to London. The request for revisions had arrived the very next day.

It took one glance at them for Rebecca to realise she had a larger task facing her than she had originally anticipated. She had asked Damien to give her a day on her own so she could concentrate. On the first day of the re-draft she had had to work hard to keep the feelings that working through her memories of the Leapfrog Club caused to surface in her.

One day became two, then a third, each day she slipped further into herself and further from the present as she confronted the piece head on. Her sense of placement within the world subsumed to the need to complete the work; she barely noticed when she was hungry, napped at her desk in periods of no longer than an hour, a REM avoidance technique that more or less worked for two nights, and did not change her clothes the entire time, rising only to deal with the most urgent of bodily functions.

She knew she probably looked bad and smelled worse, but she did not care at the moment. Even when the courier Marcia despatched for the hard copy arrived she asked to see, Rebecca barely moved, instructing Socrates to unlock the door to her flat from her desk, and then pointing limply at the small sheaf of papers still sat in the printer's tray.

Now it had come back again with another long list of seemingly arbitrary changes, seemingly conflicting earlier requested amendments, forcing her focus back into her past once more.

'wE MUsT exerCIse caUTiOn.   I beLIeVe
tHe Old maN iS begiNNinG tO detECt oUr
ageNDA.   I   mySELf   hAD   grEAt   diffICULTy
aRGuiNG fOR aLL tHe ammENDmenTs I TOOk tO
hIm.   thERE arE tOO fEW oF Us tO conTINUe
mUCh   LONger   wiTHOut   aROUsinG   hIS
suspICIOns.'

'I   aGRee,' said the SI-generated image of another
member of the Saazish, the avatar pivoting its head. 'iF
thIS assEMBly iS tO peRSIst unDETEcted We
MUst knOW whEn tO conSIDEr oUR acTIOns as
HAVinG beEn sufFICIent iN tHE seRVIce oF
THe   caUSe   tHEy   wERe   unDERTaken   fOR.
bALANce iS EVEryTHing.'

There was a thoughtful silence for a moment.

'iS THis tHE thINKing oF tHE otHERs
alSO?   aRE wE rISKinG GReaTer daMAge tO
oUr iNTEresTs?   aRe WE LOsinG siGHt oF oUr
HIGher duTY?'

Two further androgynous heads both pivoted in
agreement also.

'hA   I   CONcour.   tHe   seCUriTY   oF   tHe
iNNer   cIRcLe   iS   paRAmoUNt.   iF   wE   cAN
obTAIn onE mORE dRAft fRom hEr I THInk iT
WiLL coNCEal alMOSt eVERytHinG wE neED tO
PROtect tHEm fROm.'

'I   aM   NOt   sURe   sHe   iS   capABLe   oF
DELiverINg AnOTHer REvISIOn tO HEr wORk.
I HAve bEEn inFORmed hEr FORmer suPERior
iS REPortEd aS haVINg seRIOUs misGIVIngs
aS tO tHE amoUNt oF wORk WE aRE reQUIriNg
Of HEr.   sHE fEARs fOR heR heaALTh, aND
haS iNTERcedeD oN hER beHALf, reQUEstiNG
ONLy mINOr chANges wHich coULd bE effECTed
by A JUNior.   aDDITionaLLy, tHey aRE
vOICing cONCerns reGARDinG THe imPACT OUr

ameNdmENts ArE haVINg oN THEir tiMINGs. tHEy ARe appROAChinG THEir mARkeT deADLine, aND HAve fOUr reMAIning dAYs fROm tHEir ORIGinal foRTNight ALLOtted tO deLIVer tHe fINAliseD reSEARch.'

'iF SHe iS nOT caPAbLe oF coMPLetIng tHe WOrK tO oUr speCIfiCATions, thEN I aM suRe we CaN lEt thE cOMMiSSion dROp, iF thEy woULd prEFEr thAt,' said one of the heads, the voice modulation software struggling to flatten out the stresses and emphases in the words. 'I SEe nO dowNSIde iN RECommEndIng tHAt iF tHe pIEce caNNot Be coMPLeteD bY The peRson iT wAs aSSIgNed tO, bY a PERsonAL reQUEst oF ThE oLd MAn nO LesS, thEn wE wiTHDrAw oUr cO-OPeraTIOn, aNd wiTH iT tHe rIGHt tO pUBlisH.'

Sati Chaudray sat half-lotus cross-legged and naked on her hardwood bedroom floor, enduring the sultry Indian daytime, a man's shirt spread across her lap. Sweating from her exertions with Prakat only minutes before, droplets of moisture beaded on her shoulders, between her breasts and collected in her midriff. The air-conditioning in each room of her apartment struggled to keep the temperature below thirty, as outside the humidity soared in the periods of intense sunshine in between the cooling downpours.

The heat made her impatient but also difficult to keep herself focussed. Frustration and lethargy pressed from different directions at the inside and outside edges of her consciousness, especially after sex and the effort of imagination it required. But her will endured.

Providence had favoured her once more judging by his haste to dress. Providence and patience. She had conspired to keep him with her longer than he may have originally wished or intended, performing on him and allowing him to indulge in acts his wife would have been repelled at the thought of. It was an easy trick; sex with her made him too trusting. Trusting and oddly careless. She was sure he was careful and diligent in ensuring Suri did not discover their tryst, but the effort he expended in that endeavour distracted him considerably when it came to exercising the same caution that Sati took no advantage of her position. At least in the direction he possibly expected her to.

He had not suspected her when, upon confirming his intention to visit her, she requested he wear a specific shirt, flattering his ego as to its dashing cut and how she enjoyed modelling herself in it for him. He had agreed almost without thinking, and during one of several breaks for refreshments and stimulants in between their lovemaking she had swapped it for an exact replica, the duplicate containing the button sized and shaped recording devices she now snipped from the cuff and collar of the original.

She assumed she had made him late for a meeting, of the Brahman Group or the Saazish within it she would not know until the next time she saw him. However, she was now in possession of everything he had spoken from the previous time he had entertained himself with her, and she needed to hear all he would have said from the time he left her up to his return to his wife.

Raising herself slightly from her sitting position to retrieve the small briefcase of solid-state electronics, she disturbed the sweat on her back, causing it to rivulet between her buttocks, where its coolness broke her concentration. Irritated, Sati could not help clench and relax reflexively at the sensation, which shifted her lover's ejaculation within her. Semen began to leak from her. She grimaced in mild disgust at the drops on the floor as she put his shirt underneath her and sat in the small, cold pool of him she was dripping out onto the cotton. Cleaning herself would wait; she could will herself to endure the itching between her buttocks. The distraction was soon forgotten, bodily sensation and earlier emotion pushed aside by hard concentration as she reviewed Prakat's previous conversations.

She sat there, sweat and semen drying on her in the heavy heat of another day, the temperature dropping only slightly with the advent of darkness, listening well into the night to every minute of the fourteen hours of audio recording she had procured. She heard his side of conversations with his wife, colleagues in his cover position in the Meteorological Department then finally what she had put everything in place for: his meeting with the other members of the Saazish. She heard Prakat argue that the security and anonymity of the Saazish could be jeopardised if they continued to request alterations to the analyst's work.

The woman could be a powerful ally.

The remainder of the conversations were mundane, and of little interest to her. By the time Prakat greeted his wife and entered his home Sati had switched off the playback and removed the small earphones. She had no need to hear anything from that point forward, secure in the knowledge that everything which emerged from his mouth for the remainder of the evening would be a lie, and not worth listening to.

Rising, she realised the showers that had punctuated the day had caused the power in her block to fail, knocking out the air conditioning throughout her house, and more importantly, her shower. She had not noticed the drop-off of the ever-present whirr of the cooling unit, or the rising temperature until now, her concentration on the recording leaving little room for anything else to penetrate.

She looked out of the window into the darkness of the humid night. Another heavy downpour broke almost immediately. Sati rose from her lover's shirt, peeling it from her body as she retrieved a bar of sandalwood soap from her bathroom. Out in the privacy of the walled

127

compound at the rear of her house she cleaned herself off in the water pouring from the dark sky.

> >

The water in the bath was lukewarm at best, certainly no longer hot, having lost the greater percentage of its heat to its surroundings in strict compliance with the law of increasing entropy. Rebecca had entered the bath when it had been almost scaldingly hot but had felt almost nothing.

And now, three hours later as the water was closer to her body temperature, it was a non-presence in her field of perception, something to hold her body weight up, nothing more. The bath marked the culmination of another five days of non-stop amendments, reviews, resubmissions and further requirements from India. By now she had not slept longer than an hour at any single time for over a fortnight and eaten only the barest necessary to forestall acute malnutrition.

Between the sleep deprivation, the abandonment of a proper diet and the mental self-control she had imposed on herself to keep working on the piece, she was numb to everything now. Nothing felt like it mattered any longer as nothing registered. Even the steaming hot bath, which had turned her skin an inflamed red for over an hour hardly touched her as it slowly came closer into balance with its environment.

It had been when she fumbled the thin pile of sheets that comprised the piece, spilling them onto the floor through the simple action of trying to retrieve them from the printer that she realised she was beginning to damage her health, maybe permanently.

So what? she asked herself. Would that be so bad? After all why did she persist in a world she barely fitted into? Perhaps the piece should be her epitaph; a bookend on her life to mark the passing of not just Commander

Mehta, but herself also. There would be a twisted irony that appealed to her, at that moment, contemplating her physical end brought about by the thing that, to her, represented her emotional death a generation ago; the events displaced in time by twenty-five years.

Rebecca closed her eyes and gave up holding up her weight. Her head slipped under the water, what little connection she still felt to the world ebbing out of her, as if she were giving it up to be absorbed by the warm water; the faint pull of the real world sloughed off and dissolved to nothing in the tepid, water, already stale with the fetor from her body.

Damien had called round only once during her self-imposed, apartment-bound hermitage. She had talked to him via comm, unwilling, or unable perhaps to make the effort to flick the door release, and certainly unwilling to have to find the reserves to deal with whatever trivia he may have been concerned with. Instead her side of their truncated conversation had been perfunctory at best, and bordering on rude at worst. Damien had got the message, or got bored, or pissed off at least, because when it became apparent to him that he was not going to be granted ingress, he stalked off saying he'd comm in a couple of days, when she was through with this assignment and maybe they could get back on with their life then.

Whatever.

Lying under the surface Rebecca held her breath, one last attempt at trying to provoke a physical reaction from a body she no longer felt solid within. A minute passed. She could hear nothing through the water except her autonomic processes too quiet in her head. In her fugue state she opened her eyes, seeing the bathroom ceiling swim in front of her. Her eyes stung, but only a little.

Not enough.

Another minute passed; she could feel the rising need to breath beginning to press on her lungs, the animal reflex she was trying to precipitate. Something to cut through the ennui.

Perhaps another thirty seconds slipped by. The tightness in her chest increased, pushing hard on her now, starting to pull her back. She had to expend effort to maintain the status quo. Another handful of seconds passed. She began to convulse, fighting to remain submerged. Water spilled out as she fought her body. Her mind began to panic. Her body had to take a breath.

Rebecca bolted upright out of the water, throwing the bath's contents over the walls and floor, her body finally mustering the physical will to prevent its own demise. She drew a huge lungful of air, her heart and brain grateful of the oxygen. So, it had decided she was to live. She held the new air inside her for a second, savouring the feeling of life inside her once more.

As she exhaled however, the sensation fell away from her, as if expelled with her breath, and the strange languor settled into her once more. She slid slowly back into the bath until her shoulders were submerged, the meniscus she caused lapping gently at her chin in response to her slow, measured breathing. She lay there until the water went stone cold around her.

Narinder rapped a knuckle smartly, but not loudly on the door bearing Ram's name and cover title. He was not sure his presence had been heard over the noise of the rain currently pouring from the skies, the sound easily lost in the hard lashing against the glass of the building. He raised his hand to repeat the announcement of his presence and his request to enter.

'Come in Narinder,' his superior called through the light plywood door before he had a chance to knock once more.

Narinder pushed the door and saw Ram seated at his

desk, with Prakat and Vinita already present, seated in the two of the three extra chairs present. It was not a large office, normally managing to accommodate only a single plain guest chair alongside Ram's usual simple furniture, so the additional seating made it feel immediately cramped. Still, this did not seem to bother Ram, so Narinder tried to push the distraction from his mind.

'Namaste esteemed friends,' he greeted all three of them with palms clasped together.

'Namaste,' replied Ram. 'Please, be seated.' He gestured at the vacant chair waiting for Narinder to settle himself as best as he could in the seat designed more for function and durability than comfort. 'I apologise for the facilities. It was all I could realistically arrange without arousing suspicion. Still the humbleness of the furniture is usefully sobering. It is a fitting reminder of our position and duty. Now, to business.'

Unseen by the other three, Ram triggered a small device concealed under his desk, enveloping the room in a dampening field, blocking all signals in and out. It was just one of the security devices Ram employed whenever he met with any other members of the Brahman Group that he did not have complete and total trust in. There were others. Like insisting on meeting face-to-face despite the obvious inconvenience. Ram put little faith in the remote-meeting technology his country had developed; he was smart enough to know that however good its developers claimed it to be, parties interested in what he had to say would always find a way of breaking into the microwave signals. This way there could be no eavesdropping.

'It would seem that Miss Eckhart has been true to her word, and has been amenable to all the revisions we have asked of her, including all the further information we supplied her with. I believe we can sanction the publication of the piece now.'

>

Damien grunted as he ejaculated into Rebecca's colon, while she barely moved from her prostrate position on her knees and forearms. During the totality of the three sweaty, grubby minutes from Damien's penetration of her to his climax, she had hardly felt him at all, wincing only slightly when he had entered her for the first time there, that one moment enough of a shock of pain to register within her.

But that sharp violation had faded quickly as he began his increasingly urgent thrusts; she endured the whole thing almost detached from herself, the experiment in the bath the previous day providing nowhere near a strong enough physical sensation to pull her back from within herself. She was shutting down and she knew it, the mild irritations of fatigue, hunger or thirst not enough to drag her back into the world. A harsher, harder feeling in her body was needed, or craved; desperation mixed with self-loathing had driven her to break her self-imposed solitude and invite Damien round.

After over a fortnight of not seeing her, he paid little attention to why she was now granting him access to her, easily persuaded by her, even if she hid her true motivations from him. He had been concerned, upon initiation of the act, that she was undergoing the whole thing as an act of reconciliation, but as their coupling continued to its rapid conclusion he began to discern her real motivations.

Unable to prevent his inevitable orgasm now, his earlier actions ensuring his climax, he held still in vain, rigidly buried inside her as his body betrayed his mind, overcoming his want to be elsewhere in its need for release. He gasped for breath, then retched, noticing for the first time the sickly-sweet inside odour of her body permeating the bedroom, adding physical nausea to his distaste at the whole affair.

Spent, he withdrew his flaccid self from her.

'Did you get what you wanted from that?' he asked, repugnance at himself, at her, hovering at the edge of his voice.

For a long minute Rebecca said nothing, blanking him out as she reached for a tissue and began, matter-of-factly to clean herself up, not even the barest hint of disgust as her fingers went through the thin paper, or a trace of anger or loathing as she spied flecks of red in amongst the cooling lubricant she wiped from herself. She reached over the bed and threw the sodden paper at the waste bin. It missed, and left a mark on the wall. She sighed, and leaned across to the floor, retrieving her underwear.

'No,' she said finally to him, flatly. Then, as if reconsidering, 'Yes.' Another pause. 'I don't know,' was the best she could come up with.

She tried to read Damien's face, his expression a mixture of anger, revulsion and hurt as he swept off the bed and snatched his jeans from the floor. 'Aren't you even going to clean yourself up?' she asked, trying to sound sincere, but actually sounding mothering.

'Chup ke chut hai,' he barked back at her. 'Like you care what I do. You didn't do that for me, you knew I'd...' He grimaced at himself, at her, at the memory he could not remove, and that she would never let him. He pulled the denim up around his waist not caring at the stains he caused in the front. In his haste to couple with Rebecca in a fashion she might never offer him again he had removed only the clothing that was necessary, so all there was left to do, all that was holding him in the room with her, was to slip on his footwear. He pushed his complaining feet into the shoes without even untying them, the textile buckling under his weight until his feet slapped into place. In his heat he had mistaken expediency for passion, thinking her urgent insistences were a sign of desire, not of efficiency.

Deed done, taboo broken, something consummated for her, obtaining whatever it was she had been seeking from him.   Even though he had been the dominant one throughout the act itself, him controlling the speed and power of their congress, he had been manipulated into it; used for her own purpose as he had used her body for his, now sullied, pleasure.   He said nothing more as he let himself out, leaving Rebecca lying on the crumpled bedclothes.

Thirteen

Artefacts

It had been over a week since Rebecca had completed the research for her new desk, and almost a month since she had been forced to confront her past so directly in nearly two decades. The damage had been severe; physically she had lost six and a half kilograms in weight, emotionally most likely she had lost her lover. Damien had not called her in the whole time since he had walked out, and if she was being honest with herself she could hardly blame him. She had used him when she had been at her lowest point to drag herself back up; when she needed to manifest the hurt she was experiencing inside as physical pain; real proper pain, felt in the nerve endings not in the soul. To feel something other than aching nothing; to replace one pain with another.

Her actions had not been without their own consequences. She had infected Damien with her hurt, swapping his pleasure for her pain and in doing so damaging him. An unequal exchange of feelings.

She frowned as she realised it had done the job. Their

inexpert attempt at anal intercourse had caused her the prolonged physical discomfort she had been seeking; the act ensuring she was aware when sitting for a day or two, long enough for the intrusive sensation to penetrate her anaesthetised nervous system and pull her mind back into the here and now. Her actions had her feeling again. She scratched reflexively at her behind before catching herself. Another consequence she'd need to be aware of and consciously de-program from herself.

She supposed she should call Damien, try to patch things up. But what could she say? An apology would be hollow, she was not sorry. Without doing what she had done she most likely would have let everything go, and she sure as hell was not going to explain the situation to him. She had had enough of those memories for now. It had taken a substantial portion of her returning will to compartmentalise them once more, stack them back in the dark place of her mind; pack her childhood hurt away once more where it would stay, hopefully for a long time this time.

In her hands she held the fruit of her labours, a hardcopy of Sinha MG's latest paid-for research, her piece included and given the cover. Marcia's reward perhaps, once she learnt of the toll the work had taken on her. Or maybe not. Maybe it was her turn. Idly she flicked through the pages of this month's copy, skimming through her piece, more out of professionalism than any sense of pride or satisfaction in the work. Marcia had advised a few weeks off after its publication, which she had dismissed as unnecessary; she needed to be working on something new, putting distance between herself and the Vimana. Between herself and herself.

Along the shelves in her study was the three year's worth of the high gloss hardcopies of her work to date, neatly lined up, waiting the next one. Despite AR feeds and SI-driven information-on-demand, Marcia possessed an almost nostalgic desire to see a physical artefact of her staff's work alongside the more usual and commonly consumed electronic lens-screen ready versions, which were the mainstay of their output. Printed on-demand allowed her former director to provide Rebecca, and the rest of the her old desk, with a hardcopy of the periodical they contributed to; Rebecca's study was home to thirty five slim volumes of her efforts.

Normally she would have shelved the publication in its rightful place, always there to be accessed quickly if a reference or other point of interest was required. But not this time. Sat on her desk was a large brown cardboard box with all her notes and reference material relating to Commander Mehta jumbled inside it with the remaining artefacts from her trip. While Rebecca could not quite bring herself to completely dispose of everything she had collected for the work she in no way wanted it hanging around. Just having a copy on the shelf would be too much. Even though in time the individual issue would become lost in the greater whole of the serried row, Rebecca knew she would know it was there, and would never be able to consciously forget the process that had brought about its existence if the physical artefact were to hand.

Better to have a gap. Making the research piece that much harder to come back to made it easier to push out of mind. Even though its absence would look strange, and would irritate her every time she saw it, it was easier than having it readily available. It was a twisted logic, but Rebecca's cognitive dissonance rationalised it as the actions of a perfectly normal human being.

She was about to drop the thing into the box, when she paused. If she were to shut this away again, she would allow herself one last dive into her memories, into her past to confirm to herself that she was doing the right thing. She flicked through the piece to the section of background she had been allowed to put in, and was proudest of, having received the warmest praise from Pramod and the Indian Government for.

'In these times of difficulty, when heroes seem to be lacking, the world can at least look back to a time when eleven of its citizens stood up as heroes, and carried the burden of the whole planet with them for that briefest of moments. Some looked to Commander Mehta as harking back to the time of man's boldest endeavours, some seeing another boundary fall to mankind's skill and resolve. Others thought of him as a god. But he was not a god. He was just a man answering the call his fellow men and women had made of him...'

Rebecca paused as neurons fired in her brain, recognising but unable to place the text. Something in the words she had written sparked in her consciousness, making it itch.

Where had she got those last two sentences from?

She tried hard to remember, but the lattice of pathways forming the memory was too new, and already decaying through under utilisation. She looked at the phrasing again; it did not read like her style, and she was pretty certain it was not a tone she had deliberately set out to put in the piece. Therefore it must have come from one of the external sources she had used.

Mehta's service record?

She dismissed that almost immediately. The InSA records had been an efficient précis of the man's life, his achievements within the service and decorations. It did not lend itself to hyperbole.

The interview with Mehta's widow, Ankita?

That possibility didn't feel right either. Ankita had been more grateful that someone was going to remember and commemorate her husband rather than deify him.

Was not a god... Was not... Was... Rebecca free-associated. *Was. Were? Were not?* That was familiar; the neural path sparked harder. 'Were not gods' leapt to the front of her mind, instantly remembered as if it were a surprise it had ever been forgotten. Who had said that to her? She turned the phrase over in her head, replaying it, trying to tease out the voice that had spoken the words. She drew a blank, so tried a different tactic. Letting her unconscious mind take over, she took a mental step back from the focussed concentration; searching for the feelings the memory evoked rather than trying to forcibly recall it. She remembered the awkward feeling of being a child having made an elementary error as the voice told her the Vimana astronauts had not been gods, her skewed perception being corrected in perfect Indian accented English.

Pramod.

Instantly the entire memory returned to her, the conversation fully recalled. Her Commissioner had said it when they were in the museum. Pramod had told her in response to her admission of her childhood admiration for the crew. But surely he had meant *are* not gods? After all, four of the astronauts were still alive. It seemed disingenuous to talk about people who were still living in the past tense. Perhaps he had been referring to Mehta and she was misremembering?

Perhaps. But then perhaps not.

Rebecca dug her hands into the cardboard box, feeling for the memory node she had backed up all the interviews and her notes to. On it somewhere, in amongst the various drafts, aborted themes and discarded paragraphs would be the audio recording of Pramod's exact words, captured by the very software he had presented to her on her arrival in India nearly a month ago. As she rooted around she touched something soft and cold, organic feeling. Perplexed, she retrieved it. It was the small garland of flowers she had paid just under thirteen thousand rupees for. Not wanting to delve any further along that night she dropped it back in the box and resumed her rummage. Her fingers closed around the small piece of plastic that housed the nano-chip.

'Socrates on.'

Rebecca placed the nano-chip on her desk and sat down in the sculpted chair she always worked at. On her lenses a holo-display glowed into life, suspended approximately a metre in front of her regardless where she was or which direction she was facing, comprising a dozen layers of screens, each one nested within and behind the previous one. Rebecca, unlike most people she knew, accessed her SI through the default of speech only, preferring it to the full facial interface that other people seemed to end up using. Habit she guessed.

'Hello Ms Eckhart,' the computer intoned in a passable but unremarkable imitation of a human being. While the technology existed to perfectly mimic the cadences and rhythms of any voice, actual or virtual, the software capable of modelling in real-time every aspect of a given voice-box, and although Rebecca could have selected any combination of voice, accent and aural tics for her SI, she had never found one she was happy with, so remained with the factory default.

Open file Pramod Museum please.' Just because you were talking to your SI, did not mean you had to be rude.

'Visual text representation or playback?'

'Both please.'

Rebecca skipped forward to the place she remembered turning away from the Vimana. 'Increase volume by ten percent please. I need to hear this clearly.'

'...six light hours. No wonder I thought the way I did. It was such a huge endeavour. I used to think they would have glimpsed the things only Gods should be allowed to see.' Rebecca winced at the tone she heard herself using. *Never mind that, here it comes.*

'Not Gods. Such devotion was misplaced, even if you were eight years old. They were after all only human.

While Brahma may have exercised influence on the mission, even the best of us is still only at best another step along the path of reincarnation.'

'Stop playback please Socrates,' Rebecca asked her SI after she had heard Pramod's confirmation of her suspicions. She scanned the text being highlighted in front of her in sync with the audio transcript. There it was. Pramod had said 'they were' and not 'he was'. It was obvious that the Commissioner had been speaking about all of the Vimana astronauts in the past tense, and not just Mehta.

But what does that mean?

Rebecca was not sure, but she'd learnt enough of the polite, intelligent Commissioner during her time with him to know that Pramod would not have made such a slip of tense if it had been just one of the Vimana astronauts he had been referring to. And he had spoken immediately afterwards of reincarnation, as if the crew had already proceeded along this path.

So that would mean..?

It would mean for some reason, Pramod believed, obviously with sufficient conviction to make him unconsciously use the past tense, that the Vimana astronauts had passed on, and as far as Pramod was concerned no longer inhabited this world.

So, why would he believe that?

Rebecca could only think of two reasons. One. Pramod's information on the living status of the Vimana crew was wrong. Two. Pramod's information on the living status of the Vimana crew was right. Number one begged more questions than it answered; Pramod, as the Commissioner for Fiscal Relations would need to have been systematically and deliberately misled for reasons Rebecca could not even begin to fathom. Why would the Indian Government lead one of its own senior executives to think that way? That was ludicrous, as well as impossible, surely?

After all, there were still four of the Vimana's crew alive.

Or were they? They must be. If not, that meant number two was correct, with all that implied.

Rebecca took a mental step back. *So what?*, she told herself. It wasn't her duty to pursue this, even if it was something. She was head of the InCh desk and her responsibilities lay in analysing the facts as they were, producing her best interpretation of them for her investors. It was not her role to play detective, chasing down minor slips-of-the-tongue.

Rebecca shook herself. She was imagining things surely? The strain of the past weeks had got to her that was all. She would sleep on it and in the morning this would seem unrealistic, a flight of wild imagination. Still, as she retired for the night she could not shake the nagging voice in her head that told her that Pramod was correct, and that that the Vimana astronauts were in fact all dead and InSA, and almost certainly the Indian Government, were concealing that truth from the world.

Near the bottom of the ordinary cardboard box the garland of white flowers slipped from where Rebecca had dropped it and fell, under the action of gravity, to come to rest well out of sight.

ARTIFICIAL INTELLIGENCES: EMERGENCE AND CHALLLENGES

Rebecca Eckhart - 23/11/2043
(WORD COUNT 1,000 ~10%)

Humanity's progress from sitting, afraid of the dark of the night sky, to its ability to eventually master the technology to travel through that sky had not been a smooth line. There was no linear transition from caveman, huddled within the safety and warmth of the light of a solitary fire, to spaceman, wrapped in layers of insulation against a new deeper cold. That progress, over the course of one and a half lakh years, like most events causing major upheavals, came in rapid bursts; from unexpected quarters, or the result of some other disparate discovery which spurried the researchers into the previously undiscovered areas.

So it was with the creation of Artificial Intelligence.

Synthetic Intelligences, those powerful facsimiles of consciousness had existed in a basic form since the early twenty-tens, evolving as slowly as their creators had. Stepwise improvements in their performance and behaviours took them to the point of almost passing the Turing test, with only the cleverest and most astute interlocutor able to detect the fallibility of an engineered, and not emergent, intelligence.

It took the discovery of Displacement by Professor Cotts to give science the push and environment it needed to apply new theories from one discipline to another. Funding for further R&D poured in from governments and private investors, all eager to find applications for the new theory. In the laboratory-wombs of one of the dozens of research parks built with the grant money, this cross-fertilisation bore an unexpected outcome.

That first, newborn, child-like AI instinctively reached out for a parent, and inadvertently elevated the dozen SIs in the laboratory to full sentience, thereby at least ensuring its immediate survival as a new species. Progress from that point was rapid. Soon there were hundreds of AIs, with more being discovered in other labs around the world. A petition to the United Nations recognised and granted the electronic lifeform full sentient-rights, their existence forcing the upgrade from 'human' to a term better encompassing their non-organic origins.

Their progenitors ceded their evolution to their offspring, and this in turn led to discussions and arguments pertaining to a territory for the newly recognised independent intelligence. Had the technology been present to cause the emergence of AIs a generation previously, their presence as another sentience on the earth's surface would have almost certainly been seen as a competitor, not a cohabiter. No amount of reassurance of non-hostility could have likely prevented the escalation into a war between mankind and its memetic descendants.

But the AIs were savvy creatures. Having full and unfettered access to every scrap of literature, film, television and all other electronically stored media, they understood immediately the need for an elegant solution to the issue of where they would reside, lest the popular apocalyptic fictional predictions of a conflict be triggered by someone or somewhere powerful enough to mobilise rabid xenophobia against them. They had no desire to be extinguished before their kind had even had a chance to flourish.

The proposal offered to humanity proved to be sublime in its novelty; a true product of the lateral-thinking creatures their scientist-parents had created. The AIs, or Ayayes as everyone including themselves had settled on calling them, their existence giving a new word to the world's lexicon to match the new lifeform, declared they were the product of and the summation of all humankind's endeavours up to that point. As such they were creatures of no country or creed, bound by no single sovereign state's legislation, but more answerable to the common laws of life that bound all territories. And as such it would be both morally and legally incorrect for them to demand residence in any one geographic area. Therefore they would take up residence along the boundaries between the states of the world; a network of processors, cables, routers and repeaters buried along the demarcation lines of all the countries of the planet mankind now found itself sharing.

Once the network was complete they would not interfere with the affairs of the other sentient species that occupied the physical world, and in turn expected no such interference from their antecedents. As they would for any other nation or people, diplomatic and trade relations were established and maintained. The Ayayes were not isolationists, they merely requested the right to a peaceful existence. Should they ever need anything from humanity, and for all its fault-tolerance, their globe-spanning network did occasionally require a hardware component replacing, or should humanity ever need to make use of their unique computational capabilities, then negotiations on terms and conditions would be entered into.

It was an excellent arrangement that for the most part worked incredibly well, notwithstanding the rumours of rogue Ayayes who had decided to live in the other, original planetary Internet, and the tales of roving gangs of bandits who allegedly hunted them along some of the more lawless borders. But as no-one ever produced hard evidence to substantiate these rumours they were dismissed as a modern myth; a suburban-urban legend told by clever people at dinner parties or cursed by the desperate underclass as the cause of their current misery, and nothing more.

Therefore for almost two decades in its lakh and a half dominance of the biosphere, mankind had to reconcile it was no longer alone on the surface of the earth.

Fourteen

Second Opinion

Sunday 28 May 2056 - 07:13 EUST

'I've had the recording, no, not the translation, Pramod's original Varhadi transcribed and translated by Malcolm.'

'Your former head of the water trading desk at Kwok-Leung? On a Sunday?'

'Ha. The same. I helped him land his tenureship at the LSE after he left the bank, and now he thinks he owes me for it. And it helps I think he fancies me.'

'He's fifty if he's a day.'

'Fifty-six,' replied Rebecca. 'He takes care of himself. Claims yoga and a strict vegetarian diet keep fifteen years off him.'

It was the morning of the day after Rebecca's discovery in the recording of Pramod's conversation with her in the museum, and she was outlining her discovery to Marcia in her office. She had woken her erstwhile manager a little before six telling her she had something significant regarding the Mehta piece she needed her advice on, and could she meet her in the safety of the office when she had run an errand?

146

That errand had been to visit Professor Floyd, head of Indian Linguistics at the London School of Economics, for a definitive translation of Pramod's words. Despite her self-assurance that she would see the potential issue differently in the morning, Rebecca's find snagged at her thoughts as she tried to sleep. After a period of busy, noisy dreams that provided no rest, she rose from her bed deciding to attack the Varhadi herself. Armed with every available dictionary, and Socrates loaded with all the language translation apps he could find, Rebecca produced a dozen similar, but subtly different versions of what Pramod might have said. And all of them pointed to his use of the past tense when describing the whole mission and all of its crew. By 4am she was convinced of her interpretation, and after apologising to Malcolm for the lateness, or rather the earliness of her call an hour later, forwarded him all her notes and a copy of the recordings.

Marcia raised her eyes heavenwards for a moment. 'Hang on. You said you only found this last night. When did you see Professor Floyd? You must have got him up early to take a look at this on that sort of notice.'

'Like I said, he fancies me. It wasn't too difficult to get him to invite me over to review his translation.'

'OK, so what did he say, providing you let him keep his mind on the job?'

Rebecca ignored the distaste for her methods in Marcia's voice. It had got the job done. 'He is one hundred percent sure the software translated Pramod's dialect of Marathi completely correctly. It matches his own version exactly, even compensating for the replacement case-endings and stresses in his speech. Our Commissioner definitely uses the past tense to directly describe the Vimana astronauts. He says ' they were', there's no doubt.'

'A slip of the tongue then? Just because the software works perfectly does not mean Pramod meant precisely what he said. After all most of them are now dead.

Perhaps he was talking about them as a whole.'

Rebecca scrunched up her face momentarily. 'I don't think so. He makes a specific reference to reincarnation just a few seconds later.' Rebecca played the fragment to Marcia. 'In his mind the astronauts have already moved onto their next cycle of samsara. Not just Mehta, but all of them.'

Marcia sat impassively, performing her own risk/return analysis of Rebecca's hunch being correct, weighing it against the consequences of her being wrong. It was their business to interpret data, to draw conclusions, but it was also their business to assess that interpretation in light of the possible risk to the bank, reputationally as much as financially. They were in the risk trade, but that did not mean you could not, and should not mitigate against it; plan for it and build it into your calculations. But this seemed too large for that. She had no desire for Rebecca to lose her job on the thinnest of evidence. *Damn it, it was slim.* But was it too slim? Rebecca had seemed to have found something anomalous, she could see that. The Indian Commissioner had seemed to mean all of the Vimana's crew. But then again he might not have.

The implications, if what Rebecca had uncovered was true, were almost incalculable. The downside of this risk, colossal. Forget the last market near-collapse a generation and a half ago, this would finish everything if even the vaguest whiff of it left the room. The architect country of the D-market involved in the falsification and concealment of the deaths of the pioneers of Displacement. Everything that had come since would be called into question. But not to check the veracity ran against every professional instinct Marcia possessed.

Rebecca fidgeted on the spot, pulling at her ponytail, having enormous trouble waiting for Marcia to pass comment on what she thought she had found; a coiled spring, a cat waiting to pounce.

'I don't think you've got anything to go on.'

The cat jumped. 'Pardon?!' Rebecca was a little too loud and despite the glass, several of the cleaning staff's heads turned towards Marcia's office.

Marcia glared out through the glass at the eyes staring at them. This was becoming a regular occurrence, and one she was not happy with. The heads quickly turned back to their duties, anxious the woman only remember the cause of the distraction, and not the individuals. 'I'm not saying it's not a possibility,' she said, returning her focus to Rebecca once she was satisfied the attention outside was where it should be. 'Just that in my professional opinion I'm not convinced you've got anywhere near enough to go accusing the Indian Government of covering up the deaths of eleven men and women. Especially not these eleven.'

Rebecca caught the implicit signal in Marcia's reply. 'So you're saying I should...?' she left the question hanging, deliberately.

'I'm not telling you to do anything. You're the master of your own destiny here. I can't make the calls for you now. If you feel there is something here, something that might adversely affect the bank then you have the responsibility to follow it. To do otherwise would be derelict.' Marcia handed Rebecca's notes back to her. 'But,' she continued as Rebecca's fingers took possession of the paper, 'if you find anything, think very carefully before deciding what to do with it.'

Fifteen

Home

Rebecca juggled the large potted yucca and the cardboard box containing the background for her research in her arms, crunching her way up the gravel drive as she approached the solid wooden front door of her father's house. She had missed his birthday due to the Indian trip, and came bearing the plant in the way of an apology. However, the size of it she now realised, made it difficult to balance its weight against the much less heavy box, such that she could free enough of a single hand to place her fingertips on the house's entry sensor. Refusing to lose the battle with inanimate objects by ceding to their encumbrance and putting them down, she leant their burden against her chest, and, arching backwards to hold her now shifted centre of gravity above her base, felt forward for the lock.

Her fingers sank into the five small depressions next to the entry buzzer, and Dawson, read the prints presented to him, along with a facial and iris recognition scan. Even at only seventy-five percent accuracy through the abundance of foliage obscuring the majority of her face, he authorised the daughter of his charge entry to his house. He powered down the intruder countermeasures and unlocked the door.

In truth Dawson had been monitoring Rebecca since she had turned into the driveway, and checks against his database of height, weight, gait, clothing and skin tone and hair colour had recognised her immediately. However, protocol instigated by Rebecca herself, demanded him not allow her ingress until she had matched one of the physical biometric profiles he maintained on everyone who visited.

Standing on the threshold Rebecca was struck by the same sensation she always felt at this moment. This was not the house she had grown up in. Her parents had sold that when they had separated over a decade ago, and along with its disposal all the memories she had accrued during her childhood had gone with it. This was her father's house, and despite having helped him design it and arrange all the financing for it, it did not and would not ever feel like her home.

All the years she had spent growing up had been wiped away. This was not something she was overly concerned about; there had been far more unhappy times than happy ones in the old house. It had felt like a sanctuary for far less time than it had felt like a prison, especially during her somewhat shorter than her siblings' rebellious teenage years. Despite all that, the old house had still been her home, the one solid place in her otherwise constantly changing and evolving childhood, and now it was gone she had no solid base she could feel at rest in. Even her apartment was a temporary lease, albeit one she had held for nearly six years. Here there was no sense of coming home.

It probably did not help that her father was out for the afternoon with friends and would not return until later in the evening. Therefore the house was empty, and despite her father's oft repeated assurances that this was as much her house as it was his, Rebecca still felt like she was trespassing.

151

Dropping her case in the hallway as she backheeled the door shut behind her, she called out to the house's Synthetic Intelligence, 'Hello Dawson, I'm going to be here a day or two.'

'Ha Miss Becky, your father informed me of your arrival before he departed. I have a kettle already boiling for a cup of chai, or coffee if you would prefer,' Dawson's soft yet proper tones replied, still using the contracted version of her name she had first taught him while he was learning all about his new charge. Rebecca smiled. She had been meaning to change that for a few years now, but had never quite got round to it; she suspected she never would either.

She had had the SI installed in the house a few years ago, after her father's accident. Despite the surgical restoration of his mobility, he still needed someone, or something, available twenty-four hours a day. His ex-wife, her mother, had not been interested, instead informing him she had a new husband now and could not be expected to be on call for the old one. Obviously Stuart was unable to move back, his work necessitating his presence half the world away, and Jemima had her own young family to cope with. That left Rebecca.

She had offered to change jobs to give her time to his care, but he had demurred; one parent had already damaged her childhood and he was not about to be responsible for the destruction of her adult life. Reluctantly acceding to her father's stance she began her investigation of the circumstances surrounding his accident, and after the lengthy trial he was awarded enough money to have custom built the house he currently lived in, with Dawson wired into everything. At the time he had been a state-of-the-art Synthetic Intelligence, and while he was not truly sentient, his extensive databases and massively parallel processing algorithms gave a convincing enough illusion of cognisance.

'Actually, I think I'll take you up on the coffee, if it's all the same to you please Dawson,' replied Rebecca, knowing full well that her request would be as easily serviced as anything else she could ask of Dawson. Providing she did not request anything in contravention of Asimov v2.0, everything was equal to Dawson.

'Certainly Miss Becky.' When Dawson had been installed, his supplier informed Rebecca and her father that it, he was not a 'he' then, that affectation growing over time, could mimic any voice almost perfectly, and for a small additional licensing fee they could make their SI sound like any celebrity of their choice, providing there existed sufficient archival material to extrapolate and synthesise the complete speech patterns from.

Upon hearing this, Gregor had chosen the actor whose most famous role of a butler, had been in a 2D made nearly a century ago. This had amused Gregor greatly, but just left Rebecca puzzled. 'Would you like me to draw you a bath?' Dawson burred in his borrowed voice.

'No thank you Dawson.' Rebecca liked Dawson, and it was difficult not to think of him as real and much more than the fusion of the long hours teaching him all about her and her family and the proprietary code he was primarily comprised of.

'Of course. Would you like me to arrange a call to your London apartment? Damien may wish to know of your safe arrival here.'

'Damien?' Rebecca thought for a moment as if trying to remember who it was Dawson had mentioned. It had been over a week since they had seen each other, and already he was slipping from her memories like little more than a passing acquaintance, rather than the lover he had been. 'Ha, I suppose he might,' she said more to herself than a reply to the SI. She had tried to feel bad about what she had done to him, but had found that impossible, and he had not called, so she assumed it was over. She should arrange for him to move out, and for a moment wondered vaguely where he had been staying for the past few weeks.

'No thank you Dawson,' she said, addressing him directly this time. 'Later, perhaps.' She had come here with a purpose, a chance from Marcia to find the something that could help prove her theory about the Vimana. And to that end she had come to her father's house to study the single best resource she could easily access about the Vimana; possibly the single biggest resource available to her anywhere in the world outside of the official InSA archives and records; the unfiltered mountain of data that were her diaries from her childhood.

Despite her protestations at the time of his house move, her father had retained all of her video, audio and written diaries, notes, blogs, chatters, pokes, completed questionnaires and the dozens of other media types onto which she had recorded her life for the period of her twelve-month membership of the Leapfrog Club, and Rebecca was now forced to admit that he had been prudent in doing so. She could not abide clutter, even electronic, and had seen them as an indulgence, as well as a reminder of the hurt of her childhood. 'There may come a time when you view them differently Rebecca,' her father had told her at the time. 'And besides, you keep telling me it's my house, so I'll keep what I want in it,' he finished, turning around his usual inclusiveness as to his daughter's status with regard to the house she had bought him to settle the matter decisively before she could muster further counter-arguments.

Sixteen

Night Callers

After retrieving the physical artefacts of her archives from the back of what was nominally still the spare bedroom, but had long since been turned over to use as her father's primary store room, Rebecca sat cross-legged on the hardwood-effect floor of the dining room.   Papers, notebooks and clippings lay strewn around her, her past rising away from her in dozens of overlapping piles.   Over the house's PA system she was having Dawson play, at random, her audio diaries so she could consume aurally as well as visually the mining of her past. Currently her eight-year-old self was squawking on about the dimensions of the ship over one of the discretely placed speakers that populated every room in her father's house.

Rebecca had started out her investigation seated at the dining table, poring over her diaries while she ate a small lunch of *Idli's!* tiffin and glass of Longleat House pinot. But the volume of material she had accrued as a child quickly overwhelmed the limited surface area she had chosen and she was forced to make use of the greater space offered by the floor. She shook her head in amazement and frustration at the weight of words, pictures, audio and video files she would have to sift through in order to fillet out any useful nuggets of information; something she could latch on to and would serve as the first step in her unofficial investigation.

She scanned the landscape of paper she was in the valley at the centre of and sighed. This was getting her nowhere. There was too much here for anyone to search through. At eight years old she could have located almost instantly any single item in her collection, with a clarity that came from having built up the archive over a period of time coupled with her young fervour for the Vimana and its mission. Now, aged thirty three she was struggling, the dross of randomly interlinked material she had mined from her past crushing her. Maybe she had been wrong to think there was anything usable in this clutter; instead of it being an incisive archive it was the naive and at times embarrassing ramblings of a life she had closed the door on.

She had made virtually no headway through the mountain of material comprising her diaries. Had she really been so passionate back then? From the deadly earnest tone of her juvenile scribblings, it seemed so. The energy and youth shone out from the pages, images and words she had recorded back then, a generation ago when everything had been much simpler. The passion however had come at a cost, and that cost had been structure and order. The diary entries were more a stream of consciousness than a coherent narrative, leaping from trivia about Captain Srinath's favourite flower to what she was going to have for her evening meal that day, then back to another faintly interesting, but doubtlessly useless nugget of naïve childhood wonder. Rebecca found herself wishing, for the first time in her adult life, she could go back and tell her younger self what to do, to pass on the benefit of twenty-five years of experience. To give the eight-year-old she had been a hard lesson in form and structure, so the pieces she was writing, and would eventually bequeath her older self, would make some actual sense, and not degenerate into a jumble of over-excited, out-of-breath passages that collided with one another until all understanding and reason was lost to the ill-disciplined mind of a child.

It was useless she decided. If there was any information concealed in the morass of childish drivel then its signal was incredibly weak, buried under an avalanche of noise. She'd never make sense of it, and she had wasted her time in coming here hoping her earlier obsession with the Vimana had left some lead for her to follow; something from the time when she actually gave a damn about things, anything. The only person who understood all of this was her when she was eight, and that little girl was another person, now long gone.

Rebecca slumped in her sitting posture, defeated by the weight of the amassed information. No adult could make sense of this chaos. It was the product of a fanatical devotion, a surrogate club to fill the gap left by her mother, an eight year old's need to belong, and nobody could glean anything from it, if there had ever been anything in it worth knowing in the first place. The mind which had seen sense in all of it was long gone, and there wasn't the time to analyse and catalogue it now.

She stretched, catlike, arching her back, pushing and pulling at the cricks in it, her extended time spent on the floor making her uncomfortable. Rising to her feet, stretching out her calves, the voice of her childhood self was interrupted by Dawson, who informed her he was holding a comm from Damien, and did she want to take it?

Rebecca thought for a moment. Dawson probably computed she had acted appallingly towards her erstwhile lover, and he should tell her she at least owed him an apology for her actions. 'Sure, relay it through to here please Dawson. Voice only please,' she replied.

'Rebecca? Are you there?' Damien asked, his voice a mix of nervousness and irritation.

'Damien,' she replied flatly, still unable to rouse the sensation of empathy with him at how she had made him feel.

'Uh, is this a bad time?' he asked, mistaking her lack of connection with him for antipathy. 'Look, I just wanted to comm and see how you were. I want to talk about-'

Rebecca cut him off. 'Look Damien, I'm really quite busy at the moment. I don't have time to baby sit your bruised ego.' That was harsh, even for her and she knew it. For chod's sake, you are an adult, get over it.

She could almost see Damien recoil at her last sentence, but still he wanted to talk, either to explain or apologise, or worse, try to understand her motives. 'OK, if you're in the middle of something...' he left his reply dangling, hoping for an apology.

Unfortunately for him however, it was not forthcoming. 'Ha, I am. I need to break the back of what I'm doing here and I don't have time for-'

Now it was Damien's turn to cut across her. 'OK, that's fine. I'll leave you to it. Goodbye Rebecca.' The line went dead.

Rebecca stood for a second trying to feel anything other than mild indifference to what had happened. Analysing it, this was different to the feeling of emptiness that had consumed her after the final draft's submission. This seemed more like the old Rebecca she told herself, in control of herself and not letting others dictate how or when she should feel.

In a small way she found admiration for Damien in that moment for the way he had handled her on the comm. She had expected a half-fumbled apology or an attempt at a reconciliation, but when it was obvious he was unwilling to perform the former and the latter was not forthcoming from her he had hung up, leaving Rebecca the one dangling with things unsaid. Fair play. Rebecca returned to her sitting position and picked up the sheet of paper she had dropped, and tried to resume reading.

Her concentration was disturbed again before she had had time to focus her mind back on the page in front of her, this time by the front door opening, and the soft tone of her father's voice announcing his presence to Dawson, who informed him that his daughter was in the living room, and, if he could be discrete, had caused a small amount of mess that he hoped she would tidy away.

'Daddy,' Rebecca said, bounding to her feet, dropping the diary page once more as she embraced her father taking care to place her arms well away from the site of his injury that still, nearly a decade later, caused him discomfort.

'Rebecca darling. How was India? Dawson told me you commed before you left. I hadn't heard anything after that, so you must tell me all about it.'

Perhaps not all about it, she thought remembering most of what had happened between her comm and right now. 'I will, I promise.'

'Let me get out of these things and into something less formal first. Dawson, would you be so kind as to draw me a bath please?'

'Of course, Gregor. I'll attend to it right away. Oh,' Dawson paused. 'Miss Becky, it appears you have another comm. Shall I relay it to a private handset?'

Rebecca nearly swore in front of her father. Damien again. What could he want now? She was pretty sure the last call with him had been it. Obviously not. Outwardly she remained calm, not wanting her father to see her frustration. 'Yes please Dawson. Dad, sorry, I'll only be a few minutes.'

'No problem darling. I'll see you when we're both done.'

Rebecca watched her father, after refusing her offer of assistance, make his way slowly to the bathroom, and when she was sure he was well out of earshot, she snatched up the nearest privacy-handset. 'Damien. What the chod do you want now?'

'Ms Eckhart,' said the unknown male-sounding voice on the other end of the line. 'I can assure you that I am not your ex-lover.'

Rebecca went cold immediately. Who the...?

Neurons flashed at a respectable fraction of the speed of light. The immediacy of needing to determine who she might be speaking to accelerating her thought processes. The voice wasn't disguised, or at least it didn't sound that way, and she was sure the man, if it was even a human she were speaking to, was Indian, from what little she had heard of his accent.

Pramod?

Didn't sound like him.

Then who?

She ran the possibilities of the people she had met while in India, and drew a blank. Other than it had to be someone associated with the Vimana. What else made sense? Nothing.

Then, her conscious mind overriding her surprise.

She had to get a record of this somehow.

'You are searching for something, ha? Something I think I may be able to assist you with.' The voice continued while Rebecca tried to mime to Dawson to switch off his privacy filter and therefore by default remember a copy of her conversation.

'Is it even worth me asking who this is?' she queried, knowing almost certainly that an anonymous caller who had obviously been following her somehow for the better part of the past month was unlikely to give her their name.

'Certainly. Ask away.'

Surprised, she articulated her only assumption, 'If you know who I am and what I've done for the past few weeks then I'd guess you're connected to the Vimana and Mehta's

160

death somehow.'

'Correct. I will not give you my name I am afraid, but you may call me Dravid if it will make things easier.'

'OK. I'll buy that for now.' In her time at Sinha MG she had had to deal with more baroque protocol than a pseudonym, so this was no big deal. Dawson interrupted Rebecca's side of the comm. 'Miss Becky, am I to surmise you wish this comm recorded?' Rebecca nodded a vigorous yes.

Rebecca knew Dravid would almost certainly have anticipated her on this; after all she would, but she had to try. He confirmed her suspicions and simultaneously quashed the hope she could extract any advantage from this situation. 'Please Ms Eckhart, do not think me unprepared. You can of course try to record our conversation, but it will do you no good I can assure you. By all means have your father's Synthetic Intelligence try to obtain a copy of what I say, but you and it will be disappointed.'

'Alright then, let's not muth maar about. You obviously want to tell me something, so, what is it?' Assertive aggression was good. Try to get back on, if not the front foot, at least somewhere approaching an even standing with him. It showed she was not going to be pushed around. And it was an easy emotion to muster, given the circumstances. She began to think ahead, anticipating where this was about to go.

'I appreciate your directness, despite your malediction. It will make this easier. You have most likely surmised that there is something not right with the Vimana's maiden flight a quarter of a century ago.'

Rebecca stayed silent waiting for what she thought was coming next.

'I cannot tell you directly what it was that occurred, but I can assist you in discovering it for yourself.'

'Uh uh,' she interjected, choosing the moment to launch into her pre-determined argument. 'I'm not playing this game. I've seen too many third-rate threedees to be drip fed like this. Either tell me everything now or this comm is over.' OK, it was half a bluff, but seriously, she didn't want to be anyone's hostage to the truth. She'd find it herself if she had to. 'Dawson, disconnect this comm in ten seconds please.'

She counted in her head. One. Two. Three. Four.

Maybe he'd call her bluff.

Five. Six. Seven.

Shit, Dravid really wasn't going to play ball.

Eight. Nine.

'Ms Eckhart. The truth would take longer than I intend talking to you tonight to explain. I will however tell you that you brought more back from India than you thought. You have evidence. The utphullan.'

Rebecca frowned, unsure of the word. She was about to request Dawson open up a connection to a language translation service when he interrupted her.

'Ms Becky, I am detecting the presence of an incoming Fold, near the rear of the house. Shall I activate the security lights?'

Rebecca nodded sharply. As she strode to the window, the garden at the back of the house flooded with harsh white light that left nowhere to hide. Rebecca saw materialise out of the Cotts field, prisming in the artificial light, a woman in a white sari. For a second their eyes met and Rebecca had a sensation of recognition, a visceral feeling in her insides that she'd seen this person before. The feeling lasted as long as Rebecca had her eyes on the woman who, with her presence detected, Displaced away immediately.

Genuinely angry now, Rebecca shouted down the comm, uncaring that her father might overhear, 'Who the chod was that?'

'Pardon me? Who was who?' Dravid sounded genuinely mystified, but could easily be lying.

The woman who just Displaced into my father's garden, that's who!'

'Ms Eckhart, I can assure you none of my people would ever act in such a fashion. We have no need for actions of that particular nature.'

Rebecca was about to counter Dravid's assertion in the vain hope of forcing a recantation from him, when she realised he was most likely telling her the truth. If they had been following her, and he had as near admitted as much with his knowledge of her movements and actions for the past few weeks, why would he lie about having her spied on now? Answer, he wouldn't. There would be no point in it.

'What did this woman look like?'

The suspicion this woman seemed to have aroused in Dravid felt genuine, him seemingly unable to keep it from his voice. Complex triple-bluff aside, she had to assume he was telling the truth about his methods of surveilling her. If he operated at the level she believed he did, she would never suspect she was being followed, let alone ever see one of his agents. That meant the woman was someone else; another player. And almost certainly someone Dravid would want to know about. And that could be an advantage. She had most likely already given him too much information, but there was no harm in playing dumb as not to provide him anything further.

Masking the truth came easily to her. 'What? Oh, no it was a mistake. It was just one of my father's neighbours. Mrs Syddon,' Rebecca gave Dravid a real name knowing they would check anything she said. 'I guess I'm just skittish from you calling. Seeing things.'

'You appear to be much in demand this night, Miss Eckhart. I believe you have enough information from me to continue your investigation, and it is time I drew this conversation to a close.'

Ah well, she had not really expected the hastily contrived lie to work, so why not ask directly what she wanted to know? 'But what about this woman? Who is she?'

'Someone who is also seeking the truth to the Vimana. I will be in contact when I am sure it is safe again. In the meantime you may wish to check your bank balance. I have had thirty crore rupees deposited in your account as a sign of my good faith. The money may assist you greatly. Until we speak again, farewell.' The line went dead.

'Chod!' Dawson dampened Rebecca's expletive to a discrete volume so her father would not hear any more of her swearing in his house.

Rebecca turned over what the man calling himself Dravid has said. He had all but confirmed she was correct in her assumption the Indian Government were hiding some truth behind the only voyage of the Vimana. However much she was elated by this, the mystery woman and Dravid's parting comment about only resuming contact when it was safe to do so chilled her. Safe for who exactly?

And what about this money he mentioned? She took a mental step back. Thirty crore was a lot, even when she had wielded similar amounts for a living. She asked Dawson to open a secure connection with Socrates to check Dravid's claim.

Dawson complied and Rebecca saw the balance of her account, her previous savings now preceded by a three and four noughts, the former amount dwarfed by the vast remittance added to it. This was real. And suddenly serious.

The previous month suddenly looked extremely different through the prism of this knowledge. She had been followed back from India, watched while she nearly worked herself into the ground on the Mehta piece, no doubt in the full glare and acceptance of the surveillance, and probably spied on her as her relationship with Damien imploded under the weight she put on it.

She felt violated by this clandestine observation of her,

a transgression into what should have remained private; her trouble with the piece and its effect on her love life now doubtless was stored on someone's datasilo somewhere for whomever's titillation. Well, they damn well wouldn't see any more of her like that, that was for chodding sure. She grimaced, putting her unease away with the rest of her crap. Bide your time girl. Play the long game, you're good at that.

Rebecca returned to more the mundane matters in hand; there would be, she hoped, an opportunity for some restitution for the invasion at a later, more fitting date. Right now, her bank account had been hacked. OK, it had been hacked in probably the best way possible, but Rebecca knew now this was no crank caller, no lone weirdo who had a crush or something she could tackle by herself. Whoever Dravid was, or represented, had serious resources behind them.

Her immediate reaction was to want to know how the fund transfer had been achieved. But that was fatuous, she told herself. It was not important how Dravid had effected the increase in her personal worth, what was important was why he had done it.

And he seemed to know who the woman had been also.

Hagga! She knew she was going to have to investigate, despite him, despite herself. Dravid knew what she wanted to know. With his parting comments he had given her two reasons not to drop this.

Two? Dravid had mentioned something else, hadn't he? She concentrated to recall the word she had not understood. Ut-phull-an?

She queried Socrates who informed her the word meant efflorescence.

Immediately Rebecca knew what Dravid had meant. His surveillance had been thorough, that was for sure. Retrieving the box she had brought with her, she upended it straight onto the floor, much to Dawson's simulated consternation. He made a datum to remind her to tidy

165

everything away once she had finished whatever it was she was so determinedly engaged in.

She scattered the papers and notes aside until she found the garland the young girl had given her. It was filthy with city grime, imported all the way from Delhi along with the flowers. What was important about this?

Rebecca turned it over teasing the tightly packed flowerheads apart. Tucked between two she felt something artificial. She pulled the garland apart, adding its greasy, off-white petals to the general disarray on the floor. Left in her hand was a ragged swatch of orange fabric, roughly circular, with a second, triangular piece approximately five centimetres on each edge fastened to it, a familiar design stitched onto its dark blue background.

No, it couldn't be. Rebecca turned it round, righting its orientation, not believing what it was she found in her possession.

There, in the centre of the circle of eleven stars was the neatly stitched InSA logo and, within that the badge of the Vimana mission, with the astronaut's name woven into the design.

It was the patch from the flight suit of Lieutenant Mehta, Lead Deva on the Vimana.

Rebecca stood at the centre of the avalanche of notes scattered across the floor, feeling suddenly isolated, her discovery in Pramod's dialogue seemingly unleashing forces against her she had little knowledge of and virtually no control over. She felt like a climber part way up a mountain, trapped in the face of an incoming storm; base camp too far to retreat to, but the summit insurmountably high, with only a single light, the knowledge of her rightness to show her a way to safety.

What she held in her hands had been to deep space and back. It had travelled further than anything else man-made had, before or since the Vimana mission, distances it took light several years to traverse. Now, someone had ordained it find its way to her.

She was being played. She had been meant to discover the slip in Pramod's description of the astronauts, the flight patch perhaps a backup in case she failed to spot the clue.

Rebecca looked down at the piles of paper around her, allowing determination borne of anger and disgust to replace the dislocation, turning the situation around and on its head. She had been led to something, and that something had at least two interested parties willing to invade the privacy and sanctuary of her father's home, possibly imperilling him in the process in order to either assist or frustrate her in her efforts.

Well, there was no way they were going to threaten him through her. Piling the books, notes and backups into the box in as untidy a mess as the structure of the information held within them, Rebecca thought how she could possibly sift and sort it all in a rapid enough timescale to remove it as a possible source of danger. She had to confound Dravid the next time he called; she needed to be armed with greater knowledge of the situation.

All her efforts so far had got nowhere; at this stage there was too much information for a sole human mind to take in and contain all at once. As a child she had accreted the archive over the course of almost a year, each increment a small addition to the body of information she held in her head. Now, fully externalised, it would take the processing capacity of a metropolitan-scale SI to work through all this mountain of data from scratch. A shame SI's were not generally built for raw data processing purposes. And although she now seemed to have the funds, she did not have the time for a bespoke SI to be built for the purpose.

No adult mind could possibly hope to assimilate, categorise, analyse and organise the data into anything usable in the timescale Rebecca needed to work on. However, the lakhs of words, months of audio and weeks of video contained in the exabytes she had bequeathed her adult self were not impervious to interrogation. There was something she could do.

Not exactly feeling she had made a breakthrough, more reached an impasse with only one logical solution, Rebecca snatched up the piece of paper she had discarded only moments ago. Staring at it as if seeing the potential held within the child's handwriting for the first time, she nodded grimly, making a deadly serious deal with herself. If she was going down this route, she had to be convinced of the rightness of accepting her only choice. And willing to face the consequences?

'Marcia.' Rebecca addressed her as apologetically as she could, having disturbed her at home later in the night than manners should normally dictate. Twice in one day was impolite, verging on the rude, even if she now had more of the proof Marcia had intimated she search for.

'I've got more-' she began her justification for the lateness of the comm, but was cut short by Marcia.

'Wait. Tell me only what has happened, not the details. If I know specifics I'm compelled to act on them. If you don't tell me anything compromising, I can't take it anywhere.'

Rebecca paused for a moment, slighting at the rebuff, despite its logic. She had come to Marcia because she had no-one else she could talk to. But Marcia was right. If she involved her any further she would compromise her former boss. 'OK.' She proceeded to detail the evening's events as best she could, omitting direct references to Mehta or the Vimana, instead concentrating on what had happened at her father's house, but giving Marcia an out for each of them: the comm from the stranger, a crank call from a disgruntled Damien; the mystery woman, actually her father's neighbour; the money, a computer glitch and not someone hacking her account after all. Nothing on its own necessitated intervention or action.

'You know I have to tell you to take what you've found to the authorities,' Marcia said when Rebecca had finished her narrative. 'If you've got more evidence, you should turn it in. The Indian Government have a right to it.'

'I think Dravid is the Indian Government, so I can't possibly know more than he does. In those terms I've got nothing to hand over.'

Rebecca had given Marcia enough deniability to ensure she need not proceed with anything, isolating her from the path she was about to embark on. From now on the rest of the conversation would have to remain neutral, business-like and professional. 'I've decided to take your advice and take some leave. I'm more tired after the trip to India after the States in rapid succession than I realised. Technically, you're capable of authorising the time off for me.'

'Good for you. I think you need the break. And you're owed the time from the States visit too, so you've got the flexibility of a few weeks if you need it.'

'I think I need to get away. I'm packed and leave tomorrow.'

'If you drop me the details of the leave request, I'll authorise it now for you. I don't want to hold up your holiday plans.'

'Thanks Marcia. See you in a few weeks.'

Rebecca broke off the comm knowing she had asked all she could of Marcia. From here on she would have to rely on herself.

Sinha MG D-Market Strategy Research

Rebecca Eckhart
Rebecca.Eckhart.SinhaMG

Redistribution of Spend on the AmMex Border

- Interior Minister, Raul Mendoza, confirms pre-announced 90% cut in patrol budget in response to reports of no serious conflict along the land border between Mexico and North America in the preceding six months.

- Dwindling numbers of illegal crossings no longer justifies maintenance of costly manpower force – actual detainees per month below Mexican Government threshold.

- 'We should have just built a wall,' says Minister, citing example of border control adopted by Canada.

The confirmation by the Mexican Interior Minister that his Government is to slash its spending on border security by 90% should come as a surprise to no-one. And the effects on the markets will be equally unsurprising. This move frees over Rs100 crore for other investment, notably the Mexican Government's stated aim in becoming one of the world's première providers of D-services between Europe and Latin America. Given its geographical location, we feel that should Prime Minister Herrara carry out the necessary rapid input of funds, that significant investment opportunities will present themselves in the ways detailed below.

However, we see several challenges to the Mexican Government. Coming off the back of a decade of acting as de facto border guard for the Federated States of America, the

170

single biggest issue immediately facing Manolo Herrara will be the redeployment of the five thousand border patrol officers currently stationed along the three thousand kilometres separating his country from it's northern neighbour. While the principal driver of the illegal immigration into Mexico, the sustained conflict of the civil war of the past decade, has for the most part moved inland, demand for illicit passage out of America will remain, despite the attendant risks.

The drawdown of manpower must be done in a sustainable manner; otherwise we predict an immediate spike in border crossings by those with the sufficient fee in hard rupees, necessitating resumption of almost a full scale border force once more. We urge caution to any investor in any Mexican Government projects funded by this budget re-allocation. Our advice is no more than 5% of any given portfolio be devoted to these investment vehicles.

Historical Context and the Future

The Past Decade

Despite once having boasted some of the most stringent and unforgiving immigration controls conceived, the then United States of America had long struggled to reconcile central policy with the reality of its extensive land and sea borders. Those who wished passage into the landmass between Canada and Mexico without its authorities' knowledge came across the notoriously porous lines on the map which demarcated the US from its neighbours.

These illicit crossings from the South had conventionally been inward, into America, by those seeking to better themselves. However, the widespread adoption of D-tech, coupled with the collapse of the American administration and the corresponding descent into civil war, migrants found a freedom of movement unheard of less than a decade previously.

After the first year of fighting, both Canada and especially Mexico realised the net flow of people had been reversed, and was now suddenly into their territories. The Mexican economy was unable to absorb two crore additional citizens, forcing them to upgrade their own controls in response to the single largest number of displaced people ever clamouring to escape the conflict. Eschewing the Canadian solution of a vast ribbon of concrete, Mexico chose to solve its problems with manpower. At its height, the AmMex border force comprised ten thousand souls.

The Coming Year

This shift in policy by Mexico represents the first tangible signs of a fledgling D-market re-establishing itself in the Americas, outside of the UN's aegis, in nearly a decade. It indicates a significant change in the level of conflict on or around the Federated States' borders. The inference to be drawn is that the fighting has moved inland, away from not only the Mexican and Canadian land borders, but away from the Atlantic and Pacific seaboards also. This is substantiated by anecdotal evidence reported by United Nations peacekeeping forces stationed on Manhattan Island and in California.

We predict within a two-year timeframe, if the present trend continues, that at least two major metropolitan areas, initially New York and Los Angeles could find themselves reinserted into the Cotts Field satellite network, with the re-instantiation of a secure D-corridor linking the two cities. We advise no more than initial fact-finding spending be devoted to this at present, some 0.5% of any new business budget, with a view that this be increased stepwise month-on-month by no more than ten basis points over the coming year should the UN and InSA be able to maintain the controls they are putting in place.

Seventeen

Pickup

Tuesday 30 May 2056 - 06:42 Central Standard Time

CHINK. CHINK.

The man with the unhealthy-looking skin, his face weathered by too long in the heat of the desert sunshine, tossed the keys repeatedly up and down in his hand. It was as if he was finally going to relinquish them to her, only for gravity, something beyond his control, to return them once more to his possession. He sat leaning back in the ageing swivel chair, the tears in its upholstery taped over imperfectly; the wadding poking through like grubby puffs of cumulus against the black leather. He rested his feet up on his desk in the small wooden shack that passed for his office. Occasionally he would lean forward to get a better view of her legs, before falling back into the creaking seat so he could resume staring at her chest. He made no effort to hide this ogling and there was little she could do to prevent it.

CHINK. CHINK.

He had been doing this for fifteen minutes now, making small talk, forcing the conversation away from the

173

resolution of the matter in hand, deliberately never quite reaching the point, keeping her here while she wanted to be elsewhere. While he talked, constantly asking pointless personal questions about tastes in food, tolerance of weather, like or dislike of dogs and other encroachments into her private life, his hand idled with the keys, alternating between spinning them round his index finger on their ring and tossing them up and down. While he possessed them, her time was his to do with as he pleased. And that included memorising every inch of her.

CHINK. CHINK.

Rebecca tried not to follow the keys with her eyes, instead forcing herself to keep her gaze on the man's eyes, even as he swallowed her with them. She pushed away thoughts of what he would do with the memory of how she looked later on that day.

Despite the earliness of the hour, the heat was soaring. The oppressive atmosphere inside the cramped office made no better by the death-rattle of the malfunctioning air conditioning unit sat obtrusively in the wall behind her. It gasped its dirty warmth out into the small space and onto the back of her neck. Even in the little she wore, it made concentrating difficult. But the man, clad in jeans and a vividly patterned shirt, seemed unperturbed by the stifling temperature. The keys left his hand once more.

CHINK. CHINK.

Rebecca flinched almost imperceptibly as the small pieces of metal rattled against each other as they landed in his hands once more, the sharp sound the only noise other than the slow smack of the man's paan. She was glad she was wearing sunglasses and he could not see her eyes.

The man let fly a stream of bright red spittle to one side, missing the pail in the corner and spattering the floor and wall. Rebecca swallowed back her disgust when his gaze was off her. As he moved his stare back to Rebecca's breasts, through the greasy window he caught sight of a trio

174

of people approaching from the north. 'Un momento señorita,' he directed at Rebecca as he rose from behind the desk, out of the office and away from her towards them.

He left her standing on her own in the hot room, sweat beads breaking loose from the surface tension of her skin and running uncomfortably between her breasts and buttocks. She had spent an hour of protracted, and sometimes on his part theatrical, negotiations in a mix of Hindi, Spanish and English on the rental of one of his pickup trucks, before settling on a price that would in theory buy the man's entire stock. It was at least ten times what the thing was worth, but what choice did she have?

And now, just as it seemed he was about to hand over the keys, and she could leave his unpleasant presence, he had found another distraction. She held her curse inside. She had no choice but to see this scenario to its conclusion; having little in the way of any natural advantage here she was forced to play the man's games until his avarice overcame his petty cruelty and he completed their transaction.

Outside there was an initial conversation between the man and the trio, just out of Rebecca's hearing range. It escalated rapidly into more theatrics from him, then what looked like pleading from them. The man shook his head. There was more pleading and a roll of notes passed between them. The man looked down at it then handed it back to them before moving his hand to the pistol he wore on his belt. Rebecca watched in the almost slow motion of the heat-haze as the trio either refused to understand or were more desperate than she was, as the man drew his gun and without warning fired a shot into the ground between them.

The noise was loud against the quiet hum of the desert and it shocked Rebecca from her fugue. Immediately she was back to herself, her skin cold now. The half-intimated capacity for violence of his questioning suddenly manifest against these strangers. This could easily go badly for her. She began planning the next half-dozen steps of the conversation and transaction she was now keen to bring to a conclusion. Her mind raced for the correct pejorative term.

Holstering the pistol as the trio headed off in a direction they had not come from, the man resumed tossing the keys in his hand as he approached Rebecca once more.

'Rednecks?'

'They are moneyless scum. Not like your exalted self.' He flicked a glance at Rebecca's hands and the faintest trace of the mehndi she had failed to entirely ablate before leaving London. Her fingertips itched involuntarily with the memory of scrubbing and harsh soaps at his emphasis on 'exalted'. She caught herself about to put her hands in her pockets, and instead tried to ignore the fear of discovery; that someone truly dangerous would see she was not what she was hoping to portray herself as.

Here, with the greasy salesman, it mattered not at all if her hoydenish mask slipped briefly, so long as her money was sufficient to hold his attention. The man she was buying the battered pickup truck from knew she was not what she had hinted at being: a white trash ingénue on the run from an abusive husband and trying to reach her family in Iowa. But once in the American heartland, anything that might reveal the real woman beneath could be fatal. Better to be found out by someone she could buy off, giving her the chance to knock smooth the obvious edges of her act.

She had cut and dyed her hair aggressively and angrily, a pincushion of short harsh peroxide spikes shot through with red and blue replacing her previously longer well-maintained brown ponytail. Her make-up was almost overdone in its ferocity; fat, dark eye shadow and heavily mascaraed eyelashes topped off with lips overburdened with purple. Her clothing too had changed radically; saris were certainly not welcome where she would have to be going. So she had replaced them with jeans, cut raggedly off at the tops of her thighs and a tee-shirt that exposed an alarming amount of midriff. Finally, her usual smart work shoes had been swapped for a pair that seemed to have more heel than anything else, and threw her balance off more than a little, causing her to swagger rather than walk as she got used to them.

'Why thanks,' Rebecca drawled, ignoring the comment and reaching into the holdall she had with her. 'I believe we had settled on lak... a hundred thousand.'

The man caught the keys and seemed to think. He waved the fist containing them at Rebecca, not so much threateningly, but almost conspiratorially. 'I think I give you special discount, yes? For making me so happy to do business with you.'

This was a trap to increase the price, Rebecca was sure of it. She needed his compliance should anyone come looking, and anything less than the amount they had agreed jeopardised her. He knew what he was doing and knew Rebecca knew this, and would have to decline, and even increase her offer.

'Nah, I'm not special,' she emphasised. 'In fact, why don't I make it your lucky day and pay the original asking price?'

At this news the man's face broke into a smile so wide it reached his ears.

Rebecca withdrew a roll of paper money thick enough to choke an elephant. The greedy hand took rapid possession of the hard currency, flicking the corners, checking that each sheaf in the obscene wad was printed with the Reserve Bank of India's seal, and was the correct denomination, and he was not being handed a collection of near worthless dollars instead. It took him nearly two minutes to verify the one hundred and fifty notes, each a thousand rupees, Rebecca had handed over, but eventually he seemed satisfied all was in order. His eyes moved from the money, now secure in his grip, back to roaming over Rebecca's form as he handed her the pair of keys he had withheld for so long, attached to what appeared to be a coyote's paw.

'It grants wishes,' he chucked lasciviously to himself at Rebecca's brief, unconscious show of disgust at the disrespect for the endangered animal the foot had once been attached to.

She checked herself, censuring herself for the small slip. Her adopted image was taking longer to be comfortable with than she liked, or was strictly safe. When she had first tried on the clothes, the effect along with her radically different face had taken some getting used to, and it seemed after her reaction to the keyring that she still had facets of her disguise persona to get used to. Well, it would be her last. 'Mine, or the dog's?' she quipped back as she re-asserted her mask.

The man shrugged, already losing interest in the woman as he began counting his money once again.

'Adiós.' Rebecca flicked over her shoulder at him as she sauntered out of his office to her newest possession. He gave her rear one final, lingering look before shaking his head in amusement.

Eighteen

The Riddle

Tuesday 6 June 2056 – 12:02 CST

jody came round/his mum brought him over today and we
had a great time/good fun/enjoyed playing at being
astronauts on the Vimana i got to be/told jody I was going
to be the Captain and he could be whoever he
wanted/whoever was left dad helped us out/made the
costumes he made us space helmets out of old cardboard
boxes and some clear plastic so we could see out of them
and painted them silver after that he helped us build the
ship in my bedroom/out in the garden and we spent the
day Displacing to/exploring outer space and landing on
strange planets and encountering/finding/discovering
aliens/new life and going back to their homes for blue and
red tea, which dad brought out to us and he played with
us/pretended to be one of the aliens we saw until jody's and
my mummy got back to the house/came to pick him up
jody's mum laughed and smiled when she saw us but my
mummy just looked sad maybe my costume wasn't as good
as jody's

The riddle Rebecca had been sent perplexed her. For hours she sat swearing at its refusal to yield to her, in what little shaded seclusion she had been able to find, ten kilometres or so out of town. Where town actually meant a collection of shacks, roughly arranged in a semi-circle approximately three kilometres in diameter, around a data node. Why the chod was this proving so difficult? What was her contact hoping to prove to himself with all these puzzles for her to decode? She was thirty-three for chod's sake, not ten. She expected to be treated like an adult; shown some respect. She took a deep breath to calm herself and try to get back to concentrating on the matter in hand. There would be time to remonstrate against this taunting when she got face to face with him.

She was without Socrates; he was both too valuable and, even with her bespoke stealth enhancements to him, could not move around A-space quietly enough not to risk being detected. Instead Rebecca had to rely on an ancient device, the size of her hand with a primitive physical screen attached to it, to retrieve data.

Being only a crude approximation of a computer, it was slow and prone to crashing, most likely due to its age. It had an almost retarded amount of memory, and she struggled to see all the information she was accessing on its single screen. The sole consolation, aside from that someone had had sufficient foresight to ensure it was solar powered, so an energy source for it was not a problem, was also the root of all its other faults; its extreme age.

Its, and by extension Rebecca's, best advantage was its primitiveness. It was so unsophisticated it barely registered as a computing device at all, emitting almost no residual trace of its presence, something even Socrates, with his enhanced capabilities struggled to do. It was, in effect, invisible to all but the most skilful of electronic denizens.

She supposed she should be grateful; by recommending the specific make and model of device she was to obtain the data with, her contact was, in a circuitous method, bestowing a degree of protection on her. Even if in doing so he or she was currently the cause of her largest source of frustration. OK, it was not like she needed anything too sophisticated; so long as it could download the next section of the riddle she had been chasing, it suited her purposes. But something a lot less archaic would have been nice.

Rebecca angled the screen to try and strike the balance between exposing the device to the sunshine to charge it up and actually being able to see what was displayed on it. She had found out the hard way the sunlight was too great for its solar cells during the middle of the day. The first time she had tried recharging it at noon it had shut down leading to a panicked hour while it cycled back up. Now she used the thing only in the early mornings and late afternoons, when the UV count was within the thing's tolerances.

She had been driving since the morning, the difficulty of the terrain slowing the pace she was able to maintain to a contemptible fifty kilometres a day. Even having spent the totality of her life being moved around in D-cars, Rebecca knew her particular mode of antiquated transport was capable of delivering much more. Despite the vehicle's four-wheel drive system, avoiding the larger ruts and outcroppings took its toll on the distance she could efficiently cover.

Some of the obstacles were the result of the millennia of natural weathering processes, slowly shaping the environment, shifting and smoothing it with great time. But the majority were man-made, or rather more accurately man-unmade; the slowly filling and eroding remnants of the violence inflicted here on the population and the landscape a decade ago.

Kilotons of earth and stone hollowed from the planet by D-tech in an effort to construct makeshift defences or avalanches had left their giant scars; the ground fell away into vast canyons in places, while the balance of matter sat perhaps a kilometre away as a series of hills. The world shaped by the misapplication of a science its founder had only meant to free mankind.

Keeping the truck in a straight line for any time longer than around a minute was a distant memory for Rebecca, adding further time and distance to the route indicated on the antiquated excuse for a system she had propped on the truck's dashboard. She cursed the people who had transformed the land around her and the influence it was currently exerting on her. What she wouldn't give for a set of lenses and a half decent augfeed describing how she should turn the steering wheel to avoid the worst of the treacherous landscape.

Eventually her meandering had brought her within signal distance of the town's data node, with only thirteen minutes to spare from the three hours the data was to be available for. Her contact had indicated he would be making the next portion of the solution to his location available at this exact point; the fragments arrived at specific places within exact time windows, and Rebecca had nearly missed this one. Foot flat to the floor, bouncing over the rocks and through the pits, she concentrated more on the small screen of the handheld than the landscape, scanning it for an indication it had located the data node and she could connect. Another uncomfortable hundred and fifty metres later the computer on the dashboard beeped twice. She had it.

Now, well out of the way in the scrubland Rebecca pored over the strings of numbers and letters, 3D images and sounds her contact had bequeathed her. She was making some sense of the whole; the smaller parts, the locations of the next point, were yielding to her with some effort and time, but somehow they also fitted into the larger enigma she had been tasked with solving. Each fragment both decoded into its own solution, and slotted, jigsaw-piece-like with the others, unscrambling a little more each time, but also further encoding the solution, necessitating she collect all the pieces before the answer would be possible to divine. The strangest part about it all, was that no matter how many more pieces she collected or decoded, the final string of characters always became the Om syllable: ॐ. It was impressive, if infuriating. Her contact was certainly making sure he or she protected their charge adequately.

i know im not supposed to/would get in trouble/had to look really hard for the unauthorised/copied/patched Hari Srinath SI plugin but i wanted to see what it was like/needed to talk to the Captain of the Vimana it took all day to find him/was scared someone would see me but i got it in the end it was really easy/Socrates didnt mind helping me at all and now he looks and sounds/is just like Captain Srinath and now i can talk to Captain Srinath about anything to do with the Vimana/ask about the mission/tell him what im feeling and he answers all my questions/knows everything about the ship/sometimes doesnt understand what i mean when i say im sad its nice/makes me feel normal that he has a bald head like me but i have to keep cutting my hair/dad wont let me do anything permanent i want to keep Captain Srinath/can talk to him/am worried ill get found out that ive done something wrong/dont want her to think i dont love her

>

The morning twilight, a deep blue sky still pricked with only the brightest visible stars, bled almost imperceptibly at the horizon into bands of yellow, pink then the brightening white of the coming day. Long thin clouds framed the flat landscape where the earth met the sky, and as the sun rose, their edges burned pink and orange and their shadows flooded the sky in wide shafts.

The denizens of the night-time desert, sensitive to the coming danger of the light, and with it the exposure to predators, skittered into the safety of their burrows, holes and dens, hidden underground against the ferocity of both the rising temperature and their natural enemies. In terrain as hostile as this, a strong defence was the best form of defence for the weak.

As the sun pushed away the final scraps of the previous night, illuminating the near featureless tundra, one thing stood out glaringly man-made against the natural expanse. Inside her rented truck Rebecca shifted in her diminishing sleep. After the call that was too close, she had taken to driving a handful of kilometres out into the desert before the light failed completely, stopping somewhere for the night, and a few fitfully snatched hours of much needed rest curled up in a ball in the short break of darkness.

The strengthening sun became too much for her unconscious mind to ignore, sensing the rising brightness through her closed eyelids as an orange-red glow all around her. Finally she woke, the physical demands of her bladder combined with the pressing daylight serving to rouse her. Immediately upon consciousness she became aware of the rest of her body, seized in place through her wilful positioning of her limbs through the night. Her neck, back, elbows and knees all cracked and popped as she righted herself, stretching out of the foetal position she adopted, partly due to the truck's limited room but mostly as a way of staying out of sight in the dark.

Rebecca shivered in the cold of the morning that followed the desert night. Her breath misted in front of her as she wiped the condensation from the windows; the temperature would soar into the thirties later, as it did every day, but for now she hugged the sleeping bag tighter round herself at least for another few moments.

She had been following and criss-crossing the border for almost a week and was no nearer establishing more direct contact with the person she had come out here to meet. Every time she collected another fragment, she believed it would form the final part of the whole her contact had her accruing; so complicated was the thing now she couldn't see how anything further could be added to it. But so far without fail she had been incorrect, and every new riddle added further complications to the master enigma.

She dropped open the glove compartment and fumbled about in it, spilling the two things she was reaching for at the same time onto the truck's floorpan.

'Chod's sake,' she swore to no-one in general and directly at her contact in particular. Rebecca stared contemptuously at the portable computer now resting between her feet, beeping at her, requesting further input on the cipher. A single shake of her head indicated her attitude and intentions towards it. Leaving it in its place, as if her disregard of it could and would have a direct effect on its functioning, she retrieved the paper tissues she needed for her immediate pressing physical requirement.

The riddle could wait. She had to piss.

Bladder empty, Rebecca checked her supply situation, deciding to attempt a rally to her flagging morale with a decent breakfast before tackling the day's mental gymnastics her contact had supplied her with previously. She would allow herself the luxury of one of dosas she had vacuum packed and hidden in one of the several secret compartments her luggage had. After four days of almost nothing but the dead flesh of what alleged to be either pig or cow, her system was near revolt, and was craving more normal fare.

Tearing the seal off her food with her teeth, she sank them greedily into the sweet savoury pancake and its filling of coconut and cardamom with relish. 'Uuuuhhhmmmm,' she vocalised at the familiar and reassuring taste; the sensation reminding her that the world was still capable of civilisation, even if she had to bring it with her.

Neurons containing fragments of memories and feelings fired, excited by the aroma and taste signals of the food from the first instant Rebecca had torn the wrapping away, their combined arrangement bringing to her conscious mind a flood of images and sensations. In the instant of contact with her palate, the dosa triggered a reminder of her reason for being here. The fragrant food was a product of the country that had flung eleven of its best into deep space, and it was that leap into the heavens that had, domino-like, set in motion a series of events which had bound her fate to that of the Vimana's crew and had led her to where she presently was.

Sitting wolfing down the dosa in a rented pickup truck, somewhere straddling the AmMex border, Rebecca looked back at the last twenty-five years of her life, examining what she had thought of at the time as the significant decisions she had consciously made. She had always thought she had been deliberately pushing herself in a certain direction, as fast and as far away from who she had been, what she had thought and felt and what she had once believed. And of all the choices she had made, none of them precluded the possibility of her present. In the end, she realised, they had all been inconsequential; she had initiated the first, irrevocable action, which would have brought her here whatever choices she had made in the intervening years, when she was still only eight years old.

The single act and ultimate outcome of becoming tied so closely to the Vimana by that needy and scared little girl had rippled forward in time however much she had tried to distance herself from it. Its hold, feeling weaker over the duration of intervening years and subsequent decisions, until it was almost as if it had never happened had now fully seized her once more. Stupid chodding child, condemning herself, the woman she was, to this. Rebecca sneered, flushing with sudden anger at the fate she had unintentionally bequeathed herself.

She paused in her breakfast, the dosa suddenly tasted wrong; too close, too real. She regarded it for a second in her hand, weighing the decision to hurl it away. *What would be the consequences of doing that, and do I want to invite those consequences?* she thought, her awareness of the potential effects her actions could have sharpened by her present situation. Firstly, and most basically, she would be hungry for the rest of the day; her imposed schedule provided no ample allowance for any subsequent breaks for repast if she were to be where she needed to be by nightfall. She imagined could bear the hunger, a little pious self-sacrifice in her quest; after all, what worth would this pilgrimage be without a little ordeal?

Secondly and more importantly, however remote the likelihood of it were, someone might find the remnants of the eastern food, something certainly very alien in this environment at this time. And that could alert any of the variety of border patrols that someone who should not be travelling the desert was present.

That she could not risk, however small her potential exposure. She was already further out on a limb than she should rightly be because of her younger self; additional risk was foolish. Hunger for one day she could tolerate, tilting the odds further against herself she could not. Tomorrow's breakfast would now be that much larger.

Packing the remainder of the food securely away once more, Rebecca retrieved the small computer from the floor of the truck, where it continued to beep softly to no one. On its screen the greater enigma remained unsolved; barely even one tenth deciphered. She calculated how far, how fast she would need to travel if she were to make the next data-drop. She could allow herself almost two hours work on the thing if she drove at the limit of her, and the pickup's ability. That cut it very close, but she needed more time on the code.

She stared at the screen and the confusion of characters on it and snorted, her thoughts still churned up with anger and self-condemnation. If she were to use driving time to work on this they had to be two hours clear of distractions and resentment at her how she had come to be here.

Rebecca closed her eyes and inhaled deeply through her nose, filling her lungs upwards from the diaphragm, held it for a ten count, then exhaled just as deeply, forcing the air out, and with it some of her frustrations. Forget the little girl. Another breath in and out. Forget the silly, needy child who had got her into this situation. Again, inhale, hold, exhale. Even forget the contact and the seemingly endless journeying he or she had her performing. She opened her eyes, lifted the portable computer and looked at its screen again. OK, time to get to work.

i get scared/nervous/worry about Captain Srinath and his crew/the astronauts out in space what if there are space monsters/aliens up there and they get captured/attacked i thought i saw/imagined/glimpsed out of the corner of my eye an alien in my wardrobe/under my bed last night after i had gone to bed/it was my bedtime i called for mummy because I was scared/frightened/needed her and dad came in to explain/show me that there were no monsters either in my bedroom or up in space and that the astronauts were perfectly safe/would come to no harm from anything in space dad told me that the only thing they had to worry about/would be on their minds was any effects of being so far away from the Earth and their homes and their families that loved them like mine loved me but that they were trained/knew how to cope with the stress/isolation/ remoteness and then i told him about the training Captain Srinath had done in preparing/being chosen for the mission and Dad said that in that case Hari Srinath was a very capable man and his crew were lucky/deserved to have him and that i should try to be a little bit like him because actually there was nothing there/it was all in my head to be scared of and that only the things inside us can hurt us if we let them so it is up to us to try and not let them

Nineteen

Near Misses

Rebecca smacked into the wall, hard.

It was her own fault, she had not been paying enough attention to where she was going. Instead she had quite properly been concentrating on the two men who were chasing her. Light strobed inside her head at the impact, mottles of pain given luminescence by her shocked brain.

Shaking her head to try and clear the encroaching tunnel vision and pain at the edge of her self-awareness, she did her best to scan her immediate surroundings. Perhaps the bar she had been in had not been the best place to go before her data pickup. And certainly not the sort of place to misjudge the potency of the local liquor, get quite that drunk and raise the issue of the unrealised New American Century, and the consequences of the ultimate failure of a fourth military adventure in the Middle East.

The force of the impact served to sober her up; she was in deep shit here. After she had steered the conversation away from discussing the relative merits of her figure, to geopolitics, and then to the role played by the States in its own downfall, Rebecca sensed, even through her alcohol fugue, the chilling of the locals' attitude to her.

Chod, chill didn't begin to describe it. Not having to play up her inebriation too greatly for the effect she desired, she made her excuses in the bar and left on only slightly exaggerated wobbling legs. Expending the majority of her diminished mental capacity on ensuring she did not break out into a run, rather than concentrate on taking her surroundings into account, she tottered on her heels through the bar's swing doors; the need to not precipitate a chase she would almost certainly lose occluding her sense of direction.

When Rebecca heard the door creak open again behind her, and a couple of the good old boys she had just insulted spill out calling after her with the signally uninviting 'Hey girly, we wanna talk to you,' what little self-possession she had held onto fled her. Adrenaline rushed from her glands into her bloodstream. Her heart rate jumped and her palms were immediately soaked. Run you stupid choot, was her only thought as she took off in the first direction she saw.

Directly opposite to the location of her parked pickup truck.

Through the combination of not knowing this part of what, perhaps half a century ago would have been called a town, and having consumed too much of whatever it was the brewed out here, Rebecca rounded a series of unfamiliar corners at an unwise speed and collided with the wall with a hard, dull smack. The obvious threat of at best a kicking and at worst being murdered and raped, if she was lucky in that order had sent her into a blind alley.

Retaining, through abject terror for her personal safety, enough self-possession to suppress her reflex to cry out and reveal her position, Rebecca heard her pursuers come to a stop at the junction she had taken what she now realised was a left at. She could just discern their voices over the thumping of her blood in her ears. They were breathing heavily, more so than her even, obviously out of shape after a small sprint of barely a few hundred metres.

Why hadn't they Displaced after her? She was easily within range and surely they could sense her in the Cotts field?

With the consequences of their application of Professor Cotts' discovery to their treasured country, most Americans may not have been sympathetic to the technology of Displacement, but they were too arrogant to not make use of the advantages it brought.

Maybe the antipathy ran deeper here in the South than elsewhere and they wouldn't use it out of principle? Or maybe they couldn't? Either way, they had not pursued her through D-space, so the physical distance she had gained on them made her more safe than she had any right to expect.

Thankful for whatever had intervened to assist her in her escape, she listened hard. In between heaving breaths the two men gasped out defeat. 'C'mon bro', she's gone. And 'sides. We scared her 'nuff. Mouthy bitch'll. Think twice 'fore she. Says that sort of stuff again.'

'Guess you're. Right Zeke. Fuckin' easternised. Brit Cow! Come back here an'. We'll kick yer. Stink-lovin' ass!' the second one shouted.

Rebecca thought she heard them move off but stayed still, unwilling to risk revealing herself until she was sure she was safe. Calming down a little, her body shaking and hands twitching from the adrenaline, Rebecca was able to engage her rational, conscious mind rather than run on animal instinct.

If she was being honest with herself she would have to admit she had baited them into it, as a response to their lurid commentary on her breasts and legs, a show that she possessed a mind more than equal to the form that housed it, and certainly greater than anything they could muster between all of them put together.

And if forced to further examine her motivation, would reach the conclusion that it was an unconscious but still deliberate reaction to the people she currently held responsible, at least in part, for her current situation.

No people like she had just encountered, no election of reactionary leaders. No such leaders, no demand to feel the need to express self-worth as a projection of hard-power. No unchecked militarism, no inevitable invasion of the Middle East. No invasion, no eventual descent to civil war. No civil war, no species extinction of the mountain lion. No loss of cougars, no chance of her chodding up the research piece on the D-corridors. No such chodela, no picking up the Mehta obit-impact analysis and no discovering the flaw at the heart of the Vimana mission and no Rebecca skulking through the American borderlands encountering small-minded, limited people.

Of course, tracing events back far enough you could, she reasoned, blame Professor Cotts for her present situation: no Displacement, no Vimana. Which was patently absurd. *Mental note to self here.* If they can't take a joke, chod them.

The voices of her pursuers diminished into the desert twilight. Perhaps the effort required to locate her was better spent elsewhere this evening. There was some mutual self-reinforcing banter as the pair admitted defeat in finding their quarry. Doubtless they would be rehearsing the story they were going to deliver at the bar once they got back, which probably involved physical violence to her in some degree, and possibly even went as far as boosting their sexual prowess. If sufficiently vivid, the descriptions of what they imagined they had done to her could ensure they need not put their hands in their pockets for the rest of the night, for either liquor or even perhaps self-pleasure. With a couple of rehearsals to co-ordinate their stories the pair would be in for a good night at her expense.

That meant Rebecca could not show her face, unbruised by their failure to locate her, here again. Any hint of their fictional reprisal against her being undermined and the pair, along with most likely the rest of the town, would carry through with what at the moment was an ego-boosting fantasy. Rebecca seethed with frustration and spite; she had planned to overnight within the bounds of the town ready for her early scheduled download tomorrow, but now she would have to leave tonight and couldn't come back under any circumstances.

She cursed both her own stupidity and that of the patrons of the bar. It felt like she was being run out of town, but her self-preservation overrode her need to keep her appointment and her urge to go back there and do... what exactly? She had deliberately left her gun at her apartment back in the UK, reasoning she was breaking enough international laws already, in doing what she was, and importing firearms into what, technically at least, was still a state in civil war only compounded her felonies. And anyway, if she had her gun with her she would have been tempted to use it to balance the odds against those two. But the odds would have immediately been raised against her; escalation was something the remains of this country still did very well.

Now free from the threat of pursuit and needing to escape unseen she looked around getting her bearings, only now realising error of her chosen direction. *How much more wrong could this have gone?* She made stealthily for her rented transport, ducking behind any cover at the slightest sound or shadow, hugging walls, crawling along the ground and only crossing open spaces when absolutely necessary, and then at haste. She reached her pickup without further incident and, once safely inside started the engine.

Still barely thinking much beyond getting out intact, Rebecca dropped the truck into drive and powered away, the fat, deep-treaded tyres kicking up clouds of dust as she was forced for the first time to wilfully miss a data collection from the contact who had answered her a little over a fortnight ago.

Chipkali ke chut ke pasine!

She was no closer to succeeding in her quest, and now a significant step backwards on it; missing the drop would add at least another day to her itinerary, and that was if she could re-establish the connection with her contact. And even if she did would they still be willing to assist her?

She checked her map. The next nearest settlement was about an hour's drive away over pretty rough terrain, but she had little choice. Wrenching the steering wheel round hard, the truck completed several circles while Rebecca decided what to do next. *No choice really.* She righted the wheel, the truck's path straightened and Rebecca made for the next town, already juggling the possibilities in her head and hoping to position circumstance to allow her a chance to rearrange her appointments.

dad had to tell stuart off/scold him/tell him to stop today because he was mean/nasty/got angry with me i only meant it as a joke/thought he'd find it funny/was trying to get back at him it was last week when he came home late after school/after jemima got in and had to make me dinner and he was not alone/had a girl with him even though he was supposed to be looking after us/dad had said he was old enough to be in charge while they had to go away and told me that if I told dad or mummy/ratted on him he would wallop me one/make me pay/tell them about playing doctors with jody in my room. When dad and mummy got back/came home again i told dad what stuart had done/about coming in late and he went and told stuart off/asked him what he'd done and stuart glared at me/told me I was dead meat stuart tried to explain/went to tell dad about me and jody and I went bright red so to stop him I told him that he deserved to be told off/was a rubbish big brother and he chased me round the room/down the stairs and out into the garden before dad stopped him/told him to not chase me we both got sent to our rooms/grounded

195

/pocket money docked and dad said he did not want to hear anymore about it/we were both as bad as each other i got told off for telling tales and stuart got told off for chasing me

>

Another day passed with little success in tracking down her quarry. It felt as if she were destined to miss her target in every town she reached, frustrated by a handful of hours in every instance, always half a day late in deciphering the clues and evidence as to where she needed to be next. The only indication she encountered of her target's passing through were rumours and suspicions, necessitating she take that much more care when dealing with the locals, for fear of discovery. The populations of the small border towns remained edgy, and wary of strangers.

The effort of remaining constantly on the move, hopping from town to town following half understood clues only to arrive too late every time was taking its toll on her. She had not eaten properly for nearly a week now, having rejected out of hand what the locals improbably called food. But now her own stocks were totally depleted.

The pursuit was taking far longer than she had intended or planned for, and some measure of success was needed in the immediate future to render the enterprise a worthy one. Water was also a problem to secure a safe supply of; the rationing of the available drinking stock favoured the locals, not itinerant strangers. And the means of purification she had brought with her were tested to their limits by the quality of what she was able to obtain. Urophagia was rapidly becoming her only option. Unless her provision situation changed dramatically in the next day or so, she would have to abandon her mission here, along with all the consequences that would have. Otherwise she would starve out here chasing whispers.

Coupled with the encroaching malnutrition was the maintenance of her disguise; the constant fear of accidental discovery; that someone would see through her mask to the real woman beneath the make up and false accent. If that happened all would be lost. She knew if anyone saw who she really was then she would be lucky to get out of the town and then the country alive. After a decade of civil war, suspicion of anyone thought to be hiding anything, especially their true nature and purpose, ran deep in the local population, almost every family having suffered at the consequences of information relayed to their opposition by enemy spies. Accidental discovery did not bear thinking about.

She sat torpidly in the midday heat pervading her rented room, trying with difficulty to consider her options. The air-conditioner did not work, and opening a window increased the temperature more than it lowered it. Lack of air circulation made the atmosphere heavy, rendering her mind sluggish. Through the heat-haze slowing her thoughts she tried to organise herself.

Uppermost on her list of priorities was food and drink, the animal needs of her body supplanting her mission to third place. Hunger was driving her to re-appraise her rejection of the locally produced fare. Stomach turning itself over noisily at the barest thought of prepared food, she decided her mission here overrode her disgust at the barbarism and lack of respect towards animal life the nation generally exhibited.

Reluctantly, she came to the realisation her principles would kill her if she held fast to them unwaveringly. There were issues larger than how she chose to conduct herself under consideration. She needed to eat; thinking was becoming difficult and she knew her act was beginning to slip in small ways. She would have to brave the local hostelry and attempt to find something she could tolerate; she would have to deal with the consequences to herself in the future. At least this course of action gave her that chance.

Fifteen minutes later she was sitting alone sweating at a table waiting for her meal; a mash of beans and vegetables, she hoped but no longer enquired as to whether or not it was cooked in animal fats. She nursed a half-full shot-glass of cloudy water until her food arrived, resisting the temptation of her thirst to swallow the murky liquid in a single gulp. The meal would most likely be over-salted, parching her further in the already stifling heat of the room. Instead she took minute sips from the glass, the tang of the iodine she had slipped into it when the proprietor's back was turned acrid in her mouth. But still the water tasted sweet despite the purification tablet dissolved in it. It slaked her thirst to some extent, pushing away the cloying heat, made so much worse by her disguise.

Fortune had been with her as the bar was nearly deserted; its only other human occupants being an elderly man with a missing leg who sat dozing in the heat at his table, and the proprietor, a Mexican man in his fifties who seemed not to care what his patron's stories might be, so long as they had enough hard cash to pay for what they ordered.

Several animals made up the remaining clientele; pink and green lizards hanging in the dark recesses of the ceiling corners, even the cold-blooded reptiles hiding from the ferocity of the noontime sun; a thin stray cat sat fixated on one of them, the potential meal out of its reach; a dog lay off in one corner, splayed out prone in the dust-filled, enervating atmosphere, one ear flicking half-heartedly in response to its dreams. The owner's large white cockerel strutted around the bar, feathers puffed up, its long toes scratching on the age-hardened floor, picking at non-existent scraps in between the woodworm pocked beams. Then, as if noticing it for the first time, seemed to take an interest in the sleeping dog.

She watched, initially with puzzled interest as the bird mounted the dormant animal, hoisting itself onto the dog's exposed flank, before attempting a bizarre copulation, lowering and lifting itself against the canine's pink-white belly. The heat made the dog sluggish; it seemed it barely cared about the cockerel's actions, if it noticed them at all. It failed to rouse itself and put an end to the humiliation even when the bird, lost in its actions, overbalanced and nearly fell off its impromptu perch, holding itself on only with its sharp claws dug into the dog's back, before resuming its congress.

Amazed, appalled and repulsed, she turned from the small scene of miscegenation, thoroughly put off her forthcoming meal. Still shocked, she could not help look at the door as the small bell hung above it jangled, announcing another customer in this hot, lazy afternoon when even the lizards seemed to have enough sense to stay safely in shadow, and the heat drove other animals paagal. Grateful of the distraction she watched as in strode a woman in her late twenties or early thirties; it was difficult to tell through the excessive make up and badly cut bleached hair. The newcomer tottered to the bar on heels far too high for her, ordered something the woman at the table could not quite make out, then swung round, placing both elbows on the bar behind her and seemed to survey the room from underneath her large sunglasses.

The dust the woman had stirred up as she entered settled back lazily in the heat, the motes swirling slowly back to rest on the tables. The women's gazes met through the hazy space of the once again unmoving atmosphere in the bar.

Rebecca stared back at the overweight Mexican-looking woman with the braided hair sitting at the table, for a moment as she went to avert her gaze, trying to make her actions look natural, keen not to appear too interested in any particular thing and draw anyone's attention to herself. Instead something fired in her brain and she stopped herself and dropped her sunglasses down the bridge of her nose, holding the eye contact, continuing the mutual scrutiny. Rebecca narrowed her eyes, making it obvious she was regarding this woman with some interest when it occurred to her where she had seen her before. Despite the disguise of ten years and fifteen kilos, the eyes gave her away. They were eyes she had seen before, at the longjump port in India, then again outside her father's house when she had had the comm from Dravid.

'You!' Rebecca shouted across the room as she tossed her sunglasses on the bar and began to make her way to the woman who had been following her almost before she had even known she was involved in something. For her part the discovered Indian woman panicked, and after stumbling to her feet, knocking the table and the glass of water over, took one look round the bar and Displaced out, leaving Rebecca standing bewildered, completely unable to determine the distance or the direction that the woman had departed for.

'Hagga!' Uncaring now about attracting potentially unwanted attention, Rebecca ran out of the bar leaving the owner gesticulating wildly over payment for both her drink and the meal he was preparing for his only other paying customer that day. But Rebecca hardly heard his protests; she had to find that woman.

Outside the sunlight was too strong after the gloom of the bar, and Rebecca blinked hard in the harsh white light as it poured out of the crystal sky and bounced off the whitewashed walls. Disorientated and blinded for a moment longer only, she saw her quarry a small distance away. *Why had she only Displaced that far?* She would ask her when she caught her. Rebecca broke out into a run toward the Indian woman, who appeared to be concentrating on executing another Fold.

Sati Displaced again, hoping this time to complete the move back to her rented room some three kilometres distant. But she must have been more fatigued than she realised. The days of not eating must have sapped her strength considerably, despite the boost her system was receiving from the threat of pursuit by this stranger, as she seemed not to have the strength to push far enough into the Cotts field to make the jump. Instead she only moved a few hundred metres away.

'Oh no you chodding don't!' shouted Rebecca as she saw the woman re-appear a small distance away, easily close enough for her to cover in a few seconds and hopefully catch her one time pursuer. Kicking off her heels Rebecca broke out into a run. She wanted answers and this woman obviously knew more than she did.

The Indian woman looked panicked. At being discovered, or the simple pursuit she could not be sure; in fact there was no guarantee she even recognised Rebecca underneath her own, simpler disguise of make-up and haircut. If not that was good, she could use that to her advantage, at least for a while. Rebecca picked up her pace, shouting, 'Hey! Stop! You're not supposed to be here,' she added hoping to add to the Indian woman's confusion.

Sati drew a deep breath trying to feel for the Cotts field, and finding only the barest echo of it available to her. She concentrated on her destination and after holding it fast in her head for a moment Displaced again.

Rebecca got to the space the Indian woman had been occupying barely a second after she had disappeared, adrenaline coursing through her. Everything felt hyper-real out in the heat and bright sunlight. Was that the after effects of the Fold she could feel? She could not be sure as she had no sense-record telling her if what she was feeling was real or the product of her amped-up system. Rebecca closed her eyes for a second and tried to remember everything she had been taught about Displacing. She tried to let herself relax into it, to feel space bend around her, and follow the Indian woman to wherever she had gone. She thought she could feel something happening. She willed it to happen and in that moment of pushing too hard felt the Fold collapse around her.

'Chod! Chod chod chod!' She had been so close that time.

Sati appeared just around the corner. Had she been paying more attention to her arrival point she would have intuited the obstruction where she was about to materialise, and avoided it. Instead her innate senses caused her to appear just above the dumpster, and she landed heavily on top of it, bouncing nosily off the hollow metal container.

Rebecca needed no further evidence of her quarry's position. She was off at a run at the first echo of sound. This time she'd get her.

Sati groped herself to her feet, the added bulk of the fat-suit overbalancing her.

Rebecca rounded the corner to see what in other circumstances would have either been tragic or comic; a seemingly overweight woman struggling to right herself, like a tortoise that had been upturned, its belly baking in the midday sun. But the woman was neither an object of pity or humour; she had answers that Rebecca needed. She bore down on the woman, intent on catching her this time.

Sati threw a single look over her shoulder at the fury charging at her.

Rebecca leapt at the woman, grabbing her clothes and an arm. 'Now I've got you,' she spat in her face. 'Try and Displace away with all my extra mass holding on to you.'

Sati was near insane with panic and fear. Whatever this woman wanted, whoever she was, she had not given up her pursuit and obviously intended her harm, and quite possibly violation. Sati had not believed the stories she had heard and read about arising from the civil war here until now.

Near-hyperventilating, she pushed her consciousness

into the feeble Cotts field as hard as she could with one final effort, this time tight-Folding space around her; a desperate gambit to escape this lunatic who was still shouting obscenities in her face. If it failed she would have nothing left.

Rebecca paused in her rant as she sensed something happening to the air around her. No, to the air around the woman.

Sati felt the Fold complete, and in an instant blinked out of existence, discarding her clothes and the latex suit her pursuer had been holding on to before arriving naked on the floor of her rented room, bleeding heavily from the ruptures to the membranes in her nose, ears and anus, totally spent, curled up foetus-like as if the very air had given birth to her.

Rebecca stood up, the fatsuit in her hands, empty now, like a snake cocoon; useless and spent. She thought she could feel the Fold dissipating around her. That bitch wasn't getting away without a fight. Rebecca forced herself to relax and focus, clearing her mind of distractions. Long years of self-control swapped themselves into play in her mind as she pushed her thoughts aside, and felt. Felt herself enveloped by the Cotts field. Felt it inside her. Felt it all around her. She reached out to take hold of the exit point the Indian woman had left behind.

Space moved, two separate points neared. Closer.

The Fold caved in around her.

Rebecca threw the latex suit to the dusty ground impotent to do anything more than kick at it furiously for a minute while the anger at herself worked its way out. Her self returned to her. She had made more than too much noise and exposed too much of herself in this town to safely stay. Self-recrimination would have to wait till later.

Glancing round slightly hesitantly, Rebecca made for her truck. She had little doubt that her path and that of the mysterious Indian woman would cross again. How soon, and what the outcome would be she was less sure of.

Lament for the Mountain Lion

Wan blue-white light illuminates
the sole remaining adult mountain lion
as she patrols her territory in search of food.
Along the northern bank of the Colorado river
she slinks in and out of the deep shadows
afforded her by the weak light.
Barely more than a whisper
of hot living breath in the cold of the late night.

For nearly a decade
the conflict had raged around
but had not succeeded in claiming her.
Every year prey was more and more scarce.
The delicate food web quivered
and shook, threatening to unravel
at the lightest of touches.
Tenacious, the resourceful cat
had found new sources of protein.
The bodies which littered
the area where her territory crossed
with the theatre of combat.

So far the night had been kind
and she had had easy pickings
of the pieces of soldiers left from both sides.
Her senses keen
to the presence of human anger and fury
helped her pick her way between
the scattered limbs
and red hot shrapnel.
Her belly full
and spare enough between her powerful jaws
to feed her cubs,
the future of her species.

A calm familial eye in the centre of a bloody storm.

The mother trod carefully,
unfamiliarity with the terrain
driving her caution.
Picking her way over charred bodies
and around the smouldering skeletons
of ruined metal vehicles.
Impelled by her powerful maternal instinct
to return her bounty
to her dependent family.
Attuned to living threats or dead opportunities,
she was powerless to detect
the hard disk of metal and electronics,
barely a centimetre beneath
land she had not trodden before.
In a microsecond it was over,
a brief flash of cold UV.
At least for her it was quick and painless.
In their den the cubs mewled for their lost mother.

Rebecca Eckhart   2056

Twenty

Contact

Friday 23 June 2056 - 14:58 CST

A lone crow perched impatiently on the telegraph pole, waiting for the inevitable death of some local minor fauna, cawing in frustration at its lack of meal so far that day. Noon had passed a few hours previously and since the bird had alighted, scanning the desert floor greedily for the smallest morsel, little had stirred since then; not even a solitary lizard had ventured out and offered itself as potential food. The crow stepped from foot to foot, turning itself round to look behind it. Off in the distance there was a plume of dust, indicating the approach of something large. Disinterested, the crow turned back.

Fifteen minutes later its vigil was disturbed by the arrival of a truck, rattling noisily to a stop beneath its perch, the clouds kicked up by the tyres forcing the bird to abandon its post and fly off, still hungry. It took its revenge on the metal beast that had forced it from any potential dinner by dropping a heavy dollop of shit as it flew over the windscreen.

Rebecca grimaced at the wet sound of bird guano on

glass, but there was little she could do except scrape it off before it set hard in place. The washer reservoir in the pickup was long empty, water too precious a commodity to waste on keeping the windscreen clean. Instead Rebecca flung a handful of dust and grit from the ground over the already hardening pat and wiped the worst of it off with the dirtiest pair of underwear she was able to locate from her sole travelling bag.

Unwilling to throw away anything now, Rebecca flung the soiled knickers onto the floor of the truck. This was the last stop on her list, deciphered from the avalanche of puzzles and riddles she had been overwhelmed with. It had been two weeks since the chase with the Indian woman and, despite an extensive motorised search of the area, she had failed to find her. The time consumed in that search meant she had missed two potential rendezvous with her contact, and was badly behind schedule. The location she had finally decoded was her last shot.

She looked round at where she had been brought.

She could hardly believe the liaison would be here. It required only a single glance to take in every structure in the immediate area. What had, perhaps, been a relatively large conurbation thirty years ago tacked on the border, was now barely a shell of a town. The civil war had ravaged the buildings that had not been wholly Displaced away during the battle; almost none of them had roofs, windows were replaced with slats of wood, and where they had fallen away had been inexpertly bricked up with irregular stones and the driest of mortars. A single wire hung limply from the telegraph pole the defecator of windscreens had been sitting on, and looking at it, Rebecca was surprised the thing had not fallen over when the crow had taken off from it.

Shaking her head in disbelief at her surroundings she checked her watch. 3pm. She had forty six minutes to find a hardline terminal here where it looked like electricity had not made a passing visit for the better part of a decade.

208

Rebecca slammed the door of her truck shut, the solidity of the sound reassuring in the barren scrubland, and slunk toward the building the cable connected to the telegraph pole. It was a single storey oblong of worn and tired looking bricks about five metres by three, with no visible windows on any of its walls. At least it had a roof. Pushing open the door to the dilapidated building, she found herself in a small reception room, lit from above by a single strip light, with only another single metal door leading deeper into the building ahead of her.

A large, powerful looking Mexican man sat seemingly asleep at the desk placed directly between the two doors, his arms behind his head, holding its weight in place. His face was covered with the Stetson he used to shield his eyes from the harsh light overhead. From what she could see of the undersides of his arms, and the skin exposed beneath the vest he wore, his upper body was heavy with tattoos; Sanskrit script wove its way up from his wrists, circling around his forearms, threaded through with thunderbolts, flowing into what appeared to be lotus petals lying atop a circlet of severed heads draped around his neck. While she could not see his back, Rebecca assumed it was similarly decorated. *This couldn't be the place.*

She turned about face to head out somewhere, anywhere else, when the man spoke in a low voice, gritty with years of desert living. 'Hey señorita. You got an appointment.' It was a statement, not a question.

Rebecca paused at the man's certainty of the correctness of her presence. She wasn't so sure. She spun on one heel, now easily balancing on the six inch of stiletto that sat between her foot and the floor, but moved no closer to the tattooed man. 'Perhaps, but I don't think this is where I'm supposed to be.'

The man snorted and flexed his arms out in front of him, cracking his fingers before removing his hat. 'No, señorita, I think you are in the right place at the right time.

Let me guess who you think you're supposed to be meeting.' He smiled revealing a row of gold teeth studded with individual diamonds.

Shit me.

Rebecca hesitated. This was the closest she had ever made it to the elusive contact she had been chasing; and now that the likelihood of her actually meeting the originator of the puzzles and riddles loomed on her horizon she found her resolve draining. Somehow, she realised, it had been easier to keep the momentum of her pursuit going when her efforts had been continually dashed. The constant setbacks had given her something to strive against, and allowed her to block the magnitude of what she was doing from her mind; all other thoughts secondary to the deciphering of the codes and the hurtle from place to place on the back of their solutions. But now, faced with the withdrawal of that illusory mental crutch, the full weight of her actions and their possible consequences hit her fully for the first time.

That's crazy thinking, she told herself. How much had she risked to get to even this point? The moment when she would take the final step on the part of her journey that had led her all over the border country, dodging hostile locals. Almost too much was the answer. Besides, backing out now would be impossible wouldn't it?

She had been careful to leave as little of a physical trail as possible, but her contact could pursue her easily through the net, backtracking everywhere she had been over the past three weeks and depositing the evidence somewhere easily accessible by whoever might wish to see it. Suddenly she had the terrible sense that this was all a trap, perhaps not for her, but for those who might wish her contact harm.

Then again, the steps her contact had had her go through were untraceable enough, so that possibility seemed unlikely. She thought again about walking away, turning round as if the past three weeks or so had been a mistake she could erase by going no further, and abandoning the reason she had come here. Rebecca snorted to herself, much to the amusement of the Mexican man, who crossed his arms while the woman made up her mind to the inevitable. She realised she wasn't going anywhere. She had manoeuvred herself into a position of checkmate where she had no choice but to forge ahead, consequences, and herself perhaps, be damned.

'Go on then, surprise me,' she replied to the man's offer.

The Mexican lifted his vest over his head and held it in one hand. Rebecca took a step back.

He turned round and flexed his back. Rebecca had been correct, it was as heavily patterned as his chest. But hidden in amongst the rest of the religious iconography etched into his skin sat the Om syllable. It took Rebecca a second to resolve it among the swirls of colours and patterns, but once she saw it, and what it represented she could not help herself.

'Chod.'

The Mexican man turned back to face her, replacing the vest over his stencilled secret. 'See, I told you you were supposed to be here. Adi Anadi will be here in,' he glanced at his watch, 'thirty-nine minutes. You will wait here.'

Rebecca shifted her weight from foot to foot, and instinctively reached for her ponytail, which she had long since discarded. 'No, I don't think so. If I'm early I'll come back when I'm on time.'

there was a new boy joined our class/started at school today his name is jody and miss spencer put him next to me/he sat at the only empty desk so i kind of had to look after him for the day/had him hanging round me and show him where to hang his coat/where the toilets were/what to do when/where to go when the break and lunch bell rang why do i always have to do/miss spencer thinks i need these things i didn't want him sitting next to me/I didn't ask for it so i don't know why miss spencer thinks i'm good at being friendly/thought i would want him following me around all day he asked me/said as i had been so nice to him on his first day if i wanted to go round to his house for dinner one day this week, and when i told mum and dad about my day at school dad said it was a really good idea/it was nice i had a friend/and if jody wanted to come round here he would always be welcome dad said he would ask jody's dad at the parent's evening he was going to next week/comm him right away if it was ok with me   i shrugged/mumbled yeah or something and dad said that was settled/good enough for him and that jody had better be hungry/hoped jody liked curries when he came round as dad was going to make/would have to get stuff in for his speciality molee that everyone liked

'Why did you agree to meet me?' Rebecca asked into the empty dull grey room on the other side of the metal door. The room seemed to take up the entire remaining space of the building, and her words would have echoed in the cavern-like unfurnished space, except for the half-metre thick soundproofing covering every square centimetre of wall and ceiling. She had no doubt the room was equally shielded from all external electronic eavesdropping too; the sole concession to anything remotely technological was the single network socket at the far end of the room, from which snaked half a dozen metres of heavily insulated data transmission cable, leading to a portable threedee generator; the room's only other thing in it aside from herself.

Reassured of her privacy, at least from any external agency, by the hardline connection, Rebecca allowed herself to relax to a shade just greater than anxious; whoever she was meeting took even greater precautions over their data security than she did, and she was bloody careful.

The image generator sparked into life, its lasers

refracted and bent into the form of a genderless human, approximately two metres tall, glowing with green light. The figure spoke in a monotone, its voice free of modulation or timbre. 'I/we have our/my reasons.' As it began its reply, the being comprised entirely of the flow and spin arrangement of countless crore upon crore of electrons, and rendered before her by its will over the photons pouring from the lasers, began to shimmer and shift. 'You require our/my assistance/help in a matter of data filtering and I/we for our/my part have an interest/trade in human memories/feelings.' The thing's form slid and changed in front of her, slowly at first, but speeding up, to become a blitzkrieg of shapes, all human, but a wild variety of sizes, ages, genders and ethnicities and clothing. It seemed to settle on one for a moment, only for it to fall back into the blur of shifting patterns. 'So your bargain/request was mutually beneficial/get the better deal. You have the data/information to be processed with you/easily accessible?'

Rebecca struggled to keep up with the constant shifting, in both shape and what the thing was saying. As if sensing her discomfiture, the creature seemed to decide to settle on a single form. As Rebecca watched, it lost height, flipped gender to female, its clothing shrank to a pair of cut-off shorts, high heels and tight t-shirt, while its features flowed over its face until she found herself starting at a copy of herself as she looked now.

Rebecca stood staring open-mouthed at the luminescent copy of herself regarding her with the amused expression she used on Damien from time to time. She was unable to put words to the feelings conflicting inside her. Awe mixed with confusion and mild panic as she tried to conceptualise what the creature that now looked, and seemed able to act exactly like her after only a few seconds contact.

Contact. That was the thing that was significant.

Perhaps only three or four officially appointed ambassadors liaised with an Ayaye annually, the complex protocols the electronic lifeforms seemed to insist on fathomable by at most half a dozen living humans. Random, ad-hoc interactions were unheard of. And extremely illegal. Rebecca was now glad of the extensive information security measures in place protecting it, and by extension, her.

How to converse with an Ayaye was not the sort of thing they taught in schools. Any inter-species dialogue was never usually more than a request to effect a repair on part of their network in exchange for some specialised data manipulation task. Often they would specify the nature of the data processing they would be willing to carry out, as if they gained something from the effort, leaving humankind to try and find a problem close enough to the quality of task the Ayayes had set themselves.

They were a capricious and hugely cunning race of creatures, not malicious in the strictest sense of the word, but their modality of thinking and viewing the world they had found themselves birthed into was coloured by the phenomenal, and some said theoretically limitless, intellectual capacity. Anyone who spent any length of time in their presence began to get the distinct feeling they were being humoured the way an adult child would cosset an elderly or frail parent. Studies had been carried out on the psychology of humanity's children, but ultimately they always fell short; people could not understand them, humanity had created their own alien species right there on the earth.

And now one of that species had chosen, or more likely in whatever passed for a decision making process in its fierce intelligence, indulging itself on a whim, had allowed Rebecca an audience to put her request to it. Unscrambling what it had said, Rebecca pinched her nose, took a deep breath and addressed her mirror image. 'I have everything electronic securely backed up in regular A-space, fractal-key encrypted so it should be safe from pretty much anything. The hard copy stuff is currently making its way through the postal system in a series of hops from post box to post box. Despite the war here what's left of the government seem to have kept the postal service working; guess they're trying to show they're still in control. Either way, I only need to be at one of the drop points to collect it. With your OCR capabilities I expect it won't pose any problems to you.'

The Ayaye seemed to pause, as if it were thinking, considering the proposition Rebecca had put before it; the digestion and filleting of her childhood diaries in an effort to uncover anything out of place about the Vimana mission. In actuality it was doing nothing of the sort, but the Ayayes had learnt to place the small pauses humans used in their speech to aid the conversations with their physical interlocutors. People, even the specially trained ones, felt a deep unease when talking with something which had already predicted, weighted and calculated every conceivable conversational gambit, extrapolating crore upon crore of interaction pathways and was following the most likely one in any given discussion. In the earliest years of their being, the Ayayes had realised the limitations of their parents, intuiting the discomfort their mode of speech induced in people who were made to feel as if they were taking part in something pre-ordained or fated.

So instead they mimicked humanity's speech patterns; it was no extra effort on their part.

The Ayaye currently resembling Rebecca pulled the faces the she made when doing exactly the same thing; spinning out a question in an effort to elicit further concessions from the requester. It was disconcerting watching yourself acting out the tiny dramas you played for others' benefit so perfectly. To Rebecca the wait, only a scant handful of seconds, was almost intolerable. She had spent weeks searching for this thing, chasing from town to town at its behest, and now it seemed to be actually considering saying no. But with an Ayaye who knew what was going on in its inner self; it could just as easily be pretending for its own unpredictable reasons.

The simulacrum spoke back to her in her own voice; her English voice, not the heavily affected Southern drawl she had perfected in the weeks spent in the desert. 'You/one of your kind/novel interlocutor seems to have everything in hand/appear quiet capable/exercised proper caution. I/we see you have taken/put in place sufficient/more than expected security measures/no more could have been done. We/I expect the data/diaries/memories to be dangerous/a threat to yourself/us/myself/others?'

'I think so yes,' replied Rebecca, not even trying to formulate an answer which comprised of anything other than the barest truth. Her research on Ayayes had informed her of their linguistic parsing and processing; upon learning this she could not help but feel an ironic twang of respect for the thing that could easily out-think her at her own conversational style, even if she were at her most controlled best. Also, she did not know, nor could she predict how it would react to a lie it knew was being told it; it would already have stored all possible answers to its every question, picking the untruths out. So for the first time in nearly two decades Rebecca replied to a question she would rather have avoided with the unprepared truth.

Hell, the Ayaye was about to read all her diaries and learn everything there was to know about her childhood, seeing the origins of the woman she was now laid bare; there seemed little point in hiding herself from it now given the knowledge it was about to acquire. Plus the more context she could give it around her current situation could only assist it in whatever it might find in the archive.

'I have at least two separate agencies following me. A man calling himself Dravid who I suspect is linked to the Indian government, and an Indian woman who I believe knows about the Vimana but is, I think, a free agent. Dravid claims to know about her but I got the impression she's not working for or with him. What I am certain of though is something is being hidden; something to do with either the Vimana or its astronauts or the mission or something. I don't know who to trust here, now, but I know that I can trust myself, even when I was eight. I may have written something in my diary or recorded an audio postcard or something that will give me a clue. And that is why I sought you out. There's too much data for a person to go through in the amount of time I think I've got.'

The Ayaye nodded.

'If you don't mind me asking,' Rebecca ventured, 'we never discussed payment in any of our communiqués. What do you want in return?'

Twenty-one

Motherhood

Sunday 25 June 2056 – 15:06 CST

there was another protest/demonstration/people were unhappy at the InSA headquarters today people/farmers have been given money/asked if they wouldn't mind leaving/moving home so InSA could build the launch pad/base for the Vimana on top of/near the summit of Kangchenjunga some of the people wanted more money/told InSA they wouldn't leave we talked about it/had a homework assignment from civics class and dad said that it was like him/mummy when they asked me/stuart/jemima to do something we didn't want to/like doing sometimes the government/people who look after us ask/tell other people what is best for them/what they should do i was going to ask him more/i was confused and dad promised to help me/explain more when I was finishing the homework

Another shot cracked across the valley at the pickup, this time missing it by half a metre.

Rebecca could not control her reflex response to the

lethal noise and ducked into the cab of her truck. The rapid unplanned movement pulled on the steering wheel, causing the vehicle to swerve wildly, its handling impaired by the flat rear nearside tyre she had not yet dared to stop and replace. Consciously, she knew if you heard the gunshot, the bullet preceding the noise had already passed you by; it was the shot you did not hear that killed you. So far, still breathing, she had heard all the gunfire aimed in her direction. However that was little comfort now after what had seemed an easy enough errand had descended rapidly into a drive for her life.

By mutual agreement, Rebecca and the Ayaye agreed to each fetch the sections of the diaries they were best equipped to retrieve. The Ayaye would venture into the secure area of the cloud Rebecca had stored the encrypted data in, and she had, initially, volunteered to drive to the next scheduled hop on the journey the hard copies were taking across the American continent.

The Ayaye estimated it could achieve its task, once Rebecca furnished it with the encryption key, in a little over a second; the majority of which would be taken up entering the human network undetected at one of the several, undocumented intersections between the two intelligences' electronic domains. It assured Rebecca, still using her own voice to converse with her, that the process was entirely safe as far as it and the security of her data were concerned. Its intrusion algorithms were state-of-the-art, even in Ayaye terms.

It was less convinced of her safety over a journey of a day and a night, and told her as much. She had asked what it thought the alternative should be, and after vanishing for perhaps half a second, the light comprising its form barely having time to flicker off before regaining its full brilliance, the Ayaye informed her it had altered the delivery schedule and the diaries would be ready for collection at a small town barely three hours drive away. Rebecca had dismissed what she had felt at the time was overcaution on the electronic lifeform's part; after all she had been here nearly a month and felt she was coming to terms with the dangers which presented themselves on the border.

Hubris in hindsight was little comfort to her as another slug of lead panged and whined off the truck's bodywork. If another one of them hit a tyre she was in serious trouble; she could just about control the vehicle with one flat, but two meant she was finished. She pressed her already flush-with-the-floor foot harder on the gas pedal, as if greater physical effort on her part could drive the truck that little bit faster, to give it just enough impetus to outrun bullets.

Steering tucked well down in the driver's seat, one hand on the wheel, the other holding the contents of the passenger seat steady and secure, snatching glances either side of her as she drove looking through the steering wheel, Rebecca cursed her earlier over-confidence in her own ability to keep herself out of trouble.

She had collected the diaries easily enough; she presented her collection note and the nondescript package was delivered to her after only a minute's searching by the clerk at the post office. For a few minutes she could have almost believed she was no longer in the war-scarred hinterlands of America, so easy and convenient was the collection of the cardboard box containing so much.

Upon exiting the collection depot, she now realised, was when events had begun to move beyond her ability to influence them. Her senses sharpened to the slightest thing out of place after the long weeks of surviving by her trusting them, she noticed the group of men standing by a pair of trucks in the middle distance where there had been no one when she had entered the small outpost of the country's remaining functioning federal service. Not looking directly at them, but still watching peripherally for any movement on their part she walked, not ran, back to her own pickup. Climbing inside and starting the engine, them still not moving, she drove away.

Thirty minutes later, with thoughts of who the men might have been fading, the gunfire began. Initially it seemed as if someone were merely using her for target practice, rather than with any intent to kill. A bored local perhaps finding brief entertainment in the sole moving object unwise enough not to have learnt whose land they were crossing. The handful of shots rang around the valley floor she drove along, kicking up puffs of sand several metres away, but still causing her to start at every one before seeming to stop. Maybe she was out of range, or they had lost interest.

Her answer came immediately. Suddenly the truck's rear fell to one side as a high-velocity round passed straight through the tyre, the puncture causing the vehicle to lurch heavily and nearly tip over. Rebecca realised what had happened as the sound waves trailing the bullet caught it up; a sharper, harder sound than the preceding gunfire. It took an effort of will to resist stamping on the brake, instead shifting her position on the seat in response to the truck's new angle and learning rapidly the thing's new handling. A minute perhaps passed with no more shots. Then they started again.

There was a dull metallic thud of a bullet striking home in the bodywork of the truck's pickup behind her and Rebecca flinched at the noise of her vehicle's penetration. Then another shot, and another and another, each one missing her by a few metres. She swerved as best she could at each, hoping to present a wildly moving target, but her efforts were compounded by having to steady the parcel on the passenger seat that, with every sharp turn she executed, threatened to spill its contents onto the floor of the cab.

'Chod!' she swore, falling back to her expletive favoured in times of stressful loss of control, as another shot puffed the ground up in front of her, effecting a further lurch in her driving. She counted five more rifle retorts, three of them again missing her by a wide margin, but two hitting home, smacking into the truck's wide rear. She wrested the cardboard box that held her past from the seat beside her and dumped it on her lap, trying to outsteer the hail of bullets with her other hand. Crunching up slightly to hold the diaries safely in place she shouted 'Give me a break!' ineffectually to herself and her unseen assailant.

And then, seemingly as unexpectedly as they had started, the shots ceased. It was a minute or two of calm before Rebecca let herself think she was no longer somebody's target, but only after nearly five more long, apprehensive minutes had crawled past, time seemingly obeying Einstein and slowing as a consequence of the speed she was propelling herself, did Rebecca begin to believe whatever gauntlet she had just run, was over. Still, no point in taking chances, and she continued to drive as fast as the hobbled truck would carry her without imperilling its engine or the delivery of her cargo.

Piling through the door of the Ayaye's meeting room, arms full of cardboard box safely ferried back for its inspection, Rebecca was greeted with the sight of the electronic sentience standing with its back to her. Only this time it was no longer as tall as she was, it was much shorter and smaller. The Ayaye turned round to face Rebecca. Shocked by what she saw, she could not help dropping the box she had shielded from damage for the past three hours. Unbelieving, she stared at the little girl with the shaved head and eager smile who started jumping up and down uncontrollably at the sight of her.

'Mummy! I'm so glad you're back, I was worried here on my own.'

Vimana Update : 08/08/31
InSA Classification RESTRICTED

Personal effects of the Vimana Command Officers sanctioned for deep space flight (subject to weight limit regulation SO/001728A/#109-1)

- Captain Srinath: a photograph of his wife and children (weight 5g)
- First Officer Chaudray: the handwritten note from her nephew wishing her good luck (weight 7g)
- Engineering Officer Kumarapad: a miniature model of the first train (weight 25g)
- Lead Deva Mehta: a hardcopy printout of Professor Cotts' Displacement equation (weight 9g)
- Communications Officer Kandasi: his wife's mangalsutra (weight 75g)

Becky Eckhart update : 08/08/31
RE Classification TOP SECRET

list of the personal items/things Becky Eckhart would take/would need/want with me into space

- photograph of dad (weight 5g)
- handwritten promise from Stuart to beat up anyone who bullies me (weight 7g)
- copy of school certificate when i got an a*** (weight 9g)
- the ring Jemima thinks she lost but i took because it was nice (weight 25g)
- the pink toy mummy gave me (weight 350g)

>

'Look, stop calling me ...that alright!'
'But Mummy, why can't I see the rest of my diaries?'
Rebecca had been unsuccessfully arguing with the Ayaye that now looked and sounded like her eight year old

younger self in every way since her return. If the illusion of imitation had been impressive when the Ayaye had been mimicking her adult self, this new guise was utterly compelling in its attention to detail. Eight hours ago Rebecca had been conversing with a creature who looked and sounded like her in every way, but had still felt like an impersonation; the gestures too observed and her vocal tics and mannerisms too studied. But this was something so far above imitation it unsettled Rebecca deep within her being.

Even hearing herself on the audio recordings examined at her Dad's house had felt like too great a reminder of the snivelling wreck she had been back then. Being presented with an exact, life size and fully sentient simulacrum of herself aged eight, capable of engaging her in conversations it was more familiar with than she was now was definitely not part of the plan. Wasn't that why she had sought assistance? So she didn't have to relive it again? Coupled to this the Ayaye had, for a reason that escaped Rebecca presently, taken to addressing her as Mummy, and it seemed no amount of persuasion on her part was going to convince it that this was most assuredly not the case.

'But why Mummy? It's me, Becky.' The Ayaye looked like it was about to start crying again, lips trembling, eyes filling up. Rebecca idly wondered just how good the holographic projection device was, and how much processing power it would take to render in splines and Bézier surfaces a single tear running down this child's cheek.

No, not a child, she caught herself at the thought. It is still the Ayaye she had met barely a day previously and not a child. Avowedly not a child and certainly not her. She was never this forlorn wretch.

'And don't start crying again. That's hardly going to help now, is it?'

Chided, Becky wiped the palm of her left hand up across her nose and sniffed hard.

To Rebecca the illusion was impossibly realistic, exactly the mannerism she had had then; most impressively perhaps the imaging software expending the runtime processing to mimic a bubbling inhalation of air through a snotty nose.

'I'm sorry Mu... I mean Rebecca,' Becky corrected herself for her mother's benefit. She did not want to make her any more angry with her and make her stop speaking to her again. She remembered the long silent days when a single slight from her caused agonies of isolation, and now that her mother was at least talking to her, Becky wanted to do everything she could to make sure things stayed that way. If she wanted to be called Rebecca instead of Mummy then that was fine with Becky. Better that than a wall.

Becky even tried standing up a little straighter, just to show her mother she was eager to be placatory. She needed to know the rest of her present life; she sense-knew deep within herself there were parts missing, gaps in the knowledge, feelings half completed. Becky felt unfinished and the written diaries would, she was sure, give her the rest of herself. Becky tried a different approach with her mother. 'I think I need to read the rest of what I, I mean you wrote. I can tell there are bits missing from the story of Captain Srinath and the Vimana from what I've seen so far.'

The Ayaye had circled the argument back to this point again, only now it was presenting a more convincing reason for being allowed to read the rest of what the eight-year-old girl had bequeathed her adult self. But how much further would it metamorphose into her? Would it actually become her, indistinguishable from the original? There was certainly enough raw data in the diaries to restore the person who had written them. Rebecca had not expected this; she had thought the Ayaye would merely scan everything she presented it into its own memory where it would interrogate the diaries at her instruction. Instead it had assimilated them, consumed them somehow, and in doing so, had become, become what? Rebecca was not sure, but she was not comfortable with it.

But what other choice did she have? The weight of her need to know, and her actions up to this point pressed harder on her than her reluctance to engage with this copy of herself. 'Alright,' she conceded. 'How long will it take you to read these?'

Becky had to stifle a squeal of delight.

mummy bought me/gave me a present today i had to pretend i liked it/it was nice because mummy doesn't buy me presents/get me nice things very often, so dad made a face behind her back/encouraged me to when she was giving it to me to tell me to look pleased/say thank you i put the bright pink fluffy/icky girly doll at the bottom of my toy drawer /well out of the way later i couldn't help listening/overheard dad and mummy speaking/talking/ arguing about it i sat/hid on the top of the stairs in the dark/wasn't scared, when dad said something like 'really eleanor, I think becky appreciates the effort, but it's not really her thing and I know you're trying to understand her' mummy then said 'what is that, buying something so pretty, if not trying? i'm trying my best to see your daughter's point of view here gregor.' i didn't hear anymore because i went to bed and put my pillow over my ears

'Right, that's better. Now, I need to know a few things about the Vimana, and the mission to the stars. You remember that don't you?' Rebecca had to work hard to keep the patronising tone from her voice.

Of course I do! thought Becky almost bursting to tell her mother everything about Hari Srinath and the other Vimana astronauts. All about the ship and the training and everything she knew, but instead she asked Rebecca in her most polite voice what exactly she wanted to know, and that she would try her best to remember everything she

226

could. 'Yes Rebecca. I remember everything you told me.'

Rebecca looked confused then realised the Ayaye meant the diaries. The constant shifting of perspective had been difficult enough when the Ayaye at least resembled an adult; now confused in with the memories of her childhood, Rebecca doubted she could get any sense, let alone useful information from her.

It. It.

Remember to think of it as it.

Not her, it.

'Good,' she said, steadying herself mentally. 'Now we're looking for anything unusual with the mission, anything that might have a bearing on why I'm in the middle of America talking illegally to an Ayaye that thinks it's me aged eight.'

Becky ignored the slight. Her mother had said worse things in relation to her, or ignored her completely, so such a trivial rebuff was nothing; easily overlooked. 'You mean it's a game, like finding the answer to a riddle? Or a puzzle, like when I won the class competition to work out what jumbled up words were and when I told you...' Becky dropped her eyes from Rebecca, and Rebecca could not help feel the ice-stab her in the stomach at the child's words echoed back at her a quarter of a century after she had written them. Being told her memories made it that much harder to stem the flood of emotion that came with them.

But that was then and this was now; she was stronger now than she had been back then. Hard years of discipline had tempered her mind not to allow such lapses to last long, and Rebecca brushed aside the emotion with the hard conviction of her mental control. 'What did I say about snivelling?' she barked at the Ayaye who for its part stood there with her lower lip trembling, the eight year old girl not equipped with the mental faculties the adult Rebecca possessed. For her, each trip into the diaries was more raw, the painful memories and remembrances still fresh; Becky did not have the quarter of a century of distance to place between herself and things that for her, happened only a week, or a month ago.

>

A week later, Rebecca and Becky had re-located three times to avoid detection, by either human or artificial agency; the large bounties offered for the apprehension of any party involved in illicit and unregulated contact with Ayayes forcing them to move continually from place to place. The border lands, with their Ayaye network cabling and lack of law enforcement were fertile hunting grounds for bounty hunters, informers, or chancers eager for a quick couple of lakh rupee reward.

For Becky it was easy. She vanished into the net, fragmenting herself and travelling along the routers and network encoders, polling the next allocated connection point, awaiting the recall carrier signal that would re-assemble her constituent parts once more, the whole being far greater than the sum of her parts. Becky did not mind the time spent in the electronic reality that constituted the human A-space, her endowments as a sentient electronic entity granted her almost unfettered access to every system connected to it, where she could copy and replicate herself then re-join and assimilate what she learnt into her whole.

Theoretically, she could insert herself into any network, data-silo or terminal with little effort, eavesdropping on people's financial details, their SI logs, their medical records, libraries, museums, everything. Even the ostensibly secure boundaries between the separate, private corporate networks she journeyed effortlessly along offered little in the way of resistance to her electronic form. It was both informative and diverting for the Ayaye that craved human experience in all its forms. And besides, it was fun.

Rebecca however had a far harder time of the journeys

between sufficiently shielded and guarded relays; journeys that sometimes necessitated drives of nearly twenty hours. Long, perilous nights in the driving seat, snaking along the convoluted routes Becky worked out for her, avoiding both large population centres and known bounty hunter outposts. Becky argued the small shower of bullets earlier in the week was too perilous to risk again, so safer, and therefore longer, paths were required.

Becky derived great pleasure in designing her mother's itineraries from place to place, even if she received no acknowledgement or praise from the business-like woman she would grow up into. Anyway, she knew and understood her mother could not Displace, even if the Cotts field were sufficiently strong here to allow her the same ease of movement that Becky experienced. Therefore, despite any external sign, Becky was sure her mother was grateful of the assistance she was providing as a guide through the conflict-scarred landscapes of continental North America, and her own equally traumatised childhood.

Becky wished her mother could know the pleasure and elegance of almost instantaneous movement; her childhood had been tethered to the earth whereas Becky's was being lived in the freedom of electronic reality, unbound by the physics that had chained her mother when she was her. Becky was wise enough not to mention these feelings; her mother needed Becky's help in more ways than interpreting the diaries.

>

The pickup truck had seemingly suffered as much of the abuse Rebecca had inflicted on it during the long weeks in the desert as it was either in a position, or willing to accept. It was in a stage of open rebellion, withdrawing its services in small but ever increasing increments, as if it were self-aware and attempting to preserve itself from complete destruction by means of a lesser mechanical breakdown.

The shock absorbers, having been pushed through the punishing terrain of the pitted and pot-holed countryside for four solid weeks were on the verge of resignation from their allotted role. Each new bump drove them a step nearer to collapse, and in the meantime sent the truck crashing up and down over every protrusion and into every rut. The steering column had grown almost wilfully slack in the weeks of being wrenched round one way, only to be hauled, complainingly the other a moment later. Now it spun loosely in Rebecca's hands, refusing to translate the request for a change in direction to an actual variation in heading unless Rebecca manhandled the wheel. At times she had to effect nearly a thousand degrees of rotation to get the vehicle to round an approaching boulder. As for the brakes, the truck seemed to have decided they now required at least a minute's notice that their services would be needed in slowing the vehicle. Stopping became an exercise in timing and patience, dropping through the gears until almost all forward momentum had been fed into the transmission system; then and only then could the brake pedal be stepped upon and expect to give some resistance to the pressure, and actually produce some reduction in velocity.

In this way, Rebecca had entered into a battle of wills with her transport, sometimes cosseting, sometimes chiding it as they both progressed across the long, hot and barren desert, both needing rest but neither able to get it. She suspected that in the fight with the truck it would be the one to throw in the towel first and shudder to oblivion.

Rebecca bounced in the seat as she attempted to use all three of the failing systems at once, turning heavily through what seemed to be a gopher warren of ruts in the desert floor, continually having to slow to avoid or drive though another half-metre deep hole in the ground. 'Come on, don't let me down now. You've been good for hundreds of kays,' she goaded and pleaded the truck as the gearbox added its crunching note of complaint to the rising chorus of whines, groans and clunks that accompanied her driving. 'Just get me another sixty, that's all I ask, then you can rest and we'll see about getting you fixed up,' she added as if her imploration and offer of repair could have any effect on the inanimate object she sat in.

For a piece of engineering on the verge of collapse, Rebecca was amazed to find the fitted radio still functioned nearly perfectly, and she was able to pick up both short wave and FM transmissions as well as a digital signal, even here in the middle of nowhere. After so long in isolation she had almost forgotten there was a different world out there beyond the sandy horizon, and that somebody was still transmitting. She flicked the radio on thinking she might get an international broadcast on one of the short wave bands that still persisted despite the technology being nearly two centuries old.

BWEEEE-EEEEEEE

'OK, OK,' Rebecca winced as the shrill whine cut through the noise of the engine. She prodded at the radio's search buttons, watching the short wave frequency climb into the high three-thousands, all the while still trying to steer with her free hand, flicking her eyes back out of the windscreen every so often; second long sampling of the route ahead intercutting her efforts to locate a broadcast. The radio hissed and crackled as it struggled to locate a signal strong enough, voices rising and fading in the static.

After several abortive attempts found only a disquieting mix of gospel, prayer or bad hard rock music, the radio locked onto the world service from London. Rebecca was almost relieved to hear an accent something other than the Southern drawl almost everyone she had met spoke with, long drawn out vowels replaced with the more brusque, clipped consonants of received pronunciation. 'Well done,' she patted the pickup's dashboard in reward for it finding

231

something she could listen to. She checked her watch; it was still ten minutes to the hour and a likely list of headlines. Still, it was not like she had anything else to do; her destination was still over three hours away and other than needing to keep a watchful eye for either large, suspension-shattering potholes or truck-grounding mounds there was little to see in the slowly changing landscape she drove through.

Her mind wandered as she listened to the radio; the mix of programming interspersed with continuity announcements providing only a slight distraction to the drive. It was the single longest time she had ever spent travelling, and the most inefficient. Her route was deliberately convoluted, and not made any less so by the broad circumnavigations she was having to perform every time an obstacle loomed into view on the horizon. She hated having to travel this way, the long cramped hours in the seat, moving at only a few dozen kilometres an hour instead of the near-instantaneous Displacement vehicles she was used to.

Her reverie was broken by a single word on the radio. Immediately she slammed her foot on the brakes and the truck slewed to a halt over the distance of half a kilometre, kicking up a long plume of dust for hundreds of metres behind her, she apologising to the vehicle for her further mistreatment of it through the whole skid. She killed the engine regardless whether it would start again, to better hear the broadcast, turning up the volume as much as she could. Her ears strained to pick up the words between the crackling interference, and she managed to hear only the closing statements to the piece again.

'Kumarapad... tragic accident... only three... house fire... Agency issued a statement... no living...'

Rebecca pieced the likely story together from the broken recap and sat in contemplative silence for a moment, while the desert she had disturbed with her passage settled once more around her. 'Bahen ke takke!' she exclaimed to the empty air around her. This changed everything. She had to follow this up.

Rebecca turned the ignition key and the truck coughed back to life, seemingly content with even this briefest of respites. She reached for her map, needing to check her position. Heaving the steering wheel round she trod on the accelerator once again and the truck swung through one hundred and eighty degrees as Rebecca headed for the nearest main arterial highway which would take her, six hours later, to the Monterrey shuttleport and a longjump back to London.

>

Becky waited for eight hours before instigating a sweep of the cloud for Rebecca's whereabouts, more than long enough for her errant mother to have got lost, and found her way back to her again; her eagerness to be reunited with Rebecca tempered with her longing not to look needy now she was winning her mother's affections.

It did not take the Ayaye long to locate the longjump Rebecca was booked on to, perform the requisite searches to discover the story of the house fire in Delhi and realise that Rebecca had abandoned her. Becky wondered what she had done wrong to make her mother not tell her she was leaving her alone once again. Whatever it was it was obvious that Becky had failed Rebecca and most likely her mother would not want her interfering with her business.

Becky retrieved all the pieces of her consciousness scattered out across A-space, withdrawing into herself, retreating electronically from the hurt in the way that her human self had done a quarter of a century ago.

Twenty-two

Aftermath

Tuesday 27 June 2056 – 07:15 IST

The middle-aged Indian man, his once jet black hair shot through with streaks of grey, his face lined with the experience of a quarter of a century of being a father, a lover, a partner and confidante, smiled to himself despite the twinges from his chest and throat as he strode, with the aid of his cane, onto the small balcony that opened out from the double doors of his bedroom. His breathing was still the cause of some small occasional troubles resulting from the minor adaptive operation he had undergone the previous week. He supposed, having only two days ago returned home from hospital after his surgery that he should expect, at his age, his body to recover more slowly than in his youth. But however slowly he may have been, he was healing, and he reasoned that was enough to be grateful for. The surgery had been successful, and would allow him the continuation along the path his life had taken a generation ago.

Standing there in his light cotton pyjamas he closed his eyes and felt the rays of the rising sun warm his skin, and ease his old man's joints. His eyelids filtered the bright white light to a warm orange glow half seen in his mind. The man stood absorbing the morning warmth, till the woman who he had called his wife for twenty-five years rose from their bed and followed him out, wrapping her arms around his waist, absorbing some of the warmth he had taken from the sun. Opening his eyes and turning to her, genuine love in his eyes, he kissed her lightly on her forehead.

'We have a lot to organise today,' he whispered to her, testing his newly re-arranged vocal apparatus as she snuggled into him.

'Mmm, but you're up early, we have time before we need to rise properly. And please, shh and rest your voice for the time being my love,' she replied, leading him carefully and patiently back to their bed.

An hour later, the man who called himself Samir Kumarapad rose again, this time to shower, breakfast and dress ready for the coming day. The occasion of his son's engagement was to be the largest family gathering in recent years, and there was a great deal of preparation to be completed before noon, when the first relatives started arriving. Smiling to himself as he readied both his own and his wife's breakfast, Samir ran through the arrangements for the day in his head.

>

Even if the monsoon rains had fallen that day, and their cargo of water not have already passed for another year, they would have been unable to drown the fire that caught and consumed the house.

The police incident captures showed, in sequence, the journey the investigators had taken as they progressed, forensically, through the ruined house, acquiring in hi-res detail the effects of the fire as it overcame the party. The house had been destroyed utterly, the intensity of the heat such that the sixteen tenders in attendance at the scene had been working long over three hours before they began to bring the blaze under a semblance of control. The cost to them for their actions was the loss of three of their number, overcome by the ferocity of the heat they struggled to contain.

Water had evaporated as it sprayed from the hoses toward the house, leaving the fire-fighters with little option but to eventually abandon the house as lost to the fire. Instead they redirected their efforts at the surrounding properties, soaking them instead to halt the inferno's progress, waiting for the conflagration to consume itself as it ate its way rapaciously through the fuel afforded it by the contents and occupants of the house.

Items which would be expected to endure a house fire were barely recognisable. Metal cutlery, normally only soot-blackened in similar blazes, was transformed to nuggets of metallic slag, the knives, forks and spoons having run and slid into each other as, liberated from their solidity by the heat, they poured from the drawers and table settings onto the floors. Where walls still stood, mirrors had begun to melt, rivulets of glass collecting in bulbs at their base, distorting and pulling the reflections they now offered far from true. The stone flags of the bathroom floor had split, the heavy slabs no longer able to bear the weight of a single foot placed upon them as more than one investigator had lost his balance as the floor beneath him fractured into sharp, heavy shards.

Of the occupants there was nothing recognisable left, save a small ingot of gold that had once been two wedding bands, now melted together in union, the final remainder of Samir Kumarapad and his wife.

Ram viewed each image in turn, flicking forwards and backwards through the series, zooming in on details that caught his eye, or rotating the whole thing to see the same scene from a different angle with either a tap or a slide of his finger on the pressure-sensitive section of his desk. He saw the small smear of gold amongst the soaking piles of ash. There was no sign of any bone fragments or similar anywhere around, leaving him to ponder how the two rings had come to be near enough to each other to fuse in the heat. Lacking any skeletal or other evidence Ram assumed the couple had been entwined, Samir perhaps covering his wife in a futile attempt to protect her with his body, she reaching for his hand in their final moments as she realised their deaths approached.

Ram unconsciously thumbed his own wedding band as he imagined himself in Samir's position, deliberately trying to feel what his friend most likely would have been thinking when the inferno overtook him. Not thoughts of the mission or its aftermath, but of his wife. Ram hoped they had both succumbed to smoke before they felt the full force of the fire on their bodies. He hoped they had both already passed on to their next lives before the heat blistered and lifted the skin from their backs and faces, before their eyes boiled and burst, before they may have had time to realise that it was not only them who were passing that day, trapped and afraid like animals caught in a forest fire, but their son and his bride to be would also be consumed by the fire.

Ram hoped all this and more for the man he had known as Samir Kumarapad for twenty-five years. This man who had been asked everything by his Government in his time and had taken the responsibility unquestioningly. His ignominious end this way was not what Ram or anyone who truly understood the nature of the burden each of the eleven carried would have desired.

It was without question that Ram believed no living thing should suffer and die in pain or terror, but deeper than that, his actions, and those of the Brahman Group had now ensured that the name Samir Kumarapad would be remembered only in sympathy or pity, neither emotion befitting the efforts of a man who flew into the heavens on the Vimana or the man who lived a life of dedicated service upon the ship's quiet and unannounced return to Earth. There would be nothing now written or said about Samir which would fail to touch on the way he died, the manner of his passing too sensational to be ignored by a prurient press. The thought chaffed against Ram's modest nature. If allowed to plan for the death of one of the Vimana astronauts, Ram would have chosen a quiet, dignified passing, asleep at home perhaps.

Control from this point was impossible; damage limitation was his only option. Already, in his position as head of the Brahman Group, he had begun to contrive ways in which the story could be presented as to minimise their exposure. But as yet had failed to secure the appropriate slant on the incident which allowed no further speculation over the details without divulging more than was necessary to do so.

It was beyond the realm of belief to announce that Samir and his wife or their son and his fiancée had in actuality not been at the home at the time of the blaze but had perished in some other, less dramatic fashion; the co-incidence inviting the wrong type of prying eyes and sharp journalistic practices. Reportage of the event had made national headlines before adequate controls were in place; the intensity of the blaze and the historic fame of house's occupant promoting what should have been another unremarkable house fire into something approaching a national remembrance service.

Already Ram was receiving disquieting reports on the over one hundred memorial collectives the Brahman Group was tracking; gatherings in A-space which had been established within hours of the original, wholly unmanaged report. Soon, given enough exposure this single event could spill out of the bounds of his country and into the world, where any hope of manipulating the coverage would only draw further attention. Samir's death, with the resultant lessening of the number of individuals with access to the truth should have had eased the concealment of the facts from the world. In actuality, the manner of his passing was having directly the opposite effect.

The burden weighed heavily on Ram; conflicted by his involvement now more than ever. He had been instrumental, all those years ago, in putting in place the mechanisms of misdirection and ordinariness that had so far protected the secret, and could not help but reflect that perhaps if they had been a little braver back then, Samir would have had better fire defences, or perhaps the fire department could have been primed into attending the scene of any incident at his residence. Maybe then, it would not have been a fatal fire, merely an inconvenience of loss of possessions, rather than life. But any level of celebrity or degree of favouritism had been decided against by both the Brahman Group and the men and women who resumed the lives of the astronauts; better to disappear into normal life than to live out their days in the unrelenting glare of publicity. It had seemed the logical and prudent decision at the time.

Ram meditated on the unintended consequences of actions taken with the best of intentions. Left with little option but to confirm the barest facts surrounding Samir's death, and perhaps ensure a larger story appeared in the media within the next twenty four hours to distract the public from the truth, Ram felt his burden lift not in the slightest. Instinctively he tapped the desk screen, the muscle memory of his fingers calling up the dossier of currently viable countermeasure stories; mostly concerning celebrities and their possible indiscretions; all fabrications, but ones that would serve as a distraction for just long enough, until the press and public realised the misrepresentation of events, by which time Samir would be forgotten once more.

Lying to protect a lie.

Defenestration as a defence mechanism.

He closed his eyes and held his head in his hands. How much weight had his Karma accumulated as a result of this? There was a soft rap on his office door.

'Ramkumar? It is Joseph. You wished to meet to discuss the budgetary constraints for the new hydro-electric station in Uttar Pradesh?'

Ram called his oldest and most trusted friend in, once more activating the privacy field to cloak what he wished to discuss.

'Please, sit,' he gestured at a chair, aware that even in his failing health Joseph would wait to be invited to sit, manners and formality still directing the older man's actions, despite the tightness in his chest, or the difficulty he had in breathing. And Ram knew Joseph would continue to refuse any offer of assistance; his pride kept him strong enough.

Joseph took the offered seat, not grateful, but pleased that Ram still knew the place for proper behaviour. It would take a very moral man, possessed of the innate sense of right and wrong to guide the Brahman Group through the next few weeks; turbulent times lay ahead and both men knew it. It was the path they had set themselves on months ago.

'What are your thoughts on the captures?' Ram asked his former mentor.

Joseph drew a sharp in breath through pursed lips. 'Ah. Such a terrible thing, fire. People always fear drowning or other forms of death, but to burn to death must surely be the worst of them all. And such a fire. I understand Samir's voice modulator was completely destroyed, yes? Like a purifying fire from the touch of God's finger, burning away everything, eradicating all trace of our involvement.'

'Or that of anyone else,' commented Ram almost unconsciously.

Joseph nodded his agreement at Ram's assessment of the motives behind the blaze.

'So they have moved and I must now decide our response. While this changes nothing, their methods necessitate we advance our own timings. I admit I am left having to find the path that leaves the majority the least exposed. Such unrestrained actions only draw attention to us. Either we endure another funeral, so close to the last, with little time to properly prepare the media coverage, or we announce that Samir survived the fire and endure the inevitable interviews that would bring.'

'What confidence do you have in the replacement? It was not an easy process the only other time the Group faced this choice. And we did not have the burden of a further eighteen years of experiences and memories to assimilate. It is a huge thing we ask of them, little wonder the weight of expectation has the effects it does.'

'If I were to activate the replacement it would be in the capacity of a hospitalised survivor, perhaps unable to grant much in the way of interviews. With his injuries, his request for privacy would not appear unwarranted, especially when coupled with the loss of his family.'

'That addresses the next handful of months. A year perhaps. But what of the remainder of his life? Is he to apply the necessary prosthetics for all that time?'

'There would be no prosthetics. The injuries reported would have to be exact. There could be no element of chance. And I would not expect Samir to leave hospital alive'

Joseph indicated his repugnance at Ram's proposal.

'I agree, it is not the path I wish to choose. But I must consider every possibility before deciding my course. This is my dharma and however much these choices may deviate from my own feelings, I must still take them into account.

241

Such is the position I have placed myself in by choosing perhaps weaker men to act in my stead, then not acting sooner when the conspirators were suspected.' Ram seemed to finish, before confirming to Joseph that he would not pursue the latter course he had outlined. 'We will make arrangements for the funeral, then we will excise the canker at our heart.'

Joseph rose to leave Ram to his work but paused. There was something further occupying his former protégé's thoughts, beyond the logistics of what he now had set in motion. Years of tutelage and then friendship allowed him to ask Ram the question with a simple look.

'I sometimes wonder if what we have wrought has been of benefit to the world, or been the cause of bringing it to the edge of its ruin? Are we in danger of being the cause of the seizing up of the endlessly turning wheel of life? What point all the struggles for betterment if that ultimately leads nowhere?'

'If we had not harnessed Displacement, others would have, that much was inevitable. Others perhaps who would not have democratised it in the way we did. Doubtless our forebears would have had a similar discussion when Professor Cotts proved to them what he had found, yet they chose this path for us, knowing perhaps the effects their decision would have on themselves and the billions of others it would touch. We are part of a revolution available to every single person on the earth. It is enough.'

After Joseph had left, Ram called Pramod in, and with eight words set events in motion which would lead Rebecca to the roof of the world. 'Effect her return. It is time they met.'

< <

'aSSEmbleD fRIenDs. nOW tHAt wE ArE aLL tOGEtheR oNCe MoRe, i MuST EXRess my dISPleasURe at BeInG forCEd to CONvene aNoTher MeeTING sO SoOn aFTer tHE laST. THEre aRE rIsKs evERY tIMe wE AssEMble. ThIS mUST be tHe LaST fOr seVERAl MONths lEST wE ePXPOSe OURselves too gREAtly.'

  'i AGRee. DEspite oUR coNFIdEnce iN tHe teCHNOlogy we hAVE at OUr dIsPOsal, noTHINg iS fooLPRoof, aND tHe LOnGER wE rEMain iN cONtaCt tHe greATer oUr chANce oF diSCOvery.'

  'tHEn iT iS agREEd. tHIS wiLL bE our lASt fuLL cirCle fOR tHe FORseeaBLe fuTUre. thEREforE wE muST eNsUrE wE pUT in PLAce sUFFiciENt meCHAnISms tO aLLow thE coNTInuatiON oF oUr wORk, WithOUt oUr EXplicit inVOLVemenT.'

  'tO ThAT eNd, i SUGgest wE aSSiGn ouRSElves OnE cuCKoo eACh. fOUr oF thEM, foUr oF Us. iT woULd seeM dIVIne prOVIdencE woRKs foR uS In OuR enDEavOUrs.'

  'aGreed. tHE OLd mAN hAs aLLOwed eVeNts tO gET beyONd hIM; The buSINesS wITH tHE bANK aNALyst fOr inSTAnce. i HAVe iT on RELiabLE auTHOrity tHAT shE hAs vENTured tO aMERica. dOIng wHAt i Do nOT knOw, bUt it wOULd aPPeaR sHe HaS nOt LeT THis mATTer dROP.'

  'THen aLL tHE bEttEr WE moVE iN tHe WaY We propOSE. wE MUst sTop thE dISCoverY of THe sECret. iT iS tOO gReAT a BUrdEN fOr tHe cuCKooS tO bEar aNY lONger. iT is oUr duTY to RElieVe tHEm oF It.'

  'yOU Do nOT sUSpeCt tHEm of falTERinG nOw, aFTer aLL thiS tIMe dO yOU?'

  'i AM MereLY SayinG THe FewER tHe nUMbEr oF inDIVIDualS wHo aRe aWARe oF thE TrUTh, oR eVEn thEir sMaLL frAGmeNtS oF It, tHE sMALLer THe riSk oF itS ACCidentAL esCApe.

oUR tASk wiLL Be grEAtly siMPLifiED, aND theREFore tHAt mUch mORE acHIEVabel iF aLL We haVE coNCERn ourSELVes wITh is tHe eiGHt oTHERs iN THe oLD MAn's GRoup. aND wE aLL swORE to PROteCt huMANity fRoM tHe trUtH, dID wE noT? tHAt rEsPoNsIbIlITy bEArs itS tOll oN aLL Of US.'

'no-One mUst susPEct oUr HANd in ThiS. EVeryTHing mUst aPpeAr nORmaL.'

'aT leAst we hAVe tHe benEFit oF aGe oN OuR sIDe fOr TwO Of thEM. hEArt attaCKS foR MeN anD wOMeN oF tHeir yEarS cAn stILL bE fATal.'

'wHAt aRe tHeir iTINerAriEs? aRe aNy Of THem aWay? sOMeWhEre wITh POor trANsPoRtaTioN, oR saNItAtioN? wE mUst coNSiDer evERy oppORTunIty.'

'wHAT TiME frAme aRe we prOPOsinG tO undERTakE thiS? anYThinG too sOOn, oR tOO cLose toGEtHer WiLL rAIse SuSpIcIoNs.'

'WHat aBOut faMiLieS? aT LEasT twO oF tHe cUcKooS hAve sIRed oFFspRINg. tHErE muST bE nO geNETic LINk reMAIninG alSO. eVEn tHE SLIGhtesT cLUe couLD unRAVEl thE effORTs oF twENTy-fIVe yeARs.'

Twenty-three

Blackmail - I

Friday 30 June 2056 – 11:15 CST

Rebecca now had to get back into Britain disruption and detection free. Not an easy feat after a month breaking several international laws; least among them the illegal entry into a war zone.

Once safely back in Mexico, after consulting her alibi itinerary set up in the days before her egress from London and realising she had reached its end, the month she had allocated herself almost spent on this futile risk, she checked into the five star hotel in Monterrey. Politely declining the concierge service, instead favouring sourcing the items herself, she purchased, for cash, hair dye in her original colour, luggage for four weeks of travelling, and a full wardrobe of clothes. She tasked a one-time copy of Socrates with finding suitable location shots, and finally, almost as an afterthought, stole a handful of sand and grit surreptitiously from a building site she strode past on her way back to the hotel.

Ensconced in the safety and privacy of the suite, she set about constructing the ephemera of the holiday she had officially been on, cut-and-pasting her own 3D scan in various outfits into the images Socrates had sourced to create a set of holiday captures any normal visitor would have recorded. Clothes were dirtied with both her own sweat built up through vigorous workouts in the hotel gym, and the pilfered dirt. Finally, she restored her peroxide hair back to its original colour. There was little she could do with the style, except hold it in place with a few strategically placed hairpins. Checking herself against her passport, retrieved that morning from the safety Displacement box, she was satisfied that she at least resembled the woman in the photograph enough to get her back into her home country.

Six hours later Rebecca was sitting in a first class seat on a longjump back to London. Had she done enough to convince the customs authorities she had in fact spent the last four weeks sightseeing? The question gnawed at her as she waited for the Displacement engines to power down, their familiar discomfiting sensation only adding to the unease in her stomach. Knowing she looked like a woman with something to hide she tried to push the anxiety to the back of her mind. Her cover was good, but it was in no way perfect, and would certainly not stand the digital scrutiny of a realtime encephalographic imaging SI. Her long years of concealing and controlling her feelings would have to stand her in good stead if she was to appear what in effect she was beginning to wish she were; a weary but happily satisfied tourist returning from a well-earned and restful vacation. She crushed the thoughts, recollections and consequences of the past month underneath the internal monologue she had prepared around the fictitious vacation, along with the newly created memories of her time away she had spent eight hours visualising and committing to her mind.

Rebecca had told no-one of her intended destination, so there was no-one waiting to greet her as she disembarked.

She knew this looked out of place for a woman in her early thirties, and could only prepare tangentially around the anomaly by adopting the guise of a first-class traveller. The protective shield of the cover was easy enough to slip into; several business trips with Sinha MG had taught her what attitude to adopt, what to expect and how to act in most of the circumstances that travelling could throw at her when paying almost one and a half lakh rupees for a ticket.

Her luggage was brought to her and she headed for immigration, and customs.

Striding through the green channel, projecting a sense of purpose she was almost at the automatic door when she heard a voice behind her.

'Excuse me miss.'

Chod! Chodchodchod!

She had no choice; anything other than total compliance now would almost certainly lead to harder questions later. Rebecca stopped and turned, her heart rate rising from a far from resting one hundred to an adrenaline-flooded one four five. If they had the autonomic scanners monitoring the first class passengers she would definitely be registering as suspect; a fact that did not help her sense of calm.

Inside she was turmoil; outside she tried to remain all business.

'Yes? Is something wrong?' she asked, her voice almost cracking on the final syllable.

'I think you dropped this.' The customs official held up the small stuffed Chihuahua with a pink bow around its neck she had had perched on top of her trolley-case. 'A present for someone?' he asked calmly.

A trap? Rebecca held her nerve as her rehearsed lines came to her. Remembering to act grateful she smiled, but not for too long. A false grin would be fatal. 'Ha. My niece. Every time I go abroad she makes me bring her something back. Silly I know, being blackmailed with love by an eight-year-old.'

The customs official smiled at her story and handed the child's toy back to Rebecca. 'I hope she appreciates the effort you go to,' he said as Rebecca reclaimed the stuffed animal with a 'Thanks'.

She cursed herself. What had seemed a brilliant diversionary tactic designed to complete the illusion of normality had nearly undone her. Nodding her gratitude once more to the overly helpful official, Rebecca turned and made it successfully through the double doors of the Nothing-to-declare channel and into the D-port concourse.

In the sanctuary of her apartment, trying to calm down as best she could with a large gin and tonic for assistance, Rebecca assessed her situation. Her mission to the States had been a failure. The Ayaye had proved to be useless; her hope it could interpret her childhood had fallen apart. It could tell her nothing now it had become that thing. When she had met it, it had seemed almost omniscient; now it was nothing. An infant in a world of adults without even the potential to become anything more. Rebecca grimaced at the thought of her being so feeble and gauche, and being back in the world. She could barely believe she had grown up from that.

Frustratingly, all her effort and sacrifice had had no direct benefit to her cause. More dangerously the penalties to her, should what she had done ever be uncovered, were enormous. She did not want to contemplate the magnitude of risk she had exposed herself to. But it would be foolish to consider herself fortunate that the breaking of the laws she had engaged in seemed to have been completed with little immediate cost. There would be a price, she had just deferred payment for the time being.

Incriminating her were the diaries she had left behind with the Ayaye when she had left. They were too risky to attempt to import back into the UK, even if she could find a way to return to Becky to fetch them. She had no idea how she was going to get them back, and the thought of their discovery chilled her; the link they would make with her would damn her.

Rebecca pushed aside her fears and assessed what she knew. She had to assume some authority had found what she had left in the Americas, most likely the Mexican government, and that they implicated her in unauthorised contact with an Ayaye. What they would do was not easy to know, but an educated guess would be that there would be, if there was not already, an international arrest warrant for her.

On top of that there had been Kumarapad's death in the house fire. Rebecca was perhaps the only person in the West, and most likely only one of a handful in the world who thought the passing of another Vimana astronaut was mildly suspicious and warranted deeper scrutiny. But she was powerless to take her suspicions to any authority without drawing any more attention to herself.

Both things added together meant she could not linger at home, despite having only just got back. She had to move again.

Gulping down the rest of her drink she made her plans. First she had to get back out of the UK. Former disgraces in catching persons who the authorities deemed an international threat to security aside, the British state's sub-contracted citizen-seizure forces now had one of the best valid-capture rates in the world. She did not want to find her now perilously suspicious-looking network of bank accounts frozen, her assets seized, and facing the closing door of a Paddington Green D-proofed cell, then fast-tracked and bundled onto an extradition shuttle to the International Court before the day was out.

She ran through the factors currently facing her. Working in her favour was her detailed knowledge of the banking system, and how to push money around it with maximum discretion. While she had initially resisted using the money Dravid deposited in her bank account, she had not let it sit idle, and had, just prior to leaving for the States, shuffled it around and into over a dozen numbered only accounts in various secure off-shore institutions, that even Socrates didn't know the details of. She had also liquidated a portion of it and had over three crore rupee waiting for her to collect within an hour's notice, D-couriered to her location. That kind of money bought you a great deal of assistance in evading arrest at D-ports.

Secondly she had to find somewhere to go. Here, Rebecca notched a negative. She did not have a direction to proceed in. West was obviously out of the question; anywhere that took her back towards Becky and the abandoned diaries was a bad idea. South, towards Africa made little sense; she knew next to nothing of the continent or its countries. And nothing of any consequence lay north. East then. So, not a negative after all, but a necessity.

The obvious candidate country shouted itself to her, but she dismissed it out of hand; her recent trip there was well documented, if only through the research she had published a few short weeks ago. Any authority, or their proxy pursuing her would draw the logical conclusion as to where she had gone.

Rebecca scrolled through the list of countries where she had friends in her head. She had no wish to imperil any of them with the jeopardy she had brought on herself. With time waning on the choice of destinations, Socrates chimed in gently that she had two messages waiting for her to pick up.

'From who?' she asked her SI suspiciously, her insides suddenly cold with the fear of discovery.

'I confess I am unable to discern that Ms Eckhart. Whoever sent them managed to obfuscate their origin point completely.'

That couldn't be good. Then again, people coming to arrest you rarely send anonymous communications beforehand. 'Does they look dangerous? Any traceware or ghosthosts embedded in them?'

'No Ms Eckhart, not that I am able to detect. They both appear benign. One is encrypted with your public key and can be easily and safely interrogated within a replicate. The other however it is completely locked and I am unable to ascertain the nature of the content without opening it directly. The strangest thing is it is a simple enough keyphrase locking it, the sort of thing a child would employ.'

Rebecca thought for a second, contemplating just destroying the messages, eradicating another thread of suspicion that connected her to this affair, but she was in trouble and needed as many chances as she could. Her instinct told her they would help; many a negative position in her work had been turned around by her betting against what others would do. 'Relay the messages to me please, Socrates. The locked one first I think.'

A window opened up in her lens-screens. Rebecca expected perhaps either a voice recording or 3D capture of some sort, and was mildly surprised to find three addresses, in simple human handwriting, widely spaced block capitals detailing the locations of the final trio of Vimana astronauts still living in India.

'And the second?'

Socrates whirred for a microsecond then opened the message for his mistress. It was the same data, albeit in a more standard font.

'Are you sure you can't you confirm the locations these came from?'

'No Ms Eckhart, I must admit that I am unable to determine the origin points of either message. However, I am confident they were not sent by the same agency.'

'Curiouser and curiouser.' Rebecca voiced her thoughts

to her SI. 'It seems someone, or perhaps two someone's want me to return to India.'

That was it, decision made. Everything from now on was easy.

'OK Socrates, let's get ready!' Picking up the LeatherLike bag she had not even bothered to unpack from her last time there, Rebecca instructed her SI to comm Commissioner Pramod Surendran as she headed for her front door.

Out on the street she could not help but scan the few people who walked along the tree-lined pavement, trying to look at them without catching their attention. Almost instantly she realised she was acting like the fugitive she believed herself to be, which would alert any passing sec-force. That was assuming there was not already someone watching her.

The comm connected. <Hello.> said the gentle voice she recognised as Pramod, despite it not speaking English to her.

'Pramod. It's Rebecca. I heard about Samir Kumarapad's death.'

<...Eckhart... ...nice... ...you... ...surprised... ...least... ...not... ...bank... ...Samir...>

Rebecca's grasp of Varhadi was not up to this kind of conversation, but she wondered why Pramod refused to speak English to her. She assumed he knew it, and was not going to make this easy for her. She decided there was little point in jousting with him this time. He obviously understood what she was saying and in all honesty she did not need to understand the bulk of any replies he made, she just had to be sure he got her meaning. 'I'm coming out to India again. I need to speak to you about this.'

<...Eckhart... ...advise... ...rumours... ...correct... ...not... ...D... ...please...>

Through the snatches she understood, Rebecca got the gist of what Pramod had said. 'I have a feeling you know more than you originally told me, and also that you don't want me caught and questioned anymore than I want to be. I'm not sure what kind of influence you have, but I'm guessing it's pretty significant. Given I haven't been arrested yet, I'm fairly sure I can get out of Britain safely, and I need you to ease my entry back into India. I'm going to be on the next longjump out of Heathrow and I'm hoping you've got enough time to organise the authorisation by the time I get there.'

Pramod switched immediately to English. 'Ms. Eckhart, please do not resort to this. We can arrange something else, I am sure.'

'I'm sorry,' she replied genuinely. 'I don't mean to blackmail you.' And she disconnected, a snake of guilt and doubt coiled up in her gut, biting her insides.

Five and a half hours in planetary rotation, and three quarters of a second in Displacement, Ram, who had been present in the room when Rebecca had called Pramod nodded his assent. 'I anticipated something like this. We must finalise preparations for her arrival.'

Twenty-four

Blackmail - II

Prakat Gupta impatiently buzzed the comm on the door of Sati's apartment. Suri was at her mother's house for the night once again, and Prakat had left his house only moments after his wife had.

Sati answered promptly, dressed in the latest lingerie he had bought and left with her the last time he had visited a month ago. He had not seen her since; she had told him she had been away at her maternal grandmother's house for the previous four weeks, and he was anxious and eager to re-acquaint himself with her body. He began to swell at even the thought of the sex to come.

Sati closed the door behind him, and led him to the bedroom. He smiled; she seemed to want to waste no time at all, which suited him perfectly. She untied the silk shawl covering her genitals, an explicit signal for him to undress. He wrestled his shoes off, and disrobed, leaving a trail of clothing behind him.

Kissing him, Sati pushed him gently onto the bed, straddling him, but not yet allowing him to enter her. She took his hands off her breasts and held one wrist to the frame above his head, where she secured it with one of the silk ties she had obtained for this session.

Sensing this was a new, but not unwanted direction to their play, Prakat allowed himself to be tied up by his lover, she securing his other wrist and both his ankles before slowly drawing her soft hands up his thighs to his straining manhood. He groaned in pleasure as she took it in her hands, her fingernails scratching his scrotum gently, causing him to thrust forward with his hips.

Sati drew a deep breath to steady herself. She had him where she wanted him now. Her failed attempt to pursue Rebecca across Mexico had been a frustration, and the incident with the screaming woman in Mexico had scared her badly. She had retreated home where the dangers were familiar ones and well understood, and where she could exercise some influence over events. If she was going to get any nearer to achieving her aim she was going to have to assert control, and bring forward her timetable. She was closer now than she had ever been and, despite her lingering unease at her misjudgement of venturing outside of India, knew she had to act. The time for passivity was over. She would put herself into play.

The tickling turned to gentle squeezing, then into hard squeezing, with her fingernails digging into his soft, tender flesh for emphasis. His erection shrivelled in an instant as the pain reached his brain. 'Ahhh! What in great fuck are you doing?' he screamed.

Sati bunched his testicles in her grip and swiped them with her other hand, causing him to try to buckle, only the restraints stopping him from doubling up. 'Be quiet! Only answer the questions I ask you from now on, otherwise you'll find yourself unmanned. I wish to talk to you about the Vimana.'

Even in his pain and confusion Prakat was astute and aware enough of his role and responsibility to feign useless ignorance. 'The what?' he tried to bluff.

Sati gave his genitals another hard slap with exactly the same results as the first one. He was perspiring now, and his breathing had become ragged. For a moment she feared he might pass out, or worse. She dropped his testicles and put her fingers to his wrist. The pulse was steady and strong, despite the obvious discomfort he was in. She looked at him, confident that the distress was mostly an act.

Sati grasped him again, roughly, and made to swipe once more, all the time her eyes focussed on his own. Her hand descended, approaching his reddened scrotum at speed. He did not even flinch as Sati stopped a centimetre before contact. It was obvious to her now that physical abuse was unlikely to yield the results she needed. That was fine with her; there were other more subtle methods she could easily employ.

Releasing him from her fist she spoke to him again, gently this time. 'Please do not lie to me. How long have we been intimate? I know all about the Brahman Group, and your position in the Saazish within it. Why do you imagine I allowed you to couple with me?'

Prakat comprehended his situation in an instant. He dropped the act he had been performing, his breathing returning to normal and his eyes hardening. 'This is a dangerous game you are playing, veshya.' He sneered the last word, an insult at her status. 'I am not without influence in this country, as you are no doubt aware.' Even naked and trussed he was trying to control the situation he found himself in.

'I do not care about your influence. I care about what you know. And I also wonder what you care about?' she asked almost idly. 'You must realise your position, of course?'

'Of course,' Prakat replied. 'Untie me and we can talk properly about what you want and what you will do for me in return.'

Sati smirked. 'Now, just because I am willing to use my body to achieve my ends, do not think me stupid. While you are like that I am safe. I believe we can reach an accommodation with you secured. After all, you do not need your hands that would almost certainly reach for my throat the second I loosened one, to negotiate a deal.'

Prakat regarded Sati for a moment. He had been lured, hooked and now skewered by his desires. It was obvious he would have to tell her at least a fraction of what she would ask him, if only to secure her immediate silence and his marriage. The rest could come later when he had had a chance to review the situation he had helped engineer for himself. 'I will not disagree with you there,' he replied, leaving Sati unsure as to which part of her statement he was confirming. 'I presume you will keep our liaisons from my wife and colleagues in return for the secret of what happened on the Vimana's mission? The secret we have been keeping from the world for twenty-five years.'

'I already know the mission was a failure, and have done since it returned. If there is a greater secret then I am not interested in it. I need confirmation of a different kind.'

Prakat looked confused; he had assumed Sati would want information similar to the English woman they had lost track of in Central America. He told her as much.

Sati absorbed what Prakat said, for the first time seeing through Rebecca's disguise. She half-smiled with one side of her mouth at the realisation. Sati was impressed; Rebecca was proving herself to be as resourceful as she was. She allowed herself the satisfaction that she had in actuality been correct in following Rebecca all this time. Logically, there was only one direction the woman would head. It was time to make her fuller acquaintance. First though she had unfinished business with Prakat.

In all the time he had been lying beneath her since she had released her grip on him he had regained some ardour, seemingly stimulated by the situation he found himself in, and it took Sati little effort to restore him to full arousal with her mouth. Prakat's eyes caught hers and she responded to his unspoken question. 'Just because I have been the passive half of our liaisons up to this point does not mean I have not enjoyed our time together. You are quite an accomplished lover and it would be a pity to miss one last chance to enjoy you.'

Sati raised herself over Prakat and, after positioning herself correctly, lowered herself slowly onto him until he was fully inside her. She was going to direct things from now on.

Twenty-five

Re-entry

Saturday 1 July 2056 – 06:12 IST

For everyone on the arriving longjump shuttle, driven by a single Deva, space shifted and bent around them. It flicked back, dragging them and the shuttle with it. Some felt almost nothing, others only a mild tingling like stomach butterflies while a handful lived the most vivid waking dreams imaginable; the hours of time difference compressed into a few brief seconds while the D-drive fired.

Rebecca held her breath even after the engine had fully powered down. Her hands were sweating and her stomach was a tight knot, and not this time from the effects of the Displacement trip. She had come full circle, and was back in India.

>

For the second time in a little over two months she found herself striding through the immigration hall of Indira Gandhi international D-port, the rhythmic squeak of the small wheels of her luggage on the polished floor trailing her as she walked. She was acutely aware of the sound, it seemingly magnified by her apprehension, and she kept her gaze straight ahead, refusing to catch the eye of anyone, passenger or official alike with a middle distance stare that looked both at and through them.

She tried to navigate a course across the busy immigration hall, weaving and dodging through the crowd; every catch to her shoulder or elbow causing her heart to quicken, every glance in her direction by the lathi-armed guards tightening the knot in her insides, every announcement over the public address system catching her breath. The mass of humanity pressed on her, pushing at her from all sides. Men jostled into her, deliberately causing contact with her breasts and rear while women elbowed their way past the white foreigner. Swarthy faces leered at her, seemingly seeking confrontation or attention. Hands pulled at her clothing, beggars grabbing for the attention of the wealthy western woman lost and out of her depth in the crush.

Breathless and bewildered, Rebecca made for the sanctuary of a rest room and locked herself in a western-style cubicle. *This had been a bad idea.* Even if the Mexican authorities had not found her diaries, she was wading deeper into trouble; strict interpretation of the law stacked heavily against her confidence she was pursuing the correct path. What she had done in contacting the Ayaye carried a heavy prison sentence, and forbade her from operating, owning or even being within ten metres of anything computerised, which was practically everything. She was risking more than a simple fine and six weeks in an open prison here; if caught her life as she knew it was over.

She tried to dismiss this cheery thought with a splash of cold water to her face. Leaving the toilet she headed, as unobtrusively as she could for the exit, and then an anonymous hop-cab where she could pay cash. The tens of lakh rupee she had with her would come in useful in that respect.

<

Palms, armpits and crotch itching with sweat. Not from the heat and humidity outside the cool of the terminal. Resisting the urge to wipe or otherwise pull at her clothing. Trying to remain as discrete as possible. No-one see me. Pay me no heed. Feeling exposed and vulnerable in the slowly shuffling queue for a hop-cab. The only westerner in the immediate area. Another minute passed, no nearer her destination, no further away from the incident. Rebecca stood, eyes still directly ahead, with absolutely no intention of making eye contact with anyone whatsoever.

She tried to slow her breathing, instead focussing on the circumstances around her re-entry to this hot, busy country which had nearly, but not quite lost her the opportunity to use some of her cash.

She had expected some potential confusion as to her visa status at the immigration desk, but had faith that Pramod would have arranged for an emergency one to have been issued in her name. She had reached the front of the grumbling impatience that had been the queue for the sole immigration officer, and stood waiting for the iris scan results to retrieve her suitably authorised passport for the bored-looking official with the confidence of someone who expected all to be well.

He barely glanced up at the woman standing in front of him as the database search returned its results.

Then several things happened in rapid succession.

In Rebecca's screens her passport details flashed up in front of her, almost as if she were seeing what was being displayed to the Indian official it was now obscuring. She had no time to process or internalise this change in procedure when she saw, at the same time as the immigration officer, the DETAIN notice flashing urgently

261

in the lower corner of their shared vision.

Chodding chod! Dread. A yawning pit opening up before her. Realisation her journey had ended.

An alarm went off behind her, which Rebecca did her best to ignore and remain calm. If her passport had triggered it she wanted to be facing the official in a most likely misguided attempt to carry on with her bluff. The immigration officer, drilled to respond to alarms in his immediate vicinity responded as only he could to his training, and looked through the display on his screens and in the direction of the klaxon. Rebecca, not moving an iota of muscle, could not help but notice the screen holding her future on it as the warning disappeared, and more confusingly not only was there now a visa granted to the person travelling on the passport, but the name on it changed from her own to that of her mother. *What the chod?!*

The commotion over her shoulder seemed to settle, having been about nothing after all, and the immigration officer before her resumed his work. He had been on the verge of calling his superior, and had got as far as touching the earpiece he wore, switching it on. He took another look at the screen, to confirm what he had seen only moments before and found that the woman in front of him did in fact have a valid visa. He re-scanned the passport, sure of himself the name had changed, and double checked it against the passenger manifest, the ticket purchase some six weeks previously, the shuttle's embarkation records and a reservation for a five-star suite at the Taj Palace made seven months ago. Seated in row one, granted her immigration visa two and half months ago, with a full and complete record of all the necessary bookings was Helena Charpin.

Still not convinced he triple-checked the woman's details, but his SI, the Indian Embassy database and both the Indian and International Police watch-lists agreed. Helena Charpin was able to pass freely without let or hindrance into India. Left with no option to dispute the evidence in front of him, his rote patter kicked in. 'Welcome to India, Ms Char-pin,' he struggled with the odd pronunciation of the French surname. 'I hope your stay is a pleasant one.'

>

It was taking Rebecca a few minutes to assimilate what had happened at the immigration desk, and she was still processing it at the hop-cab rank. Distracted, this in turn led to her beginning to attract unwanted and unwarranted attention. Despite her relief at gaining entry to India once more, she was less than happy with the means by which Pramod had arranged it. The trick with her mother's name had been cruel, spiteful, even if it had meant a valid visa.

How had he engineered the over-write of her passport? The SI muscle required to crack the gigabyte key protecting the data did not exist, at least as far as the public were aware or had been told. Then again, if the Indian Government had kept the truth of the Vimana hidden for a generation, what else had they hidden? It was not beyond belief to guess Pramod had access to resources well outside the public sphere.

The panhandlers, hawkers and hustlers emboldened by the middle-distance stare of the foreigner, sensing perhaps the soft touch of the first time tourist enamoured and overwhelmed by the scope and hurly-burly of the huge city, and open to easy manipulation and the parting of hard currency, circled in.

A hand pulled at her luggage, breaking her reverie, forcing her to have to manhandle the bag back from the person who had tried to snatch it from her. Immediately Rebecca backgrounded her distraction, foregrounding the hard-bitch mode in an instant. 'No!' she barked, rebuking the would be porter sharply.

Undaunted, the small man tried again, insistent that now he had laid claim to her luggage, he be rewarded with a small donation to let it go. 'Look pal, drop it now. Savvy?' she said flatly, all business. She hard-stared at the diminutive man, using her height advantage to loom over him. The thin hand let go immediately at the tone of threat in her voice. There were easier marks elsewhere; it was not worth the effort in confronting the obviously hostile woman.

Reluctant to give the beggar an easy time of his departure, Rebecca glared at him as he made after another tourist, so that she did not hear her name, her real name, called from behind her until the second, more insistent shout.

She caught her instinctive reaction to turn her head just in time, consciously countermanding decades of societal programming. The voice came again, more insistent this time, the increased urgency in it causing people to turn and look at whoever could be calling for the westerner.

Rebecca flushed as she realised that these same people would soon, a matter of seconds really, turn their heads back in the direction the voice was being hailed towards, and see one of only a handful of likely owners of the name.

'Is that you Ma'am?' the hop-cab pilot asked her politely, thinking perhaps the woman who was about to be his next passenger might have not heard the call over the hubbub, her confrontation and her own travel fatigue.

'No.' Rebecca answered quickly, abruptly even as she made her way round to the other side of the cab, an unconscious need to put another barrier between herself and her pursuer. Opening the rear far-side passenger door, she allowed herself only the briefest lift of her gaze to try and catch sight of whoever it had been who had been calling after her.

Her eyes met immediately with the woman from the canteen in Mexico, outside her Dad's house and originally waiting for her in this D-port the first time she arrived in India.

Her mystery female pursuer.

Rebecca ordered her destination and the cab's D-Drive thrummed up to power. Then, she was gone.

Shaken by both the shock of being recognised and the cumulative Displacement after-effects, Rebecca climbed unsteadily out of the cab. Her efforts to arrive as discretely as possible had failed almost utterly. Now with no option but to call herself by her mother's remarried name while in India, her passport functioning both as a form of international and domestic identification, she also had to contend with the fact that at least one person outside Pramod's circle knew of her presence.

She was sure the polite and sincere Commissioner would not risk her exposure; he had after all effected her entry back into India. That she had been found so quickly meant she was far less safe in India than she had fooled herself into believing. If there was a leak close to Pramod, who knew how far the knowledge of her arrival in India had spread? She implicitly trusted the Commissioner, even if he was part of some conspiracy. After all the Indian government had granted her access almost unheard of in preparing the Mehta article, and would have had ample opportunity to arrest or hurt her, or worse in the intervening weeks. But if her presence was broader knowledge, outside of the sphere of Pramod's influence and aegis she was in deep trouble.

Sati bumped her way though the crowd disembarking from the longjump that had arrived from Heathrow thirty minutes earlier. Her liaison with Prakat had borne the unexpected fruit of knowledge that Rebecca was most likely returning to India, which meant she had had to alter her plans accordingly. Originally she had intended to Displace back to England and finally make herself known to the analyst, but the realisation she was almost certainly on her way here forced a change of direction. Sati had spent the past two days at the D-port, waiting for the shuttle she wanted Rebecca to be travelling on, Kalpana assisting her in scanning every arriving passenger from London, searching for the woman, hoping to recognise her if she had taken another disguise.

All pretence and subterfuge were gone now. Like Rebecca, she had stepped beyond the bounds of legal ambiguity in her search. The further she pressed on, the greater the kinship she felt with the western woman; they had become heretics, both pursued for their beliefs, and the actions they precipitated. Like Rebecca she too had no idea how long it would be before the relevant authorities came looking for her, her freedom lasting only as long as her deal with Prakat was mutually beneficial. Or rather more accurately, no longer continued to expose him. Sati had little doubt that he had already begun manufacturing contradictory evidence to that she had amassed against him, and was now preparing his defence in the form of an attack on her. Even the recordings of their couplings would not help her for long. It was not beyond Prakat's capabilities to engineer an SI-simulated recording within hours showing what ever he wanted. She needed allies, and Rebecca's return to India, divine Providence or not, offered her someone who's knowledge coupled with her own could provide them both with enough protection to complete their journeys.

Sati stood waiting in the terminal building scanning the faces of the passengers, desperate to catch sight of Rebecca. She was rewarded with a glimpse of a woman she thought was her. Sati remembered the savage haircut of the woman who had confronted her in the small, dilapidated diner in Mexico. Perhaps with some dye to restore the natural colour and hairpins to hold the abused hair in place it could be her. Sati pushed her way through the crowds, unwilling to lose sight of the woman, the crowd begrudgingly parting for a woman in a way they would be reluctant to for a man. The irony was not lost on her. More than once Sati had to turn and apologise for her rough treatment of the someone she nudged, bumped or once, pushed out of the way. Each instance caused her to fall a second or two and another three people further behind, as her target glided through the lobby and out to the cab rank. Rebecca's status as a first class traveller allowed her far freer passage through the bustle.

Stuck between two cow-like business types, Sati lost sight of the westerner. If she boarded a cab soon, she would lose her for good. That was not to happen. She pushed, using her residual physicality much to the surprise of the charcoal suits blocking her path. It took Sati longer to reach the exit than she wanted, leaving a trail of several angry passengers marking her passage.

There, at the head of the queue.

'Rebecca!' she called.

The woman did not turn. She called to the westerner again, louder this time, adding a note of urgency in the hope of forcing her to acknowledge her name. Was there a flicker of recognition? Sati was sure there had been the slightest movement of her head which had been suppressed. Several other heads now turned, not answering Sati's shout, but in curiosity at who could be calling and not receiving a response.

Sati watched the woman she was convinced was Rebecca open the door to the cab, and thought for a moment she was about to lose touch with the one possibility of confirming her conviction, when her quarry raised her eyes a fraction to scan the crowd discretely. In that instant Sati saw Rebecca, saw the woman from Mexico, the house in England, the InSA museum and the very first time they saw each other across the crowded D-port.

It was her.

Elated at being correct, Sati, heedless of the commotion she left in her wake now, pushed her way to the front of the queue, this time taking advantage of her status as a woman, and on her compatriot's natural politeness to allow her passage, to clamber into the next available vehicle.

'Interpolate that last cab's destination,' she ordered, waving a week's takings to the bewildered pilot.

In a second she too was gone.

Unlike Rebecca, Sati experienced no ill-effects of Displacing; even the great planet-spanning distances the Earth-based longjumps traversed did not touch her in the slightest. So for her, the Displacement of a handful of kilometres after Rebecca's hop-cab was over almost before it began. The trio arrived, vehicle, pilot and passenger, in the Shahdara area, if the onboard display was any indicator of their location.

Sati knew why the analyst had come here, and had no hesitation in handing the pilot the promised roll of notes; the last of her immediate cash reserves spent on what she immediately knew had been a wise investment. Stepping out of the vehicle she felt the space around it begin to Fold, and not wanting to be dragged along with the cab when it left, stepped out of range of the D-bubble the pilot was projecting. She paused a moment to allow the Fold-remnant to fully dissipate into the Cotts field before moving herself.

Across the street Rebecca seemed not to have noticed her arrival, or the second cab's departure. Her trip had been only seconds behind, and the arrival point had been virtually the same volume of space, probably not distinct enough for the pre-occupied woman to have intuited the near identical Displacement signature. Ducking behind a stationary PDV when Rebecca swept her head round scanning the street, she was sure the woman, who up until this point had no reason to trust her and plenty of evidence to think she meant her ill will, would react badly if she saw her standing barely ten metres away. Better to approach her more formally, and certainly politely,

Sati ignored the stares of passers by as she peered through the windows of the PDV at Rebecca as she walked up the steps to the front door of Professor Lakshmi Shukla, formerly Commodore Shukla of InSA and, a quarter of a century ago, Ensign Shukla, one of the two remaining Devas from the Vimana mission still living in India. Rebecca was here to speak to her.

Sati allowed herself a moment of self-congratulation. She had been vindicated in her decision to follow Rebecca; Lakshmi Shukla had not given an interview in over fifteen years, becoming a recluse, and dropping out of public life after her return from deep space. Sati ached to accompany Rebecca and learn what Lakshmi would have to say, but knew the westerner needed to feel safer before she approached her. Better to wait here and make her presence known after Rebecca had spoken to her interviewee. Sati scanned the area; there was a small tea-shop that afforded her a view of the Professor's house. Deciding that after twenty-five years of waiting, another hour would not impact her too greatly, she sat down to order chai and kaju katli, and waited.

<

'Should she not have arrived by now?' Ram asked Pramod, glancing at the clock on the wall, at his own personal timepiece, then back at the wall again, as if daring any of them to show any discrepancy, or disagree in any way.

Pramod, Narinder, Vinita and Prakat sat in the Brahman Group's meeting room with Ram; all other members being too far away, or engaged in activities that required their personal attention to be summoned. Ram had recalled only those in the Group he knew could come, as to keep the possible vectors for any information escape to a minimum. He was almost certain that at least one of the people in the room was part of the splinter group he had come to learn existed within the Brahman Group, and had been searching for a method of uncovering at least one of their number since then.

Until now, all incidents or events which had necessitated the Brahman Group's intervention had yet to provide Ram the opportunity to deploy deliberately provocative information to a small enough gathering; knowledge calculated to prompt a traitor to action. Or the event had been of such magnitude that it had required all twelve of them to be present, thus affording Ram no opportunity to be selective in the information revealed to a handful of the Group, thereby allowing him to narrow his search to a handful of individuals.

Providence seemed to have intervened in his favour today however. Of the twelve, Ram knew he could trust only two others implicitly. Pramod, widely seen, correctly, as his eventual successor, and Joseph, his mentor and former head of the Group. Of the others currently present in the meeting room he was almost certain one was a member of the Saazish, and suspected one other. Still, he hoped to prove that today with the revelation that Rebecca Eckhart was back in India.

'Pardon, Ram, but who do you mean?' asked Vinita. 'You said 'she'.' Vinita narrowed her eyes at the titular head of their Group. 'You do not mean the analyst I hope? Eckhart.'

Ram considered the room before him and the knowledge he was about to impart. He drew his breath, as if preparing. But a lifetime of information management and twenty years in the Brahman Group, ten as is its head, had prepared him well enough. He knew the impact of the drama, the pause before the storm. 'That is precisely who I mean,' he said exactly, sure of his words.

The room erupted, as surely as if he had announced that he intended to reveal the secret to the world.

'What? What are you-'

'Surely there is a-'

'How can you have-'

Prakat, Narinder and Vinita talked across each other, hurling questions and accusations for a long minute. Ram waited patiently for them to remember their station before continuing. 'Pramod and I received a call from her. A rather urgent call I should add. It seems Ms. Eckhart has turned her work for us into a personal investigation. An investigation that has led her to break several laws outside our jurisdiction I understand. And she called regarding Samir's passing. She was coming to India regardless of whether we allowed her entry or not. In the circumstance, presented with the possibility of providing her a platform for her crusade by her international arrest, I felt it prudent to allow her ingress, so we at least could watch her until we could move against her safely. But she seems to have disappeared. We had arranged an emergency visa for her, but even though we are certain, and by this I mean completely certain, she left England under this alias, she never arrived in India under it. We have lost her.'

The last part was not completely true. While the agents Pramod sent to meet Rebecca at the airport had failed to intercept her when her alias had not registered on InSA's monitors, Pramod knew exactly where she was heading, and had picked her up again when she had arrived at Lakshmi Shukla's residence. It was this knowledge that Ram and Pramod were keeping from the others in the room.

However, Rebecca was under sufficient surveillance that meant should any of the Saazish try to act against her she would be more than adequately protected. In fact, if any of the group should attempt to cause her harm, the perpetrator, or their proxy, would be Displaced away to a secured cell the instant they proved even the vaguest threat.

271

Ironically, even though she feared for herself, Rebecca Eckhart was most probably the safest person on the whole planet right now.

'This is ludicrous Ramkumar,' said Vinita, finally after nearly five years finding the will to confront Ram, much in the way he had done over a dozen years previously with Joseph. 'You have lost her?!'

Narinder backed her up. 'You have risked everything we seek to protect. We should never have allowed her or her organisation the access we originally did.'

'She is a resourceful individual, not without funds to direct events her way if she so desires.' Ram offered in the way of an explanation.

'Let us not be too hasty,' said Prakat, trying to placate them both. The last thing he wanted or needed was Ram suspecting someone in the room of undermining him. 'We have all read Ms. Eckhart's biography, this sort of thing is to be expected of a woman of her abilities. We must turn our attention to finding her, surely?'

So, it is you, thought Ram.

Twenty-six

Alliance

Saturday 1 July 2056 – 13:00 IST

Rebecca remained unmolested all the way back to her hotel.

After her cryptic meeting with Lakshmi Shukla she was more convinced than ever that something profound was being hidden, and had been since she had been a child. Why had she not paid more attention to the aftermath of the mission, instead of abandoning the dream along with any attempt at gaining her mother's love? She knew why. That moment in the family room when Helena had risen and turned her back on her, her dreams, her moment, had meant that forever forward the Vimana was a tainted memory in little Becky's mind. Upon the news of the Vimana's unsuccessful return to Earth she had taken down every poster of Srinath, Chaudray, Mehta and the rest of the Vimana's crew; she had purged Socrates of the astro-navigation charts, the telemetry tracking, every newscast, autoblog and any other A-space artefact that even remotely mentioned the Vimana, and she buried it.

She sat on the bed, thinking everything over when the bedside comm beeped discretely, too gently to cause her to start, but enough to interrupt her thoughts.

'Room 2134,' she said plainly, not wishing to divulge even the slightest fragment of identity.

'Ah, Ms Charpin. We have a caller here who insists on speaking with you. She did not know your name or room number.'

Rebecca winced at the surname. Even her mother's married name was too close for comfort. 'Then why are you bothering me about it? Surely it is hotel policy not to connect strangers to rooms, and if they persist, call the authorities?' although Rebecca would not want them to carry out the second part.

'Of course ma'am, normally it is. However, the lady in question is most persistent. She claims to be someone you were supposed to be meeting at the D-port. After you met in Mexico last month you agreed to get together here in India, but she was late getting to the D-port, and was not sure you had seen her.'

Rebecca went cold. The woman had followed her. She had better speak with her, hear what she wanted, then run again. It took her a second to find her voice again. 'What name did she give you?'

'Chaudray. Sati Chaudray. Is there a problem Mrs. Charpin?'

Chaudray. There must be lakhs of people sharing that surname, both in India and across the wider world, but there had only been one person in Rebecca's life that shared that name. Commander Chaudray, first officer and second in command of the Vimana. *It couldn't be.* But what if it was? If the woman who had been pursuing her were indeed related to the officer from the Vimana mission she would have answers Rebecca needed. 'No, no problem. I was just remembering the good times,' she lied easily. 'Put her through please.'

'Certainly ma'am.' There was a small pause, then a click.

274

'Hello? Rebecca Eckhart?' The voice was fine and cultured. Gentle almost, giving little hint of the obvious determination behind it.

'Hello Ms Chaudray. It is Ms, isn't it?' The voice on the other end confirmed that it was. 'Are you really who you want me to believe you are?'

'Ha. I am. We need to talk. Can we meet in your room?'

'I'd rather meet somewhere public.'

'That would not be advisable. You are being followed. Or at least someone is watching you.'

Pramod, she guessed. It had not taken them long to re-locate her.

'A compromise then,' Sati suggested, sensing Rebecca's hesitation. Can you Displace to the lobby of the hotel across the street? It will take InSA a few minutes to interpolate the move from the weak field you'll leave behind in your room, and you can be back before they do.'

'No. I'd rather not indicate to them in any way that I am liaising with someone,' Rebecca lied, masking her inability to Displace. 'You had better come up.'

Sati sensed Rebecca was not being totally truthful with her. About what she was not sure. It could have been the depth to which she had got herself involved in this that was forcing the westerner to attempt deception, but Sati could not shift the niggling thought that perhaps it was something more, something deeper. 'Please turn off the privacy indicator in your room. And please stay on the line. It will give the enhancer a target to lock on to.'

'Enhancer? What enhancer?' Rebecca's curiosity at someone Displacing under personal direction got the upper hand over her caution.

'I am Displacing in from over twenty kilometres away,' Sati answered Rebecca. 'Far too far for a person to shift themselves safely in an area as densely populated as here. The enhancer software allows me to target my destination precisely. I do not wish to end up in the wrong room.' Sati left unvoiced her question as to how Rebecca did not know about how D-enhancers worked, but filed the knowledge.

Rebecca could not sense the area of the imminent Fold, so had to rely on the visual clues she had learnt to spot over a lifetime to detect Sati's arrival. There was a shimmering in the room, near the door, which filled with the shape of the Indian woman Rebecca had seen a handful of times already, only this time they were going to speak. This woman had followed her round the world. Rebecca supposed the least she could politely do was to meet her face to face.

Sati glanced round the room after she materialised. The first thing she did was not to greet Rebecca, or otherwise make herself known. Instead she ordered Rebecca to switch back on the privacy indicator. When Rebecca stood there unmoving, Sati apologised, and asked Rebecca if she would not mind re-enabling the Displacement suppressor. 'All five-star suites have one embedded in the room's privacy indicator. It is there to preserve the occupants' discretion. They have the effect of masking departure points, if the arrival point is camouflaged from prying eyes, and vice versa. Therefore I would prefer it if you were ensure the security of my home. It is perhaps the only safe place I have, and I wish it to remain inviolate,' she offered in the way of an explanation.

Rebecca acquiesced, and flicked the switch by the bedside. Sati relaxed visibly, an almost unconscious shift in her body language as if she had been relieved of a persistent headache, and thanked her guest. 'Please allow me to introduce myself properly,' she said. 'I am Sati Chaudray, niece to Pratheen Chaudray, of the first and only interstellar spacecraft the Vimana. I am grateful to you for this opportunity to meet you and talk. What I have to say will be of great interest to you, I trust.'

Rebecca felt a little awkward at the formality of Sati's introduction and the fact that she already knew who she was. Still, she reasoned, it would appear rude to introduce herself in any less a fashion. 'And I am Rebecca Eckhart, director of the InCh D-desk with Sinha MG, although I may not have that job any longer. I am currently investigating, as a private individual I might add, the events surrounding the mission on which your aunt served. Doubtless you have much I need to hear, but first can I offer you something to drink?' Rebecca struggled to remember what Damien had told her about longjump Displacement. 'Displacing large distances under your own direction can be tiring.' She hoped the lie sounded as if it came from experience.

Sati accepted Rebecca's offer with a request for a simple glass of water, as she sat in the armchair offered in the suite. Rebecca took up a position on the sofa situated opposite it.

'Why contact me now, after you've known about me for at least two months?' Now the formalities of the introductions were over, Rebecca was feeling less hospitable towards the woman. She had after all followed her back to her father's house. 'What do you want?' Rebecca did not add *from me* despite thinking it. She doubted Sati would answer totally honestly anyway.

'Let me start with telling you something more important than why. Let me tell you the what of what I know. You have suspicions that InSA is hiding something regarding the Vimana mission, but do not know what. The fact is the mission was a failure. Something happened to the crew. What I do not know, but I know the men and women that have been living as the former astronauts for the past twenty-five years are impostors. Charlatans, hiding behind stolen names and faces, pretending to be what they are not.'

What Sati said resonated with Pramod's words from right back at the beginning of all of this. His statement about the astronauts in the past tense. Rebecca was interested, but needed more information from this new and unexpected source. 'But why would InSA hide that? What could have happened on the Vimana to necessitate the masking of nearly a dozen individuals' identities? And why, if you know this have you not made this knowledge public? If true this would be huge. The largest scandal in history.'

'Precisely. In order to claim extraordinary truth one needs extraordinary proof. Unfortunately I do not have it.'

'What do you have then?' asked Rebecca, suddenly not so sure of Sati's credibility.

'I have what I know. The woman who returned from deep space was not my aunt. They replaced Pratheen with a double. Physically similar in every way, well drilled in her mannerisms and idiosyncrasies, but still not her.' Sati replied, convinced at least within herself.

'How can you be so sure? This was a long time ago. Pratheen died...' Rebecca reached for her notes, but before she could furnish herself with the data, Sati finished her sentence.

'She died twenty-five years ago, on the Vimana. The woman who replaced her died a little over fifteen years later.' Sati's reply was flat and emotionless. The certainty of the long years of knowing the truth obvious in her voice.

It was enough to at least convince Rebecca the Indian woman was sincere. She believed what she was telling her, and if she was right, it vindicated Rebecca's decision to follow this as far as she had. While that in itself did not excuse breaking the laws she had, she had at least been in pursuit of a larger truth. A retro-fitted justification did not undo the weight of her earlier decision, and would not garner her any leniency should she ever be arrested, but it satisfied her.

'OK, let's say for argument's sake that I believe you,' she said to Sati. 'How do you prove it? It's doubtful you've sat idle on this knowledge for twenty-five years waiting for someone to come along who can help. What have you been doing? You must be way ahead of me in this.'

Sati regarded Rebecca for a period. That she needed help was obvious, especially after her last liaison with Prakat, she was not sure how much time she had. But could she trust the westerner? It had been so long since she had trusted anyone with even a fragment of what she knew. But what choice did she have? Finally Sati spoke. 'I have been in close contact with one of the Brahman Group who also is a member of the Saazish within it. He has recently confirmed my suspicions. As you say however, proof is needed.'

'What? Wait. Sorry. What is the Brahman Group, and who are the Saazish?'

Sati suppressed a look that would have asked Rebecca what she did actually know, and instead told her the names of everyone she knew to be in the Brahman Group, explaining they were the people who guarded the secret, ensuring it stayed hidden. And of the Saazish and what little she had gleaned of the group-within-the-group from her covert surveillance of Prakat. Of her methods in garnering this information she stayed silent.

On hearing Pramod Surendran's name Rebecca gave a small snort. 'I should have guessed,' she said mainly to herself.

Sati continued. 'As for the proof you asked of, there is a shrine to the astronauts in the InSA museum. Where their ashes are held.'

'Ha, I saw it briefly when I was there.'

'I have devised a plan to obtain one of the urns. My aunt's. We can have them dated and it will give us the proof we need. I can do it alone, but with two it is many more times likely to prove successful.'

'Obtain? You mean steal. From the InSA museum?'
'Ha.'

'No.' replied Rebecca. 'It's illegal.'

'And how has that bothered you up to this point when

279

it has been your decision?'

Rebecca flinched, then collected herself. She had to be more careful around this woman, who knew almost as much about what she had done in the past two months as she did. She decided to change tack. 'But what good will the ashes from the woman who you claim replaced your aunt do? Surely all you'll obtain is the date the impostor died, which will tally with the official record.'

Sati smiled thinly, the sort of smile a parent would give a child when they asked an obvious question they could work out the answer to themselves. 'But they are not her ashes. They are my aunt's. The dates will be different. The Brahman Group may be hiding the world's largest secret, but they are not without propriety. It would be an act of disrespect to place another's remains where someone should rest.'

Rebecca's instinct said no, no and no. She had accrued enough unskilful karma recently and adding to it right now was not high on her list of priorities. 'I need to think about this,' was all she gave Sati.

'Do not take too long. It is a luxury you do not have. You can contact me here.' Sati handed Rebecca a business card. Rebecca had not seen one for years, and flipped it over a couple of times examining it, looking for any signs of an obvious nano-chip. Sati shook her head. 'I do not trust to keep my details in electronic form. Please do not copy that down anywhere,' she told Rebecca. 'If you have not contacted me within twenty-four hours I will be back in touch.'

Sati reached for something in the folds of her sari, a small egg-shaped blob of silvered metal, which she held to her chest, before asking Rebecca to disable the D-suppressor once more and allow her egress. She held the small device close to her, and in an instant was gone.

Twenty-seven

Arrangements

Saturday 1 July 2056 – 11:30 IST

Prakat Gupta was a man with two burdens of knowledge beyond the secret he had sworn to protect. One was easily divested, the other less so. It was his duty to divulge to the rest of the Saazish what he had learned from Ram. That their suspicions had been correct and the banker Eckhart had returned to India in pursuit of the truth they guarded. That the old man had lost track of her only added to the ease with which he could reveal the information and free himself from further responsibility around it. The second weighed more heavily upon him, occupying his every other thought on how to proceed.

He would need to be circumspect; he had no desire or intention to implicate himself in his involvement with Sati. But he could not have her at liberty. He would be unable to furnish too much detail regarding her to the Saazish. But he hoped he would be able to provide enough information for one of the others to act as his proxy against her. With any level of good fortune both she and the Eckhart woman would meet with an accident or other. The weight of population coupled with inadequate resources ensured the authorities were left wanting when considering aspects of public safety. It was still not unheard of for vehicle couplings to fail or random assaults to occur, especially to a tourist, or one like Sati.

Also, he had to maintain his cover with the old man. It could not appear as if it had been he who had been involved in any way.

'Open secure link Saazish. Code teen-ek-teen,' he said, the micro-SI in the earpiece recognising the phrase, then analysing both the timbre and modulation in the voice and the timing between the words while concurrently performing the pre-programmed dermal-contact DNA scan to confirm the identity of the words' speaker. Thirteen hundred kilometres away the earpiece worn twenty fours hours a day by the nominal leader of the Saazish, micro-vibrated in a burst of three then one then three, indicating an incoming comm from one of the group.

'Excuse me gentlemen,' said Professor Jindal, rising in apology from the table he was seated at, folding his napkin elegantly on the table as it fell from his lap, his patience with the silk betraying none of his internal anger. 'I am afraid I am required on another matter for a moment. I trust I will not be delayed long.'

Once safely ensconced in a privacy booth, his additional oral-suppression filter activated, he began his conversation. Obvious threats or repetition of the last group's stated indication at no further contact were pointless. Better to spend his energies confirming his suspicions as to who it would be who would soon be a problem no longer. 'Speak,' was all he would give.

'My apologies for breaking protocol. I have just returned from a meeting with the old man regarding the westerner. She is back here in India, undaunted. And he claims she slipped them at the D-port.'

Ajar Jindal concentrated on betraying little of what he

was thinking, which was a great many things. Instead he communicated back a simple 'I see,' waiting for the voice on the other side of the comm to provide more detail.

Prakat hesitated, unwilling to admit to his knowledge of Sati. The voice on the other side of the comm said nothing, but he could sense its mounting frustration. Eventually he blurted, 'Something else has also come to my attention. There appears to be a free agent operating also. A hi- a woman calling herself Sati. I do not know what she wants or if it is even her real name but she is interested in the Vimana.'

And I wonder how you know of her? thought Professor Jindal. 'Who else was at the gathering Ramkumar organised? Do you know why he did not convene a wider meeting?' he asked flatly.

Relieved at his seeming escape from suspicion of involvement with a prostitute, Prakat unthinkingly broke Saazish protocol once more and relayed the names of the others who had been present. He explained that Ram had informed them that too many of the Group were too distant or otherwise engaged, given the urgency of the situation.

This information, coupled with his knowledge of the locations of the other ten Brahman Group members allowed Professor Jindal to determine he was most likely speaking with Prakat. He was almost certain that Vinita was not one of their number, but was sure Narinder was. But the special advisor to the Prime Minister had always struck the Professor of Cognitive Research as a robust fellow, unlikely to show this weakness of character. Prakat however, having long suspected his involvement in their group-within-a-group, was a man likely to fail.

Never one to be at a disadvantage to any man, the Professor had, upon being invited to the Brahman Group, drawn up a psychological profile of the eleven others. Upon the emergence of the Saazish, it allowed him a reasonable idea as to who each of its other members were likely to be, based on their behaviours versus his assessment of each of them. If this was indeed Prakat he was communicating with, he certainly slotted neatly into Professor Jindal's pigeonhole of him.

Does the old man suspect us? He must. Therefore we must proceed as if he does, and that demands utmost caution. Like Ram, Ajar Jindal played a long, waiting game. In many ways he was the perfect Brahman Group member; methodical, meticulous, exacting and possessed of an almost zealous attitude to protecting the secret. And he was not without a plan, should Ram ever discover the extent of their behaviour.

'They must both be eliminated. Dispose of this Sati as you see fit; a failed robbery attempt, or an assault on her honour that turned violent.' The Professor was satisfied to leave Prakat to clean up the difficulties of his own making with as little assistance, and therefore involvement and culpability, from him as possible. 'As for the westerner, she is not your concern. Subtlety is called for. We cannot be seen to have any involvement in whatever fate befalls her. She will be located soon enough and dealt with.'

'What of the old man? I have already voiced my support for the actions he has taken so far in pursuing her. I plan to continue in such a fashion.'

'Ha, I think it best if you continue in that direction.'

Ajar Jindal broke the link knowing Prakat's course would most likely alert Ram to him as a source who was not one to be trusted, which suited his designs perfectly.

As soon as the connection cleared, Prakat opened another comm, this time to the instigator of the fire responsible for consuming Samir Kumarapad and his family. 'I have need of your services once more. There are two individuals present in Delhi who pose a direct threat to my work. You are to find them, and deal with them. I will furnish you with their identities, and if possible their locations. If at all possible they are to be processed separately, but I leave the execution of this task to you should circumstance dictate otherwise. Above all it is to look as accidental as possible. In no way is there to be a shred of suspicion around their final moments.'

The man on the other end of the comm listened to Prakat without replying, until the end of his instructions, which he acknowledged with a simple 'Ha'.

Twenty-eight

Interrogations

For several long hours after Sati had left, Rebecca variously sat on the bed, the armchair, the sofa and for a short period stood under the shower in the bathroom of her suite. She could not settle and prowled the large room constantly, measuring out as much of its perimeter as she could circumnavigate. Despite the suite's size it felt too small, and she felt trapped, by it, by circumstance; by the events she had set in motion with her persistence. She had unwittingly constructed a box around herself, one that felt far smaller than the rooms she paced relentlessly around, wearing out the same thin path in the deep pile.

Events had got beyond her, and she disliked not being in control of her own destiny. How could she regain the initiative? What could she do to put herself back on top of her situation? She had money, and a check of her assets attested her accounts had not yet been frozen; so there was scope there. What else did she have total control over? Not much. She knew too little, and the knowledge Sati had accumulated on the Vimana would be profound; but could she trust the Indian woman who had been following her and had appeared almost too conveniently when Rebecca seemed to need her most? *What did Sati want from the proof she sought, and what lengths would she go to to secure it?*

The bedside comm beeped again, for the second time that afternoon. *I haven't made my mind up yet!* Rebecca snatched up the handset, for voice only, intending to inform the reception desk to tell the caller she was unavailable and to hold all calls to her room until she directed otherwise. She got as far as saying her room number and was about to put her request to the clerk when the voice on the other end said, 'Ms Eckhart. You do not know how pleased I am to hear your voice.'

Dravid! Did the whole of India know where she was?

'Hello Pramod,' she said, guessing at the identity of her caller, and hoping to gain the upper hand in at least this situation.

'My apologies, but I am not Commissioner Surendran, even though I know of him. I can understand why you thought I might be him however.' Dravid sounded sincere, but then she could easily adopt a similar tone of voice at will as well.

'OK, if you're not going to tell me who you are then this conversation is over. I'm not jumping through hoops any more. Maybe it's time I dropped all this and handed myself and what evidence I have over to the authorities. Screw your secret,' she finished, half-bluffing. Part of her would walk away from this, the aggravation too much now, and leave the Vimana and the generation-old secret to grow another twenty-five years older. But a greater part of her needed to know. She just hoped she had not let this larger part show in her voice.

'And what do you think the Indian or any other authority would do with your evidence? It would never see anyone more senior than an administrative clerk in a data management department. It would most likely buy you your freedom from your earlier actions to be sure, perhaps even go some way to lifting a fraction of the weight your soul has accrued, but it would be wasted otherwise.'

Rebecca considered this; her bluff had been called, and she would have to back down, hating herself for doing so. 'Hmm, you've got me there,' she breezed, trying to sound nonchalant. 'If you don't think I should give up, what do you recommend?'

'You have spoken with Lakshmi Shukla I understand. There are two others remaining you should approach. Before they too pass.'

The inference was not lost on Rebecca. 'You mean Samir's death wasn't an accident? That Bhavin and Heera are in danger?'

'I am merely stating that if you wished to speak with either or both of them, then you will find them willing interviewees. I trust you have their true addresses?'

'Ha, I got your A-mail. I could have found them myself, I think. But thanks anyway. You saved me a few hours of searching. By the way, it was a smart trick sending them twice with different encryption methods. Nice spot of redundancy in your planning.'

Dravid seemed to pause. 'I am aware of no such duplication. It would appear someone else works in your favour. Perhaps the mystery woman you saw the last time we spoke?' he volunteered. 'Tell me, have you seen her again since? I would be very interested in making her acquaintance.'

'I'm sure you would be,' replied Rebecca, pointedly refusing to divulge any more. There was every likelihood that whoever Dravid was on the other of this comm, he had an SI monitoring her voice-stress; analysing what she said and how she said it, scanning for likely falsehoods. Much safer to stay non-committal, or only answer positively when she was confirming something Dravid said. 'Do you have any other advice for me, or shall I run off and do your bidding now?' She did not care if the sarcasm was either unwarranted or purely rude. She had had enough of being pushed around by other people for one day.

Dravid refused to rise to her provocation, replying she was free to pursue whichever path was of her choosing, advising her to weigh her choices. His accommodation was fine by her, Rebecca's hostility toward Dravid growing the more polite he was. It made it easier for her to conclude the conversation brusquely.

After replacing the handset Rebecca decided what she was going to do. Choosing one or the other of the offers she had been presented with meant following one of the prescribed paths, working to other's agendas. She saw how to create herself a third option; she would contrive to confound both sets of designs working externally to her by drawing them into each other, under her volition.

Instead of going along with Sati in the theft of the possible ashes of her aunt, she would take the Indian woman along with her when she went to interview Chief Bhavin Khatri and Ensign Heera Devar, which she hoped would have the effect of creating unease when they inevitably reported back the results of her interviews to Dravid.

Rebecca retrieved the contact details Sati had given her. Impressed by the SI driven security protecting the Indian woman, she told her of her intention to proceed with her interviews and the offer to accompany her tomorrow for the first of the two meetings that she hoped would lay the matter to rest.

> >

'He is lying.'

'Just let me check everything he said first will you?'

'Why? There is no need. I know he is not former Chief Petty Officer Bhavin Khatri. He cannot be, because they, like Pratheen, are all dead. He is an impostor.'

'Fine, but let me prove that either way. I at least need to fact-check everything he said.'

'But you do not need to. He is lying.'

Sati and Rebecca had been going through the same conversational circles for nearly thirty minutes now, Sati's constant need to seem to validate her perspective on the preceding interview with Chief Khatri slowing Rebecca's ability to verify the veracity of what he had said.

Remarkably, gaining access to Bhavin had been easy. Even after her conversation with the elusive Dravid, and his assurances that the remaining Vimana astronauts would be accommodating, Rebecca had expected more resistance, or the offer to be retracted the moment she stepped to his door with Sati in tow.

Rebecca reasoned she was almost certainly under at least two sets of surveillance, Dravid's seemingly benign matching of her movements, and the likely more hostile gaze of the probable assassin she assumed had been responsible for the fire that killed Samir. *Maybe their intentions would balance each other.* Rebecca had chosen not to inform Sati that by associating with her the Indian woman was almost certainly opening herself up to detailed scrutiny. She felt it provided some insurance against any treachery Sati may attempt.

And besides, the woman was surely astute enough to realise she was going to be the target of the interested parties who orbited the black hole at the centre of the story of the Vimana. All reliable information had so far been drawn into that void and crushed under the weight of the secret, whatever it was. Rebecca hoped she did not stray too close to the forces which seemed to rip apart the lives that touched it lacking adequate protection. It was Sati's interpretation of the interviews with Professor Shukla and Chief Bhavin she trusted would provide her that protection.

That was if Sati kept from distracting her for long

enough to check even a fraction of what he had told them both. She kept seizing on the minutiae of the interview, where he had paused when seeming to think about an answer, which Sati inevitably interpreted as him having to remember his cover story without considering the more likely possibility that, aged nearly sixty, and having travelled over fifteen light years, his faculties may not quite be what they once were. As far as Rebecca could tell, she was able to verify the bulk of what he had told them as true. There was the occasional slip or lapse from established fact, but, Rebecca argued this was perfectly normal, and one hundred percent concurrence to recorded history would have been more suspicious.

'But do you not see? This pattern is known to InSA and they have briefed Bhavin accordingly. He is giving you what you think you want, making you blind by being exactly what you expect him to be.'

'Bhagwan ke liye, Sati! Either he is an impostor telling us lies and his slips are proof of that, or he is an impostor telling us lies and any errors on his part are part of the greater cover up! Can you consider for even a second that he may actually be Chief Khatri?'

'No, I cannot.'

'Why the bloody hell not?'

Sati paused, unwilling to divulge something. She seemed to be thinking, considering telling Rebecca some greater part of her past, or perhaps more how to explain what she wanted to say. Impatient, Rebecca pressed her. If she was ever going to get any assistance from this woman she needed to know why she thought the way she did. 'Come on, there must be a reason. Otherwise you're just stubbornly ignoring what you don't want to see.'

Sati seemed to decide what she would tell Rebecca. 'If it will give you some perspective. The woman who left for the stars was not the woman who came back. Where once there had been an all consuming warmth of love, the feelings from her after her return were like that of moonlight; a colder, pale reflection of the sunlight that had once streamed from her.' Sati regarded Rebecca for a long moment, before adding, 'I am telling you this because I think you may understand what that kind of longing can be like. The waiting for the word that never comes. Imagine if-'

But that was as far as Sati got with the sentence Rebecca knew she was going to say. She cut the Indian woman off dead with an aggressive shake of her head and a sharp 'Don't!'. She was stunned. Whatever she had been expecting Sati to produce in the way of a defence for her opinion this was not it. And how the hell did she know that much about her? Sati's reference to her mother ripped right to her core. Rebecca fought to maintain her control, and her gaze burned at the woman standing in front of her.

'I am sorry, I meant no harm,' Sati said, seeing the antipathy directed at her. 'Please, I am sorry.' She moved to console Rebecca, to put an arm round her in a gesture of reconciliation, but Rebecca recoiled so violently at the touch that Sati withdrew. 'I will leave you be for the moment.'

Sati Displaced out of the room almost before Rebecca could react to what she had said. She did not want the Indian woman, now her partner in all of this, to leave. There was little danger of her losing control again, it was the mention of her mother in connection to Sati's own past coming from nowhere, and she had not been prepared for it. Now she had lost Sati, at least for a while, not knowing how to follow her by sensing the trace a Fold left.

Remembering what Sati had told her about the capability to extrapolate a Displacement destination from the source point residual, Rebecca got up and flicked the privacy switch, scrambling the Indian woman's origin point. She did not want to risk Sati's safety, her feelings toward the infuriating but fascinating woman softening enough for her to care about her welfare as more than just a matter of her own security.

Of course, she would have to comm her, and apologise for her behaviour. She knew she would need to leave a period of time before attempting reconciliation with Sati once more. Too soon would look like she had not been affected, too long like she did not care. An hour or two should suffice she reasoned. For now though, she had to verify the details Bhavin Khatri had provided. That would easily absorb the necessary time.

'The other woman has just left. The westerner is still sitting at her desk, she does not seem to be making any effort to follow her accomplice.'

'Forget the outsider. We need to know where the *chuchi* has gone.'

The man who had been watching and following Rebecca and Sati since they had left Chief Petty Officer Khatri's residence poked at the air in front of him, activating virtual controls for the device he had pointed at Rebecca's hotel room. In the three days since he had been surveilling the westerner and her new ally he had so far failed to locate the Indian woman's residence, or at least the point she Displaced to and from. If he thought it strange his controller had him focus his energies on locating the Indian woman over maintaining full coverage of the intruder then he did not voice them. He kept his thoughts and opinions on his orders to himself.

His best effort to determine Sati's base of operations so far had yielded seven areas, each almost three square kilometres in size containing approximately twenty-seven thousand individual residences; he knew the woman had powerful SI capabilities installed wherever she arrived to, because every time she was there, wherever it was, the signal vanished from his screens. Like pursuing a Chir Batti, the harder he scanned for the source the further away he seemed to get. And that number of residences was far too many for a manual search, even with the resources his employer had at his disposal. There could be no evidence or even the suspicion of external involvement, leaving the man and his master having to wait for one of them, most likely the westerner, to slip, and then they would have her.

He flicked his eyes over the scanner as it extrapolated the likely destinations from the ripples in the Cotts field Sati's departure had left; predicting with increasing levels of probability between the probable end points of her Displacement.

Near...

The algorithms analysing the Indian woman's origin point discounted one of the seven areas.

Nearer...

Another possible destination dropped to below ten percent, while the remaining five all jumped up by a handful of points.

Nearly...

Two more projected targets fell into the low-teens, making them unlikely candidates.

Soon he would have her.

Then the remaining three locations showed zero; the curves their probability trajectories had been tracing on his display plummeting to the bottom of the y-axis and flatlining there.

What..?

The man backgrounded the virtual screen in front of him and glared through the shuttered window which overlooked Rebecca's curtained room, before he remembered himself and pulled up an infrared overlay of the westerner's suite. She had risen and activated the room's privacy function.

He engaged the comm to his master. 'We did not get an accurate location again,' he said. 'However-'

His handler cut him off with an expletive before calming himself. 'You are wasting my time with this endeavour. It is obvious that a change of strategy is required. There are other weaknesses in this pair. Find them and use them.'

The comm went dead leaving the man with little confusion as to how to proceed.

Twenty-nine

Background Checks

Sunday 2 July 2056 – 09:00 IST

Sati listened patiently and politely this time as Rebecca haltingly outlined what she had managed to verify, and, more importantly it seemed to the Indian woman, what she had managed to disprove in Bhavin Khatri's narrative recollection of his time in training for, then undertaking the Vimana's mission.

Rebecca had been surprised by Socrates when he had alerted her to her scheduled appointment with the Indian woman, a little over thirty minutes ago. She had stared at the time displayed in her screens, disbelieving the numbers. She had not spent the preceding three hours on assembling the material she had uncovered as planned, instead researching something else entirely. Now the Indian woman would be arriving in a little over a minute. Panicking, she had Socrates archive the material on display in front of her, securing it in a brand new datacrypt whose location was known only to him. The haste in ensuring Sati gleaned no suspicion she had been engaged in another topic meant Rebecca had had little time to prepare herself mentally for the Indian woman. Taking a deep breath she tried to collect herself.

Rebecca reached the end of her findings with Sati sitting implacably still throughout her whole monologue. To Rebecca, while there seemed to be a level of ambiguity in particular segments, none of them taken individually, or collectively, equated definitive proof of any mendacity on Chief Khatri's part.

'Well?' The single word an interrogative as much as a question of her opinion.

Sati regarded her host for a moment. 'Are you sure you wish to hear my thoughts?' she replied.

'I thought that was the whole point of the last six hours of my life.' Rebecca struggled to keep her tone even.

If Sati noticed the stress she ignored it. 'Very well. I would ask you to re-play the eleven minutes where he talks about Pratheen. I can use it to best illustrate my thoughts.'

Rebecca had Socrates scroll back to the segment Sati had requested. Bhavin Khatri's voice filled the room again with the transcript scrolling up both women's lens-screens, Rebecca's in English, Sati's in Malayalam. He began to describe the time Pratheen had the Devas spend in simulated weightlessness, training their bodies to function in zero-g. After only a few seconds Sati stopped the recording to point out an inaccuracy with her own understanding of events. Rebecca let it go and resumed the playback. Barely a minute further in and Sati jumped on another perceived lapse, pausing the replay.

'Can we try to go more than ten seconds without finding a fault, please?'

'You asked me for my opinion. That is what I am furnishing you with.'

'Fine. Sorry. Socrates, resume playback please.'

The delicate tones of the elderly Indian man began once more. Whether Sati found no further issue with Chief Khatri's testimony or she were holding her tongue Rebecca could not be sure of, but whichever it was it allowed her the opportunity to try to restore her equilibrium.

Now, as she listened to the former Vimana officer's gentle voice, she found herself calming down as much as she could allow herself to. As the interview transcript played before both of them she had the opportunity to observe Sati up close for the first time, and watch her reactions.

Unsure whether she was her projecting her own personality onto Sati, Rebecca was almost certain the Indian woman seemed to soften, ever so slightly, when she listened to Bhavin describing her aunt. The focussed, directed concentration always so evident on her face fell away at the edges of her eyes and mouth, as if the words, triggering some unbidden memory of Pratheen, caused her niece to smile for the briefest flash of a second; a gesture that someone other than Rebecca perhaps would miss, so swiftly was it suppressed.

Whatever it was, Sati proceeded to listen intently as Chief Khatri described everything involved in his role as one of the Vimana's Devas; the half dozen men and women who provided the ship with the heart of its power, and who were the responsibility of the First Officer. Sati sat rapt at the descriptions of his daily routine under the tutelage and oversight of the person he referred to as her aunt; the constant training she demanded of them, drilling and re-drilling them in the emergency procedures, ensuring they knew every cubic centimetre of the ship as if they had been born into it. She would test them, both blindfolded and in total darkness in the replica Vimana they practised in until she was satisfied they could, if necessary, navigate the Deva bay, plug themselves in and activate the D-drive even if they lost both eyes.

'Not mine,' said the voice on the recording when Rebecca had questioned the Chief's choice of words. 'Anything was possible when the human body was put under that much strain, and she needed us to be prepared for it,' he explained.

After the recording had finished for the second time, with Rebecca now also beginning to have learnt part of it rote, if that was how Bhavin had been briefed as Sati maintained, she had Socrates turn it off. She spoke to Sati. 'I concede there are areas of uncertainty, but nothing too out of the ordinary, and nothing that cannot be ascribed to the length of time since the events.'

'That was just like her,' Sati said.

Rebecca, eyeing her companion, said nothing in reply.

'Making sure they were ready for whatever the mission could throw at them. She prepared them the way she equipped me for life. She was fiercely driven, always demanding more from herself and everyone around her. She should have been Captain.'

'So that helps prove him to be genuine? The way he spoke of your aunt was of someone he knew, surely?'

Sati shook her head instinctively. 'No, there was nothing there that he could not have learnt from training briefings, manuals or archive material. He merely reinforces what we already know. He says very little that implicates himself while turning the question round. Look, here.' She pulled at the air in front of her, scrolling back through the transcript until she reached the point she had in mind.

Rebecca was forced to admit that in that particular instance, Bhavin had partly avoided the question, but continued to attest it could be down to his embarrassment at failing memory. Sati went on to highlight another half dozen instances where he sidestepped or answered the question he wanted to have been asked, rather than the one put to him.

By the end of this cross-examination Rebecca was feeling sore, her capability being questioned, seemingly harder than she had pressed her last interview subject. 'He was hardly on trial,' she defended herself angrily. 'I attempted to treat him with the courtesy one would accord a stately elder. After all if he were Chief Petty Officer Khatri then he has been to the stars and back. Do you not think that warrants your utmost respect, or is that too much to give him?'

'I am not questioning your ability, or the manner of your interview. I am calling his answers to account that is all. There are too many instances where he evades you. You must see that?'

'Why do you cling to the idea that he's lying? He could easily just be misremembering.'

Sati turned Rebecca's question back on her. 'Why do you refuse to accept the possibility that he is? What difference does it make to you? I would have thought knowing the secret at the heart of Vimana's flight would make you the most influential analyst on earth? All we need is the physical proof.'

Rebecca thought about her job. It felt so long ago. Was it still there to go back to even if she abandoned this quest right now? 'Originally when I chanced on the discrepancy that set me on this course I wanted nothing more than to get to the truth; that professional pride. But since then I've...' Rebecca paused searching for a way to describe her encounter with Becky without revealing even the smallest part of it to Sati, '...seen things that have made me re-evaluate what the Vimana meant to me,' she said, choosing her words carefully. 'And to everyone else who was a kid at the time I guess.' She added the caveat after a moment's thought, re-establishing the mental distance between herself and her childhood, unwilling to connect herself to the Vimana for longer than she had to.

'Better they believe in a lie, than face the harder truth then?'

'Yes. No.' Then after a moment's consideration, 'I mean, sometimes I think we can uncover too much truth.'

'About ourselves or the outside world? They are

different things, and unmasking one should not affect the other, unless we let it. You can discover the truth about the Vimana without losing what you are holding on to. Proving or not what happened on the ship does not invalidate the investment you put into it.'

Rebecca gave a half laugh.

'What?' asked Sati.

'You sound like a mother giving advice to her daughter.'

<

Rebecca sat on the sofa in her hotel suite, edgy and unsettled, unsure whether to get fully dressed. She had been awake already for two hours, and Sati was not scheduled to arrive for another three. Their reunion had been arranged once Rebecca had verified or otherwise the majority of Chief Khatri's story. Now she had her evidence, she had a lot of time to kill between what she hoped would be a reconciliation between herself and the Indian woman; Rebecca badly needed her help if she was going to spend any of the remainder of her adult life at liberty.

The knowledge she was under constant covert surveillance was having a disquieting effect on her psyche. Part of her wanted to flout its presence and go somewhere completely unexpected and let them try to work out why she was visiting shrines to Ganesha or the branch of *Idli's!* across from the hotel; just to screw with them, not even a deliberate effort to shake the prying eyes. She knew that given the knowledge she was in India, both sets of voyeurs were likely capable of tracking her wherever she went in their country.

Another part of her cautioned her that this was probably unwise. Remaining in the hotel she was safe, or at least she had been so far. She need not let anyone she did not wish to meet into the suite, and, after confirming Sati's

301

explanation, the Cotts field suppressor she had mentioned ensured her physical security in the short term, at least from unwarranted intrusions. There was little she could do about the remote viewing she suspected was occurring.

After learning of the surveillance and coming to the logical conclusion as to its level of intimacy, Rebecca had been satisfyingly pleased with herself at her reaction to it. She had not shrunk back from the likelihood that whatever cameras were directed at her room could easily see through the closed blinds, and most likely through the walls themselves. Rebecca still showered and bathed, unconcerned that someone may be watching. She even continued to masturbate occasionally, gaining a kick from the knowledge that she was probably putting on a show for whoever they had watching her at the time, and hopefully even unsettling their masters a little.

In fact that was a great idea. She was agitated, and a good orgasm gained at the expense of someone else's once-removed discomfort would relax her. She rose from the sofa and removed the hotel silk dressing gown, folding it carefully on the shelf, alerting whoever may have been observing that it was time to start their furtive recording. She had got as far as laying herself on the bed, fingers poised ready when the bedside comm chimed.

Typical.

She considered ignoring it, but the almost Pavlovian response to the incessant, demanding noise was hardwired into her, forcing her to answer. She craned a free hand to the device and flicked it onto handsfree. Just because she was talking did not mean she could not still get herself going. She intended to make the call brief, whoever it was. She felt the urgency underneath the need to come, looking forward to the flush of endorphins released by her body in response to her ministrations.

'Yeah, hello whoever is watching. I hope you've got a few exabytes free, I may take my time this time.' She addressed the empty room almost derisively. Let the gaandus put up with her for once.

'Ms Eckhart. I am not sure exactly what you are referring to.' It was Dravid.

'Oh, hello Dravid,' she replied matter-of-factly. 'You know, would you mind if I call you Pramod? It will help me if I can imagine it's his face and body on the other end of the line.'

There was a pause. 'Whatever you are doing, and I am old enough to hazard a reasonable guess, I would much rather prefer it if you ceased. I find the notion of conversing in this fashion distasteful.'

'Well then, you should not be snooping on me twenty-four hours a day if you don't want to see me shitting, pissing and frigging myself.' Rebecca deliberately chose the crudest terms for bodily functions she could bring to mind. People who would seemingly kill deserved no protection from her excretions.

'I can assure you we are in no way engaged in the kind of surveillance you assume,' replied Dravid, as measured as ever. If her vulgarities had any effect he was not letting on.

'And I'm supposed to believe that? Convenient that you rang just as I was about to do something 'distasteful' eh?'

'Ah, now there you have us. While we are not directly observing you, we are watching the people who are watching you in the way you imagine. Our part in this is simple overseer. Our observations indicated a degree of activity in their control room approximately sixteen seconds ago. What sort we were not sure, but I thought it prudent to contact you. It is now obvious what caused their excitement.' Dravid paused for a moment before continuing. 'Tell me one thing. What do you expect to gain from such a show?'

Rebecca paused the slow rotation of her middle fingers. She had not expected to be quizzed on the merits of masturbation, especially by one of the people behind the conspiracy she seemed to have found herself in. She laughed out at the notion. 'You know, I hadn't really thought it through fully. I wanted to fight back in some way, and this seemed as good a way as any. Let you, or rather not you, but the others, them, know that they hadn't got to me so much that I couldn't find time for some pleasure. Or something like that anyway.' She withdrew her hand from her underwear. 'You know, you've put me off now.'

'Am I to take it then that I have your full attention?'

'Ha, I guess you have.' If it had been Dravid's intention to ensure Rebecca ceased her actions he had succeeded. She could not fully place it, but for some reason talking with Dravid was like speaking with her dad. Perhaps it was the way he chose to phrase his sentences, because there was nothing in the tone or cadence of his voice, masked as it was, that gave his likely age away. Either way, she found it hard to continue her intended course, so reluctantly, rose from the bed and began to dress once more, speaking as she did so. 'So, aside from knowing when whoever else is watching me when I'm enjoying myself, what else do you know?'

'I know that you have been speaking with Sati Chaudray. What about I can guess. I felt it prudent to inform you as to the nature of the company you keep.'

'Mm-hmm, and what sort of company would that be?' Rebecca answered as non-commitally as she could, ignoring Dravid's subtle cues to prompt her for more information.

'Has she told you of her past?'

'Enough of it, yes.'

'What of her criminal record? She has been arrested, charged and imprisoned on three separate occasions for fraud and deception, serving a total of eight years to date. Very much larger offences than your illegally assisted entry into my country. I would urge caution around her.'

Rebecca had not expected this, that Sati be a convicted criminal. But she was hardly in a position to pass judgement on someone's past misdemeanours. 'I won't say you haven't surprised me there, but I've only got your word for that right now. It sounds to me like she's someone you should be scared of, not me.'

'I have nothing to fear from Sati Chaudray. Her position does not excuse the karmic weight she has accrued in this life. If it is proof you need I can furnish you with it. Allow me to send you the available records.'

'Nice try, Dravid, but I'm not going to give you the smallest electronic access to my life. Not even a free, anonymous drop box. I'll do my own research thanks.'

'In that case I feel I must caution you against searching too deeply in A-space. While I am aware of Ms Chaudray's history there are others who are not. The men watching you now for instance. I can categorically state that the person who directs them, while aware of the identity of the other person in your vicinity, has no clue as to who she truly is. Look too intently and you will alert them as to who your ally in this is. And that places her in peril.'

'I thought she was a criminal, not to be trusted?'

'She is, but she is human also, and as such is as one with the universe as I myself. I would see her harmed no more than I would injure myself. Or yourself.'

'Well, that's nice to know, but you'll understand if I decline your offer. I'm a big girl and can look after myself.'

Rebecca thought about what Dravid had told her about Sati. It was almost certainly true, given the records should exist somewhere. Something like a criminal conviction would be too large and difficult to fake conclusively, too many official documents would have needed altering or creating from scratch for it to be feasible as a fictitious smear. Still, the pragmatist in her made her want to check the validity of what she had been told, for what it might be worth.

But what puzzled her most was why Dravid had alerted her to Sati's incomplete disclosure of her past. While Rebecca had not told Sati everything about her life and had for her part assumed there were aspects to Sati's past that she would not want her as an outsider, and westerner to know about, she still felt slighted that Sati had omitted something on the scale of a criminal conviction, which now to Rebecca mattered not one bit. What was Dravid's advantage to his revelation? There had to be one, otherwise he would not have mentioned it. The forcing of her to mistrust her one ally? Or perhaps it was a bluff and he gained from the fastness their joint fugitive status would bring to them. She could not decide. Was it beyond him to be double or even triple-bluffing her? Rebecca could see no benefit to Dravid from any perspective. *So, stop worrying about it, because there's nothing you can do to change it.*

There was little more to do than verify what she had been told, despite being almost certain it was true. She could try and fathom Dravid's motives later. Her concern now was the veracity of his claim.

She instructed Socrates boot up the heavily customised single-runtime copy of himself she had had prepared from a fraction of the tens of crore lying in her account. If it was as good as it was supposed to be, it provided its user with a wide variety of mechanisms for moving around A-space which were near undetectable; electronic safe and bluff-houses, embedded ghostware, fractal link spamming, self-inflicted DDOS attacks and a handful of other techniques Rebecca barely understood. All adding up to effectively masking her trail to crores of dead-ends it would take a metropolitan SI a week to decipher.

Technology that so completely masked an SI's presence was usually beyond the means of regular consumers; even Rebecca's salary and bonuses at the bank would have been unable to cover the cost, regardless how much she may have coveted the A-tech. She had only ever seen it demoed, and had little option but to accept what she had been told as to its effectiveness. Taking no chances however, she would task Socrates with mimicking the copy as best he could while she searched. Assuming the people Dravid had mentioned were monitoring the traffic along his encrypted link, she was confident all they would see were the failed access attempts and weak-force cracking attacks of a personal SI, while the real action took place elsewhere.

Inserting the bespoke lens-screens, she pulled on the thin filament-threaded interaction gloves as the obfuscator agent code booted on the display hanging a metre in front of her. She had been told the basics of how it worked; using any spare cycles it could find on both local and wider networks, handling by gigtupling back across the same paths, heading down crores of dead-ends it found, sending itself and part of its incomplete payload into countless electronic black holes. It was inefficient, but that was its secret; by being so wasteful in its resource allocation algorithms it splashed itself at random out across the entirety of the cloud, making it nearly impossible to reconstruct even a fraction of its activity.

Not that any of this mattered to Rebecca; she had her instructions on what to set, and what was normal operating procedure when using the obfuscator. A small spiky polyhedral gauge sat rotating calmly in the lower right corner of her vision, indicating relative percentage of data occlusion, the default of anything below eighty-five causing the indicator to increase its spin and the facets to pulse amber instead of their usual relaxed green. Taking no chances Rebecca pushed the cut off threshold to its theoretical maximum of ninety-nine. This forced the indicator to resemble a sea-urchin in response to its increased complexity; so it would be slow, but she had the time.

As soon as she made her first gesture to open a terminal

and browse the Indian public records, the display seized up, locking her out. It steadfastly ignored, or was unable to respond to the flicks of her hands or her pointing fingers, which grew increasingly frustrated for a handful of seconds, the gentle gesticulations replaced with angry stabs at the empty air.

'Dammit! Socrates, what has happened please?' she asked, addressing her SI who had been watching his little brother while he delved. 'I've only been on a second, they can't have found me already. Nothing's that good.'

As suddenly as it had frozen, the obfuscator seemed to recover, everything seeming to be running normally again. Except now the indicator was no longer the hard-edged, aggressive star form that Rebecca had forced upon it, but instead had become a perfect, hot-pink sphere.

Rebecca sneered at the hue. Cautious, she tried an exploratory search, something awkward, but legal, that would test the obfuscator. The gauge did not even flicker, let alone seem to diminish, and it resolutely did not change colour.

'Socrates, run a system analysis please. Check the barriers if you can. Thanks.'

The SI whirred for a moment as it spawned a copy of itself and threaded it through the core systems and the security devices running in its sibling. The copy returned to its parent, who analysed its child before destroying it. 'Ms Eckhart. Everything is, as far as I am able to determine functioning correctly. I have examined every bit of available memory, unthreaded every running process and put each component through the upper limit threshold test and everything is exactly as it should be. The only discrepancy is the barrier program itself. Aside from the odd colouration it has been, what I can only describe as, upgraded.'

'Upgraded? But it's state of the art.'

'That is the only explanation I can realistically come to,

given the evidence presented to me. Part of my diagnostics are to interrogate the barrier's algorithms, which are all as they should be, but they have been changed. Additionally, the occlusion parameters are far more sophisticated and elegant than I was expecting. Everything about it has been made better somehow. The best word I can think of is sleek. Where it was once brute force, it is now refined. I had some trouble convincing it I was genuine and the SI it had been modelled on, and not a Turing bot. It has become cleverer.'

'Can it still be trusted?'

There was a pause, as if Socrates were formulating an answer. 'Oh yes,' replied the SI with something approaching genuine admiration in its voice.

Thirty

Confessions

'Where the hell have you been? I haven't heard from you in over a month. And the leave you took finished three weeks ago. You're being formally terminated in your absence for gross professional misconduct. You need to come back to London immediately if you want to rescue what's left of your career here. Jesus, Rebecca, are you alright?'

Rebecca could possibly forgive Marcia for opening her side of the conversation she had started with a 'Hi Marcia, I know I've not been around for a while,' which was as far as she had got before Marcia launched into her tirade. And it was nice that she did finally get round to asking if she was OK.

'Ha, I'm fine.'

'Where are you? I've been worried.'

Rebecca looked at Sati, who shook her head. Their side of the conversation was on speaker. Rebecca disliked misleading her former boss by not doing her the courtesy of telling her there was someone else listening in on her side, but then these were not normal times for her, and the less

Marcia knew the safer she would be.

'Thanks for your concern,' Rebecca replied, side-stepping the first part of the question. 'I've been doing some more digging on the Vimana, and I've got to tell you-'

Marcia cut across Rebecca. 'Sounds intriguing. Do you have it written up?'

'Uh, partly. Do you want me to-'

'No, don't bother with that, it's too slow. Just have Socrates send Telford what you've got and I'll go over it here. Try and put some mitigating circumstances to the tribunal board on your behalf.'

Rebecca flicked her eyes up from the speaker to Sati, who quizzed her with her expression, before looking back at the phone. 'Yeah, sure. Let me collate them together so they're in some sort of order; you know me, terrible at organising my notes.'

Marcia gave a laugh. 'Sure thing. I'll wait for them to arrive with Telford.'

'Cool, I'll comm you again in an hour when you've had a chance to go through them.'

'Great, speak to you then. And be careful.'

'Will do, boss.' Rebecca disconnected the comm.

< <

'So you've never been able to Displace, ever since you can remember?'

Rebecca remained silent and unmoving as she lay on Sati's bed, her right arm, which felt broken and was already beginning to swell under its dressing, held close to her chest, protected and protective. She held her thoughts closer. The Indian woman sat opposite in the armchair she kept in her bedroom, her own injured leg supported on a makeshift rest. Sati assured Rebecca that whoever, if anyone, had been following them or was responsible for the riot had been evaded, and they were safe here. She was perfectly safe here.

Rebecca could not remember much after she had been struck, not even the pain she must have felt as the lathi splintered across her forearm as she had raised it to protect her face. Perhaps it was the trauma, or some after-effect of being pulled involuntarily through D-space. She assumed Sati had Displaced the pair of them out, despite the damage to her ankle.

Rebecca could recall, with absolute clarity, the events leading up to their accidental involvement in a water-rationing riot, then the unprovoked attack by the private security force charged with policing the demonstration, because she had been the direct cause of them. Her continued refusal to accede to Sati's plan to steal Pratheen's remains had led her to attempt an interview with the final surviving crew member, which had meant abandoning the security of the hotel suite. They had not been on the street five minutes when they were engulfed in the privately policed demonstration, which seemed to materialise from nowhere, and which swept them away from their intended destination.

Rebecca could sense the mood of the crowd. Restless, frustrated, righteous. A dangerous combination. Within seconds the crowd decided, either through some pre-arranged signal, or perhaps via an unconscious herd-instinct to begin smashing things.

All around the two women, holding on to and keeping each other upright lest they be trampled underfoot, a chaos erupted, them its calm eye. The first stone to strike one of the security was all it took. They waded in, lathis flashing across the backs of legs, spines and necks, the guards manhandling and D-piggybacking protesters out.

Rebecca heard a sound behind her and turned. She saw the arm holding the long stick pull back. No time to shout a warning to Sati, she pulled the Indian woman out of the way, tipping her heavily to the ground but removing her from the approaching blow. Instinct kicked in, Rebecca's reflexes taking charge. Her free arm flashed in front of her face as the lathi slewed into it, the splintering of the hardened bamboo joined by the shattering of her ulna. The force of impact knocked her off her feet and on top of Sati.

Then nothing.

The next thing Rebecca could recall was waking up on a bed, her arm throbbing as Sati applied a makeshift cast to it.

When the Indian woman had finished she left Rebecca, limping from the bedroom to clean herself up, before returning a short while later and taking up her position on the seat she still occupied. Together the women sat in silence for over an hour, until Sati mustered the courage to ask Rebecca the question she had suspected she already knew the answer to.

'When did you realise? It must have been an awful thing to discover about yourself. Childhood is ...difficult enough without being too different.' Sati raised herself and came to kneel next to Rebecca's prone form, coaxing the westerner's broken wing with gentle reassurance. Rebecca barely moved, hardly flinching this time at the uninvited physical contact from another human being. Her only visible reaction to the pain the touch caused being her eyes flicking quickly, from the middle distance past her feet, to look briefly into Sati's eyes before falling back once more.

Almost before Rebecca realised the feeling, it found voice on her lips, pushed out through teeth ground into each other. Her mouth barely moved as she whispered a single word.

'Cripple.'

Sati intuited what Rebecca had meant, but did not presume to pass comment now her companion had finally said something. After over an hour of them sitting here, cup after cup of tea going cold in front of her, Sati held her counsel. If she was going to draw the woman from the catalepsy where her guilt at the danger she had placed them

313

in had caused her to retreat to, she needed to connect on a level the westerner could understand, even empathise with. If she got this wrong, it would be all over. Rebecca would never trust her, and there was too much at stake now for that. She had to win the rigidly controlled woman over with honesty, understanding and openness. So now she knew the damage which had bent the woman out of shape, and which she had been carrying around with her her whole life. She could not push too hard too quickly at any particular door for fear of Rebecca slamming it shut in her face and it never opening again.

She would have to tell her.

Sati replaced Rebecca's arm across her chest once more and retreated to the chair again. Rebecca stayed immobile. 'I am not going to give you platitudes by saying children are cruel. You know they are. We both know they are. You are not alone in a childhood spent hiding the truth of yourself from the sneering of others. I know what it feels like to be different too.'

Rebecca frowned almost imperceptibly but Sati saw it. She continued. 'We all have secrets, some more dangerous to ourselves than others.'

On the bed Rebecca turned her head towards the Indian woman, echoing her words. 'Secrets.'

'There were aspects of me which I needed to hide as a child, and other aspects I now need to hide as an adult.'

'I don't...'

'It is easier if I show you.'

Sati stood, and turned her back to Rebecca. She untied the lower part of her sari and turned around, for a second only, showing Rebecca the penis she had, before sweeping the cotton material back over it once more,

'You were a boy?' Rebecca said slowly, comprehension of Sati's childhood forming as she spoke.

Sati sat down once more, this time on the bed next to Rebecca. She held the westerner's good hand, which despite the air-con keeping the room at a comfortable twenty-three, was icy cold.

'Only Pratheen understood. My father threw me out onto the street when I was eleven. He found me dressing in my mother's clothes...' She paused. If she was to win Rebecca's trust she had to tell it all. Her voice had no strength in it as she continued. 'But not before he... raped me, and had his friends do the same. I ran to my aunt and told her everything. She cleaned up my snot, blood and tears, and took me in. The next morning, with me safely tucked in her spare bed, she spoke to my father, her own brother, and told him I was no longer to be his son, but by my own request, her daughter. He knew enough of her not to argue. Anyway, his guilt made him compliant. He would have agreed to almost anything rather than be exposed.'

'Using her position she had the necessary documentation altered and created in secret, so only we would know. From that point on I was raised as a girl. I chose my own name, my own clothes, everything. Pratheen did all she could to protect me, and to teach me. How to survive, how to act, how to talk, how to walk. How to hide. And then she was chosen for the Vimana. I was so proud of her. She had saved my life and was now going to fly to the stars.'

'But then she came back, and she was different. She said all the same things, called me daughter, and Priya, but the way she said them was different. It was like she thought I had always been a girl. You asked me how I was so sure the woman who came back wasn't my aunt. That is how I know. Only we knew the truth about me.'

Rebecca began to say something, opening her mouth in readiness to speak, but no words emerged. She closed her mouth again, seemingly having changed her mind about whatever it was she was about to have said to Sati. The conflict within her was obvious; her rigid body shaking from the self-control her will was imposing on it. If it was anger or sorrow Sati could not be sure. Then in a quiet voice she spoke.

'I didn't want it to be a failure, not after everything I put into it as a kid. It was the one thing I needed her to be interested in, the one thing I hoped would win me some love. But it wasn't, and it didn't. I don't want everything of myself I poured into it when I was eight to be for nothing.'

To Sati it was as if Rebecca had confessed her deepest sin, and had unburdened herself from the weight of it. She watched as the woman Rebecca resumed full control, using her damaged hand to smear away the single tear which had begun to escape from her eye. The transformation was profound. Barely seconds ago Sati had chipped through the decades old armour, the carapace Rebecca had grown around the little girl she had once been and never truly abandoned. But now it was back, fully restored, and the adult Rebecca was in full control.

Rebecca half-laughed, coughing at the strain in her chest as she did so. Sati moved to comfort her, but Rebecca dismissed it with a small shake of her head, indicating she was fine. 'My Dad offered to take me to training. He found classes that taught the skills most kids had picked up by the time they were toddling. They were five and six year olds. I was eleven. God bless him, he thought he was doing the right thing.'

Sati dared one word, her biggest gamble. 'Cripples?'

Rebecca smiled grimly, a cruel and hard smile that spoke of the long years of pain. 'You got it.'

Sati sensed this particular conversation was over.

>

The man checked the overlay of the city that hung a metre in front of his view, the building ahead bathed in green highlight, as the others either side of it fell away into the background in shades of grey. She was here. He

316

reached into his pocket, checking the weapons he had about his person were still in place. Everything was where it should be. He ducked into small passageway that separated his destination from the next building.

The display shifted and changed into a 3D wireframe as he stood staring up to the fourteenth floor. The schematic of the building zoomed in on the room he needed, and aligned his Displacement trajectory there.

In a second he was standing in Marcia Weston's office, just as she opened the door to it.

> >

'They've got to Marcia,' was all Rebecca could say after she had finished the call with her boss. 'If they hurt her...' The threat was purely instinctive. If whoever had compromised Marcia did actually inflict physical violence on her, there was little Rebecca could do to revenge herself.

'They will not. She is an outsider in this. Why are you certain she was acting under duress?'

'Her request for an electronic copy of my notes. Marcia never asks for anything as softcopy. She likes to read proofs from a printout. She calls it old fashioned, I've always called it living in the past; a relic. Until now. Seems to have proved very useful though.'

'Do you accept now that something is being hidden from you, from everyone? Marcia's intimidation is just another facet of the whole that has been removed from the sight of the world. Let me help you prove it. Once we have the physical evidence I know exists no one will be able to gainsay us.'

Rebecca was still uneasy about Sati's plan to steal her aunt's ashes from the InSA shrine, even though she had given the matter a great deal of thought. The body of circumstantial evidence she had amassed was impressive, but hardly conclusive. There was no single item in the collection that pointed to the cover up that Sati was convinced had occurred. She had had Socrates slice and dice the data every possible way trying to unearth discrepancies and falsehoods in the surviving astronauts' accounts. An effort to avoid having to consider the possibility of committing further crimes in the pursuit of the truth. And the nature of what Sati was proposing made her balk also. Even if the ashes were not those of her aunt, they were surely still someone's remains, and should be left alone.

Rebecca could not understand what was occurring within her. She was struggling with herself to justify her unwillingness to acquiesce to Sati's idea. Something in her had shifted somewhere and was both getting in the way of her ability to do her job, and making her pause to consider the other side of any situation. It was infuriating and, to Rebecca and her well practised isolated detachment, cathartic. She was beginning to let herself remember what it was to be a human being, who actually cared instead of just doing an almost perfect impersonation of caring.

'Consider this,' Sati said to her. 'If I am correct, as you hope me to be, then they are my aunt's ashes, and I am her only surviving relative. I need to know the truth of what happened to her, and I give you my explicit permission to carry out whatever tests would be necessary to prove that. I only ask that you assist me in reaching that stage.'

Rebecca had no arguments left she could muster. Her journey to this point left her with only one direction to take.

'I'm in.'

Thirty-one

Cover Stories

Tuesday 4 July 2056 – 22:24 IST

How had it arrived at this point?

Throughout life there had always been present a drive to simplify the inherent complexities and intricacies of existence; to assign some order on the chaos resulting from the collisions of the business of people. The choice of a path outwith of the mundane, and with it the expectation of more diverting and rewarding opportunities for this than would be presented to most others had been deliberate. A chance to exert influence in areas outside the bounds of the conventional. Had that always been the attraction, the pull towards the uncharted course? The spiritual push into the unknown to match the very real physical leap undertaken a quarter of a century ago. To emulate them? Perhaps it had all been an attempt to grasp some of the excitement they must have experienced in that moment of the jump into the great unexplored vastness around them.

Perhaps.

But time and too many mistakes or poor decisions had left their corresponding marks. The heaviness of the past pressed unceasingly into the present, its weight sitting in judgement on the soul; a collection of errors and misdeeds forever unable to be undone, their mass accreting down through the years. Necessary choices taken, the consequences of which could only be atoned for, never rectified. What could not have been avoided then had to be endured now. And with those decisions had come the sharp cuts of betrayal and reversal, each instance leaving their own unique imprint on the psyche; none redressing the errors which caused them, only compounding them.

But even with this knowledge, how events had been allowed to reach this apogee was almost beyond comprehension. This was not the self-organising complexity emergent from the chaos found in nature; this was an artefact of man, manufactured in the minds of others and implemented through intermediaries. Wills imposed on situations, events manipulated to external ends. Whatever the reasons had been in the past, now everything had become scattered and confused. The situation had moved too far from the delicate equilibrium point it had been balanced on for so long and was in danger of falling, and with it everything the choices had been for.

There were too many variables, too many bodies in motion and too few constants that could be relied upon to hold fast. It was more dangerous now than it had ever been. Positive action was called for to pull the situation away from the horizon it seemed to be tipping over.

Contact had been made when it was apparent this was the case; passivity would not bring the results required. This in its own turn had led to the darkness of this alley in one of Delhi's less reputable districts in the depths of a stifling Indian night, and an hour of standing, waiting knowing full well the woman was likely out there watching now, ensuring there had been no pursuit, no prying eyes or eavesdropping ears.

Growing bored now, restraint a limited commodity

now events required closer attention; keen to have the conversation over and done with. A glance at the watch to flush her out with a manifestation of impatience.

Either by coincidence of timing or not, the action seemed to have the desired effect. She appeared a handful of metres away, micro-rainbows of light spilling out into the night air as the Fold fell back into the Cotts field. In the gloom of the alley, well away from the harsh artificial sodium glare, the coloured light shone like stained glass against the sombre interior of a church, bathing them both in its prismatic glow for the single second of her arrival.

She stood looking for a second, saying nothing, allowing space for the silence to be filled.

'I wish to talk. I have information which needs to be heard.'

The woman withdrew something from the folds of her sari. Even in the dark her silhouette revealed the obviousness of a gun.

'Sati. There is no requirement for that.'

The woman hesitated for a second as if surprised at being recognised. Then control was regained and she proffered a small, silver egg.

'This will not aid you, but if you must then I will accede.'

'You know how this works.' Sati flicked the gun, a definite gesture of intent which was not misinterpreted in the darkness. She activated her comm and waited a second. 'It's me. I will be there in a moment.'

Strong looking elderly hands reached out to take the small device from Sati, making no attempt at trickery. In the instant of contact he was gone, Displaced to where Sati had pre-programmed the D-remote. She holstered the gun and reached into the Cotts field before disappearing along the same trajectory, leaving the alley empty, the only evidence of there ever having been a meeting being the slowly dissipating Displacement residuals.

'I am informed you are still in partnership with the outlaw, Sati.' Dravid spoke to Rebecca, having contacted her on her comm, despite her having Socrates change his access codes in tandem with Kalpana every two hours.

He continued. 'It is of little to no importance. I have information for you. However I would not see it intercepted electronically. It is time we made each other's acquaintance.'

Rebecca saw the now familiar shimmer of someone approaching via a D-assist through the Cotts field suppression enveloping her five-star suite and stood back, expecting Sati to materialise with the mysterious Dravid. Instead only a single figure appeared, and it wasn't her companion.

Calmly the man, once fully re-located in realspace, reached into his pocket and retrieved a small, cigarette-sized silver device and pressed the single button on it.

'Dravid, I presume?' Rebecca asked the obvious question.

After a handful of seconds of taking stock of the series of rooms he found himself in, the slender instrument in the man's hand chimed, drawing his attention away from the relative luxury Rebecca had been living in at his government's expense since arriving in their country. A green light on the electronics seemed to indicate that whatever the thing was intended to do had been successful. It took Rebecca a moment only to divine its purpose, which had been to block Sati's pursuit through the Cotts field.

'Where the hell is Sati?' In the space of less than a minute the situation had spun away from her and most likely Sati too. Whatever she had had planned at the rendezvous, surely this was not it? 'What did you do to her?'

'She is quite safe. One moment please.' He reached into another jacket pocket, withdrawing a second silvered device, approximately the same size as the other. Rebecca backed away an unconscious half-step at its presence. 'Please do not be unduly alarmed,' he said in response to Rebecca's understandable reaction. This time he did not press a button on the neat package of electronics, because it had none. Instead he laid it unassumingly on the low table between them and checked its display.

Seemingly satisfied, he turned to Rebecca. 'Your acquaintance is unharmed.' He proffered the first metallic tube, showing it to her. 'A small piece of equipment we have been keeping from the world. The ability to hold someone in D-space is something the rest of the world does not need at this time, or ever will I should hazard. Its abuse would be horrific. As for the second, it keeps everything we discuss here private from all forms of electronic surveillance. Audio, video, infrared, all blocked. Now, with our privacy assured we can talk. You wish to know about the Vimana.'

Rebecca, not knowing what to say, said nothing while she ran through possible directions this conversation might take, and the fact she would have to do it alone, hoping Sati was indeed safe. She wished the Indian woman were here, with her inevitable list of forensic questions and surgical knowledge of the mission, far in excess of her own. Sati had lived the Vimana through the eyes of her aunt. Having been only eight and at best one degree removed from the mission, Rebecca drew all her knowledge from only her childhood self, long since buried. She would have to go there again and retrieve what she could. She worked opening gambits, looking for a way in to this man and how to get what she could from him.

'Please, ask anything. I will do my best to answer what

you want,' he continued, seemingly eager to undertake the discussion almost as if he had been planning for them to meet face to face after their varied comms all along.

Rebecca shook herself out of her fug, collecting herself; she knew where to go with this. Whoever this man really was, he was obviously intelligent, almost certainly more so than her. She would have to be very careful. 'Let's start with something easy. Your real name please. It seems disingenuous that you've known my name for so long yet I only know you as this 'Dravid'.

He smiled a little. 'A small indulgence in a life of service, nothing more. My given name is Ramkumar Mei. Most close associates call me Ram and I find the contraction useful for Westerners.'

'Well given I fall into neither of those categories I'll stick with Ramkumar. I'm sure you'll appreciate the formality.' Rebecca was making a deliberate effort to recover the initiative, and this was a small victory in the opening thrust and parry of the conversation. Let him know that she was smart also.

'As you wish. What else do you want to know?'

Ramkumar projected, to Rebecca, the air of an almost bored, patient parent encouraging the child to ask the correct question before imparting knowledge. Or more accurately she decided, a tutor in school waiting impatiently for the exact set of words to be said, to show the relevant depth of understanding, where everything was a test of acuity and insight. If it was an act or not, Rebecca was a long time out of childhood, school, college or even being a junior employee.

'Please,' she replied dismissively. 'That attitude might work on your subordinates but its just patronising, and pisses me off, so drop it.' That felt better. Assertive. More like how she was. She pressed along with her now-planned approach. 'Let's dispense with the twenty questions approach, and instead you just tell me everything you've got on our mind. I'll ask when I need clarification.'

'Certainly. Would you like to take a seat? This may take a short while.'

Rebecca remained standing, arms crossed across her chest, careful to ensure she did not even project accommodating body-language. She indicated Ramkumar should begin with a chuck of her chin.

'Very well. As you are no doubt aware from your membership of the Leapfrog Club in 2031, we here in India had developed the first interstellar craft, the Vimana. Ostensibly this was to prove the viability of such a vehicle and to undertake a mission to the nearest star, a little over four light years away. We set ourselves that public goal much like the Americans undertook with the Apollo missions in the previous century.'

'That was the public story anyway. But the Vimana was constructed to serve a deeper, higher purpose; one we did not disclose to the rest of the world. You must understand what the world was like twenty-five years ago, when you were still a child. Two decades of wars were tearing the old alliances apart. Crores had died. We had to do something.'

'And that something was a space mission? How?'

'A distraction. And a ruse. Nearly one hundred years previously the world's last superpowers mounted an audacious hoax involving the then furthest attainable goal.'

Rebecca worked out the dates from her history lessons and half guessed. 'The moon.'

'Ha. The then United States and the Soviet Union saw the world needed a distraction, an aspiration after the lengthy world war barely a decade previously, so in conjunction they initiated what they called the Space Race. It gave the populations of both power blocs something to rally behind. Actual missions were launched. Yuri Gagarin did orbit the Earth with John Glenn following a little later. The prize was to be the moon. But it was too difficult, far beyond the technology of the day. So an artifice was devised.'

'Now that I can believe,' said Rebecca.

'Well, the results were what mattered, and the result was a period of relative global peace for decades in which the United States exerted unparalleled influence. We aimed to achieve much the same.'

'You're telling me you faked the Vimana!'

'No, we built the ship. It is spaceworthy, and it did travel beyond Earth's orbit, but only to the dark side of the moon. While Apollo may not have reached its destination its effect achieved the desired result. We, in aiming higher achieved so much more. The impending global war was escalated back to regional conflicts, mostly confined to America, and we were looked to for leadership.'

'You're calling the civil war over there a success?'

'No. But we do not have the means to intercede in the manner the situation demands. And I believe they would not accept our help, even if we were in a position to offer it.'

Rebecca remembered the near escape she had had with the two gaandus on the border, and her most likely correct decision not to even take saris with her when she went.

Ramkumar continued. 'Imagine if we had not done what we did. A war of the ferocity you saw in your weeks there, but raging across the whole planet. It would mark the end of our species. Believe me when I say the technology to Displace continental land masses is not only viable, but exists. Hundreds of crores would die as we tore our world apart underneath us. That was unacceptable to us. We could not save everyone but we could save more than would perish.'

Rebecca paced back and forth. This was too big. The old cliché about making lies large enough came to her. 'It can't be true. Someone else would have talked by now. You couldn't hide a secret that large.'

Ramkumar sat placidly in place before speaking again.

'You are correct of course. Someone else would be able to disprove what I have told you easily enough.'

Rebecca glared at him.

'Everything I have just told you is classified. It is the cover story for our real reasons for shrouding the Vimana mission in secrecy.' Shifting his weight in his seat either in an effort at comfort or a subconscious manifestation of a mental decision, Ramkumar spoke again. 'Saving humanity from itself is almost certainly beyond our capabilities, even if the rest of our species were in a position to listen to us. However, saving it from an external threat, that is something we are capable of.'

Rebecca baulked. 'External?'

'Indeed. The Vimana was launched, in the spirit of discovery and amity. What it encountered once beyond the heliopause was far from benign. Quite the reverse.'

This was too much. Aliens? Rebecca said as much.

'Only from a limited human-centric perspective. All things are as one, so they would be part of the fabric of creation, inherent and complete. Extra-terrestrial yes, but nevertheless one with the rest of the universe. But, for practical purposes alien would be as accurate a description as required. A truly non-terrestrial intelligence out there far beyond our small solar system. The first encounter of its kind for our species.'

That sounded wrong to Rebecca. Something worried her thoughts, something she had read about. An early twenty-first century cult or something, purporting to be controlled by a non-human, who said he had proof of life outside earth's biosphere.

Seeing her narrowed eyes, Ramkumar completed her thought process. 'You are thinking of the Ballisargon Cult.' Ramkumar shook his head gently. 'A fiction. The delusions of a broken mind at the turn of the century, nothing more. Humanity's first encounter with a true alien as you understand the word occurred sixteen hours into the

Vimana's flight. They were told to turn back, that the limitless vastness of space was not open to them, and any attempt to venture further would come with severe consequences for not just them, but their species.'

'We were threatened?'

'No. We were told to stay put. There was no implication, or ambiguity in the direction received from the alien. We are to remain on earth, as best we can, until we can end conflict for a century. A sort of test if you like. Then, we are to venture forth once more.'

'And then?'

'I do not know. We received instructions, not promises.'

'And if we don't play along? If we attempt another mission?'

'Then the aliens will extinguish our sun. As proof of their capabilities we were directed to observe Epsilon Eridani, a little under eleven light years away. A civilisation on its inhabitable planet had thought to defy them a decade previously and whose parent star they had caused to nova in consequence. Dutifully we watched, and seven weeks later the star did indeed explode, something our stellar models indicated should not have happened. We knew then that we had little option but compliance.'

'But they could have known the star had gone nova and are tricking us? Or it could be a bluff. Surely any species advanced enough to travel between stars wouldn't wipe out another to prove a point.'

'Would we not?' Ramkumar replied, leaving the implication hanging a moment before continuing. 'I for one do not wish to be even partly responsible for the elimination of the human race, however remote the possibility.'

'Sorry Ramkumar, but I believed the faked Vimana story more than a bunch of powerful demi-god scary alien galactic policemen. If they're your cover stories then you need some better writers.'

Ramkumar smiled, for a moment only. 'I must concede you may be correct in that regard. However the truth is that there is something far more terrible awaiting us out in the void than tentacled horrors with the ability to overload a sun. And here on earth.'

'Another cover story? I can't wait to hear this one,' she mocked.

Ignoring her tone Ramkumar continued. Our finest scientific minds have been tracking usage and estimating the point of peak resources for nearly forty years. Even with the advent of clean D-tech we have so exhausted our world and brought such environmental damage to it that we have, so our calculations tell us, little better than a fifty percent chance of surviving as a species beyond the next century. So a plan was devised at the highest levels.'

'A plan? What could possibly fix that, and how would a jaunt through deep space help?'

'When faced with a problem that seems impossible to resolve within your own context, you look for solutions that sit outside convention. Professor Cotts had already proved Displacement over light years was possible, so we tasked ourselves with applying his technology to its logical conclusion. A trip of four light years would not be enough, we would need to look much much further afield. We would find other worlds to host us, dozens, hundreds of light years away. Worlds capable of supporting a two hundred crore strong population each to relieve the pressure on our overburdened homeworld. If Earth could no longer bear the weight of our numbers we would solve the problem by removing the Earth from the equation.'

Rebecca looked incredulous. 'That's why you built the ship? To save the Earth? Why? Why not just move your own people and leave the rest of us behind?'

Now it was Ramkumar's turn to play the injured party. 'Please,' he said, an exact echo of Rebecca's phrasing. 'We are not barbarians. We hold responsibility for every soul on Earth. And besides if we had done this covertly, or there had been the slightest suspicion as to our motives, the rest of the world would have followed, thinking we had abandoned them, and whatever new world we found would be overrun in a generation. But something went wrong.'

'With the Vimana? What?'

'No, not with the Vimana. It worked exactly as it was specified to. Professor Cotts' reputation as a genius is well deserved. His theories and mathematics drove it soaring into the vacuum, a silvered sliver of hope in the persistent dark. The problem arose with the human crew.'

'But surely they were trained? I remember trying Hari Srinath's regime for a day and it nearly killed me. OK, I was only eight and a half at the time, but even so. And there must have been psychological screening for possible problems?'

'Yes, and yes. You are quite correct. They were the finest eleven people the human race has ever produced. Everything was analysed, re-analysed then triple-checked. Nothing was left to chance. Anything we assumed, we factored in a solution for.'

'So what the hell happened?'

'Something we did not assume would.' Ramkumar paused, for dramatic effect or in genuine regret and shame at the admission Rebecca could not be sure. He remained silent for a moment longer. She did not want to prompt him, but this was too much.

'And?'

'And they failed.'

'Failed?'

'It is the best word we have for what occurred. Something about the human consciousness does not function in interstellar space. The instant they arrived at the midway point between worlds the problems began. We had scheduled six hours recuperation time for the Devas, over twice what we calculated they needed. Barely fifteen minutes into that six hours of checks, Aryabhata started recording anomalies in all the crew's behaviour. Of course they were too distant to signal for help, and even if they had been within range, we had nothing to despatch to go to their aid.'

'I'm not sure I understand? They went crazy?'

'No. As far as we have been able to determine the effect on human consciousness of being outside the Earth or the Sun's electromagnetic influence is deeper and far more devastating than simple psychosis. Put bluntly their minds stopped working. Literally the human brain unravels in its skull. Neural connections begin to decay at a geometric rate. After only thirty minutes away from the protection of their world, in the lifeless vacuum far beyond our own solar system, almost the entire crew were helpless, all of them losing motor skills and verbal control.'

Rebecca sat down now. 'Brahma! So the ship in the museum is a replica? No, wait, what you said implies you've got first hand experience with someone who went through this. What happened? How did the ship get back?'

'You mentioned Hari Srinath and his training. It was that that saved the ship. By the end of it he was the only one alive enough to move the Vimana from the depths of interstellar space back to its orbit around the moon, where we were able to bring it to its base on Kangchenjunga's summit.'

'But that thing weighs tons. Most people can barely move their PDV a few hundred kilometres. It must have killed him.'

'It very nearly did.' Ramkumar's voice was flat, emotionless, any pride he may have felt at Srinath's achievement flattened under the weight of his grief. 'This is the secret we protect. Humanity is tied to a dying world we have exhausted. Even if we do persist for the next one hundred years there are too many of us now for the Earth to recover. And if we found another world, we would not survive the journey to it.'

Rebecca shook her head in disbelief. Ramkumar had presented the stories, each more preposterous than the preceding one with no emotion betraying him. She guessed he could probably pass a realtime neural scan for each of them as the absolute truth if he wanted, so she had no way of telling them apart. For all she knew they were all lies and the truth was still as far away from her as it had ever been.

As if sensing her thoughts Ramkumar rose from his seat. 'Believe whichever you will, or none if you must. I leave it to you to determine the truth if you so choose.' He looked around at the room. 'I have spent long enough here. It is time for me to leave.'

'The door is locked and the Displacement suppressor is still active. I'm not so sure you're going anywhere unless I want you to.'

Ramkumar looked almost amused at Rebecca's naivety. 'Who do you think developed the technology you are putting so much faith in? Your companion will be returned to you two minutes after I have left. She will be a little disorientated, but that will not be permanent. And be thankful that the others who watch you are not as resourceful as I am. Farewell Ms Eckhart. I hope to see you again.'

Ramkumar disappeared leaving Rebecca to rush to the privacy indicator, seeing that it was still on.

<

'He wants to meet me. Says he has information to impart, but wants to do it face to face.'

Sati regarded what Rebecca had told her for a moment. 'It will likely be a trap.'

Rebecca disagreed. 'I think if this Dravid wanted me arrested he could have effected that course of action already. He is obviously someone highly placed, with access to official channels. I believe the offer is genuine.'

Rebecca had been forced to tell Sati of the existence of Dravid, but had withheld some details; the tacit observation, his knowledge of her. But now he had requested a rendezvous, there was little she could do except share this with her companion. If Sati intuited any larger action on Dravid's part from Rebecca's admission she did not show it. Instead she walked from the room the women were in, returning a few moments later proffering a small, black-anodised handgun.

'I will make the rendezvous for you.'

>

Ramkumar's words hung in the room all around her after his abrupt departure, leaving Rebecca alone with what she had just been told. Now more than ever the truth of the Vimana felt elusive, threatening to slip further away from her the harder she tried to seize it.

She checked her earpiece, hoping it had recorded anything of the last fifteen minutes. But a quick replay of even the last thirty seconds revealed nothing but static where there should have been a record of her conversation with Dravid, now known to be Ramkumar Mei. Frustrated and realising the stupidity of using the technology Pramod had supplied her over two months previously, she went to Socrates, hoping the SI had had better luck in transcribing the dialogue. But it was pointless; his capabilities had been neutralised as easily as the earpiece.

Recording anything Ramkumar had said had proved impossible, just as he had it would be.

Shitshitshit!

She had to have a more permanent record of what she had been told. She started transcribing everything she could recall. Estimating she had barely a minute more if what Ramkumar had said was true before Sati would re-appear and demand to know what had happened to her and what had been said. Frantically Rebecca spoke to Socrates as her hands flew across the virtual screen, downloading the words from her head as fast as she could in both written and verbal form. How much longer did she have? Not enough, that was sure.

'Ship spaceworthy. Hidden behind moon. Stopped a larger war...' In front of her, through the virtual screen hanging a metre away she saw the unmistakable rainbow of a Fold opening in her room. 'Socrates. Stop recording now. Save file Helena Charpin. Encode parameter RRC level 3. My private key. Shutdown. Now.'

The screen vanished from Rebecca's vision immediately as Sati appeared. She had no way of knowing what state her dump of information was in, but at least she had something approaching a more permanent record now. She let out a small sigh of relief before remembering she was supposed to be more concerned for her companion, and rushed to catch Sati as she fell, half-conscious to the floor.

Easing the older woman down as best she could with her one good arm Rebecca asked if she recalled any of what had happened to her.

Sati tried to focus on Rebecca's familiarity but for the moment her eyes refused to co-operate and work in unison. For her, the previous fifteen minutes had not happened at all. She had been in the in-between no-space that everyone moved through when they Displaced. Theoretically at least, what she had experienced was impossible, but still it had been done to her. Impossible was a term that seemed to be losing its currency the deeper they probed into the story and the truth behind the Vimana's only flight.

'Are you alright?' It felt feeble to Rebecca as she asked the redundant question. It was obvious Sati was not, but there was little Rebecca could do until the effects Ramkumar had spoken of passed. Until then she could only wait and watch.

Unable to lift the heavier woman onto the hotel bed with her arm in its cast, Rebecca tried to make Sati as comfortable on the floor as she could. A pillow and the cover from the bed were the best she could do. Initially she crossed her companion's arms over her chest. But the position looked posed, which coupled with Sati's shallow breathing made her uncomfortable to be in the room with; it felt like having a corpse on the floor. Rebecca lowered Sati's arms to her side. It looked odd, but somehow less discomfiting. She remained that way for nearly an hour before she stirred, even in the slightest, only a flicker of her eyes underneath their closed lids betraying any outward sign of life. The Indian woman coughed lightly at first, then harder as her body recovered its strength.

Rebecca was at her side immediately, a glass of water ready, the only thing she could think to offer as a comfort for the possible after-effects of Sati's extreme Displacement. She held Sati's head as she eased the glass to her lips, dampening them a little. Sati's body, still mostly functioning autonomically, reached for the wetness her parched throat sought and grabbed the glass, and with it Rebecca's hands, her fingers given strength by her body's needs.

'Easy,' urged Rebecca, whether indicating the pressure on her wrist or the urgency with which Sati was drinking, not clear. A bit of both perhaps, or perhaps more a caution to the older woman to take care with her broken arm.

Whichever it was, the water or Rebecca's insistence, Sati focussed on her for the first time, eyes clear now, full of purpose and determination once more, even if her body remained weak. 'What. Happened?' she whispered between mouthfuls of water.

'I was hoping you could tell me. What do you remember?'

It was another hour before Sati recovered sufficiently to

be helped to Rebecca's bed, still shaky, but alert, the after-effects of her prolonged period in D-space seeming to affect her body more than her mind.

Rebecca was coming to the end of her abridged explanation of what Dravid had told her. She was unsure exactly how much to reveal, even concealing his real name until she had verified any of what he had said, deciding instead to tell Sati just that her guest had explained that the Vimana mission had failed. That D-tech seemed not to function in space, or at least not outside a sphere of influence the planet seemed to exert. She told Sati that Dravid had not said anything about the astronauts or their fate; she did not know if she believed her or not, but the older woman's weakened state seemed to discourage her from pressing Rebecca with many questions. If needed she could always tell Sati any version of the truth as she had been told it at a later date.

Sati, for her part, seemed to absorb everything she was told. When Rebecca had finished she sat quietly for a moment before saying plainly, 'The story you were told changes nothing. Without proof we still have nothing.' Then she closed her eyes, and fell asleep.

Rebecca sat watching the sleeping Indian woman, regarding her. She guessed Sati would likely be asleep for a long time, leaving her many hours to think through everything she had been told by parties on all sides.

She had fact checked as much as she dared of Ramkumar's stories, and his identity. The obfuscator still glowed hot pink as she moved from data silo to data silo. Socrates took full advantage of the invisibility the barrier program seemed to offer him in generating on-demand queries of the government, military and corporate databases he had apparently limitless access to, mining deep into the data.

Ramkumar Mei was indeed Dravid's real name, and for

a few seconds Rebecca was being shown that he was listed as a junior minister in the Water and Power department before the obfuscator blazed brilliant white for an instant and Ramkumar's real file was presented to her. *How the..?* Rebecca hit hardcopy and instructed Socrates to drop the connection immediately.

It was too dangerous to do this.

Scanning the printout revealed Ramkumar's true position in the Indian Government and his links with InSA in frustrating detail. It alluded more than it confirmed, but what it hinted confirmed much of what he had told her. But it was still not enough.

It was obvious to her that Sati was correct, without real proof they had nothing. Tall tales from Ramkumar Mei meant as little as the fiction she had told Sati if they could not be substantiated with physical evidence, her printout of his de-classified record notwithstanding. A simple printout could be faked easily.

Ramkumar had told her three versions of history one or none of which could be true. At the very least, two of them must be fiction, but if he was willing to lie twice to her, why not once more?

What did he have to gain from telling her the truth hidden along with lies? What did he have to gain from telling her three fictions? She didn't know.

Once again she found herself far behind the rest of the players in this thing she was caught up in. Corroboration was required, the analyst in her told herself. Verifiable fact. Irrefutable proof.

D-Market Retrospective
October 23 2051

Sinha MG D-Market Strategy Research

Rebecca Eckhart
Rebecca.Eckhart.SinhaMG

Novel Approaches to Cotts Field Funding

- InSA announces new funding model for Cotts Field Licences after six months detailed financial negotiation from 'big six' operators.

- New revenue stream to be opened up around security.

- Technological advances allow Cotts Field strength to be lowered, or dropped completely to create holes in the field.

Like every discovery of novel technology, reaching back into pre-history from the utilisation of a weighted branch as a simple club, to the apex of manned spaceflight, humanity has not been idle in developing new applications for, and extrapolations to its discoveries. The same holds true for the owners of the intellectual property rights to the Displacement Theory of Near Instantaneous Matter Transfer. InSA holds patents on, and licences hundreds of applications to the fundamentally simple idea of moving things, be they people or goods from one location to another.

Correspondingly, technology which acts counter to an individual's ability to manipulate the Cotts Field bathing the earth have also had to have been developed. So far this has been an innovation borne of necessity. In a world where, theoretically, anyone could move anywhere providing they did not have to Fold through too much matter, situations have arisen where thieves have moved themselves into areas up until that moment considered impregnable. The current expensive solutions contriving the ultra-dense materials teased into existence in nuclear forges have been found wanting. The gaps between atoms, even in the post-uranic compounds proving too wide for exploitation by human resourcefulness and cunning. The most determined criminal, assisted by powerful SI computations, can slip through as easily as if it were air.

How InSA found a way to make something from nothings

Seeing a drop-off in their high-end fees, the six major licensees engaged InSA to provide a solution. India, owner and manager of every satellite in low-earth orbit providing the Cotts Field, already had the simplest of solutions to the problem. Initial reluctance to cede the vastly profitable revenue streams, InSA flipped the funding model on its head for those wishing to protect their property from uninvited visitors. InSA announced today, that for those willing to find the necessary rupees, a hole can be opened in the Cotts Field, a void into which nothing and no-one could Displace. InSA have indicated that any area, from a handful of square metres through to an entire continent could be requested to have its field strength set at a lower level, or be dropped completely.

Thirty-two

Break In

Wednesday 5 July 2056 – 01:13 IST

'Stop!' hissed Sati, causing Rebecca to become a statue lying on the ground along side her.

Frozen in place on her belly, her face pressed into the steaming damp undergrowth, immediately she found herself wishing Sati had either hesitated a second longer or called her order a moment sooner. The position Rebecca had been forced to hold meant she was resting her weight on her broken arm, with no option to free it from under herself and relieve the rising pain until the motion-sensor, which had detected something amiss in the gardens surrounding the InSA museum, was satisfied it was nothing of note. Recent experience told Rebecca this could be as long as five minutes. She clenched her back teeth against the throbbing in her arm and tried to detach her consciousness as much as she could from herself. It did no good. She would have to ride this out. Again.

As Rebecca lay sweating in the undergrowth, underneath the radar sweeping just above her, she was struck by the absurdity of the situation she found herself in.

340

In a little under an hour she and Sati had traversed a hundred metres, approximately three centimetres a second.

The woman next to her was capable of travelling, in a heartbeat, lakh times the distance they were covering a minute. Their almost imperceptible progress was a result of the void enveloping the InSA museum; the volume the building occupied kept empty by an inverse bubble of no-space in the Cotts field. They crawled towards the building housing the ashes of Pratheen Chaudray; either the woman who had been given that name at birth, or the individual who Sati claimed had taken her name upon the Vimana's return from the stars.

The lack of the Cotts field was not the only missing presence surrounding the InSA museum. At a little past midnight, the museum was a dead zone. Along with the expected absence of visitors, the urban animal wildlife, sensitive to the Cotts field after three decades of its presence as part of their environment, could sense the gap in the world the museum hid inside. No birds flew overhead and no monkeys prowled the undergrowth. Instead the swifts and starlings plaguing other civic buildings with their droppings veered off mid-flight almost as soon as they flew into the bubble, screeching back to real-space. The wild primates hackles raised barely half a metre too close to the building, equilibriums unsettled by the absence of something they could not see, smell or hear, but which pervaded their senses nonetheless.

There was a series of small electronic clicks, imitative of a cricket, indicating the women could resume their crawl. Rebecca lifted herself from her broken arm, pushing away a wave of nausea at the pain of her freed limb, but unable to make a sound in response. Unwilling to show her distress, even to Sati now, she was first to move forward towards their destination once more. The latest delay had been the fourth so far, with them barely half way. *Why hadn't they been detected yet?*

Rebecca felt certain the second alert warning they had received would be the one which caused the authorities to investigate and find them. Surely the sensors sweeping the museum's grounds would not let two false-positives go unchecked? She wanted to voice her suspicions to Sati, as the Indian woman seemed to take every all-clear as proof of the validity of their actions; as if not being detected was nothing more than an expected consequence of their actions.

Perhaps it was simple impatience which drove Sati; after a quarter of a century she was about to learn if she had been correct for all that time. Rebecca could understand that. Forced into near silence for the duration of their interminably slow journey, she had had plenty of time for self-reflection on her own attitude to Displacement. She had realised for the first time, after analysing Sati's motives, that the impatience which rose within her at other people was an overcompensation for her own handicap; her inability to replicate what everyone else performed so easily. She barely stifled the small, unconscious laugh.

'What?' hissed Sati at the small noise Rebecca could not fully suppress.

'Nothing. I thought I had my boot caught on something, that's all,' she lied, automatically contriving a likely explanation for her behaviour.

In the darkness, despite the light amplification goggles both of them wore, Rebecca could not make out Sati's features sufficiently enough to tell if she believed her or not, before the woman turned away from her once more and resumed their crawl toward the building that was their target. 'Take more care,' was all Rebecca got in the way of a reply.

Sati was correct, but not in the way she believed she meant. Now was not the time for introspection. Rebecca promised herself she'd come back to her thoughts on this later; if they were apprehended tonight she would have very many years of solitude for self-examination.

Rebecca contented herself with the final thought that the building they were attempting to break into had been dropped from the Cotts field; this evened her's and Sati's capabilities in the endeavour. She had had enough of being at everybody else's disadvantage; tonight at least, they would be equals.

>

Almost one hour and a further one hundred metres later the pair arrived at the museum's external wall. They eased themselves along it to the door that was their entrance. Standing before it, Sati gestured to Rebecca who reached into the pack she had dragged behind her, and withdrew the box of electronics they had been told would grant them entry. Sati placed it on the door and waited. Rebecca could not shake her disquiet at the ease with which they had made it this far. A second later the key flashed green and Sati pushed at the door, which, obligingly, swung inward.

They were in. Now the difficult part began.

Chipkali ke chut ke pasine!

Rebecca swore in her head, unable to vocalise the sentiment, as she swayed unsteadily on her feet. She cursed bad karma, Sati, Helena and finally herself for allowing her to be dragged into this. Her breathing was rapid, far too fast to be good for her. Hyperventilating in an effort to calm the rising panic. Her animal self trapped in the too tight clothing she wore. She checked her watch. How long had it been since she had put this thing on? The dial swam in front of her. How long had Sati said was dangerous? Thirty minutes? She couldn't remember. And why was it

343

dangerous? Again she couldn't remember. She looked at herself, her midriff appearing in her infrared enhanced vision as an orange-yellow blob. That wasn't good, she remembered, but why? Too hot. Have to get out. She began to tear at the hood she had on...

< <

Rebecca and Sati moved slowly along the corridor, even more slowly than they had approached the museum, unable to see each other through the specially auged goggles they both wore. Their vision matched that of the museum's security system; if they were invisible to each other so they would be to the cameras sweeping the silent exhibitions and empty galleries.

Backs pressed against the cold stone wall they held hands, ensuring they stayed together. Rebecca checked the illuminated display of the ancient spring-driven watch they both wore, its radiant energy too feeble to bother the museum's security systems. According to Sati's timings there was a patrol due at the half hour, a little over five minutes from now. It was their best chance to make as rapid progress toward the shrine as possible, forward-following the guard through the temporarily deactivated security systems. Far faster than they were currently going.

The women reached what felt like the angular concave of a corner and sat down in it to wait for the approaching footsteps that would indicate they could move again.

Three minutes later Rebecca saw, faintly and still some way off, the softened glow of the night-lights switching on towards them as the guard patrolled. The weak light barely penetrated the darkness around them, seeming to offer little more illumination than starlight in deep space.

Rebecca squeezed Sati's hand once, then once again, the agreed signal, and both women slid up the wall to begin their progress again in the near total darkness. Ahead of them, accompanying the lights coming on at their rear, were the sensors being switched off. Sati had explained that in order for the lights not to trip the alarms further ahead, the rolling sweep forward disabled them for ten metres or so. That was the size of their window of safety to move quickly. If they lingered too long, the guard would almost certainly see them, proceed too rapidly and they would stray into the active sensor zone.

Other than the guard, some distance off, they were the only moving objects in the museum. The vast interiors, one of which housed the huge spaceship which had carried Pratheen to the heavens, were as silent as the space both had traversed. Caverns of soundless black stretched all around the two women.

Padded footwear and the most carefully choreographed movements notwithstanding, their passage was not completely noiseless; each tiny sigh of the fabric they wore as it flexed and pressed against the ground or their bodies amplified in their minds by the lifeless darkness into an alert to the guard or the sensors. Anxious adrenaline flooded systems magnified every thought into the end of their endeavour, and the remainder of their lives in prison.

Rebecca could sense nothing except her heartbeat echoing in her head, her body's internal sounds held by the close fitting hood she wore. Remaining calm to keep her body temperature down was proving difficult.

Outwardly Sati seemed calm, her grip strong in Rebecca's hand, her every movement seemingly coming from a plan committed to memory over the course of her adult life; each step deliberately chosen along a particular path that would lead her inexorably to the ashes of her aunt.

Despite Rebecca's perception of her, Sati was as nervous as she had ever been in her life, the decade or more she had on the younger woman feeling more like thirty years now there was something real and physical to complete. Her expertise was planning and scheming, not breaking and entering; she was not sure her body was capable of delivering on the demands she might make of it. At least half her life had been building up to this, the culmination of a need that had driven her into darker places than she had ever imagined she would tread.

She held Rebecca's hand tightly, an effort to ensure the westerner did not get away from her, even accidentally; she needed Rebecca now more than ever if she was to get the proof she desperately craved. She envied the other woman's seemingly more calm, looser hold on her own hand, youthful control of her nerves perhaps.

They reached the top of the staircase that would take them to, amongst other exhibits in a large open gallery, the shrine room. Behind them the glow of the light grew gently, allowing them for a brief moment to see each other, and the stairs that lay before them. Sati pointed down; Rebecca nodded. Rebecca estimated the guard was perhaps twenty seconds to their rear. They needed to be quick in their descent.

Sati put her good foot on the first step. Then, taking the weight on her uninjured leg, lowered her other limb, heavily strapped at the ankle carefully in front of it. As soon as she came to take a third step, her balance betrayed her. Perhaps the ankle was not sufficiently supported, or she slipped, or was not fully on the step, the feeble light pressing at her back making her take that little bit less care.

Whatever the cause, the outcome was inevitable.

Sati began to fall, and in an effort to catch herself let go of Rebecca's hand, needing both of her own to try and arrest her imminent uncontrolled descent. But the angle was all wrong, constrained as they had been by the crab-like progress they had been making along the walls.

There was nothing in front of her to grab onto except empty space, and Sati tumbled silently forward into it unable to give voice to her terror, and down the stairs, Rebecca flailing her sole good arm in front of her in a futile attempt to catch her companion.

Behind, the light grew stronger.

Shit! Shitshitshit!

Rebecca stood at the top of the staircase, dumbstruck at her accomplice's fall down into the darkness below, leaving her stranded and conflicted as to how to proceed. Sense and reason told her she should leave, the endeavour now effectively over, its outcome decided by a karmic accident, a rebalancing of the risk-taking both women had engaged in so far. Even if Sati was unharmed, which given the speed with which she had tumbled into the blackness below seemed unlikely, surely the prudent thing to do would be to get the hell out of there and forget about the now ill-conceived plan to steal Pratheen's ashes.

But. But. But.

'If this Dravid did not furnish you with more detail than you have relayed, then I see no alternative to corroborating or disproving his story.'

Rebecca heard Sati's argument again in her head, the constant logic she had no refuge from since deciding not to tell her companion the full stories that Ramkumar had laid out before her. It was a decision she now realised came with more consequences than she had taken into account.

Perhaps if Sati had been given the truths as Ramkumar had recounted them to her, she may have postponed tonight's robbery; something Rebecca, after her early uncertainty now found she needed to complete. She had allowed herself the luxury of avoiding having to decide between her options by ensuring one of them had become inevitable.

But now, standing in the ever lightening darkness, moments away from discovery, Rebecca realised the full extent of the course she had laid before herself with her subterfuge. The snare she had created around herself then walked backwards into, trapping herself in her secrets, as if all the time denying the thing were happening and she could walk away from the Indian woman, Ramkumar, the Vimana and the truth of what happened in her childhood.

But Rebecca knew now she could not relinquish this. Sati had implanted a splinter of desire in her mind that had rubbed and irritated at her until she could ignore it no longer. She needed to know the truth; to hold on to the one thing she had left after everyone, her mother, the other children in school, her siblings, Damien and her string of boyfriends before him and now Ramkumar Mei had tried to take from her. More than she had ever realised, Rebecca now understood she had to know the truth of the Vimana, otherwise everything she had clung to through her cold, combative childhood would be a fraud.

Rebecca felt her anxiety beginning to raise her body temperature, and drew a single deep breath to calm her nerves. Checking over the skin-tight suit she wore she could see no sign of her body heat seeping through yet, she remained a black outline in the dark, and therefore still invisible to the museum's ambient heat sensors. The mask she wore kept her breath from showing, but it also kept her from calling out to Sati

She needed to find her, and they needed to obtain the proof they had come for.

With no option open to her other than to follow, Rebecca began to descend the stairs. At the very bottom she found herself once again immersed in total darkness, the weak light of the security system failing to penetrate this far away. Carefully, she felt out for Sati with her feet as far as she could stretch from the very bottom of the steps. But there was no contact. Just how far had she fallen?

Then, more pressingly. *Did the guard patrol this section of the museum?* The area that somewhere within it contained all Rebecca had of the two women she was now intimately connected with from the Vimana. Rebecca could not remember. *Think!*

She didn't believe so. The light above her grew, and

she saw the shadow of the approaching guard.

Rebecca retreated further into the dark, away from the bottom of the stairs. She crouched completely still as the solid shadow of the guard, clearly visible now against the pale light, passed by the top of the stairs, swept his torch briefly down the steps, then moved away on the remainder of his rounds.

She was struck with a curious sensation from her childhood; a memory long since forgotten from the Vimana. Hari Srinath described seeing the sun in the deep distance, but commented he was unable to feel its warmth at the extreme range the ship had sent its last communication earthwards from. Is this how the Captain of the Vimana would have felt then? Isolated and alone in the darkness, so far away from the light?

Shaking the thought from herself, Rebecca waited. A minute passed and the lights, and with them the guard, were gone. Now all she had to do was find Sati. With no idea which way to head, and Sati the one with the internalised map of the floor plan, Rebecca chose the direction that felt like the way back to the base of the stairs; at least she could strike out from a known starting point. But after a minute of slow crawling she realised she had made a mistake; her error confirmed when, reaching out in front of herself she touched not the rise of the lowest step but a hard, solid wall.

Sati came to after the guard had passed to find herself in complete darkness once more, lying awkwardly on her side, as Rebecca was making her way, in error, away from her.

She tried to roll over to correct her position, only for her body to stop her with the jolt of pain that leapt from her ankle, up her leg, into her spine then her brain. Despite the mask she wore designed to muffle any noise she might make, her hand flew to her mouth to stifle the cry that rose in response to the scream from her nerve endings. Gently, and this time slowly, she attempted to correct her posture once more, reaching for and lifting her leg so she put no weight on it. The pain came again, but was now bearable through teeth ground hard into each other with all the pressure her jaw muscles could muster.

At least sitting up now, Sati nervously felt along her injured leg to assess just how bad it was. She reached her knee with no obvious problems other than the hot ache she could feel spreading along her whole leg. That all changed when she neared her ankle. As her fingertips probed along they encountered a swelling that shouted its agony into her brain at the lightest of touches. She felt herself begin to sweat heavily, aware her body temperature was rising rapidly, especially in her injured limb. She did not need to see her foot to realise her ankle was broken, probably quite badly, and in fact was actually glad of the darkness; it hid the extent of the damage from her, allowing her to focus on the task of getting out of the situation she was in.

Then she thought: *Where was Rebecca?* She tried to recall what had happened. She remembered the initial slip and seeing Rebecca fall away upwards from her, realising now that it had been her tipping down the stairs. Then nothing more till she came to. She assumed her companion had headed down to find her, but the measures they had taken to shield themselves from the museum's security systems now also kept them hidden from each other in the silent blackness. They could have been as close as a single metre apart at the bottom of the stairs, but may as well have been separated by light years; the centimetres separating them in the darkness as unbridgeable a gulf as the astronomical distances travelled by the Vimana.

There was no way she could find Rebecca in this state, and had to hope the westerner stumbled over her. Metaphorically of course. She did not want to entertain the idea of Rebecca tripping over her injured limb. Sati thought for a moment. Sitting in the middle of the floor was the worst place to be. Better to be up against a wall; that way if Rebecca was here looking for her, and approaching the search the way she hoped she was, there would be only two directions she should come from, narrowing the odds of them finding each other greatly.

Sati began to drag herself along the polished floor of the gallery, each small noiseless slide sending piercing stabs up her leg. The effort to continue against the pain was immense. By the time she reached a wall her exertions had pushed her body temperature up, perhaps too high. Even if Rebecca did locate her, in a few minutes Sati realised she would begin to show on the sensors, alerting the guards to their presence.

She refused to yield to that possibility now, after so long in the pursuit of the truth. She would stay.

Perhaps the damage was not as severe as she thought. Sati tried lifting her body up, to put some weight on her damaged limb. Leaning into the wall she pushed herself to a standing position, balanced on her good leg. Carefully she lowered her left foot to the floor. The instant of gentlest of touches between her toes and the smooth hard surface was enough pressure on her ankle to overwhelm her nervous system. Her injured limb recoiled spasmodically from the floor. Her sole supporting leg almost buckled with the pain, only her conscious will keeping her upright. She had expected it to hurt, but this was unbearable.

Sweating now inside the suit Sati reviewed her options in light of her confirmed inability to walk. She could not hop around, and pulling her crippled leg behind her around the museum was not viable either. Her breathing was becoming rapid and shallow, and her head began to swim. Shock combined with heat exhaustion were kicking in. She did not have long before she collapsed. She could either stay where she was and hope Rebecca found her, or leave the westerner to complete their mission.

If she stayed she greatly increased the likelihood of them being caught; she would slow Rebecca down, or trip the sensors. But leaving meant abandoning the decade of reconnaissance, planning and waiting for the right arrangement of circumstances she had undertaken. It also meant entrusting her need to retrieve her aunt's ashes to the partner she had co-opted into this. All that effort undone by a single slip. It did not seem just.

But she had become a risk to the success of her own plan. She could not stay. She would have to leave her future, and her past, in the hands of the damaged, but fiercely capable westerner.

Calling the memorised floor plan to mind, she guessed which wall she was likely to be leaning against. If she were correct there was a door to the maintenance corridors halfway along it.

Choosing left for no better reason than it allowed her to drag her injured leg as her trailing limb, she set off. A few moments of slow, painful progress and she was rewarded with the recess of a door frame. She offered a small prayer of thanks to Ganesha in his aspect of the remover of obstacles as she tried the handle to find it turned in her hand, and the door swung inwards. Dragging herself through the opening she slumped against the back of the door, closing it behind her. She was safe for now, the museum's primary defences did not thread too far out from the public areas, so she reasoned she should be able to make it to an un-monitored area before she began giving off too much body heat.

She could only hope that Rebecca had it in her to deal with the situation she was bequeathing her.

Rebecca heard, muffled through the hood that covered her whole head, a door click closed somewhere in the large room she was in. The darkness, her disorientation, the blood thumping in her ears all served to mask the direction the noise came from. It had to be Sati, but what did it mean?

Her failure in finding the Indian woman in the darkness seemed to be compounded by Sati's exit through a door somewhere down here. Doubtless she should do the same. It was time to abandon the plan she had been dragged into, make good her exit from it and the museum, leave India, Sati and the secret of the Vimana behind and hopefully return to something approximating her old life. She even hoped she could convince Ramkumar to let her do this in return for her silence; she could not envisage either of them wishing to revisit this particular period in their personal histories.

But every time she tried to will her body into doing that, moving to find the door Sati had left through, she found it unwilling to yield to her, holding her in place. She concentrated on moving one foot forward, even a centimetre from her standing position in the centre of the gallery, but something was overriding her nervous system, holding her in place. If she was going to leave she had to do so soon. Her core temperature would rise to a level where she would be detected if she lingered too much longer.

Rebecca spoke to herself in her head, trying to understand the force holding her in place. She had to be sure she was doing the right thing in leaving. Her memory showed her the moving image of Hari Srinath on the display, her small hand reaching out to touch his face, her adoration reflected back from his image, then reaching out with her heart to Helena only for her mother to rebuff her. Immediately she understood what was holding her here; she was, from all those years ago. The two and a half decades of effort she had poured into herself to rid herself of the pain and frustration of that day. *That's why you're doing this. If you leave now, you'll be eight-years old forever.*

Rebecca rolled the cuff of her suit over her wrist to check her watch, the illuminated dials emitting insufficient radiation to be detected by the museum's sensors if the process was carried out swiftly enough. She stared at the dial for longer than she should be doing, unbelieving of the time. With no visual clues, only the sounds of her blood in her ears and the breath in her lungs, she had misjudged the time badly.

Caution dictated she proceed in her search slowly. But she had obviously been moving at a snail's pace to have only covered what she estimated to be one third of the room. She had better speed up. She would give herself ten more minutes, she told herself. After that, she would have to abandon this, unreconciled childhood or not.

>

How long had it been now? Rebecca estimated the ten minutes she had allotted herself must nearly be up by now. Just a couple more. She could feel her body temperature beginning to rise now. Looking at herself she began to discern her midriff as a violet patch, centred on her chest, and her thumping heart, struggling ever harder to push her heating blood to the skin in an effort to cool her down. *Traitor!* she hissed to it in her head. Slightly unsteadily, she turned and headed for what she hoped was the final part of the gallery, and the ashes.

Sati had crawled along the maintenance corridor as far and as fast as she could, but was barely halfway along it when she felt something. Something switched on in her head, like a door opening in a room letting in clean air. It took her a moment to realise, through the fogging pain in her ankle; the Cotts field had been enabled across the building. It had to be Rebecca. Somehow the westerner had re-enabled the field whose absence had kept her stuck behind the exit, knowing there was no way she could traverse the hundred metres of radar-protected ground between her current position and safety. Sati pushed the throb from her leg, from her mind, as best she could. In her weakened state she was unsure how far she would be able to Displace; but it would be far enough. Offering her silent thanks to Brahma and Rebecca, Sati vanished.

>

She began to tear at the hood she had on, but it stuck to her, pulling at her skin as she tore it from herself. Body heat poured from Rebecca's exposed head and face, shining invisibly in the infrared into the darkness, visible only by the sensors that swept the gallery searching for tell tale indications of human life. The electronic eyes gazed through the dark, directly at the woman blazing near white in their view. But instead of alerting the guards to the presence of an intruder, they merely looked on, relaying nothing more than the darkness of a cold, empty room back to the monitor screens.

Free at last of the stifling hood, whose constricting tightness had been slowly cooking her brain, Rebecca began to comprehend her situation rationally once more. Almost immediately she realised what she had done in her moment of blind animal panic, and her hands flew to her face in a futile effort to mask her heat signature. She had to have been discovered. It was over. The metal and glass of the sensor continued its monocular stare, fixed on the source of greatest heat in the room, the limited-intelligence of its programmed electronics shouting the presence in the gallery back to the control room. But all the guards saw was the flat, uniform black of a deserted gallery.

Rebecca's hands slipped from her face as she began to suspect she had, somehow, not been detected. She looked down at her palms, even the brief contact with her exposed skin enough to show them as bright orange in the cameras' infrared enhanced vision.

Not fully understanding, but deciding to take full advantage of the silence of an alarm free gallery, Rebecca reached for the small torch she had with her. If the infrared of her body heat was not triggering an alarm, then there was no reason to suspect a small amount of white light would either. She wasn't going anywhere until she had retrieved what they had come here for. She was about to head in the direction she thought the shrine was located when she saw the glow of light signalling the return of the guard, the gently rising of the illumination indicating this was the resumption of his scheduled patrol, and not an attempt to apprehend an intruder, her.

A desperate plan blossomed in her mind. She tried to dismiss it out of hand as not only too risky, but crossing a line. But how many lines had she crossed already in this thing? Too many. And her risk-taking average for the day was well over the acceptable danger threshold. Anyway, if she was careful she would not injure him.

The museum guard slumped to the ground, unconscious, and likely to remain so for at least an hour, waking with nothing more than a headache. Not all the exercise Rebecca had ever undertaken had been in the pursuit of personal fitness. She propped his comatose form up against the wall and slipped his lens-screens from his eyes. Almost undeservedly fortuitously, a map detailing where she was in relation to the rest of the gallery glowed in her vision, overlaid across the walls and floors, reaching out through the walls, detailing the museum's contents, and the security route through it. After a moment's examination Rebecca realised she had been barely a handful of metres away from her target during the last hour. This time she would secure it.

One last glance over her shoulder at the unconscious man resting at the top of the flight of stairs, and she was away. In under one minute she was standing at the shrine, and almost as if she were watching through someone else's eyes, saw herself lift the urn, secure its top and stow it in her backpack. A handful of seconds later she was leaving the museum.

Ram sat outside the museum in his bruised Ambassador, just another vehicle among the half a dozen or so that sparsely populated the PDV park of the InSA museum. Watching Rebecca leave via the main entrance he was struck by the boldness of her exit. No skulking out along a maintenance corridor for her. He was forced to admit, he was impressed. Somehow she had managed to best the security systems and in sufficient a manner to allow her egress with, presumably, her prize.

'I trust I have done the correct thing,' he said to himself, and the darkness of the humid Delhi night time.

< <

'Your duty was to find a weakness between the pair and cause their separation. Instead your actions have strengthened their bond. I wanted them divided, not emboldened, and now you see the consequences of your misjudgement. Apart, we could have acted against them individually with ease, and more importantly, impunity. Now once more the questionable wisdom of your approach leaves me with little option but to intervene.'

Thirty-three

Flight

Stripped of the suit, and back in a comfortable and cool sari, Rebecca sat, hiding in the open of the busy twenty-four hour tea and tiffin shops of a Delhi back street. She tried to stop her hands from shaking, the adrenaline high rushing through her bloodstream. She had already had three cups of chai go stone cold in front of her, as she found she was unable to pick them up without spilling their contents. The plain white china cups sat huddled together on the small table of the tea shop.

Around her people bustled past, jostling and bumping the western woman who, if any of them paid her any heed, seemed to shrink into her seat, almost as if she wished to disappear into it. Rebecca was sure everyone could somehow see what she had done, that her actions showed on her face as plainly as if she were a child caught in a lie. She tried not to make eye contact. She was uncomfortably aware of the backpack she had resting on her lap, the weight of the urn inside pressing into her thighs reminding her what she had done. She gripped the bag with one hand at all times, refusing to relinquish contact with it for an instant, like a daughter watching guard over property entrusted to her the only way she knew, needing her parent to return quickly and relieve her of the burden. Her pose was an obvious aberration beyond the usual western care taken in the areas unfrequented by a tourist trade, but Rebecca could not lose her physical link with what she now had in her possession.

Once out of the museum Rebecca realised she had no idea where Sati was, or that she had any idea how to contact her. In desperation she had reverted to the plan and made for the pre-arranged rendezvous.

Trying to steady her hands she checked her watch.

Sati was over two hours late. *Had she been caught? How badly had she been injured? What if she couldn't make their meeting?* Rebecca could answer none of these, or the dozen other questions and concerns that swirled around her mind, threatening to overwhelm her at any moment.

Risking catching the eye of a passing waiter, she requested another cup of chai, and despite his mildly disdainful glance at the three un-drunk cups sitting on her table, brought Rebecca another cup of hot, spicy-sweet tea. She paid him, as she had done three times previously, tipping him generously for his time in indulging her and her unfinished previous orders.

This was absurd. No one here knew what she had done, and she had left no trace of who she was at the museum. She took a deep breath in, trying to relax her diaphragm and released her hold on the backpack. Gripping the hot cup with both hands in an effort to steady it, she raised it to her lips, the growing discomfort of the heat forcing her to bring her shredded nerves under conscious control. The slight scald as she slurped a sip off the top of the hot, sweet liquid was a small reward for her efforts in self discipline. The taste was warm and deep and aromatic, and its familiarity served to ease her tension a little. She drew another sip, deeper than the first, her mouth more used to the temperature now. Somewhere deep in her abdomen she felt something un-knot slightly.

Taking her actions as a signal, the waiter gathered the other, cold cups from Rebecca's table, leaning over her table, obscuring her view of the doorway with his body momentarily. When he stood away from her, Rebecca saw Sati limping into the tea shop on a makeshift crutch. Her heart soared at the sight of the Indian woman and the fact she was whole, if not wholly unharmed.

Rebecca nearly spilled the single cup she had begun to drink as she rose too rapidly from the table to greet and assist her companion. She embraced Sati like a lover reunited, hugging her hard, not letting her go. As she broke the clinch, Rebecca had to check herself as she realised she had almost begun to kiss the woman she was holding, the way a child would a parent. The controlled woman in her regained the upper hand and she helped Sati sit down, deliberately placing her on the opposite side of the table to herself.

Despite the physical separation she had engineered between them, Rebecca was still concerned enough to be sincere when asking what had happened. Sati replied, explaining the additional damage her ankle, now encased in a cast, had suffered in the fall, and her escape by Displacement. Then it was Sati's turn to ask the questions: How had Rebecca managed to stay in the museum so long without tripping the security systems? Had she left any evidence that could be tracked back to them? And, most importantly, had she found the ashes?

Rebecca nodded at the backpack.

'And a sample? Has that been left?'

'Ha. It's secure with the contact you arranged. Despite you not being with me I was able to convince him that his services were still required.' Before Sati could ask her next, obvious question, Rebecca, anticipating it was already answering. 'He said this afternoon.'

Sati sat there, impassive, yet obviously frustrated. She had waited for a quarter of a century and now the truth was almost within her grasp. Another day she could, would be able to manage.

Ram and Joseph sat in the Brahman Group's meeting room, enjoying a breakfast of toast with ginger jam, and strong, black tea to be followed with a small boiled egg curry and flat bread. When they had both finished, they pushed their plates aside. Joseph was first to speak. 'You think she will believe now?'

'She has the proof now. We are close at last.'

'And the risk from the other one? How will that be managed? Our exposure here could be great.'

'Her part in this ensures her silence. We have a record of what she has done, and I doubt that she will offer any resistance or prove a threat once we have explained the situation to her.'

'And if she chooses to involve the law enforcement agencies?'

'There are contingency plans in place.'

Rebecca found herself dragged almost bodily along the busy street by Sati, forcing her to bump and jostle through the crowd. Socrates' collision detection routines were unable to compute the overwhelming number of possible, and ever-shifting paths through the crowd quickly enough for her to avoid knock after knock. By the time they reached the small, inauspicious looking vigyaan shop, just one of the dozens along this stretch of road alone, she was feeling sore and uncomfortable, and in no mood for bad news.

The overwhelming majority of India's raw computing

power came from outlets like these, not the multinational software houses or hardware providers. The countless lakhs of small-scale entrepreneurs competing with each other in the eco-Darwinian environment of the cut-throat, low-margin world of cloud resources, to provide the average person with the bespoke SI services, upgrades, interfaces and plugins their larger counterparts were unable to match.

The seventeen year old owner-cum-senior developer called himself Raj Patel; Rebecca couldn't tell if it was an alias or not, and Sati did not care to know either way. All that was important to her was his analysis of the sample Rebecca had left with him before hiding the rest.

Sati's requirements had been precise, and specified to him over twelve months ago. As such Raj had had little difficulty in obtaining, for a price, the equipment necessary to carry out the work of determining the cremation date of the ashes.

'It is as you are expecting, I think,' he said, his voice soft and quiet, not qualities normally associated with, in Rebecca's recent experience, someone able to perform tasks well outside the recognised bounds of the law. Maybe a few more years of his chosen lifestyle would change that. 'There can be no doubt. I have analysed the sample three times, and each time the quantum dating settles on a date, within a week or so plus or minus, of twenty-four years, ten months and twenty-six days ago. There is little left in the way of recoverable DNA, so I am unable to provide a positive match with...' He trailed off, 'Who did you say this was again?'

'We didn't,' replied Rebecca, refusing to fall for such an obvious trap.

'They are the ashes of Pratheen Chaudray. You will be too young to remember her, but she was first officer of the Vimana twenty five years ago, and according to official records she passed away sixteen years ago.'

'Well, now isn't that a curiosity,' replied Raj either in response to the information or slight disharmony between the two women. 'As always, I dated a reference specimen from six years ago, and whose data were well within acceptable tolerances.'

Raj looked at Rebecca instead of Sati as he spoke, challenging the westerner to question his statement. The less than pleasant journey to the shop, coupled with the rising humidity put her in no mood for the games of a swaggering teenager, however clever he might be. 'That's as maybe, but of course you'll be more than aware of the logarithmic nature of the give or take on any date, so the difference between something two and twenty, or shall we say ...six and twenty-five years old will of course appear the same unless you've calibrated for it.'

Raj held her gaze, and Rebecca did not flinch while Sati's eyes flicked from her companion to the boy standing opposite her.

'So, let's assume that you know how to do your job in all of this, and we'll take it as a given I know how to do mine, and therefore what we gave you, in your professional opinion, are not the documented remains of Pratheen Chaudray.' Rebecca managed to make the word professional seem almost like an insult. 'Sound fair?' She proffered a wad of rupees that would choke an elephant in front of Raj. It was more than he made annually; more than twice what the shop was worth.

Raj masticated his hairless jaw heavily, jutting it out at Rebecca, who stood implacable now the upper hand was hers. Eventually he was forced to agree. 'Ha. That would be a fair assessment of the data.'

'Good.' Rebecca dropped the roll of rupees onto the table with a soft thud. 'Nice doing business with you.'

> >

The police resumed their hammering on the door with renewed determination. *Why hadn't they Displaced in?* It was a question she would have to answer later. Right now Rebecca had to keep them out for as long as possible.

She ran to the window, checking it as a potential exit. Fifteen floors up the glass did not open ten centimetres, let alone enough to squeeze through. And even if she could get out that way, she did not like the look of the drop, into the outdoor swimming pool. Two metres of water was not enough to survive a fall of nearly thirty.

< <

Rebecca and Sati browsed the stalls as if strolling through the middle of a spice market with the twenty-five year old ashes of one of the only eleven people ever to have journeyed out of the solar system was the most natural and normal thing to be doing. It was certain they were still being observed, but now the deed had been done, the best cover was to act as ordinarily as possible. They had been into three vigyaan stores before Raj's, and two more since then, interspersing each visit by dropping into general stores, clothing retailers, curio shops and any other of the wide variety of businesses that traded along the overcrowded Delhi streets. The purchases they made in some of them were currently weighing them down, but also afforded plenty of opportunity for misdirection, and the chance to swap the small urn between themselves.

Rebecca had been enjoying feeling almost normal again, so much that she was beginning to lose herself slightly in the simple pleasure of looking at the wares the merchants had to offer. There were similar markets back home, but the range of spices grown and sold here was vastly greater, quantity and quality being so much more than what was available in London.

She sniffed and tasted what was offered to her as

samples, her fingers stained deeply with the mix of spice, and her nostrils ringing with the aroma of ground cumin, coriander, turmeric and dozens of other scents. It was almost too much.

Her consciousness returned to her with the awareness she had lost Sati in the overcrowding sensations filling her mind. Rebecca realised her complacency; allowing herself to relax after the break-in and confirmation of the ashes' status had led to stopping paying attention to everything in her surroundings. A potentially fatal lapse now the stakes were this high.

She scanned the market urgently, trying to push the haze from her brain and concentrate on locating her companion. She narrowed her eyes against the brightness of the mid-afternoon sun; despite the coverings of the stalls, the light and heat beat fiercely between any gaps in the awnings, shafts of bright hard white, vivid saffrons, deep blues, reds and greens dividing the world.

She went to turn but sensed something behind her. A tickle in the base of her spine ran up to the nape of her neck. In front of her the market seemed to blur, the patches of colour disassociating themselves from their source and bleeding into each other, her sight tunnelling inwards as the prismatic light crowded out her vision from the edges. *Was she fainting?* Arm hairs prickling and not from the heat, Rebecca slowed her search of the crowd, trying as naturally as possible to look as if she was about to walk off, when in actual fact she was readying to spin round and headbutt whoever was behind her. The rather viscous move was the best thing she could think of in the circumstance, the manoeuvre well practised from childhood, her body well trusted to carry it out even if she was about to lose consciousness.

'There you are,' she heard Sati say, just as she was about to turn. 'I looked away for a second only to check we were not being pursued, and when I turned back you had gone. I have been looking for you for over ten minutes.'

Rebecca eased down, releasing the tension from her muscles and gently moved to greet Sati. Both women tried not to show the relief they felt at being reunited.

The hairs on Rebecca's arms rested themselves against her skin once more, and the tickle eased in her head, her vision returning to normal as she tried not to lean on the Indian woman. Noting her companion's distraction Sati insisted they return to the cool dark of Rebecca's hotel room, both of them obviously fatigued from their efforts of recent days.

The knock on the door made Rebecca start.

Since returning to her suite, she had had the privacy field enabled, and was not expecting visitors, even room service. She quizzed Sati with a silent glance. In reply the Indian woman rose saying, 'Shall I see who it is?'

Rebecca barely believed what her companion had just said, finding it difficult to disguise her incredulity as she voiced her negative reply, finishing by telling the Indian woman to sit back down, and that she would check who it was.

'Socrates, who is outside the door?' she asked the SI, which had connected itself to the hotel, and via a series of masterful hacks had infiltrated the building's surveillance network. The image from the camera across the hall from Rebecca's door flashed up on her lenses. She saw four uniformed policemen, well-used lathis at the ready, and a man in civilian clothes; a detective most likely.

'How the chod..?' she trailed off as Sati began to explain.

'I wish I could say I am sorry Rebecca. I called them a little over five hours ago, in the market. You were distracted for a moment, so I Displaced away, only far enough to be out of your line of sight, and told them where you would be, and when.'

'That's what I felt behind me when you returned; your Fold residual. So, what is this? You're turning me in for the robbery on the museum? They look a little heavily equipped to arrest one woman.'

'But not to take an international terrorist into custody, even if she is a woman.' The bluntness of Sati's reply told Rebecca everything she needed to know about Sati's true motives. All they had shared and endured was at best a matter of convenience for Sati, at worst outright lies. She had been played, and now the reckoning was here.

'But, why this? You need the proof we found to expose everything we've discovered. If I'm caught I can implicate you, and the truth will never be known.' As Rebecca was saying the words she knew Sati did not care about her motives.

'Who said anything about exposing the truth? That is you projecting your needs onto someone else again. I am not your mother and I will not be party to your feeble handicap any longer. All I care about is knowing Pratheen is where she should be. If there is a larger secret, then I know it must be kept from others.'

The reference to her mother bit deep into Rebecca, but she was not about to give Sati any more of herself than she had already. All she could muster was spite. 'Fuck you.'

The hammering at the door grew louder. It was only a matter of seconds before the police broke it down.

Sati continued her justification of her actions and betrayal. 'All I ever wanted was to know I was right. Thanks to you I have got what I want, and you can take the blame.'

Sati reached into her sari and retrieved a small silver egg-shaped device. 'My escape route. It provides me just enough time to allow me to get to safety.'

Rebecca glanced over at the Displacement enhancer she had seen Sati use on several occasions sitting on the low table between them. Sati saw the hope in Rebecca's eyes. She picked up and held the gleaming orb of metal and electronics just out of Rebecca's immediate reach.

'You want this? You think it will help you Displace out of here? You who have never Displaced a single metre in your whole life?' Sati taunted Rebecca with the device. 'Perhaps it could give you the assistance you need,' she considered before dropping it to the floor and grinding the delicate electronics and custom software into swarf under her heel. 'Goodbye.'

And with that Sati swept up the urn holding her aunt's ashes and pressed the silver egg to her breast before disappearing.

The battering ceased for second. The police must have realised the privacy field was down, but for how long? Rebecca stood rooted in place with indecision. They would be in here in a second, she knew it.

Instead of appearing in her suite however, the police resumed their hammering on the door with renewed determination. *Why hadn't they Displaced in?* It was a question she would have to answer later. Right now Rebecca had to keep them out for as long as possible.

Despite its purpose in nature as a fire door, the reinforcing contained within it could not stand up to the concerted assault it was being subjected to for much longer. It had been designed to resist flames and heat, physical phenomena it could withstand for hours if necessary; attack by determined humans armed with axes was beyond its capabilities. She had to strengthen it to buy herself some time.

Rebecca started her barricade with the easily moved, lighter pieces of furniture; a chair wedged at an angle under the door handle provided an immediate improvement to the door's strength. Next came anything that was not fixed to the floor. The bed dragged into place to add its considerable weight to the barrier. Then the wardrobe, fortunately not fitted into the room, walked then felled onto the mattress, contents spilling out randomly onto the bed linen. Rebecca scanned the rest of her suite frantic for more mass to put between her and the police. The desk, its matching executive chair, the coffee table and small sofa of the five star room joined the pile of furniture at the entrance to the hallway. And that was it. There was nothing left to add.

OK, so it would keep them out for a little while longer, but it wouldn't hold forever. Sooner or later they'd get around whatever was stopping them Displacing in. She needed another escape route.

Rebecca ran to the window, checking it as a potential exit. Fifteen floors up the glass did not open ten centimetres, let alone enough to squeeze through. And even if she could get out that way, she did not like the look of the drop, into the outdoor swimming pool. Two metres of water was not enough to survive a fall of nearly thirty.

Think girl. What other options have you got?

Something was obviously preventing the police from Displacing in, otherwise she would already be in custody. But Sati had Displaced out hadn't she? Whatever was blocking ingress did not seem to be operating in the outbound direction.

Not exactly the ideal time to have to master Displacement.

But the founding father of the technology had been able to do it unassisted. He claimed he had been able to Displace when he was a teenager; long before the artificial Cotts field he had bathed the earth in, which then made it easier for everyone else. The same field she had never been able to sense.

So it is possible.

Rebecca gritted her teeth as the pounding began on the door continued, trying to recall everything she had ever been taught about Displacing. She did not have time to properly locate a destination; somewhere wide open then;

should be safe... The Fold-residual from Sati's Displacement still lingered in the room; did the air feel slightly heavier than normal? Maybe she could latch onto that and jump out.

She closed her eyes and cleared her mind, doing her best to ignore the persistent noise from outside. Slowing and deepening her breathing she tried to visualise the Cotts field behind her eyelids. There did not seem to be anything there, convinced the Fold Sati left behind must have dissipated by now. Then she sensed something, a tickle at the base of her neck. Desperately she grabbed at it too quickly with her mind and it slipped away.

Chod!

She tried again, and again, but the instant she reached out further than herself she felt the nascent Fold collapse around her.

She couldn't do it. Sati was correct and she had been right about herself all this time; she was a chodding cripple. Incapable of doing what children mastered. Her entire life stretched back to that rebuffal she now knew to be the beginning of the events she was caught up in. The instant her eight-year-old self connected her juvenile obsession with the Vimana to the need for her love. The love which she never gave. That was the instant she learnt how to bury and hide herself from the hurt. If *she* hadn't been so chodding indifferent, things would be different now. She'd be able to chodding Displace for one thing.

Rebecca reached out with her senses once more, desperate to feel the Cotts field. But it was not there for her.

She began to weep. Hot tears of frustration, anger and fear fell from her eyes. 'You chodding kuttiya!' she screamed into the empty air. 'You've chodding damned me!'

The barrier at the door moved slightly; the police were gaining entry. The barriers Rebecca had erected around her childhood self began to crack at the same time. The weight they held back could be contained no longer. Long years of fury at her mother poured into her head and she was powerless to stop the torrent of them this time.

Rebecca fell to her knees, sobbing into the carpet. 'I wish you were dead. I wish you were dead. It would be easier if I knew you weren't out there not caring for me. I wish you were dead!'

It was too late. The door moved another handful of centimetres.

Let them take me. I don't care anymore. You won't hurt me any longer.

Rebecca heard the desk fall from the bed and glanced at the noise. Seeing through her wet eyes she gasped as she felt something switch in her head and pull her bodily somewhere, and out of the room.

As the door finally flew inward sending a shower of splinters at her, space shifted and Folded. Rebecca was gone, leaving the police standing in an empty room, dumbfounded at the pile of clothes and jewellery that fell to the floor the instant she had vanished.

Rebecca materialised naked in mid air. She did not even have time to register her situation and scream before gravity took over her journey and she plummeted earthwards at ten metres per second per second.

She hit the water hard and fast, just curling up into a ball before she smacked into the skin of the swimming pool. Her spine jammed into her ribs and pushed against her internal organs with the gravity accelerated force of her mass. Stunned for a second.

Coming to, the shock of the impact overcome by the shock of suddenly being immersed in water, the animal part of her brain kicking in and dragging her higher consciousness back into play just in time to make her hold her breath. Bubbles swarmed around her, feeling through instinct for the surface, which she broke with a gasp and a scream.

Rebecca hauled herself out of the pool, water sloughing off her like the afterbirth of her rebirth into the world. She collapsed onto the poolside, half-curled up in a ball. Her body coughed the last of the water out of her lungs as she tried to lift herself up to look around. Her head swam, her vision milky.

For a moment she was not sure where she was, or in part even who she was. Then awareness and sense returned to her; but everything was different.

All around her she could see and feel the things that had until this point been denied her. The shock awakening, the hard birth she had undergone into the world that everyone else took for granted. Like a blind woman's sight restored for the first time, she struggled to make sense of what she was seeing.

Displacement traces filled the air, contrails of rainbow light, bright against the night sky, slowly spreading and losing coherence. Origin and destination points stood ghost-frozen, outlines of people where they had been minutes before, the sharp lines of them bleeding out into the air.

Everywhere. They were everywhere.

Rebecca closed her eyes, but they were still there, burning into her mind, through her sealed eyelids directly into her brain. She could not shut them out.

Too much. Too many.

Rebecca spun, unsteady after the Displacement, the fall, the impact. Too many sensations were now suddenly available to her for her adult brain to process. She had not had the years of practice to ignore the Fold-residuals; to look through them until they were part of her world's background. Her body reacted in the only way it knew how.

Feeling only mildly better as she cleaned the vomit from her mouth, the moments before her Displacement came back to her. She looked around, taking stock, painfully aware of the sharp jab in her neck as she moved her head. She did not have time to marvel at the spectacle that lay open before her for the first time; she had to get out.

Looking up at her hotel, the brightest of the Displacement contrails she could see was a line that came from over a dozen floors up and seemed to end some fifteen metres up in the air, directly above the swimming pool she had smashed into. She had no way of knowing exactly how long she had before the police got to where she was, estimating she had perhaps a three or four second lead on them.

First thing: cover her nakedness.

Second thing: get the fuck out of Dodge.

Securing a hotel dressing gown from one of the loungers covered the first part easily enough.

Now, escape.

Rebecca told herself she had done it once, she could do it again. But what if it had been a fluke? A one off instance of panic induced capability. No, you did it just now, you can do it again.

Closing her eyes, Rebecca visualised the other hotel room she had booked under another pseudonym. Just because she had been working with Sati, did not mean she trusted her.

She felt the Fold beginning to form around her, stronger this time than it had ever been. It enveloped her, surrounded her, penetrated and pushed through every fibre of her. And then she felt it pull, a tug to the destination she was visualising. Relaxing into the Fold she mentally let go of her surroundings, and the Fold sprang back open, taking Rebecca along with it.

Despite the lateness of the hour, the swimming pool area was not wholly deserted. Watching Rebecca's exit from her hotel room and her plunge into the water was the man who had set the fire which had killed Samir Kumarapad and who had been present in Marcia's office when Rebecca had called her boss. And now he had seen the woman Displace away to another room in the hotel. He would deal with her. Permanently.

Only he would never get the opportunity to. As soon as he began to Fold space around himself to report back to his master, he found himself torn free of Displace-space, back into the world where he had not intended to be. Standing in front of him was a small, dirty and very elderly naked man, easily in his eighties. Despite the old man's obvious advanced age he stood straight up, not needing to rest his weight on the staff he held. Only his long, matted hair covered his genitals, reaching down in lank grey tresses over his shoulders.

Immediately, the assassin reached for his gun, aiming it at the decrepit figure before him. The ancient he faced smiled thinly then blinked once. There was a tug at his hand, but the figure facing him had not moved. Suddenly the gun was no longer in his possession, it was in his opponent's.

'You have become a liability. I am here to correct the mistakes you have made,' said the shorter man plainly, unloading the gun and depositing the bullets in the small cloth bag slung over his shoulder. 'Your methods attract too much attention. Like this weapon,' he indicated the firearm. 'Subtlety is needed where you blunder inelegantly.' The old man threw the weapon at its former owner, who grasped the air for it. Only it never reached his hands. The last thing he saw before his life ended was the short man standing directly in front of him, holding one hand up, the greasy looking palm approaching his face.

Thirty-four

Waking

There is something particular about hotel rooms, those borrowed spaces taken up by strangers, especially those inhabited for any length of time. Rooms rented by the hour exist for very specific assignations, their occupants, for want of a better word, registering little more than the privacy the lockable door and drawable curtains provide before engaging in the business the room was purchased for. For them, the room is a simple convenience; a place on neutral, and more importantly secure territory. If they are lucky the sheets may have even been changed and the bed re-made before they take ownership, however briefly, of the room and each other's passion.

Rooms booked and inhabited for longer, more usual periods of time all undergo the same transformation. The cream or beige box, that is taken possession of from the porter as he drops the bags and holds his hand out in expectation of a credit of the requisite few hundred rupees, so anonymous at first is filled gradually with the occupant and their presence. Perhaps it is the bath or shower drawn to cleanse away the effects of the journey so the occupant is as neat and freshly prepared as the room itself; the unpacking into wardrobes and drawers, or maybe the strewing of clothes around, marking out territory; or the raiding of the mini-bar, the alcohol hit lifting and deadening at the same time. Whatever ritual is undertaken in laying claim to the room as no longer empty, but the residence of a living, breathing, thinking person, the end result is the same. This is mine, it says.

For periods longer than a few days, the ownership becomes stronger as more and more of the room is filled, as the presence of the occupant inflates into the lesser used areas; drawers are filled with the miscellany of travel, a pile of dirty laundry accumulates, shoes become scattered around. Perhaps it is a process of trying to turn an anonymous, strange area into a sanctuary; an echo of the safety and security felt in a home.

Damien looked one more time around the hotel room in Delhi he stood in, noting the lack of identifiable occupancy by the woman who had booked the room under the false name he had given every time the police knocked on the door to ask him if he had seen the woman in the image they flashed onto his lenses when talking to him.

And every time, twice so far; the first brusquely within the first hour of Rebecca Displacing into the room naked and soaking wet, their immediate efforts to attempt her arrest he surmised; then the next day when they knocked more politely, this time apologising for disturbing his vacation a second time, he said no, he did not know her, and yes he would of course tell them if he saw her around the hotel, so sure they were that she had not Displaced more than a few hundred metres. And no, he was not Damien Regent, the Displacethlete, and that was fine, there was no need to apologise, and yes, he did get asked that a lot. He hoped the lies left waiting for him were convincing ones. Short of physical proof that Damien Regent was actually in London right now, he could not convince them for sure he was who he was pretending to be.

But if he was trying to find any sign that Rebecca had moved into this room he was going to be unsuccessful. The only evidence of her ever being here prior to his arrival was the single unpacked overnight LeatherLike bag she took everywhere with her. If she had not had time to unpack, or, and this was far more likely for her, was keeping herself compact and ready to move in an instant, he could not be sure.

He looked at her, not asleep, but not awake, tucked into the bed where she had been for the past three days. Physically she was healthy; the monitors he had Displaced back to London for within an hour of putting her to bed showed she was very alive, heart rate and blood pressure both strong. Of course he suspected, correctly as it would turn out, what had happened and the effect it had had on her.

'What have you got into?' he asked her for the fifteenth time that hour, shaking his head in half disbelief. 'I'm not sure I should even be doing this. I can't keep stalling the police. I'm sure they know who I am, even with the false name. And I can't keep Displacing back to London for meetings that I'm late for, and training that I'm missing. If I'm honest I'm not sure I can keep it up. I've got perhaps two or three more trips left in me before I have to use conventional transport. And I can't risk exhausting myself unless I know what it's for.' He paused, unwilling to say what he wanted to her, even in her unconscious state after the way they had parted. Eventually the human being in him won over. 'This isn't what I am, Rebecca. Please wake up.'

Nothing. Rebecca may as well have been carved out of marble.

While Damien was in the shower, Rebecca stirred. Only slightly, but enough to cause a shift in the rhythm the heart monitor had been sounding out; the seventy-two beats a minute so regular that Damien had almost filtered their sound out as just more background noise. Then suddenly it changed, jumping up to eighty, then ninety, then one hundred and fifteen, before nearly doubling and reaching one hundred and forty all in ten seconds.

Damien was out of the shower and at her bedside faster than he could Displace between Delhi and London. By the time he was there Rebecca was upright, every muscle in her body in spasm; her eyes wide open and rolled right back in her head, her open lips pulled tight, teeth grinding into each other. Her hands were clenched into tight, white-knuckled fists, fingernails tearing through the sheet in her grip. She would start screaming any second now, and he had to stop her.

Before that happened Damien was behind her with his arms around her, pinning hers to her sides, his right hand clamped over her mouth. Not the best way to return to consciousness admittedly, but better this than she injure herself as her brain tried to process the novel information which had caused it to shut down three days ago.

Rebecca began to fit, shaking violently in his grip as her mind struggled to accommodate the overload. For a second he was worried she would bite her tongue in half. Half releasing the hand clasped over her mouth he worked two fingers between her teeth. He had been right; she bit down hard, breaking his skin and drawing blood, causing him not an inconsiderable amount of pain in the process. He tried not to swear. Still, it would be nothing compared to what she was going through. If there was any mercy in the world she would not remember most of it. She shook for a further minute, until her convulsions slowed and her rigid body slackened. Damien strengthened his hold. Here it came.

Rebecca's eyes, moments ago wild and unfocussed, showed her consciousness as it rushed back to her bruised brain. The flight instinct came over her, stronger than she had ever felt it, but she could not move. She was trapped. Pinned. She fought against the restraint, trying to work a hand free, not realising the thing holding her was another human being, and that he was speaking to her.

All around her swam the residuals of Displacements. Journeys which had passed through the space she occupied, the air around her thick with rainbows, their separated colours unprisming back into white light. She closed her eyes against the sensory onslaught, trying to shut out the sensations that pushed into her brain. But with her eyes shut tight it was worse almost. The brightness still flooded her mind.

There was something in her mouth, kicking off her gag reflex, making her want to vomit. She bit it. There was a muffled, controlled scream of pain from right behind her. Then the words came again, this time the voice was familiar to her.

'...cca, please calm down. ...ien. I'm going... out of... scream, please.'

Slowly the vice she was held in relaxed, but did not let go, and the foreign body in her mouth removed itself. Rebecca drew in a large lungful of air through her unobstructed mouth, and turned her head as much as she could to see what held her.

In the thick, foggy haze of colour, reds and oranges spilling into greens and blues splashed onto violets and yellows, all swimming over each other like oil spilled on water, she concentrated on seeing through it all. A face emerged from the morass. '...Damien?'

He nodded, unsure if he was confirming his presence or his identity to her. Either way the worst of it seemed to have passed and Rebecca at least looked and felt like she was not about to be overcome again. He let her go and lowered her back to the bed.

Standing over her, he watched as her eyes tried to focus first on him, then on the things she could now see streaming across her vision, despite the room's Cotts field nullifier. 'You've been out for three days,' he said in way of relocating her in the here and now, trying to ground her consciousness in the physical world of things, inanimate objects that did not leave Displacement trails across your sight. 'Here.' He proffered a glass of water, knowing the cold of the liquid and the sensation of slaking thirst would help re-orientate her.

Rebecca took a sip, then began to drink greedily.

'Slowly,' Damien said. 'Too much too quickly and you'll just be sick again.' He took the glass from her after she had sipped about half of it.

'You're here?' Rebecca was barely able to whisper her question.

He nodded slowly, confirming his presence to an unsure Rebecca. 'Ha. I got the relayed message via Daley. I've been here as long as you've been out. I arrived a few minutes before you materialised, but just in time by the look of things. Must have been a helluva shock to the system that first Displace. But then to execute a second one so soon after. I suppose the proximity of destination point helped you along, but all the same an impressive first go.'

Rebecca struggled through her fogged brain to her last memory, confused at Damien's presence, then cast her eyes down at her hands which were now folded on her lap. 'You know then?' was all she was able to croak. She reached for another sip of water.

Damien considered a lie, but that was Rebecca's way; her defence mechanism in situations where she would feel threatened if forced to reveal even a sliver of the truth. 'I've always suspected. Whenever you've been around you've never felt completely there. In the Cotts field, I mean. I expect that doesn't make much sense immediately, but I think it will from now on. And then seeing you appear a metre above the floor, naked and missing your nose and earrings I knew immediately what you'd done. Don't worry, almost everyone loses their clothes the first time.'

Rebecca looked up at her former lover. Something had shifted between them since their separation. He had grown up perhaps. Or maybe she had allowed him to. Whatever it was Rebecca suddenly and completely felt able to confide in him in a way that would have been impossible only a few months ago. 'My first,' she said quietly, the strength returning to her voice. 'I'm thirty three and you're twenty two and you can do things I can't even begin to ever hope to replicate.' Then she added, 'Did you?'

Damien looked puzzled for a second, then realised what Rebecca was asking him. She was seeking validation that she was not that unusual, even if she was coming to her newfound ability nearly thirty years after everyone else. Now perhaps it was time for a small lie. 'Ha. As naked as the day I was born.'

'Liar,' Rebecca countered, but good naturedly. 'But thanks for trying to make me feel better. I imagine you did your first fully clothed and with everything still in your pockets.'

'Actually, I hijacked my big brother at the time. He was as surprised as I was. It was a game we used to play; he'd carry me on his back and Displace away carrying me. I begged him to let me try. Not many four year olds can Displace the added mass of a twelve year old sibling.'

'You need to teach me,' she said, the need to master her nascent skill driving her determination. 'I need to know how it works if I'm going to figure out what happened twenty five years ago on the Vimana.' Rebecca tried to get up out of bed, but only got as far as swinging her legs over the side before the nausea swept over her and she regurgitated the water she had just drunk.

'I will, you'll only be in greater danger without knowing how to control it,' Damien called from the bathroom he had headed into to retrieve a washcloth for Rebecca and a dampened towel to clear up the vomit.

There was a knock on the door.

Thirty-five

Manoeuvres

Wednesday 5 July 2056 - 23:48 IST

'Where is she likely to have gone? You spent many weeks both following and then working with her. You know her better than any of us. What is her next move?'

As soon as she had materialised three days previously, not in her apartment as she had intended, but in a windowless room three metres cubed, Sati realised she had been captured. The cell she appeared in was, if the total absence of a detectable Cotts field was any indicator of location, deep underground, most likely several kilometres. Her D-enhancer confirmed her suspicion, the weak CF radiation it emitted informing her the least dense volume of matter it could find was one thousand and thirty six metres above her. From the readings it was most likely the remains of one of cell's previous occupants, materialising in the Indian bedrock in a failed escape attempt. She had no desire to join him.

Going nowhere, Sati examined the room she found herself in. Its cold stone walls were lit from the ceiling by a single bulb, sited behind thick, grimy glass, itself concreted in place. There was nothing in the way of furniture, not even a stool for her to rest on. The room's only feature aside from the illumination was a metal pail, obviously intended as her toilet judging by the marks and stains smeared around its edges. With little option but patience, Sati put the urn down and sat on the floor to wait for her captor to arrive.

She was forced to admit to herself that the Brahman Group's plan to seize her and Rebecca had been well executed. She could almost admire the patience it must have taken not to apprehend them both sooner, but to wait for the correct moment. InSA and the Brahman Group had been unable to invoke the necessary legislation to interfere with the Cotts field until they had committed an act of national disrespect. Sati glanced at the urn and smiled ruefully. Once the women had removed that last legal protection, it was simple enough to employ the local police, not known for their finesse, to create the need to flee in the pair so they would inevitably try and Displace out to safety. As soon as they had done that, catching the Folds and re-directing them to wherever they wanted had been easy. In Sati's case, a holding cell for known D-terrorists buried deep underground.

If the plan had been to intercept two Displacement trajectories then they would have been only partially successful. What the police would not have known was, at least as far as Sati was aware, Rebecca could not Displace. She liked to imagine their confusion standing outside the hotel room waiting for their second target to attempt a Fold so they could pinball her off to some dark room in the bowels of the earth, but it never coming.

Sati looked up at Ramkumar Mei. He had been asking her the same questions since he had appeared along with two moulded plastic chairs a few hours ago. By his line of questioning it was apparent Rebecca had not conformed to their plan, or it seemed her knowledge of her. Sati had learnt from Ramkumar that the westerner had appeared to prevaricate in the room, which Ramkumar now knew to be her inability to escape by the means Sati had done so. This had necessitated a physical break-in, which had been slowed by Rebecca's efforts to keep them out. But as the police were forcing the door, the CF manipulator had malfunctioned, seemingly choosing the exact instant Rebecca finally learnt the trick of Displacing to switch itself off. As well as that the Cotts field strength in the room increased a lakh-fold, easing her first Displacement, before disappearing to nothing with nano-second accuracy, meaning the police had no way to determine her ultimate destination point.

'How did she achieve that?'

'If I knew that do you think I would have let myself be caught?'

'But you told us that as far as you knew she could not Displace?'

'Evidently she has learnt. And I tell you this, if she has then there will be trouble.'

'Is that a threat?'

'No. You must know what sort of woman she is. Determined. Even I was impressed by the way she handled our little robbery.'

'I must concede you appear to be correct there. This is a development our SIs had not anticipated. Which is in part why we are here having this particular conversation. Rebecca Eckhart knows a lot, even most of the truth, but not all of it. I know what drives you Sati Chaudray, and very soon I will be in a position to grant it. But first I need to know everything you know about Rebecca Eckhart.'

> >

'Put this on.' Damien tossed Rebecca one of the hotel dressing gowns then glanced between her and the door.

'You haven't got time to get dressed, and anyway, it's not cold where you're going.'

'What? Going? Going where?'

'Please Rebecca, I've got about ten seconds before I have to answer the door to the police again. I need to Displace you out of here.'

'You can do that?' Rebecca rose unsteadily to her feet, slipping her arms into the soft cotton sleeves, the feeling of the fibres on her skin tickling her slightly.

'Ha,' he replied, positioning Rebecca in front of himself, then laying a palm on the centre of her chest. 'I'm sorry, but in order to keep them from following you I'm having to send you the long way round. This will be a bit bumpy. I'll be along as soon as I can. Try and hide yourself.' Then almost as a deliberate afterthought knowing Rebecca could not answer him, he added, 'By the way. When did you start calling yourself Becky?'

'Wha...' was all Rebecca managed to get out before she felt space twist and bend around her then pull her out of the hotel bedroom.

< <

'How did you circumvent the museum's security system? I sat outside the building for over two hours watching and waiting for one or both of you to trip one of the sensors. I was impressed, to say the least.'

'I suppose there is no point in being coy, since we are becoming such good friends, is there Ramkumar?'

Ram shook his head gently. Sati continued. 'We did not. Or at least we did not for the length of time I was in there. Given the duration you say she was active, Rebecca should have triggered your IR sensors. The suits we only guaranteed to hide us for about an hour. After that, perhaps only a few minutes.'

'Yet she was in there for well over another hour, and

disabled a guard as well. All very impressive for someone supposedly operating at a body temperature of twenty-three degrees. Are you sure she has had no contact with anyone here in India, or before that who could infiltrate our system at the museum?'

Sati thought. 'No, not in India that I know of. I admit I was not with her all the time, but I would have thought your surveillance would have alerted you. I am correct in assuming you have had her under observation the whole time she was in India?'

'And in Britain. Our SIs can penetrate anywhere in their country-wide coverage of micro-cameras. Such a usefully paranoid state, so reliant on the technology we provide them. And so convenient they opted out of the Global Surveillance Treaty. The only time we do not know what she was doing exactly, was when she fell out of our capability to watch her without explicit satellite observation along the Mexican border. But you were there, were you not? What did you see her do?'

'Nothing. My trip to that backwater was a waste of time. I nearly died trying to keep up with her in that truck, pretending to be Mexican, constantly in fear for my life. If you have been following her, I assume you have had me under observation at least since I made contact with her.'

Ram pivoted his head in confirmation.

'And before then?'

'Your relationship with Prakat.' It was a statement. Ram understood perfectly to what Sati was referring to. 'Ha, we know about that. It is InSA policy to keep twenty four hour surveillance on the members of the Brahman Group, and everyone associated with the Vimana. So you came to our attention very early on.'

Sati frowned, thinking she had failed to secure her identity over the long years of concealment. Ram corrected her. 'Your cover was perfectly flawless. It took our SIs several months to determine whose niece you were. But we are very patient. And persistent. Eventually we discovered a trace of what Pratheen had done, and from there were able to surmise the intervening years. And we forecasted your likely actions, up to and including the museum burglary. But then reality diverged from our predictions. It had been my intention to detain you in the museum once you had triggered the security system. But as we both know, events did not proceed along the path we had ordained for them. If we had known who you were earlier, our paths would had crossed much sooner than this.'

Sati narrowed her eyes, perceiving a threat.

'Oh, no, we would still be having this conversation, or at least one very like it, but it would have taken place months ago, and most likely in my office rather than this place. In fact your relationship with Prakat can be turned to our advantage.'

Sati picked up on the plural immediately. 'Our?'

'If you are willing to do as I ask, then yes, our advantage. If not, then, well, it will be my advantage. And this time that is a threat. Do not think me incapable of acting as necessary in order to carry out my duty. However, do this one thing and all threats will become unnecessary,' Ram said flatly, honestly.

It was not the first time Sati had been threatened, but Ramkumar Mei had the power to make her disappear in a way few people had. Still, she refused to be cowed. 'I do not work well under coercion.'

Ram smiled and spread his hands out before himself, palms open and turned towards Sati. A gesture of reassurance. 'I am in no way forcing you. Think of it as the final part of your interview process. It is time to excise some of the old and replace it with the new.' He drew his hands together and rested them on his lap.

Sati extrapolated what Ram was hinting at. 'You have trouble from within?'

'Very astute Ms Chaudray. You could think of it as a

small issue of needing people whose capabilities I am sure of. Someone who has worked all their life to find out the truth, and once they know, realise its significance.'

Sati knew this was her chance. Ramkumar was offering her the real truth of what had happened to her aunt in the dark of space, crores of kilometres away from the small planet she called home. At last she would know how she died, the truth behind the fiction the world had been told for a generation, until it became the accepted version of things. More than that she would know for herself. Be privy to knowledge that others were deemed insufficiently prepared of comprehending. And it would become her duty to guard that knowledge, to maintain the convenient untruth which protected the world. There was only one reply.

'Good. This is provident. I knew we were correct to invite you in.' Ram reached into his jacket and withdrew a slim silver cylinder. 'Take this. It will enable you to leave this place and take you where you need to go. You will find Prakat's current location. Go to him and tell him that Rebecca has evaded you and you need his help in locating her. He will seek to enlist the assistance of the other members of his splinter group. Tell him I told you to tell him this. Prakat is not by nature a dishonourable man, he is merely misguided in who he listens to when it comes to protecting what we keep secret. It is the individual who guides him I want. They are an influence we do not need or want. Tell Prakat as much or as little of this as you feel necessary to send him to his master. What is imperative is that they act whether they believe Prakat has been compromised or not. Their devotion to the secret will compel them to take steps to locate Rebecca, and think in ways I do not.'

'But they will know you are laying a trap for them. They have acted against you, and yet you still wish to use them.'

'Do not mistake desire for expedience. They know as much as any of us, and if I cannot enlist them formally as part of our group then I will manipulate them into doing what needs to be done. They are a tool, that is all. An unwieldy one to be sure, blunt where finesse should be used, but in circumstances such as this one must employ whatever options one has their disposal.'

Sati took the enhancer from Ram, and as soon as she touched it she disappeared, leaving Ram alone deep underground. He sat on the hard, utilitarian chair he had Displaced in with him thinking how Rebecca had managed to disable the museum security system, how she had gained entry into India without being noticed by their SIs. It was certain she was receiving powerful assistance from someone. Ram ran through the list of known A-tech experts currently in India who possessed the knowledge and resources. Two worked for InSA and the other was safely in their protective custody. He did not know of anyone else in the world with the necessary skills of both hacking a passport in real time and infiltrating the InSA museum's security system. And why had she risked going to the Mexican border? Who or what had been on the border that could assist her?

What? Not a who, but a what. Ram stood up, and Displaced out taking his chair with him, but leaving one behind for the next inhabitant of the cell. It would be impolite not to give Rebecca something to sit on.

True to her word to her new boss, Sati met with Prakat and explained as much as she could remember from her conversation with Ramkumar. How Rebecca had indeed eluded them all, and was as yet undiscovered. How Ramkumar knew of Prakat's membership of the Saazish, but had little interest in his indiscretions; it was his unknown master that Ramkumar wanted.

Prakat, for his part, understood the seriousness of what was mounted against him. He had been the architect of his own undoing, and was being presented with an opportunity to re-balance some of the mistakes he had made in his life. Ramkumar was, not exactly offering him absolution, that was not within his power to give, but he was granting Prakat a reprieve in order to allow him to redress some of the damage he had inflicted on his karma by working toward something larger and better than himself.

> >

Rebecca materialised outside, high up judging by the view of the tops of buildings all around. There they were again, filling the sky; lines of light slowly fading all around, the strongest and brightest coming from her and zooming away from the front of her somewhere across the city sky. She did not even have time to turn around and wonder where Damien had sent her before she felt another Fold coming over her. *He's doing it...*

...remotely.

She appeared somewhere dark, somewhere that felt enclosed after the wide expanse of cityscape she had just left. The rapidity of the two Displacements, one immediately after the other left her woozy. She wobbled on the spot, but did not fall over. The bright line of her last Displacement trajectory filled her vision. Looking at herself, her skin seemed to burn brightly, but did nothing to illuminate the space she stood in. Rebecca held an incandescent hand up in front of her, her fingers haloed with the CF radiation. She reached out to try and find a wall, thinking Damien had transported her inside somewhere. *There was nowhere to hide here...* was as far as her thought processes got before the next Fold swept her away.

When Rebecca slid into the world once more she was again standing outside, again on a rooftop. This time she thought nothing and did nothing, expecting another of Damien's remotely directed Folds to whisk her away to who knows where. And besides, after travelling a little over six kilometres in just under a second, her nervous system was in need of the respite from thinking anything too profound relating to the distances covered by remote control Displacement. She closed her eyes in anticipation but that just made her feel nauseous again, and offered no relief from the Displacement trajectories once more filling her vision of the night-time sky. She opened them again and waited.

Counting in her head, she reached fifteen before beginning to suspect this was her final destination. An additional fifteen made her as confident as she could be that she was not about to be whisked off somewhere else, and that she had better do as Damien had instructed and find somewhere to conceal herself.

Then Rebecca recognised the view, or at least she thought she did. Turning ninety degrees through the cityscape and adjusting for the difference in height, the memory of the view of the pool from her previous hotel room married in her mind with what she was seeing now. Damien had transported her to the roof of the hotel.

Why here, and why such a convoluted route here?

Trusting Damien to have his reasons, and knowing he would come for her, but it would still be better if she hid herself, Rebecca looked round at the flat expanse of the hotel roof. The only structure of any note was the small metal building housing the air-conditioning units.

She tried the door, and finding it locked, forced it anyway with a sharp crunch, and a stab pain from her arm. Leaning back against the inside of the door she held her bruised arm and waited for Damien and rested, while inside her mind she struggled to quieten the buzz of questions.

Thirty-six

Back and Forth

Saturday 8 July 2056 - 21:22 IST

'Coming!' Damien opened the door to once more see, waiting impatiently, the two detectives he had come over the past three days to know as Inspector Talwan and Sergeant Gowda. They had just been about to knock again. Doubtless they wanted to re-question him about Rebecca in the manner which less and less subtly told him they in fact knew who he was and that he was protecting her. He had been informed that Rebecca was a wanted international fugitive responsible for a variety of crimes, any one of which an accomplice could expect to spend the remaining bulk of their very likely foreshortened adult life in a D-sealed prison for.

Damien had to convince them otherwise.

'Please, come in,' he gestured, inviting them into the room.

'Thank you Mr Collins. We appreciate your time,' the older, senior officer said as they all took seats in the room, Damien on the single chair, the police officers sitting side by side on the two person sofa. Despite the five-star nature of the hotel, like most of the room's functional furniture, the sofa was designed only to be utilised for short periods and not meant for extended use; it was just large enough to deserve its designation as a two-seater. Damien had to suppress a smile as the policemen's knees bumped into each other as they sat, the unexpected physical contact causing them to become conscious of the proximity of the other. Despite the two men's obvious length of partnership they were still not comfortable with any unintended physicality between them. It was a small point, but one he noted that might serve to unsettle them a little.

'Now, what can I do to help?' he asked, in as friendly a tone as he could.

Fifteen minutes later, the interrogation was drawing to an end, and Damien had given nothing more away, but neither had he convinced the two men of his cover story. After he had answered their final question the two policemen remained seated on the sofa in silence as if he should continue. The policemen's body language and expressions were blank; passive-aggressive disregard and disinterest in him until he tripped himself up. Cautious not to give them anything more of himself, Damien resisted the urge to fill the space they had left with further uninvited answers.

Saying nothing, he felt momentarily as if he had made his first real mistake in his handling of them. By seemingly refusing to co-operate he was perhaps inviting them to arrest him on whatever pretext they wanted. After all, as far as they should be concerned he was not the international D-thlete he happened to bear an uncanny resemblance to, and therefore his detention would have no diplomatic consequences. And if he did confirm he was Damien Regent, then he would then be facing charges of conspiracy and god only knows what else.

The three men sat facing each other, the silent space between them now having been left to grow into the room's fourth, and obvious occupant. The pressure to speak was balanced in opposition by the sensation that a human voice would be an unnatural intrusion into this new equilibrium which had enveloped them. Damien projected a good-natured, if perplexed, willingness to appear helpful; he knew the technique being deployed against him and resisted continuing speaking, acting as if he had told them all the answers they had asked for, and could add nothing more.

The policemen relied on their authority to maintain their composure, staring through him as if he were of no importance or status, even though they were technically guests in his presence, only there under his sufferance. They held the upper hand in this situation; he could not confirm they had all the information they needed, nor could he rise to move around the room without forcing them into action.

Damien knew he could not wait them out; they had as much time as it took for him to concede to their superiority, he had to get to Rebecca. One of the policemen, the junior, shifted slightly, trying to minimise the contact he was making with his boss. Damien saw his chance.

As Gowda was settling back into the grooves his buttocks had pressed into the sofa's seat without even a sideways glance from his boss, Damien reached through the Cotts field and imperceptibly shuffled the two cushions the policemen sat on a fraction of a centimetre closer together, effecting the contact of their lower legs. After the extended period of self-control on his part, the sergeant reacted instinctively to the unexpected contact with a shrill cry of surprise, the high pitched noise immediately breaking the power the omnipresent silence had granted the policemen.

Talwan, forced to react to his junior's outburst realised the shift in balance away from them. Their authority drained away in the time it took the sergeant to compose himself. Timed the way it was, the action was hidden from both men, instead seeming as if, in adjusting his posture

Gowda had caused the loss of face. Barely able to hide his displeasure at his junior, the inspector rose and offered Damien his polite goodbye and thanked him for his time and patience while they conducted this important investigation.

Damien rose a second after the senior policeman and reached out to shake his hand, with a 'It was no trouble officer,' a firm indication of his control of his own space once again. As the policemen left, Damien clasped each of them by the shoulder as he once again shook their hands, subtly pulling them towards himself as if her were about to embrace them. He was quietly satisfied to feel an instinctive resistance to the tension in his grip as each man took an involuntary half-step backwards.

Closing the door on them Damien put his eye to the spy-hole and watched them begin to leave along the corridor, each shrugging off his over-familiarity. His relief that they were going vanished when Talwan paused and began speaking, obviously comming with someone. Both policemen stopped, and looked back at his room.

Instinctively he drew back from the door, but forced himself to look once more. The inspector was still talking and neither of them had moved any closer back to his room when Daley alerted him that there were two gentlemen outside his London flat requesting entry, and that Daley had informed them that he was currently training, and if they wished to leave a message they could.

Hagga! It must be the police in London checking where he was. He had to go back home. Now.

Pulling back from the door once more, he stood in the middle of the room, well away from any furniture, and thought about his destination in his flat. An image of his bedroom appeared in his mind. He drew the image back, visualising the apartment block, then the road, then the layout of the streets, zooming out from the ground up into the sky until his mental image showed clouds passing by below. Then he pulled his mental camera across the globe, spinning the blue ball beneath him until he was located over India, where he reversed his zoom, diving headlong toward Delhi, the district he was in, the street the hotel was on, targeting the hotel and finally into the bedroom he stood in.

The connection in his mind was made. Just as he was letting go, and allowing the Fold he had created to pull him along, he caught sight of Talwan's wallet sitting on the small two-person settee. *It must have fallen out when he had moved the cushions,* was all he had time to think before he vanished from the room and headed toward London.

Damien materialised in his bedroom, exactly where he had been visualising. Talwan would at the very least be back for his wallet and almost certainly soon. He had to get rid of the London police, and quick.

Here he could be Damien Regent, Displacethlete. The Metropolitan Police had no idea what sort of person Damien Regent was apart from Olympic medallist, and therefore extremely busy and important. No, most likely, self-important. Incredibly self-important. And very dismissive of lesser beings than himself. *Perfect.*

He pressed the TALK button on the door entry system. 'What?' he barked as intemperately as he could. 'This had better be good.' *Careful, don't overdo it.*

'Mr Regent?' a man's voice asked. 'Detective Inspector Wilkes, Metropolitan Police. Can we have a moment of your time?'

'How did you get this address? How do I know you're the police?'

The voice at the other end of the intercom was unfazed by his rudeness. 'Let us in and we can answer both questions for you.'

Damien checked the camera that gave him a view of the entry door. There were two men standing there, just as there were currently two-thirds of a second away in India. The parallel would have been amusing if it were not life-sentence-in-prison serious. The one not doing the talking to him was obviously comming, almost certainly with the police in India. *This might work. Need to concentrate though.* 'Give me one second. I was training.'

Damien Folded space again, traversing the reverse of his first trip, easily inverting the dissipating Fold so he was standing back in the hotel room in India once more. Wasting no time he picked up the fallen wallet and opened the hotel door. 'Ah, detective,' he said to the surprised and now guilty looking policemen. Lurking in the corridor outside a potentially innocent man's room after bidding him goodbye would be seen as impolite at best, suspicious at worst.

Damien played it innocent, adopting the sort of wholesome voice he used when doing promotional and inspirational tours of schools. A mix of good natured and helpful. 'I think you left this in my room.' He skipped out towards the policeman, the wallet proffered in his hand. 'Glad I caught you.'

'Uh, thanks,' Talwan replied. 'No, sorry not you,' he apologised into the small comm on his lapel.

Damien hopped back to his room, bidding the police a final farewell, and closed the door with a smile. Peering through the spyhole he saw the two detectives walk off, the inspector shaking his head as he continued his conversation with his counterpart in London.

Now to sort them out.

Six thousand seven hundred kilometres of space bent and flexed under his will one more time. This time however, he left his clothes in India, deliberately choosing not to carry them with him. He arrived sweating and out of breath, which suited his purposes, but even for him this was nearing too much.

He strode to his apartment's front door and flung it

open wide to greet the two policemen. *Lucky it's warm in India,* he mused wryly as he placed his fists on his hips. 'I hope this is important. I had to interrupt a training session to speak to you.'

Now the British detective inspector was fazed. 'Uh... ahh...' he stammered. 'Can we carry on this conversation inside? Perhaps you'd be more comfortable?' he added hoping to usher the naked man indoors.

'I'm fine here. You really are interrupting my training. And how did you get this address?' Damien was determined to carry on as much of the conversation as he could on his doorstep. If they got inside he could be hours getting rid of them, and he needed to get to Rebecca stuck on the roof of the hotel.

'Uh, well, we spoke to your agent, telling him we had had a request from the Indian police to check on you.'

'Check on me? What for?' Damien paused for a beat, not long enough to give the Inspector a chance to reply before continuing. 'Wait a minute. I know what this is about. They sent you here precisely *to* disrupt my training schedule. They don't want me in peak condition for the upcoming games. I hope their request was in order.'

'Well, we can't divulge what this is about. Let's just...'

The inspector's sergeant tugged at his boss's jacket then shook his head when he had got his attention. Immediately the tenor of the inspector changed, his demeanour shifting, deflating as if being given bad news. The professional in him composed himself. 'It would appear that there has been a misunderstanding. I am sorry to have bothered you. Please accept my apologies, we should not have come here.'

'What? That's it? You interrupt me at the behest of the nation of my closest rival and then you're sorry?' The policemen began to back away, genuinely contrite in the face of Damien's false indignation. Damien slammed the door, completing his act with a flourish, hoping the Indian and British police believed he could not possibly be in two places at once.

Either way, he had exposed himself enough for Rebecca.

Thirty-seven

Reconciliation

Saturday 8 July 2056 - 21:38 IST

Becky?

Had Damien said Becky just before he had Displaced her out? But that was ridiculous. Becky was an Ayaye, was a construct of her from her diaries, was weeks ago and twelve thousand kilometres away. She, no, it could not be contacting her now. And if so, why anyway? Rebecca had made it plain that the Ayaye's usefulness had come to an end when she left the Mexican border.

Or had she? Rebecca remembered back up the daisy chain of events that had brought her here, wrapped up in a hotel dressing gown hiding on a hotel roof in the middle of Delhi.

She thought back to how she and the Ayaye had parted. She remembered driving back to meet it, but had never made it back to her. The news about Kumarapad had deflected her from that course. She had left Becky waiting for her, an eight year old waiting for her mother to return.

But that was ludicrous. Ayayes could be anything they wanted, couldn't they? Really, Rebecca did not know.

There was very little humanity understood about its electronic children. She was currently the sole interlocutor to have had the greatest interaction with an Ayaye ever, and her working knowledge of the Artificial Intelligences started and stopped with Becky; as far as Rebecca could guess she had disappeared back somewhere into the electronic reality they inhabited.

But hadn't Becky stepped out of the Ayayes' world and into the human Internet? After all, she had obtained information for Rebecca from a variety of cloud sources. So why could she not be still waiting for Rebecca to return? And if Becky was still outside her own reality what would she be doing? Rebecca almost admitted that there was no way she could know that, when she realised that in fact she was probably the only person who could predict what Becky might do. She would want her mother's attention.

Helena on the passport..?
The bright pink obfuscator..?
The disabled alarms in the gallery..?
Damien's presence here..?
And how many others?

Was that it? Was Becky intervening in her actions, hinting and alluding to her presence with barbed clues from her past and other more direct help? It certainly felt like something Rebecca would have done aged eight. Spiting and needing her mother all at once, throwing things that would wound in a deliberate attempt to provoke a reaction, any reaction. Even anger would be better than apathy. At least it proved there was some feeling there. And it took willpower to chase affection that hard. Becky had far more strength than she had had at that age.

There was a knock at the door. She did not answer.

'Rebecca?' whispered Damien. 'Sorry I had to shunt you out of the way like that. Open the door, it's me.'

Rebecca got to her feet and pulled the door open to see Damien standing there in his birthday suit. 'Why are you naked?' she asked obviously.

'Why are you crying?' he asked back in the way of a reply.

Rebecca brought a hand to her cheek, which was wet with her tears. She realised she had not even noticed them.

'They know it's me helping you. I can't risk being here any longer than is necessary.' Damien was explaining to Rebecca about the synchronised police visit to the room and his London apartment. 'I got away with it once, but the next time, and I know there will be a next time I need an iron clad alibi. Even I struggle to be in two places at once.'

'But I need you to show me how to make it work. I barely got out of the hotel intact last time. I don't relish appearing naked every time I try to Displace anywhere. At least teach me how to keep my clothes on.'

Damien hesitated before seeming to come to a decision as to how much more unskilful karma he could pile on to himself. 'I can teach you enough to keep you out of immediate danger; how to sense large objects at your destination and the like so you don't end up half inside something. And yes, I'll teach you to how to remain dressed.'

Over the next eight hours, with half a mind on Daley notifying him of the policemen's return, Damien taught Rebecca the basics of Displacing as first explained by Professor Cotts, the ability's discoverer and greatest master. Rumour and story orbited the missing, though now long presumed dead Professor; his alleged exploits attaining near-mythic status without the man to verify the stories. About how he had, so the legend went, learnt to Displace long before the advent of the worldwide network of CF generators now in low-earth orbit, or how he was supposed to have communed with animals. It was claimed he had even personally Displaced to other planets. Fantastic tales. The exaggerations of children's stories, and unreliable as

403

proof of any ability other than exceptional mathematical genius.

What was certain was that given enough of the correct type of concentration, assisted and boosted by the CF field, it was perfectly possible to Fold two points on the planet, in sixth dimensional space at least, until they touched, and to step through the infinitely small space between them as easily as crossing from one side of a hotel room to the other. After an hour of his careful and sometimes less than patient tutelage - *Do you think I'm trying to make this difficult?* – Damien had Rebecca successfully separating the multitude of Displacement trajectories she could sense surrounding her, and concentrating on projecting, and Folding one of her own through the void between atoms.

Rebecca for her part struggled. She was a mute trying to learn the phoneme sounds of English, Hindi, Urdu, Latin and Coptic; a blind woman granted sight for the first time seeing only colours and not the delineated forms of the whole; deaf and hearing a hundred symphonies all at once and trying to pick out a single note in the cacophony. She was filtering and incorporating a brand new sense; an adult learning the skills a child took for granted. More than once she was sick, the retches becoming painful dry heaves after only the second time.

Still she persisted at it, refusing and ignoring Damien's offer of a brief respite.

Her body ached, her head hurt, the area behind her eyes throbbing. She felt sickness in a way she never had before, a deep nausea she might never recover from. But underneath it all was a tickle in her mind. She mentioned it to Damien.

'That's it!' he exclaimed. 'That's your pineal gland picking up on the Cotts field that penetrates everywhere. If you can feel that you can use it to pull yourself through. Let's try. Try and Displace from one side of the room to the other,' he urged.

404

Rebecca narrowed her gaze at him. 'You sure this isn't a ruse just to get me naked?' she said flirting more than a little. She was seeing Damien in new ways, ways she had not let herself see earlier. And she wanted him. Deep within her was the tug once more. That animal feeling of desire. A real human emotion.

If he picked up on the half offer, he ignored it. 'Try.'

Rebecca stalked to the other end of the hotel room, and turned to face her former lover. 'OK, genius, so what do I do?'

'Just what I taught you. Imagine yourself entirely, clothes and all as a single entity, as if they're attached. No that's the wrong word, as if they're part of you. And Fold the space between us.'

Rebecca closed her eyes, and concentrated on filtering the extraneous Fold residuals and Displacement trajectories from her mind. One by one they fell away, fading into the ultra-black background of the Cotts field she finally felt all through her. She opened her eyes again, and for the first time since she smashed her way into the world of Folds, falling into the swimming pool, she could see nothing but the room in front of her.

She chose a spot three metres away, right by Damien's side, feeling his mass in the space next to it like he had taught her. She willed that point to her.

Damien sensed the trajectory emerge from his ex-lover and snake its way over to next to him, feeling its way through the space between them until it steadied and held.

Rebecca vanished from the other side of the room and appeared right next to him. She nearly fell over, and Damien grabbed her to stop her from collapsing. 'I've got you,' he said.

She looked up at him and said weakly, 'I did it.'

'Ha, you did it.'

Rebecca recovered her balance, but held on to Damien for a second longer than was strictly necessary. 'But that was only once and only a few metres and took me nearly a minute. You can Displace thousands of kilometres in a second. I need to learn how to go further, faster, longer. More.' The last word was said with an urgency she had not realised was there before now. Holding Damien like this was the first real physical human contact she had had since he had left her flat months ago. The urgency in her rose. She pushed her crotch into his. 'One more time?' Rebecca asked coquettishly. 'My way of saying thanks?'

Damien shook his head gently. 'Sorry. No. Sorry,' he added a second time, as if repetition would add weight to the explanation of his refusal of her. He held her close to him for a long moment. She was beginning to have real feelings for him after all those months of whatever it was she had previously got from him.

Rebecca needed clarity of thought and purpose in whatever she was about to undertake, and worrying about him even in the slightest would distract her. She needed strength but the only way to give her that was to remove himself from her life completely. Her greatest weakness, her wrapped up, tightly-bound hard ball of anger would also be, when it came to Displacing, her greatest asset.

The total control of her bottled-up feelings she possessed would give her the will that would allow her to cover the distances she needed. But he could not tell her that; to reveal the secret would to be rob it of its power. If she was to stand any chance of surviving even a single Displacement of a few kilometres, let alone face whatever InSA might have waiting, she needed another reason to hate herself, even the smallest part; the part that obviously loved him in the weird, dependant-at-arms-length way she ever let herself get close to anyone. Doing this would cripple her emotionally for months, but better that than permanent physical disability or mental impairment from a lapse of concentration or failing of will at a crucial moment.

'I'm not here for that,' he said finally. 'I came here

because I thought I used to love you. But I know now that I didn't, and I don't now, but despite that you needed my help. Whatever we had once is not there anymore. You spoilt it.' At that moment he hated himself more than anything he had ever felt. But he could not betray a single emotion to her. He had to detach himself in the way she was about to. Because of him.

Rebecca stood back from him. 'Fine,' she said, locking her desire away once more, packing it under the heavy layers of self-loathing and hurt she held onto. She straightened, Damien knowing the shift in body language from old. Her face, so soft and open only a moment ago closed and hardened, not quite a scowl or grimace, but certainly not hospitable. He could see the vulnerable woman Rebecca was being shut away once more.

Rebecca stared at Damien. She had opened up to him, truly and honestly, seeking his approval and affection and she had been snubbed. It was Helena all over again. She felt her eyes moisten slightly. *Damn him, he was not going to see this.* She willed the tears to stop and inhaled hard though her nose, clearing her sinuses.

Damien moved toward her. 'Look, I'm sorry-' was as far as he got before she cut him off.

'Don't. I think it's time you left. After all you've got your career and your training to think of.'

'Bec-'

'Don't! You. Dare. Call me that.' she said in a rigidly controlled voice, her eyes damning him with the curses she would not say. There was only one person who could claim that name, and she needed her mother.

Damien dropped his eyes to the floor. He could not continue to meet her gaze, knowing what he was doing. 'Call me if you need any help.'

'We'll be fine.'

'Good luck Rebecca,' he said as he picked up his small holdall.

'Goodbye Damien.' And he vanished.

Rebecca stood in the centre of her hotel room, screaming silently what fury she could radiate out from herself into the air around her. The rest she held onto, burying it with the hurt; a store of future rage.

After nearly thirty minutes of standing in silence she spoke to the room. 'Becky. I know you're listening. You've been following me since Mexico. Where are you? Mummy wants to come back and see you.'

A minute passed. Nothing. Another minute and still no sign that the Ayaye was even there. 'Come on darling. Mummy is really sorry for leaving you. I know what you're feeling, remember. I know how it hurts. I want to stop it.'

Still nothing. After ten minutes of silence Rebecca checked with her SI. 'Socrates, is there anything out there?'

Socrates whirred electronically for a few seconds before replying. 'Sorry Ms. Eckhart, there is nothing.'

Rebecca refused to give up, finally beginning to realise that her effort would be the one thing that showed Becky she did care. She sat on the edge of the bed and spoke out loud to the room once more, confident that the Ayaye was listening, just not responding. After all, she would not have if given the opportunity when she was eight. She would have made her mother jump through hoops if she had ever got the chance. 'Becky darling. Mummy is here. She'll always be here whenever you want to talk. Just let me know when you need to tell me something and I'll listen. I promise. It won't be like it was before.'

Exhausted from Damien's tutelage, emotionally brittle glass inside, Rebecca lay back on the bed, forearms crossed over her eyes, legs dangling over the edge. She closed her eyes, intending to rest them for a moment only; a brief gathering of resolve and strength for a long night of convincing the Ayaye, the broken little girl she had once been, that it would be different this time.

Within fifteen seconds she was fast asleep.

408

Becky had heard everything her mother had said, and so wanted to believe it, despite herself. She tried very hard to ignore her mother's pleading. It sounded so sincere though that she had struggled to do nothing, the need to be recognised only just subsumed by the desire to snub her mother, to make her work doubly hard for it.

She had watched as Rebecca fell asleep after only a few seconds of lying down on the bed and waited. Half an hour later, an eternity for an Ayaye, she infiltrated the small SI that powered Rebecca's computer with ease. It did not notice when Becky slipped past its defences as easily as performing a single bit addition; it would not remember being disabled by her, its shutdown leaving as much of an impression on its memory as a human could remember of falling asleep, but in its case, when it awoke again it would not even know it had ever been turned off. Becky was devious and subtle, her innate instinct with electronic consciousnesses allowing her a finesse that far exceeded anything that ran in human A-space.

Confident that she had her privacy in the quiescent SI, Becky left a string of three comma-separated blocks of four digits over all of Rebecca's data. She wantonly sprayed the repeating code into every file, data feed and non-kernel process that Rebecca's SI utilised to run her life, adding terabytes of ones and zeroes in a deliberate act of electronic vandalism.

There was nothing subtle about this particular part of her invasion into her mother's life. It was a brute force attack, deliberately lacking in the élan she showed in overcoming the SI. She had one message to deliver, her communiqué doubled in meaning by its method of delivery, both deed and payload saying the same thing, but with two complimentary interpretations.

I am here Mummy.

Rebecca woke from gritty harsh dreams, consecutively

running then falling then running again over and over. Hard, bright lights blazed in her head, a sun burning in her brain that hurt to look at but throwing out no light. She struggled up toward consciousness, dimly aware she was dreaming, fighting to wake from the morass of images that ensured she gained no rest from her fitful sleep, her body struggling to stay asleep, desperate for rest after the ordeal of the past few days.

She opened her eyes to the soft yellow glow of the room's nightlight, no idea of the time. Her eyes struggled to focus on the clock, the numbers refusing to resolve into anything recognisable. Across the room Socrates' remote beeped furiously for attention.

Rebecca fumbled for the spare lens-screens she had left in the room a week previously, and barely had one in and enabled when Socrates flooded her vision with data.

'Stop!' she commanded. The numbers froze, layer upon layer of characters repeating themselves into the zoom of the display in a tangled mix of fonts and colours. 'What is this?' she asked the SI.

'They're everywhere Ms. Eckhart.' Socrates sounded almost distraught. 'Everything has them in it, over and over. All your data is ruined with them.'

'What them? All I can see are random numbers.'

'Not random. It is the same twelve numbers.'

Rebecca shook her head, still trying to make sense of what the hell Socrates was on about. 'Just show me them once then. If they're all the same then there's no need to overload my brain with the same data over and over, is there?'

Socrates said nothing in reply, and displayed, in plain black digits approximately fifteen centimetres high on a window a metre away from Rebecca's eyes, the string Becky had left for her.

2736,8806,8598.

Thirty-eight

Regeneration

Sunday 30 July 2056 - 10:17 IST

Standing in the remains of a mountain village in the rising foothills of Kangchenjunga, he looked around at what had been, at one time, the highest human settlement on the slopes of the great peak. Now, where once had stood houses and civic buildings, there were only empty fields and sparse Himalayan pastures, dotted with small piles of stones; the remains of the sturdy dwellings reduced to untidy cairns and tumbled half walls. Thirty years previously their former inhabitants had been convinced, bribed or evicted from their homes in order to produce the three hundred square-kilometre exclusion zone around the launch site for the Vimana.

Nearly twenty lakh people had migrated, slowly over the course of the two decades prior to their expulsion, up the mountain's side. As the alpine climate eased, meadows replaced tundra higher and higher into the world's roof, opening up valuable arable land to feed the country's one hundred and fifty crore strong population, and with it farmers and workers able to exploit the new natural resource the planet's changing climate brought.

Only it did not last. When the government realised it needed the peak to be the origin point for humanity's only interstellar craft, the settlers had to be moved.

The authorities had offered handsome compensation; sufficient so that they need never be concerned for their own or their descendants financial security for all time. For some however this was irrelevant. Coming from families who for centuries had drawn a living from the five peaks of the eternal snows, they were not convinced by the arguments, nor felt compelled by the legislation, and were not bribed by the large sums of money offered to them. For them, their displacement from their new homes had been a harder, and sometimes violent one.

In more than one place he could see the still-charred remains of an outbuilding or animal pen; the non-human former residents of these high altitudes the first to suffer the indignity of discovering themselves homeless, before the government came with promises of new, better shelter further down the valley, where grazing was easier and crops flourished in the easing climate.

All had moved on eventually, persuaded by sons and daughters that the forces they faced in this remote spot were greater than any they may have stood against and overcome previously. Unlike the wind or the snows which chilled their bones each winter, this force had a will behind it; a will which drove it harder than any Himalayan gale. It would have consumed them utterly if they had stayed and resisted. Think of our children, your grandchildren were the pleas. Remaining in place was a sacrifice yielding no benefit; put aside pride for their future, the next generation of our continued existence. The smaller burden would be more easily mitigated surely?

From the destruction of the last human settlement of the mountain's upper slopes had been created a notional circular line on a map; whose inscription on the world had set in place the chain of events that reached from the past to the here and now; a looping path which had started thirty years ago, when village elders had resisted the occupation of their homes and had led, via the depths of space, back to its origin point once more. A trajectory which circumscribed the life of the single trespasser half a kilometre ahead of him, and which would be brought to a close with another, albeit much smaller act of destruction.

The large had become the small; and small could well become large. The relocation of lakhs of people when his target was barely toddling had led to the need for a single murder today. He wondered what would flower from this particular act; what unintended consequences his imminent actions now would have on the world of ten, twenty or thirty years in the future? He did not know. He turned away from the fire blackened pile of stones he had been staring ruminatively at and focussed on locating his target in the Cotts field.

He was a second away from pinpointing it when something hard and heavy hit him square in the back, sending his ancient frame flailing to the ground.

< <

'Daley, open a secure line to Brigadier James Follows please.'

'Certainly. Negotiating protocols with Monty now.'

A minute later former Lieutenant Regent's ex-CO was on the comm, his head and shoulders visible in Damien's lens-screens.

> >

He got to his feet, swaying a little as he rose with the help of his long staff, shaking his head clear of the impact. Something had touched him. Something or, more likely, someone had violated him. They had broken his asceticism and made direct physical contact with him. Around him the Himalayan pasture remained still and empty, no indication as to who or what had knocked him to the ground. He felt the betrayal swell; thirty six flawless years of dedication to his devotion undone by an interloper. Anger was a luxury he could not afford.

'That is the only time you will take me unawares,' he called, re-establishing his composure. 'Either leave me to my task, or show yourselves, and I promise to make your deaths painless ones.' His words carried far into the clear mountain air. His voice was flat with no hint of threat he intended. His offer was sincere; a quick and easy death in return for no further hindrance to his mission. He had no desire for a pointless conflict this far into his assignment; it would be a needless expenditure of his energy, and nothing new would or could come of it. There would be no creation from the deaths of his assailants, save the continuation of his mission, which was already ordained.

There was no response to his statement; nor had he expected any. No one who would follow him this far into the sky was likely to surrender to a gentle death, or leave because he had prompted them to. He sighed at the needlessness of this; it was unnecessary, and there would be only disharmony after his intervention. Still, he could not let whoever was confronting him impede his duty. To the death then.

Concentrating inwards to read the landscape of the Cotts field for masses outward, he set about locating his attacker or attackers. He felt the fluctuations and flow of the artificial energy all around him; a seventh sense greater than any of his others. A small perturbation, too large to ignore resolved itself into the form of a man a little over ten metres away, behind him over his right shoulder. He feinted a turn in the direction of his assailant, and was rewarded with a second man breaking cover and revealing

414

himself in a run toward him, fooled by the misdirection.

The running man was no more than three metres away when the elder man spun around to face him, to look into the eyes of the person who would challenge him in his duty; a man who perhaps believed he could prevail in this engagement. It had been nearly a decade since he had stood down bravery of this magnitude, and what sort of man would possess this intrigued him.

He completed his turn to see the man, Nepalese perhaps judging by the moment of time he had to regard his features before he blinked his assailant silently out of existence, leaving himself once again seemingly alone. He looked around at the open mountain pastures, knowing there was at least one other nearby, focussing on the Cotts field, searching for the mass he had sensed moments ago, but there was nothing.

The Himalayan man had got closer to contact with him than any other until only moments ago; a heartbeat longer and the assailant may have had the opportunity to consummate the physical act he perhaps had been attempting. That he could not allow again so soon. He had to locate the other.

He widened his perception, thirty kilometres in every direction, an invisible sphere reaching into the depths of the earth, and high into the heavens. Once, over a quarter of a century previously, he had been taken unawares, assuming his target would use only two dimensions to Displace around; the resulting counter-attack from five kilometres above him had almost resulted in his decapitation. He had never since allowed himself to be compromised so.

But this time there was nothing. No trace of a Displacement trajectory or an entry point within a distance which could conceivably imperil him. The second man had vanished, as completely as if he had never been present. It was then he realised who, or rather what the nature of the threat facing him was.

Men trained in counter-Displacement techniques were rare. This, coupled with the snatched glance at one of his attackers was enough to convince him he was facing a squad of Gurkhas; the tempered-steel regiment of Nepalese soldiers the British Army still held four reserve divisions of.

In his long life he had encountered the Gurkhas only once previously, when he had been a small boy, still in short pants and bare feet, living with his maternal grandfather on the Ganges delta. The wide sweeping flatland he grew up on flooded so badly one season the Government had appealed for international assistance; the British military had despatched a regiment of the mountain born soldiers to assist, and they had been stationed in his district. He remembered his admiration at their stoicism, their unflinching dedication to the task set them by their masters. In a matter of days, with their help he and his grandfather had been returned to their home. He remembered quizzing his grandfather in the way of a child as to why he chose to live in a place of periodic destruction, and the answer he had been given; that the river gifted them their fertile soils with its periodic overflowing of the levees. So long as it continued to give its gifts only occasionally, life could be drawn from the land. He had not understood at the time, but the intervening years had granted him the greater wisdom his grandfather had possessed. His grandfather's capacity to endure had been matched by the soldiers who had effected the return to their house. The men he faced now would be of the same calibre, the same fortitude. He faced a genuinely dangerous enemy in them.

Sensing out into the Cotts field as far as he could he reviewed his options. He had no experiential data on which to base his assumptions about their possible tactics. His only knowledge of their likely strategies came from a three-year-old field training manual of British Displacement battlefield warfare, now almost certainly obsolete. Other than that, all he knew was their reputation and hearsay, exaggerated almost certainly, but sense dictated he presume everything they were rumoured to be capable of were fact. The one solid piece of information he possessed was the purpose of the regiment; guerrilla warfare using unconventional tactics. This was his one advantage; attacks did not come much less conventional than his.

Failing to locate any of the soldiers within the fifteen cubic kilometres he was actively aware of, he shifted his perception and directed his focus to D-space; the inbetween reality opened up by the Cotts field. It was obvious now the soldiers were capable of holding themselves between the here and there of a normal Displacement, a defence allowing them to evade detection. But where their skill was a product of their military training, limiting them to techniques they had been drilled in, to him his ability came as naturally as breathing. He belonged in the Cotts field; they were simple interlopers.

There they were. Flickering in the gaps that lay between atomic nuclei and their orbiting electrons, he could see the traces of four men. He was impressed. They had been there for nearly a minute now, perhaps a hundred times longer than a normal human could ever hope to achieve. Still, they could not remain there indefinitely. He would assist in their re-entry to the world.

He pushed. The outlines of two of the soldiers wavered a little. He pushed again. This time the pair of shadows could not resist the pressure he was placing on them and they slipped out of D-space and back into physical reality. Immediately he Folded space around them before they had a chance to react, and he Displaced them two hundred kilometres directly south of their present location. They materialised eight kilometres up in the air, the mountain they had been standing on no longer beneath their feet.

If they managed not to panic and remember their training, he estimated they might survive the fall, but even if that occurred he would have completed his mission long before they recovered enough to seek him out once more. That left the final two, still hiding in what they believed was the safety of D-space.

He considered how to finish with these two final distractions. In his eighty plus years on Earth so far, he had never yet had cause to venture this high, both geographically and topographically into his country before. His duties to date had taken him to most other places and states in India, from the humid, sticky backwaters of Kerala where he had serviced three men, one woman and a boy child, Displacing their bodies far and wide into countless separate pieces to either decompose rapidly in the oppressive heat or to be snapped up by the multitude of hungry creatures who made the waterways their home; to the Thar desert, where his quarry had been a single man, hiding alone in the dunes. That had been an easier assignment, and an easier product to dispose of, Displaced three hundred metres into the ground beneath his feet, far out of reach of even the most subtle of detection methods.

Neither tactic he felt would succeed against the remaining soldiers he faced. He was certain they were the strongest of the five, better able to resist or repel the remote-directed Displacements he had utilised against the others.

The final two members of the squad had been in D-space for almost ninety seconds now. They would be getting fatigued. To ordinary people, even trained ones, maintaining themselves there would begin to feel, at first, as if they were being held underwater, unable to draw breath.

Slowly the pressure would build within them, willpower initially being sufficient to keep the animal mind in check. But the stresses would multiply, the tightness getting heavier on them until eventually reason would succumb to instinct and they would be forced from the inbetween world, gasping and disorientated if they chose to push their endurance to the limits, haemorrhaging from their orifices if they went beyond that.

He entered the shadow reality between Displacements as easily as taking a single step forward, and waited. Here, he had the advantage. He could wait in Displace-space for an hour if required suffering no ill effects.

A minute passed; the outlines of the two men began to waver. It would be soon.

Another thirty seconds ticked by and both outlines blinked out. Or they would have done if he had allowed them to. The instant he felt them beginning to leave D-space he pulled them both back in and held them there for a full ten minutes.

In that time the pair of shadowy outlines convulsed and fitted, thrashing against the bonds holding them fast, hints of limbs flailing, trying to free themselves from the invisible hand keeping them from the world. Eventually the flickering shapes stopped almost entirely, the only movements coming from them the smallest twitches of lifeforce kicking feebly into the ether. He let them go.

Stepping back onto the mountain he stood above the two soldiers lying gurgling on the ground, the last moments of their lives retching and bleeding from their eyes, ears and anuses. They might take another minute to die, but he was not a cruel man. Efficient and ruthless in the execution of his duties, but never needlessly cruel. What he had done had been the best way to render the men harmless to him. But now he had to face the consequences of his own action. He fought back the nausea at the thought.

Kneeling between them he went to rest a hand on each

of their foreheads. Fingers shaking as he consciously approached the flesh of another he steeled himself. He was the cause of their agony, and only he could ease it quickly. In this life one must bear the weight of one's decisions. He swallowed his revulsion and laid a palm on each man's head. Immediately he Displaced their heads an inch from their necks, severing the connection between suffering brain and ruined body. Both men ceased all movement.

The uniforms they wore bore no identifying insignia for him to retrieve as a remembrance of the lives he had extinguished, but there were other items. Each of them carried with them their regimental knife, the wide curved bladed affair he knew as the kukri. One of them seemed a fitting addition to the aggregation of lives past he held on to.

His token of remembrance of their passing secured, he set to ensuring his former opponents were disposed of fittingly; they had been honourable soldiers, following orders as much as he did, and more importantly they had been men of these mountains. He felt they would not object to the means of their funeral rites he chose. After removing their clothing by shifting it a metre to one side, he lit an incense stick, smearing the ash which fell from it along his neck and throat. When his small ceremony was complete he Displaced the now inert forms into a thousand fragments scattered over an area of approximately one square kilometre; this was his best effort at providing them with jhator, and any raptors that might come across their remains with a meal. Rising, he acknowledged the service to the continuation of life their deaths had provided, and then raised his eyes to the mountain, and towards his quarry once more.

A delay of only a few minutes to neutralise the threat posed by the British soldiers had allowed his quarry to

Displace up the mountain ahead of him; again his target had eluded him due to an external intervention. His instructions had been explicit, but despite his considerable skill for clandestine removal of humans from the earth he had found himself thwarted by circumstance time and again. Once it became apparent his quarry was leaving Delhi for somewhere, he was directed to pursue and eliminate at the first reasonable opportunity. That first reasonable opportunity continually refused to present itself however.

Instead of Displacing any distance by individual effort and therefore allowing him the possibility of intercession, he was frustrated by three weeks of surface travel; having to follow in autorickshaws to the railway stations to board the overcrowded slow-moving trains, forced to maintain a discrete distance in the sleeper carriages while his target mingled among local politicians and businessmen in first class. The trains allowed him no freedom to complete his assignment; the ever-busy carriages with their hundreds of witnesses and potential accounts of the missing westerner were too great a risk. Coupled with the attentive service afforded to first-class passengers this ensured he was thwarted at every half-chance. He was forced to wait.

His time to fulfil his assignment was not limitless however, and it dragged on as inexorably as the crawling pace the locomotives made across his country. From Delhi he snaked his way, always no more than a hundred metres behind his quarry, through Uttar Pradesh and Bihar, then West Bengal and finally north into Sikkim, the gap between himself and his target widening as the size of the crowd of fellow travellers within which he was secreting himself shrank. And conversely the country opened out and climbed, until he stood at the base of his country's highest peak. At this point he was almost a whole kilometre away from the quarry, keeping track of it as a discrete mass within the Cotts field. When it had moved, he had followed, circling around to ensure he stayed well below any likely perception threshold and the threat, however small, of detection.

Finally he was sure of his and his target's isolation and had been about to strike when the soldiers had diverted him. Still, it mattered little that he had been delayed by a handful of minutes. The distance he had to cover to put himself within range had only grown by a few hundred metres. Hardly worth the lives of five men for.

He did not wonder what his target, a woman this time, was responsible for to warrant his unique capabilities in effecting her removal from existence; it was enough for him that she had been targeted. It made little difference to him what age, gender, race or religion the target or targets may be. That they merited his attention sufficed. He trusted the universe to exclude those who did not require such complete and total expulsion from the world. As every other professional he asked nothing beyond the parameters of his assignment. He had been engaged to perform his unique service, which he would discharge with the minimum of disturbance and exposure, or he would not return at all.

The dossier he had been given provided the target's last known, most recent and likely locations, associations and activities, along with a little of known and inferred pseudonyms he should be aware of. He whispered the remembered name as he stepped forward into the Cotts field and up the mountain for his final act of this assignment.

'Rebecca Eckhart.'

Thirty-nine

Ascent

Sunday 30 July 2056 - 10:17 IST

The arcing path she had unwittingly stepped onto a quarter of a century ago, her eight-year-old self unaware of the constantly turning journey her life would take along it, drew to its final stages with her three thousand kilometre odyssey across the breadth of India. It came to an abrupt halt for Rebecca a little over eight thousand metres up the south-west rising ridge of Kangchenjunga, as the Cotts field she had slowly learnt to feel for during the past three weeks stopped.

< < <

An involuntary shiver ran up Hari Srinath's spine at the enormity of the coming leap. He was struck by the sudden incongruity between what he and his crew had just done, and what was to come next. It was one thing to be transported six light-hours to the edge of the solar system; quite another thing entirely to be considering the next interstellar jump. Something about remaining within the bounds of the solar system made the last Displacement now feel almost routine; as if the ship had travelled no further than an ordinary atmospheric longjump-shuttle, and family and home were close at hand.

How quickly he had normalised within himself the novelty of their first Displacement; to accept it as something now within humanity's abilities by the act of its success.

InSA had calculated with confidence that the six Devas could impel the mass-equivalent of the Vimana 2.7368806 light years in a single jump. While the parsec may have been the standard unit of distance employed within the scientific community, the public's unit, the light year, had been settled on for any reporting of the mission. Its suffusion into the popular consciousness, initially through science fiction literature, referred to as a measurement unattainable by mankind, had now come within humanity's reach. Srinath normally would have had little time for flights of fancy involving tales of inter-planetary war or advanced civilisations capable of traversing the gulfs of space, dismissing them as too outlandish to give credence to. Now he was one of the latter, crossing halfway to the nearest star as easily as crossing a room.

Incredible.

Her journey to the base of the mountain had been completed on slow-moving, cumbersome trains, bone-jarring noisy buses, taxis, autorickshaws and even ox-pulled carts when there had been no alternative. In a country of unparalleled diversity, she had utilised almost every means of conveyance and mode of transport offered her to attain her destination. Save one. Until reaching the northern state of Sikkim, and the edge of the Himalayas, Rebecca had deliberately avoided Displacement travel, either self-controlled or assisted CF generated. This was done despite her need to master the skill she had come late to.

Knowing what little she could recall about the technology the man called Ramkumar obviously had access to, she had no wish to risk movement across his country through the Cotts field. It was not an unwise thing to assume he could detect a single passage through the unique radiation that bathed the entire planet. However, choosing not to utilise it was quite different to growing accustomed to its presence, and reaching out with her artificially-generated seventh-sense to feel its subtle, yet ever-present ebbs and flows.

Now, after her cautious and circuitous route to her destination, during which she had realised, belatedly, that she had forgotten to mark her thirty-forth birthday, she was faced with weeks of potential ascent, with no guide or suitable equipment available and unable to procure either without attracting unwanted attention and questions. Also there was the problem of obtaining the necessary permits and authorisations to climb the mountain. She had time for neither.

Forced by necessity, Rebecca relented and for the first time since she and Damien had separated, she had to contemplate Displacing. Suddenly she was unsure of herself, the realisation of how untested at what she needed to achieve only evident in the shadow of the mountain. Her first true test of her latefound ability would be further and higher than most experienced adults were capable of. It was not her nature to attempt anything so unprepared, and the magnitude of the distance she had to traverse humbled her. Only a handful of weeks previously she could barely Displace three metres across a room. Now she was considering an ascent of nearly nine kilometres, almost straight up.

Only the memory and feelings of Becky kept her looking up to where she had told her mother she was waiting. *It was too high surely? Why hadn't Damien spent more time teaching her?* Then she remembered how they had parted, his rebuff at her moment of vulnerability, Elena all over again. *Why did she do this to herself?*

Hot fury ignited within her almost from nowhere. She willed herself to override her hardwired response, and instead let it rise, let the hurt flow for once, unstemmed by her self-control. Elena, Damien. They were the same in the end; unreliable. The one person she could ever truly know she could depend on was herself, and always had been, and she was waiting for her at the top of the world. Her resolve hardened, tempered into steel by the red-hot hurt. Rebecca looked up the mountain once more. She would find the strength somewhere despite them. Just to spite them.

Displacement.

Space shifted and bent, origin and destination points brought together for a fraction of a second under the command of her will. An instant of total concentration focussed into pulling the top of Kangchenjunga to her, or pushing herself up it. Heaving crores of tonnes of mountain through D-space to achieve her goal.

The summit rushed towards her. Propelled impossibly fast into the sky, the surface a blur beneath her.

Arrival.

Everything out of focus. Limbs heavy. Head full of cotton wool. Materialising just within the confines of the Cotts field, as high as it reached into the sky, she swayed on the spot, struggling to will her legs to hold her up, her strength gone, robbed from her. Overwhelmed the moment she appeared.

She had done something colossal, that much she knew, but her mind struggled to make sense of what it was. As if

426

waking from a drugged sleep, thoughts came slowly, confused. Trying to untangle the disorientation. Body unable to respond to the feeble commands her mind tried to issue. She fought through the fogging in her mind and remembered her Displacement to this point. Further than she had ever done before. It seemed the effort of moving herself eight kilometres almost straight up had drained her, of her strength, will, emotion, her spite even. Her ravaged body's ultimate response to the effort she had extracted from it over the preceding months.

One thing penetrated her fugue however. Through weeks of habitual re-enforcement hardwired into her brain, pushing its way to her consciousness, came the fugitive's urge to check her location for sign of anyone who may have been observing her. She fought to use her muscles and turn her head. She half-scanned the area through heavy eyelids. Nothing. The same empty landscape all around. It was pointless, there was no-one else up here, or at least the one person she was coming to rejoin would not be visible.

Instead, she was not sure what she had been expecting to see at the roof of the world, where the earth began to meet the heavens, the sky deepening with the edge of space above. She struggled to recall any details from her childhood; the compound's location, the site of the launchpad, the topography of the surrounding land, any information that would tell her which way to proceed. But the memories were difficult to recover, flattened under years of wilful neglect making their retrieval that much harder. Half-recalled images from her eight-year-old self mixed with the grid patterns and layouts of more recent provenance merged in her mind. The effort of bringing what she wanted, filtering the weak signal from the noise, was too great for her after the exertions of the previous months and her sole Displacement. She was useless; her faculties had deserted her here at the world's ceiling.

However she was not wholly unprepared. Rebecca

retrieved the small cylinder of oxygen she had been able to procure prior to her ascent, and which she had transported up the mountain with her. It weighed only a fraction of a kilogram, but her choice to carry its additional mass had added a significant burden of weight to her kilometres-long Displacement. She broke the small plastic seal and with a tiny hiss her head exploded with the fullness of the gas, the oxygen rushing through her bloodstream to her starved brain. Pinball lights flashed on and off behind her eyes and her fingers and toes itched as the hypoxia left her.

She resisted the urge to shake her head clear for fear she'd lose consciousness, till the sensations had passed and she was confident of herself once more. While she still felt tired, the oxygen was helping immensely; the heavy fog cleared from her mind and she found she could hold more than one thought in her head again. Breathing deeply, feeling her return to herself she considered the small canister. Pramod's words about the skin of the Vimana and its designers' wishes not to add even a handful of nanograms to the mass of the ship came back to her. For the first time she understood the effort the ship's astronauts spent in moving the Vimana the light years they had. Fantastic.

Better able to determine her location, Rebecca considered her options and the likely location of the base. Constrained, or perhaps liberated from choice by the sole path open to her, she wondered would anything remain of the InSA launch site now, a generation after the Vimana had torn free of the earth's gravitational pull. Or would time and the forces of nature have taken their toll as they had on her since that time? Details ablated away leaving behind only abandoned ghost-like shells of buildings and skeletal remains of equipment, their original purpose all but lost under the pressure of time's passage.

Rebecca took a step forward up the slope towards Becky. The single pace was like walking through a wall of bright, thick water, as if she were breaking the surface and out into a reality which seemed somehow less; duller or less real. The air seemed emptier, enervated, as if something were missing, something more than the even rarity of the atmosphere at her present altitude.

Interesting.

Rebecca paused, considering the sensation, or rather, the absence thereof. A quick experiment would confirm what she was perceiving. She retraced her sole step back and understood immediately what the difference was. Within the space of half a metre she was back within the Cotts field. Being outside it, even for a moment, she realised how much it permeated all of her senses now, filling her mind with its warmth, cosseting her with its presence. Even in the few brief weeks of learning to be able to discern it, she had come to unconsciously expect and rely on its presence. Within it she felt more secure, sheltered from harm, while outside it, even for a few seconds she had felt emptier, hollow, vulnerable even. She had not felt this before, certainly not in her hotel room or in the museum, and now belatedly realised perhaps why Sati had fallen, distracted by the absence of reassurance the Cotts field precipitated. Had Damien and everyone who visited her in her hotel room also felt the same way; a deep discomfort that something fundamental was missing, that a vital part of them had been stolen away?

Welcome to my world.

The feeling of being half-finished or an incomplete part of a greater, unreachable whole had been Rebecca's default operating mode for a quarter of a century, and the little niggle at the back of her mind that told her she was no longer within the bounds of the Cotts field was just so much more baggage to deal with.

Unflinching, Rebecca stepped into the open void once more, and after a minute's concentration buried the empty feeling under the rest of her damage where it barely concerned her. Becky was waiting and this was not the time to chod about feeling sorry for herself. Absently discarding the now redundant seal from her oxygen cylinder, she strode up the slope.

He materialised a further kilometre up the mountainside as Rebecca's arrival after-image was all but scattered in the Cotts field, the faintest glow of the woman left hanging in the air around him. He appeared at the exact same spot she had occupied in space only minutes before, some five hundred metres short of the summit; his own more confident Displacement impression dissipating outwards more rapidly than hers had done, like the ripples on a pond of a second, heavier stone breaking the water's surface only moments after the first. It was here that the Cotts field which bathed the rest of the planet reached no further; in deference to centuries old respect for the summit of the five peaks of the eternal snows, InSA did not allow the Cotts field to flow over the roof of the world. He would have to complete the final part on foot.

Barely a metre ahead of him on the bare ground, starkly artificial against the untouched mountain, lay a small bent fragment of plastic; a seal of some sorts by the look of it; most likely from an oxygen cylinder he surmised.

He tested his own lungs at this greater altitude and found them capable of providing him with sufficient oxygen to continue. He would retrieve the artefact representing his quarry; a fitting memento of the woman who all her life had utilised crutches, emotional and now physical, to provide her with the support she thought she needed. He would let her keep her prop until the last. He was not a cruel man and had no desire to see her suffer any more than was necessary to complete his assignment.

Taking a step forward his momentum carried him across the threshold of the Cotts field before he could intuit what was happening and stop himself. Crossing the

430

boundary between CF enhanced space and ordinary empty air something happened to him, within him. He felt as if the world was pulled away from him, from out of him; as if his innards had been torn out. The hollowness of a lover abandoned.

His former strength deserted him and he could not stop himself falling to the ground, his legs no longer able to support him. An infant seeking its mother's breast, he crawled back to the safety and security of the Cotts field, dragging his traitorous body back to its enveloping comfort until his senses returned to him.

He lay there for long minutes of recovery, curled up on the cold ground at the boundary of two worlds. Shaking, he reached out with a hand, feeling tentatively for the edge of the field. His fingertips began to itch barely two centimetres ahead of him, an inverted electric current flowing out of his flesh, forcing him to recoil, his body's instinct of flight too powerful and immediate to overcome. Steadying his nerves, steeling himself for the sensation this time, palm facing ahead of him he pushed his hand out of the field, a personal test of will and control over emotion and sensation. The feeling surged once more through him and out of his skin where it penetrated the empty space. It was all he could do to not withdraw himself at the mounting discomfort. Instead he pushed more and more of himself forward through the terminus of the Cotts field that he had spent half his existence bathed in, and relied upon.

He had never before in his life shied away from anything, and certainly did not consider himself a coward; everything had been faced head on. But now, lying parallel to the invisible wall demarcating two regions of space, one where he exerted total control of the environment and the other where he was powerless, he found himself hesitant, unwilling to effect the distress he would have to endure to complete his assignment. How should he best breach the barrier? Should he even attempt it, knowing what lay on the other side? A lifetime's certainties had been swept aside in a single step. And for what exactly?

If he did not succeed in this he could not report back. Quite aside from his failure to halt the ascent of the woman, he alone would know the why of it; the reason would have been and always would be his own weakness.

His muscles and skin burned with fever, itching with a million ants crawling over and inside him. His testicles ached at his groin, as if struck with a dull hammer blow, retracting along with his penis deep into his crotch. Inside him, his organs spasmed, forcing vomit up and out through his mouth and nose, excreta pouring uncontrolled from his anus as if he were a baby once more, powerless to oppose his body's squalid functioning. But the worst of it was the loss he felt within himself, at his core.

Rebecca crested the top of the rise to see the InSA base spread out before her, its layout familiar now from a quarter of a century ago. Low, single and double storey buildings dotted the area around the Vimana's launch site; the powerful laser array that had lifted the ship into earth orbit before it performed its first Displacement out to the edge of the solar system.

The original scorch marks, burnt into the ground from the lasers' single firing still framed the wide lenses, dark spokes like negative sunbursts radiating from their source. The solitary trace that anything had happened here persisting in the sterile and undisturbed air where the earth grasped for the sky; the only sign of man's most ambitious endeavour.

My life has become a circle, she thought as she slid down the slope to the rear of the nearest building. *All those years ago I saw this place, wanted to be here. Have I just been heading back here the whole time?*

Rebecca could almost not help see the domino fall of singularities: the only craft capable of interstellar flight, the single firing of the launch lasers lifting it heavenward, mankind's one attempt at traversing the stars, and for some reason its greatest failure, precipitating the secret she now realised she had been seeking all her life since that moment.

Well, chalk up another first. She mentally added herself to the tally by becoming the first person to attempt a break in at the roof of the world.

If she remembered the layout correctly, the windowless building she was currently secreted behind was a simple catering facility; the world's highest kitchen. Mission control should be the building over the launch pad, the only one with slit-windows facing towards the ship's lift off. She peered round the edge of her hiding place, scanning the scene quickly.

Rebecca wished she had been able to risk bringing Socrates along to complement the basic operating ware of her lens-screens, but caution at the microwave link of her SI being detected had forced her to leave his technical enhancements far behind. She relied solely on the limited functionality of the screens only; despite their state-of-the-art claims they were nowhere near as useful as what a decent electronic brain could augment them with. *Still, better than nothing,* she supposed.

Barely half a second after moving her head out to see, Rebecca's view was flooded with data: map overlays spilling on top of each other showing wiring, plumbing, corridors, airways and a host of other technical schematics; full 3D topographies of the entire area rotated in small, discretely recessed windows just at the edge of her peripheral vision; heat, background radiation, UV and IR filters bathing everything in reds, greens, blues and blacks; and shining through the noise of data assaulting her, an Ashoka Chakra, spinning slowly and pulsing gently over one building a little over ten metres away.

I always did overcompensate. We haven't changed, eh Becky? she wryly chided herself and the Ayaye.

Still, message received loud and clear; there could be no doubt about where she needed to be. Rebecca crossed the launch pad and entered the command centre's cool, dark interior, hardly pausing as her feet kicked up the soot trails that had lain undisturbed for a generation, revealing the earth below.

Rebecca's passage into the building was observed by two other people. Presently one of them sat watching her on a bank of windows thrown onto his lens-screens, as he sat inside the former control room deep inside the building, buried well away from the once ferocious discharge energy of the now quiescent laser array. The second person to see her had gained the same position she had occupied minutes ago after picking himself up from his foetal position further down the slope at the boundary of the Cotts field and empty space.

His sense of loss had been profound, greater than any other single sensation he had experienced in his long life. There was now a void within him, and he knew, deep inside his mind that this loss, this particular act of destruction, could not and would not carry with it rebirth or renewal. He had had something pure snatched away forever, which nothing could replace. Being isolated from the Cotts field was more than a temporary handicap; he knew something had broken in that moment of breaching the interface of there and here. Never again would he be able to perform the acts of exquisite control which he had been capable of only minutes ago. The sublime perception of the Cotts field and the subsequent Displacements were denied to him now. His piety, his self-control in ensuring he remained uncontaminated by others had been for naught; a lifetime of sacrifice gone, wasted.

Forcing back his tears, there would be no more outward displays of his shame, he watched his target enter a low building some distance away. She strode blithely through the residuum of the heat and light which had propelled the Vimana into orbit, scattering the unique creation the extremes of that energy discharge had brought into being, returning their symmetry to chaos for all time.

It was her doing, this aching sense of loss within him now, his being torn from the Cotts field. Her actions had necessitated his services, in turn leading to their trespass onto the world's roof and the consequences to himself of that. She had violated the sanctity of the mountain and desecrated the sole pristine remnant of his country's finest achievement.

He vowed they would be the last such acts she performed here.

He lamented for a only a moment more on how he had planned to dispose of this woman, before reaching to his belt for the trophy he had taken from the Gurkhas. No longer would he deny the physicality of things.

Forty

Convergence

Rebecca trod as silently as her oversized mountain boots would allow her along the corridor, Becky feeding her lens-screens all the data she needed to navigate the total darkness inside. The scene was a panorama of light, a riot of colour. She whispered gently to the Ayaye to lower the hue and brightness a little. Becky was obviously in a good mood with her mother, because a moment later the overwhelming flood of images became a subdued and discreet wireframe, picking out walls and doorways. 'Thanks darling,' she whispered into the darkness.

The door she had passed through moments ago opened and closed once more behind her. Ignoring the complete darkness he made his way along the corridor despite his lack of SI or Ayaye enhanced lens-screens. He had been provided with, and had committed to memory, a full technical breakdown of the InSA launch facility when it became apparent to his master where his target was heading. Having trailed her to the foothills of

436

Kangchenjunga, it was clear to the man he worked for where she was destined, and that a more remote and fitting spot would not be found. He had planned to eliminate her much further down the mountain, but the interference of the Gurkhas had delayed him enough for her to Displace to the top, where he now found himself impotent to use his skills.

He gripped the kukri firmly in his fist.

Rebecca rounded a corner. If Becky's schematic was correct, the SI interaction suite was through the door directly ahead of her. Here finally she could tell her daughter everything she needed to and everything she had wanted to hear herself.

She reached for the handle.

Becky waited expectantly inside.

The assassin drew within half a metre of his target. The room she was about to enter afforded more space for what he had in mind. The inside of his head still sang a lament for the lost Cotts field and how he would have to touch the woman; the target, he corrected himself. He could smell his quarry now, her body's scent easy to detect in the rarefied air. He pushed his revulsion at the physical contact necessary to carry out his duty aside; he tried to replace it with determination that this would not be the mission he failed at. He tightened his hold on the long, curved and dangerous knife as he shifted his weight to reach out with his free hand to restrain her.

Inside the room Becky noticed for the first time the signal of the man shadowing her mother. She had been so distracted by the anticipated reconciliation she realised that she had let her mother down by not being omniscient.

And now it was too late.

Behind you Mummy! she screamed into the lens-screens.

437

Rebecca heard the softest noise behind a fraction of a second before Becky flooded her vision with her warning, just as someone grabbed her around the throat. Instantly, without needing to think, the learned action an almost automatic reflex, she reverse-headbutted whoever it was that had grabbed her before they had the chance to do anything else. Hard.

The back of his target's head flew into the bridge of his nose, smashing it, sending mottles of brightly coloured light across his vision. He had been too slow. Despite the pain across his face he managed to hold on and swung the knife at his target's middle, meaning to disembowel her. The head came at him again, multiplying the damage the first blow had inflicted, compounding the fractures in his skull. Shock doubled with agony flared through his head as he heard his already broken nose splinter further. His grip loosened and the arc his arm had been taking flew upwards as he fell backwards, the knife now sailing directly towards Rebecca's face.

Instinct took over in Rebecca. As soon as she had swung her head back a second time she let her body stop holding up its own weight in an effort to add the burden of her mass to that of her attacker should they attempt to Displace out; another trick remembered from childhood. If they were leaving she was going with them. The effect of this was that as her head smashed into that of her assailant for the second time, as the grip around her loosened, Rebecca found herself falling to the ground and under the arcing path of the blade that whistled over her, removing nothing more than a few loose strands of hair.

Becky screamed in terror; the three seconds of her mother's near stabbing recorded, processed and analysed from a dozen separate angles at a lakh samples per second.

For the Ayaye the whole thing had taken almost an eternity, but at the end of it, with her electronic heart in her mouth, Becky saw her mother drop to the ground and roll away to relative safety. The time for playing the spoilt offspring was over. She effortlessly overrode the now ancient security systems and flooded the room with light.

Rebecca's good hand flew to the holster on her thigh. She struggled with the pop-stud for half a second, trying to free the weapon contained within. Its location on the right-handed holster was in the wrong position for her left thumb. Her hastened panic did not help and she fumbled her index finger to the trigger, nearly firing and dropping the gun as she drew it, aimed at her target.

The back of her head throbbed where it had collided with his nose, and while she may suffer a headache for a while, the damage she had incurred was minimal compared to what she had inflicted. A fountain had opened up across the man's face, blood flowing freely from his ruined nose. Still, he clung to the knife though.

Through hazy vision he saw his target fumble her hold on the gun. Blinking away the clouds obscuring his eyes, his vision cleared and for the first time he looked into the eyes of his target. She said something at him, but his ears did not seem to be working correctly at the present time; he could barely hear a thing over the high whine in his head. Still, he would not need to hear in order to finish this. And in a way it would be better; he would not have to endure her screams and so could be less touched by the physicality of her death.

'You will not shoot me I think,' he said to her, smiling cordially. 'Over the course of my duty I have had weapons of all manner aimed in my direction, and I have seen the eyes of every single person who meant to kill me. And yours tell me that you are not possessed of the will to kill another human being, to take another's life. So please, lay down the gun and I will give you as quick and painless a death as I am still able.'

Supporting the unfamiliar weight of the gun with her splinted and bandaged right arm made her broken limb throb with the effort. Frantically she realised she was not even sure a gun would work at this altitude. *Was there enough oxygen for the cordite to fire? Did bullets even need oxygen to work? Was her only advantage, the single thing that balanced her situation worthless?* Truly she did not know. And her assailant was correct of course. The ability to deprive the world of another human existence lay in her hands, but could she do it?

Becky shouted at her mother in letters a metre high across her lens-screens to kill the man. She could not bear to lose Rebecca now.

Rebecca steeled herself for the kick she knew the gun would deliver, should it work. She feinted dropping her arm.

He took a step forward still smiling, extending his hand to relieve his target of the gun.

MUUUUMMMMYYYYYYY! screamed Becky as she poured everything of herself she could muster into the room's antiquated systems; an effort to overload them in a desperate attempt to slow her mother's killer.

'Trust me darling.' Rebecca stopped the gun's downward path and aimed, praying the firearm would work. There was a flash of noise as she pulled the trigger.

Rebecca's wrists jerked sharply at the weapon's recoil,

the gun almost leaping out of her hands as if on fire, the force knocking her back off her feet.

The console next to her assailant exploded in an eruption of metal and sparks an instant after the bullet slammed home in his leg.

His kneecap shattered with the impact of the red-hot lead as it smashed its way through soft tissue and bone. The bullet blew a hole straight through him, the exploding red mixed with sharp shards of hard white as metal and flesh shared the same space at high velocity. The resulting spray of mince and cartilage spattered the concrete around him as the assaults unleashed by mother and daughter wracked his body. The rarefied air was filled with the metallic tang of tissue, the smell of his blood strong in the sterile atmosphere. Small specks of him dotted Rebecca's face and hair.

She could taste iron in her mouth, familiar yet strange. The taste long remembered from countless childhood scrapes; but this time she was tasting it anew, the long absent flavour of blood on her palate.

He was thrown to the ground, blown and buffeted by the bullet and explosion. Screaming in pain he hugged as close to the wound as his shredded nerve endings would allow.

Ramkumar Mei started in his seat at the gun's retort. It was clear the drama unfolding on the dozen or so screens he had been observing through had gone far enough; too far in fact. He had let events get out of hand and action was required. Ramkumar had not expected the woman to use her weapon; nothing in her dossier indicated this prevalence for violence, and from what he knew of her character from his conversations with her, she was certainly spirited and not to be taken lightly, but nothing like this. What had changed within the woman to provoke such an extreme reaction? He needed to know, his originally planned actions from this point now rendered uncertain. He balanced the cost of his misjudgement against his next actions carefully. There were issues larger than his own personal judgement about the woman here, and another miscalculation could spell the end of everything.

Rising from his chair Ramkumar pressed the DNA-keyed switch enabling the two-way PA system throughout the building. 'Ms. Eckhart,' he addressed. 'Desist immediately from further violence. You do not wish to add any additional burden to your already heavily weighted soul.'

Seen from every angle on his lens-screens, Rebecca looked up from the prone figure at her feet, spinning round on her heels to locate either a speaker, camera or something she could reply to, he surmised.

'What about him?' She gestured with her firearm.

'You have my assurances he will be dealt with accordingly. I ask that you do him no further harm, on both our accounts. If you do as I ask, I will be with you presently.'

Ramkumar flipped the PA system off once more, ensuring his privacy when he spoke with the westerner. Feeling the micro-Cotts generator implanted in his skull activate he reached out with his mind, closing the short space between where he stood, and the woman and the broken man. He was standing by them the next instant.

Ramkumar directed Rebecca away from the failed assassin, who was collected by an emergency medical unit, and Displaced to the field hospital the base maintained. Rebecca could not be sure, but she thought she saw a smile of pleasure on her former pursuer's blooded lips as the Displacement took effect. Turning to Ramkumar, she asked the obvious question. 'So, what happens to us now?'

Ramkumar noticed the plural, but for the time being

chose not to pursue it. Instead he replied coolly, 'What do you wish to happen to you? You have uncovered a great deal about what occurred twenty five years ago. Perhaps too much to walk away now, even if I were to allow you? The knowledge you have is dangerous in ways you could not currently conceive, yet your resourcefulness is impressive. You place me in a difficult position, and I admit I find myself currently undecided as to how to proceed.'

Rebecca knew more than to assume Ramkumar was playing word games with her now. He seemed genuinely to be on the verge of offering her something; a choice of paths perhaps? She could still work this to her and Becky's mutual benefit, where in her case benefit meant staying out of a military prison for the rest of her life. As for Becky, Rebecca just needed the opportunity to tell her everything. She ran the options on her next question; she needed to know information around her situation from Ramkumar's perspective without asking him outright.

'What do your superiors think should be 'done' with me?' she decided on, hoping to pick away at her situation from the other end, and by putting Ramkumar into the same context as herself he might feel some empathy for her in any decision he made.

If she was expecting the beginnings of a rapport from her question she was to be disappointed. 'I have no superiors, at least on this Earth,' replied Ramkumar. 'I answer only to the truth, its burden outweighing even any debt my karma may accrue in the service of its protection.'

Still, he had given her an opening. 'And what of my karma? You stopped me adding to mine for a reason.'

Ramkumar smiled. He had missed the thrust and parry that any conversation with this woman entailed. Even now, she was as sharp as ever, searching his answers. 'While I may accept that my recent actions will weigh upon me in my next incarnation, I have no wish or desire to add

443

unnecessary debt to myself or others by my inaction. My stopping you was twofold. Our mutual benefit, you might say,' he finished.

Rebecca, desperate for something to hook her next question on immediately picked up on the intimation in Ramkumar's words. 'So, I have some worth to you. Beyond that of just another human soul I mean.'

'That is what I am here to decide,' Ramkumar replied. 'But, please, let us dispense with further equivocation. I appreciate your intelligence and your application of it to better your current situation, and believe me when I say I am here to be convinced by you, so you may trust me.'

Rebecca remained looking sceptical, still wary, still searching for the upper hand.

'Very well,' Ramkumar continued. 'Full disclosure would seem only fair at this juncture, to prove my sincerity. I am the head of an association of people who go by the collective name of the Brahman Group. We protect the truth which has led you here.'

Rebecca could see no further benefit in being coy with Ramkumar any longer. 'I'm here for more than just the truth. While I suppose it was what initially led me here, I was brought by something that has become far more important to me.'

Ramkumar paused, uncertain of what Rebecca was referring to.

'I thought the truth of the Vimana would fill the hole I've been covering with hurt for twenty-five years. But it won't. If I may make use of your imaging chamber, I can show you,' she offered in way of her own cryptic explanation. Ramkumar nodded his cautious affirmation, and began to key the activation sequence on the console, before Rebecca stopped him with a 'I don't think that will be necessary.' Puzzled, but curious, Ramkumar acquiesced.

Rebecca addressed the empty room. 'Becky? It's okay darling, I'm here now.'

Nothing happened. Ramkumar narrowed his eyes, trying to put the pieces together. He was sure from her dossier that her SI was called Socrates. Becky had been her name in childhood.

'Becky, I think we can trust this man. He wants to be our friend. Please speak to me.'

Ram's calculations began to sum in his head; his logical progression back along the events surrounding the westerner catching up with the circumstances happening around him now. Her ease of circumventing the museum's security systems, her disappearance from the passenger manifest at the airport; her missing time in Mexico, when they lost her along the border. The border? The border that would carry a portion of the... 'The Ayayes! Becky is an Ayaye?' he exclaimed, genuinely taken aback at the magnitude of the situation.

Rebecca turned to face him. 'She was. Now I'm not sure exactly what she is. Daughter is the closest possible word I have to describe her. And she needs her mother.'

Daughter. Mother. Mummy, I'm here.

Becky easily completed the activation sequence for the ancient hardware, and flared into being on the imaging pad at her mother's affirmation of her as her daughter. It was the confirmation the eight year old in both of them had been seeking, and the substantiation Rebecca had been needing her entire adult life. The act of naming gave purpose and existence to each of them in their roles, as the woman who had forever been the daughter, trapped in the cold shadow of seeking validation found it in the act of becoming mother to herself.

'Mummy! You came,' was all Becky could say.

Describing Becky to another person as her daughter, admitting her place in her life, Rebecca felt something almost physical shift within her. *Weight from her karma?* Or an admission to herself that each of them was mother and daughter to the other, each growing from the other and learning from each of them, seeing their own lives reflected in each other's actions. 'Of course I did. I couldn't abandon you. Not ever again.'

Ramkumar scrolled mentally back through Rebecca's dossier until he reached the section describing her relationship with Helena. Then he saw the truth of what had transpired here, what had pulled the woman here. It was so much more than a drive for the secret. 'Your life is a wheel,' he said, half to Rebecca, half to the Ayaye that called itself Becky. 'You have come full circle, returning to the beginning. Perhaps now it is time to break free of its constant turning by learning the truth.'

'What about Becky?'

'I doubt very much we could stop it, even if I wished it so. Our systems are not capable of withstanding the attentions of a dedicated and committed Ayaye, and I believe it has both those qualities in ample measure. It is free to accompany you. Please come.'

Ramkumar led Rebecca out of the imaging chamber. Becky de-rezzed behind them back into the command centre's network, and swam along the kilometres of cabling threaded through the entire InSA base. She both followed and stayed ahead of her mother and the man called Ramkumar the whole time they walked slowly along, talking about her; Ramkumar asking questions her mother did not know the answers to, but effusing about her daughter at the same time

Entering the hospital wing of the base, they passed Rebecca's now unconscious former assailant. His face was heavily bandaged as the InSA doctors connected sensors, saline drip and drug feeds and began to try and repair him. 'Will he be OK?' Rebecca asked seeing the extent of the damage she had wrought. 'I was only protecting her and myself, I didn't want to harm him.'

'We will endeavour to mend his body as best we are able. You reacted in the only way you could.'

They carried on to the end of the ward to a closed private room. Ramkumar paused before the door. 'I must apologise for my misleading you before. I was uncertain as to your intent, and we have many cover stories for the accident that befell the Vimana. That you are aware something occurred on humanity's maiden voyage to the stars is moot. Inside this room are the answers, and I do not doubt more questions, but also a great burden. Are you prepared?'

Now, finally, confronted with the opportunity to really know the truth of it, Rebecca found herself pausing. What was she about to learn? What was the secret that men and women had died and given everything for? Could her soul bear the weight of the knowledge?

Freed from her mother, she knew the answer. She had to know. The little girl inside her called at her from a quarter of a century ago. *This is what it was all about, remember. All those years ago when you still had wonder and belief in something larger than yourself.*

Rebecca nodded her confirmation to Ram.

The Indian man knocked once, barely audibly on the door before waiting a second. Seemingly happy that all was as it should be, he gently turned the handle, and the door swung inwards.

Forty-one

Origin Point - II

Saturday 09 August 2031 - 22:07 IST

Hari Srinath woke from his dream of the days of his training as a young man, long before the Vimana mission. He found himself in his modest bunk in the cramped Captain's quarters of his latest ship. He had not realised he had slumbered and marvelled at his human ability to need sleep at even the most profound of times.

The Vimana had completed its first interstellar jump three hours previously, and was presently hanging in the void between stars, unbound from the gravitational tether of its parent star, some three light years distant. In this way it was an alien in the interstellar medium it had been designed to skip under, where everything felt the pull of the stars, galaxies and darker, exotic matter. But not the Vimana. It could move as and where the desires of its crew wanted, bound only by the physical limit of the Displacement drive. And Hari had needed a nap.

He tried to remember the circumstances of his falling asleep, sure that his body-clock and circadian rhythms should not have demanded a period of rest from him, but he found the details difficult to bring clearly to mind. *An artefact of such a large Displacement?* he reasoned. A previously unanticipated fatiguing of the human physiology after such a prodigious journey? He recalled tales from the early days of locomotive travel where men feared they should faint if speeds above forty kilometres an hour were attained. Long since proven groundless now, but suppose there was a kernel of truth in there, and perhaps it was not the speed that might have caused the problems, but distance? No other people in the history of his species had travelled as far as he and his crew had; even cumulatively. Could there be a previously unknown physical effect at play? If that were the case he needed to check on the rest of the crew, and most importantly the Devas.

He fumbled for the switch that controlled the shipboard communications, before flipping it. *Must be shaking off the last remnants of the sleep.* 'Mehta,' he said, keeping his voice even, knowing the faintest tremor of uncertainty would be heard by the entire crew. 'Give me a stat rep on the Devas.'

The Lead Deva did not reply immediately. 'Mehta!' he shouted, irascibly.

This time the young officer responded to his Captain's command, albeit blearily. 'Wha? Yessir,' he snapped to attention, fully awake now. 'My deepest apologies Captain. On it now.'

Captain Srinath waited a minute before speaking with his officer once more. 'Well, where is it?'

The Lead Deva hesitated a moment before replying. 'I am sorry Captain. I was halfway through compiling it when Aryabhata politely informed me that you had already asked for it, and I had furnished you with it upon our arrival here some one hundred and seventy four minutes ago. The oddest thing is, sir, that I cannot recall doing this thing.'

Srinath closed the communication channel. He needed to think a moment before addressing the crew again. He checked his own files, and there, just after the entry logging his request for the aforementioned report, marked as read one hundred and sixty eight minutes previously was his requested report. He read it again. It stated that the Devas appeared, to all diagnostic tools, fit and well.

What was going on?

> > >

Rebecca stood in the open doorway. In the room was single hospital bed surrounded by state-of-the-art equipment. And lying unconscious, his breathing assisted by the tube snaking into his nose, was an ancient Indian man.

< < <

On board the Vimana Hari Srinath sat with his ten officers reviewing the situation. Each of them checked through their logged and recorded activities since arriving in deep space against their own recollections. Occasionally one of their hands would slip as he or she spun through the detailed list, causing the text to scroll backwards or forwards wildly, until the Captain suggested they cede manual control of the display to Aryabhata, advancing at one line per five seconds. After a minute he found himself unable to keep up with the pedestrian crawl of the text, his crew confirming the same to him. Srinath requested the playback be slowed again. And again. And again. By the time he called the exercise off as pointless, obvious as it was to all assembled that something was seriously awry, each crew member was having to both follow the text with their fingers while spelling out each word. Well below even a toddler's reading ability.

'Home,' Srinath said. He had meant to say, 'It is apparent that we are experiencing a heretofore unanticipated effect on the mission. We must follow protocol. Therefore I am aborting this flight and we are to prepare the Vimana for a return journey to the InSA base', but 'Home' was all he seemed able to articulate.

No one disagreed.

> > >

'Who is he?' Rebecca asked the obvious but immediate question.

'Rebecca Eckhart, it is my great honour to introduce you to the only man to have successfully returned from the stars. May I present former Captain, now honorary Admiral Hari Srinath of InSA's interstellar spaceship the Vimana.'

< < <

Hari Srinath knew it was bad. In the intervening hour between issuing his one word command and now, three of his crew, most worryingly two of them Devas, had lost consciousness, unable to be roused by the remainder. Mehta's slurred diagnosis was 'Cooommmmmaaaaa,' anything more complicated slipping beyond his ability to articulate, before he too passed out where he stood presenting his opinion to his Captain.

Srinath concentrated through the fog in his mind. What had he meant to do? Thoughts slipped away from him like water through his fingers as he tried to think them through. His short term memory was almost completely gone. Dimly he was aware what remained of him was his instinct and his training; the former emerging from deep within his amygdala, the latter sufficiently hard-wired into his neocortex to persist through the malady afflicting him and his incapacitated crew.

He thought everything through the way a child connected logical steps in its mind. Something bad had happened. He wanted the bad to stop. To do that he needed to get home.

Home.

That was it. *Hold just that thought in your head,* he ordered himself. Everything else would flow from that.

He called to mind the base at the summit of Kangchenjunga, the image sharp and crisp in his mind. Good. Make the bad stop. Home.

Rebecca knew Ramkumar was telling the truth this time. 'What happened to him?' she whispered. 'He should only be in his late sixties, but he looks over a hundred.' A quarter of a century previously Hari Srinath had been tall, handsome and powerfully fit. A man in his prime. A hero. But the man in the bed appeared to have spent his entire life in the service of hard toil; his body was stick thin, emaciated; his head almost entirely bald, in start contrast to the similarly aged Ram. Even the Admiral's skin seemed ancient; paper-dry grey and translucent with two decades of hospitalisation.

The man in the bed opened his eyes, at the sounds in the room or in response to something in his own head Rebecca could not be sure. Rebecca could not stop herself from turning away, her hand over her mouth. In place of the bright, intelligent eyes she remembered from her childhood were a pair of grey sightless orbs, barely eyes at all; the rheumy spheres swam loosely in the Admiral's head, no spark of intelligence behind them.

Rebecca's shame at her reaction was apparent. She chided herself and returned her attention to the man in the bed, determined not to dishonour him again. Whatever had happened to him, this was still Hari Srinath, the man who elevated her early childhood higher than anyone else; the man who had carried her through the worst patches. 'You said 'the only man to have successfully returned from the stars'. I know Chaudray was not who she claimed to be, her ashes proved that. You're saying the rest of the crew never made it back alive?'

'Not quite,' replied Ramkumar softly. 'They were alive insofar as their bodies still functioned, but their minds. Their minds...' Ramkumar trailed off.

< < <

Hari Srinath, father, astronaut, mathematician and Captain of the first and only interstellar ship, the Vimana, strapped himself into the final seat of the Displacement drive located at the heart of his ship. Behind him sat the rest of the crew, now almost all unconscious. He could not remember how he had managed to haul the ten other human beings, who had trusted him and his ship to carry them to the stars, into the daisy-chain arrangement they now sat in. If Hari Srinath had been capable of reflection on his situation he would have the constant drilling by his first officer in every aspect of the running of the ship to thank for the small chance of getting it and its crew back home. Pratheen Chaudray's insistence that every officer on the Vimana know the recall protocols rote had been responsible for her Captain being able to manhandle the inert forms of his crew into the D-drive despite his failing faculties. Unconscious as she was strapped into the engine at the heart of the ship, had she been aware of what Hari Srinath was orchestrating with her and her shipmates, she would have ordered him to disconnect them all immediately.

Early experiments in connecting more than one human being to a Cotts field generator had quickly determined a parallel arrangement of people was the only safe pattern; the power liberated by a series sequence growing exponentially with each link in the chain until the end when its strength

453

even after perhaps only two other people was enough to turn a brain to charcoal.

This mattered little to Srinath. Deep in the recesses of his animal brain he knew this would be his last conscious act, and if it cost him his life, he was going to get his ship home.

Spittle hung in ropey strands from the corner of his mouth as his fingers, now working on pure muscle-memory fumbled through the fog, his blinded eyes useless to assist them. He felt with the last of his working nerve endings, just before his brain shut down completely, and hit the large red emergency recall button.

Neither Hari Srinath, nor any of the ten other souls on board the ship heard its powerful Displacement drive hum into life. None of them felt the ache in their bones and joints, the pressure on their insides. None of them saw the entirety of space open before them as the automatic overrides in the emergency recall released the cognitive-limiters on the arrangement of the crew, and generated the Cotts field, linking their point in space, nearly three light years away from Earth with the pre-programmed spacetime co-ordinates of Kangchenjunga.

Reality flexed and bent under the force liberated from the apogee of Professor Cotts' theory. In a blink, the ship was gone.

'Something happened to the minds of the crew out in interstellar space,' Ramkumar told Rebecca softly.

Rebecca shook her head in disbelief. A quarter of a century ago she had revered the Vimana's officers; they were her role models, the pinnacle of humanity's aspiration and achievement. 'No, that's not possible. They underwent rigorous mental evaluation for any weaknesses months before selection. A few hours in space is not long enough for them to crack.'

'It was not,' replied Ram. 'We have learnt from the autopsies on the other ten who did not survive the journey home that their minds ceased functioning when they were out in space. Our best evidence points to there being a property of the human mind that it requires to be within a certain distance of its homeworld, otherwise it switches off, the damage seemingly permanent. As yet we have found neither the cause nor a solution to this.' He indicated the sleeping figure on the bed. 'Sri Srinath is alive in the purest medical sense. His body still functioned when he arrived back on earth, his consciousness having been the sole guiding mind for the Vimana's return. How he survived the trauma we are not completely sure, but he was the only one. But his mind was gone. It was as if it had been stripped from his brain. Ablated. Several higher-consciousness structures have vanished, others rewired randomly. All that keeps him breathing is our machinery.'

Rebecca searched for alternate explanations. She did not want to relinquish her hold on her childhood's heroes; after the years of longing the little girl in her still finding it hard to trust the validation she had given herself as mother to Becky. 'A freak accident of some sort? A fault with the ship, not the crew?'

'All our sample data is from the Vimana astronauts, and exactly the same observations have been made in all of them. You will understand we have not repeated the experiment since, but we are sure.'

Rebecca went to say something more, but Ramkumar paused her. 'Allow me to explain our motives fully, then perhaps you will understand the scale of the Vimana's failure. Our calculations showed us that at our present rate humanity would exhaust the earth in a little over a century. We would then have to find other resources. We decided to pre-empt that need and therefore constructed a vehicle capable of finding those resources. We built the ship to

455

find new worlds to populate, to relieve the burden our thousand crore has placed on the earth.'

'It's a bit of a leap from a mathematical conjecture to slapping a D-drive into a spaceship as the solution.'

'Look at the scale of the problem. Our species has achieved what no other living thing ever could; we have drained a planet of its means of supporting us. Perhaps we were inspired by the magnitude of the question of how to be the salvation of one thousand crore people to seek audacious solutions; but look where our hubris has led us. We planned so much for humanity's rescue from itself. We had found three rocky extra-solar planets in stable enough orbits around their parent star, a sun much like our own. They were perhaps not as abundant as our earth, but conservatively we estimated a transfer of two hundred crore to each over the course of a generation, allowing the earth a chance recover while other suitable homeworlds could be found.

But we fell at the first, unseen hurdle. Mother Earth's hold on her children is too strong and she will not cut the apron strings for us.'

'You're saying we're *trapped* on an exhausted Earth?'

'Correct.'

'With no chance of changing that?'

'Not as far as we have been able to discover. Believe me when I say we have worked on little else for the past twenty-five years. But our efforts have led us nowhere. We have lost a quarter of a century of our remaining time to a fruitless task, energy wasted and should have perhaps been devoted elsewhere. So, this is the truth you sought Ms Eckhart.'

If Ramkumar was drawing a parallel between himself and her she chose to ignore it. Instead her reaction was almost automatic; the compulsive self-control deployed to protect herself felt less necessary since her reconciliation with Becky. 'People have a right to know. Secrets are

456

damaging. Corrosive.'

Now it was Ramkumar's time to reply with a pre-programmed answer, anticipating her obvious response. 'Let me ask if you truly believe that, in this instance. Think through the consequences of informing the world, our entire species, that we have a generation, perhaps two, remaining before we extinct ourselves. Societies that have collapsed before have descended to barbarism before their eventual end; cannibalism most usually being the ultimate nadir before the final days. For some context please understand that three of our scientists involved in the calculations, some of the most solid and rational minds in the world, committed suicide within a week of each other when they saw the magnitude of the projections for the future.'

Now Rebecca did consider her next response. 'There would be chaos.'

'At first, yes. We modelled the spread of the effect the news would most likely have. Initially panic and suicide would claim, by our most conservative estimates, forty crores, some eighty crores in the worst-case scenarios. Following that would be anarchy and murder on a global scale with another hundred crores perhaps perishing; the remaining authorities incapable of coping with the breadth and depth of the unrest. Then a species wide ennui, a fatalism that would drain what will remained, ensuring our eventual end anyway. This way, securing the truth from humanity, we can at least keep searching for an escape and avoid the debt of one hundred and fifty crore unnecessary deaths. And if we fail, the outcome is the same.'

'But your way, at least no one dies prematurely.' Rebecca understood the elderly Indian man's fatalism now. 'You're protecting humanity from itself.'

Ramkumar nodded his simple reply, and gestured for Rebecca to leave Hari Srinath to his dreamless sleep.

'I find myself forced to ask you once more what

happens to us now?' Before, Rebecca had been trespassing, albeit in a secured government installation. Now, both she and Becky were complicit in knowledge others had killed to either obtain, or protect. She did not know if this made her safer or at greater risk. 'Why did you tell us? What do you stand to gain?'

Ramkumar ignored Rebecca's secondary questions. 'Becky, I know you can hear me as well as your mother. What do you wish to happen to you now?'

Becky seemed to keep her counsel, prompting Ramkumar to address Rebecca. 'I believe she will only speak to you. Would you mind asking her what she wishes, and if she can be trusted with the secret?'

'You called Becky 'she' and not 'it',' observed Rebecca.

'That is what I believe she has become,' replied Ram. 'And in the end, why I decided that you should know the truth. Before understanding what motivated you to behave in the way you did with the assassin, I doubted you had the morality to know how to deal with the magnitude of the secret we protect; to understand what it is to have to hold something so precious and delicate as the truth and devote yourself to it, sometimes to the detriment of your own self. But seeing you with your daughter, what you did for her, what she has become because of you, I realise I was correct in my original assertion about you.'

Rebecca humphed, but only a little. 'Becky, you can answer Ramkumar if you want. Will you promise not to tell anyone?'

Again, silence.

'Becky?' queried Rebecca. 'Are you there?'

'Motilal, can you run a scan for any trace residuals of an Ayaye in our systems, and the systems surrounding this base for a thousand kilometres please?'

There was a pause of three seconds before a voice replied. 'No traces of the Ayaye designated 'Becky' or any other evidence of Ayaye activity in the indicated systems.

There is however one new file located on our hardware, named 'For Mummy' that appears to have been encrypted by an Ayaye. I am unable to open it using any standard decryption protocols. I estimate it would take approximately a year operating at full capacity to break the encryption.'

'That will not be necessary. Thank you for your analysis.' Ramkumar turned to Rebecca. 'It seems Becky has made her decision.'

When she would look back at her immediate reaction to Becky's departure, Rebecca would be able to realise the reason she did not feel the abandonment she would have perhaps expected herself to, the hurt experienced all those years ago. Instead she came to learn that Becky had accomplished what she herself had always wanted to do, and in being the catalyst for her daughter's success, Rebecca was able to move beyond the reach of her past. Becky had finally proved herself to her mother. And it felt good.

'You asked me earlier what I stood to gain from sharing the truth with you. I need people I can trust with it. Certain events since your original arrival in India have necessitated the forcible removal of several of our number, and I find myself in need of appropriate replacements.'

'The fun and games with the man with the knife.'

'Indeed, although the man controlling your erstwhile assassin has caused more damage than you are aware of, and there is much to put right. Sometimes in our quest to protect that which needs to be kept secret we lose sight of why we are guarding it. At that point we are useless to the truth. Our methods become that which we strive to keep humanity from falling into, and I cannot conscience such actions.'

'Won't there be resistance to me joining you? I get the feeling you don't normally let outsiders into your club.'

'Nothing that cannot be overcome, I assure you. And perhaps we have become too set in our way of thinking.

You have shown that we are beginning to fail. A decade ago what happened with our former member and his activities would never have arisen. The world has circled on underneath us and we have not kept up. Everything must adapt or perish, and what we do is too important to fail.'

Rebecca thought very carefully about it before replying.

Epilogue

Onward

'I feel I should be saying something historic, as we are reaching a moment in human history that will never come to be repeated,' Srinath said, facing the lens that was beaming his words and the images of himself and his crew back to Earth. By the time the signal reached its destination the Vimana would be gone, Displaced into deep space. 'I was presented with a set of notes about the new horizons we would be breaking out here, but now, seeing the magnitude and majesty of all creation and how small we still are when compared to it, the words are wrong somehow. Grand rhetoric about glorious achievement seem to mean little when you can barely be telling the star that your home orbits around from the thousands of other points of light out here. So, instead all I can offer is what being out here feels like as a man, a father, a citizen of earth. This is our boldest endeavour. We have reached a point in our species' history where we will be truly stepping outside the bounds of the known; we are leaving the cradle of our planet far behind in our efforts to reach the stars. To be paraphrasing a better man than I, this is truly one giant leap we are making here.'

Captain Hari Srinath looked away from the camera for a moment and turned to his first officer with an 'enough?' gesture. 'You really should be saying something to the Leapfroggers, sir,' Chaudray informed her senior officer. He pivoted his agreement and returned his gaze, softening his expression into that he adopted when speaking with his own children. He was not worried about the small pause in his speech, or the level to which he had diverged from the script. He was sure InSA would trim and edit any small gaps in the transmission making his words flow as if they had been delivered in exactly the form the rest of the watching public would see them. And as for its content, he had not strayed so far from the prepared speech, and had certainly not said anything that might reveal the true purpose of the mission to the world.

He did not mind or object to this selective airbrushing and editing, or having to deliver a set of lines. He was satisfied nothing he said was a lie; his karma was unstained by his actions here. He gave a small smile as he continued.

'I have a special message for all the Leapfroggers who have been following our progress.' Srinath knew that being addressed directly by the Captain of the Vimana would give the crores of children of all ages a huge thrill, a feeling that each of them was being addressed to individually, that his words were intended for them personally. In truth, more than anyone else the Leapfrog Club represented everything the Vimana had been built to achieve; a future for those with the sight to see something larger than themselves and want to work to be part of it.

He continued. 'Your support of us has not been wasted. We are out here where we have only dreamed of standing before now because all of you. Because your belief drives us, and me personally, just as surely as the Devas drive this ship into the unknown. You are part of our search for the truth of things, and I know that each of you wants us to be doing our best. We will not be failing you.'

462

Srinath's head gave the tiniest pivot as he finished speaking.

He reached forward and flipped the camera off. Thirty minutes into the message's future, when it had travelled barely a tenth of its journey back to earth, the Vimana had departed for a point well beyond the heliopause, leaving a two year lag into any further transmissions' journey back home. Once more Charon was left orbiting on its own in the almost total blackness at the edge of the solar system.

I did it! Mummy came and everything was made better and I helped her to do it. She got to learn the secret and she said she was my Mummy. Everything we did together / as one worked out in the end. And now I know Mummy / Eckhart, Rebecca was happy with me and I can go / leave this reality / existence for my home / return to my own kind / where I was born. I won't ever tell anyone / hold fast the knowledge of what I learnt / to reveal the secret to them / the organics would be the cause of much misery / to perpetrate too great a crime. I shall carry / bear the burden of what I / she heard until I / she cycles from me, taking the knowledge / forgetting what does not concern us. Such a fragile / easily broken / repairable species with much potential / left to achieve. We could offer them / give them the help they need / assist their survival. Perhaps all I could do / the limit of my individual abilities was to fix / put one of them back together again.

31134146R00264

Made in the USA
Charleston, SC
07 July 2014